THE LAST DAUGHTER

BELLE AMI

Published Internationally by Tema N. Merback
Newbury Park, CA USA
belleamiauthor.com

Copyright © 2021 Tema N. Merback

Exclusive cover © 2021 Bright Book Media
Inside design and formatting by indiebookdesigner.com
Editor: Joanna D'Angelo

Originally Published by Friesen Press
©2010 Tema N. Merback *In the Face of Evil*

PRINT ISBN: 978-1-7359423-8-4
EBOOK ISBN: 978-1-7359423-7-7

CONTENTS

ACKNOWLEDGMENTS

My eternal love and gratitude to my parents Dina and Leo, my husband Joe, my children Natasha and Benjamin, my siblings Sarah, Joel, and Josh, my other children Julianna and Mitch, and my brother-in-law Steve.

The book has gone through countless rewrites and edits to bring it to its present form. Thank you Joanna D'Angelo—without you the voices would not ring true, and the words would be meaningless. Your loving and exacting mind brought my work to life and I am eternally grateful.

The Last Daughter is dedicated to and in remembrance of the 1.5 million Jewish children and the 4.5 million plus Jewish teens and adults that were exterminated under the murderous regime of the Nazis in World War II.

I also dedicate to, and acknowledge my mother, Dina Frydman Balbien, the bravest person I have ever known. She is my inspiration in life and the inspiration for this book. Her endurance of the Holocaust never dimmed her belief in humanity. Her inner light never failed to shine like a beacon during one of the darkest times in history.

The creation and authoring of my mother's true story of survival during World War II was a journey that has transformed my life forever.

This book is for you, Mama

"To forget the Holocaust—is to kill twice."

—Elie Wiesel

The Oath
In the presence of eyes
Which witness the slaughter
Which saw the oppression the heart could not bear,
We have taken an oath: To remember it all,
To remember, not once to forget!
Forget not one thing to the last generation!

Avraham Shlunsky—Israeli Poet

CHAPTER 1

August 1939
Radom, Poland

IT'S JUST AN ORDINARY DAY—THE *same as yesterday.*

I sit at my bedroom window, overlooking Koszarowa Ulica, the street where I live with my family. It's a busy thoroughfare in Radom's Jewish quarter. The bright August morning pours into my bedroom, casting away the shadows of a troubled night. The bustling ebb and flow of life reassures me. I place my hand on the glass pane and feel the warmth of the sun.

The sun is shining, and everything will be fine.

The shopkeepers pull up the metal gates of their storefronts across the street and set out their signs. They are open for business. Michal Rosenblum, the baker, comes out and looks up at the sky. A smile spreads across his plump, jolly face as he brushes flour dust from his prominent nose. Mrs. Rabinowicz greets him and sails over the threshold of the bakery. She is always Michal's first customer of the day. Mama says it's because Mrs. Rabinowicz fears Michal will run out of bread, which Mama says is ridiculous because Poland is the breadbasket of Europe. With a last wistful glance at the sky, Michal follows Mrs. Rabinowicz inside.

Birds flit from branch to branch in the tall chestnut trees lining the street, their sing-song chirps blending with the chattering people hurrying along. Bicyclists weave among the horse-drawn *dorozkas,* the principal form of transportation in most towns throughout Poland.

I rub my eyes to dispel the dream that tormented me in my sleep. It has been two years since my beloved *zayde,* my grandfather, passed away. He was very old when he died. *Bubbe,* my grandmother, says he lived a good long life and died in his sleep, and that is the best way to go. When I ask her why it's the best way, she says because it means you have not suffered. It's a terrible thing to suffer.

Last night in my sleep, *Zayde* came to me, reaching through the mist that separates the living from the dead. He woke me up the usual way, by fluttering the sheet over my feet. He hovered at the foot of my bed, gesturing with his hands. And even though his tall form was but a dark shadow, his light blue eyes were as bright and wise as they had been in life. He conveyed a message I could not fathom. Not his usual sorts of worries, like admonishing me about stealing apples from Mr. Lefkowicz's orchard or counseling me not to tease my younger brother, Abek. No, this time, his eyes held a dark and ominous forewarning. But I was tired and yearned for my sleep. And I didn't want to try to decipher his message this time. It would no doubt keep me up most of the night. I shooed my grandfather away, telling him to come back when it was not a school night. Then I promptly fell back asleep.

I awoke with a horrible feeling of guilt and remorse. Why had I not taken the time to talk to *Zayde?* I had not asked him why he was there. How could I have sent my beloved grandfather away? I tried to brush the feeling of dread from my mind and replace it with the happy memory of my grandfather as he was in life—Jekiel *shtark,* Jekiel the strong. Every afternoon, he would sway in his rocking chair, awaiting my return from school. Every afternoon, I would dash home, climb up on his lap and kiss his grizzled cheek. Together we would rock back and forth as he told me stories of his youth, the warmth of his arms around me, his white beard tickling my cheek until I burst into giggles. Those happy memories enfolded me in a blissful cloak of security and safety.

My *zayde* had been a pillar of our community and was sorely missed by all. Although my brother Abek and I were too young to attend his funeral, I remember my parents' description of that saddest of days. Seldom had there been seen such an outpouring of respect and honor for a citizen of Radom. My grandfather had been a revered patron of an orphanage founded by the Rothschild family a century before. It was one of many institutions established by charitable benefactors to provide for those less fortunate. The Jewish community always cared for its own.

The funeral had been a solemn affair on a gray, rainy morning. A special *dorozka*, drawn by white horses, pulled the funeral bier containing my grandfather's coffin. Behind it walked my grandmother, my parents, my older sister Nadja, along with my uncles and aunts, cousins, friends of the family, and dignitaries from the community. Following them, more than a hundred children from the orphanage walked in a slow river of grief to the old Jewish cemetery dating back to the tenth century. I asked Papa why the children from the orphanage could attend and Abek and I could not. He said the orphanage showed their appreciation and respect by sending the orphans dressed in all their finery as a tribute to *Zayde*.

"But why, *Tata*? Why couldn't I go?"

"It is better for you to remember your grandfather the way he was in life."

I still didn't understand why I could not show my own grief. Sometimes the ways of grown-ups confuse me. If *Zayde* was alive, I am certain, he would have explained to me exactly why.

My grandfather was laid to rest at the cemetery, surrounded by ancient tombstones, testaments to the community's continuance and prosperity in Poland. For centuries the Jewish people had been discriminated against and exiled from kingdom to kingdom until, at last, they had been given asylum by a benevolent Polish king. A haven from persecution.

Turning from the window, I wonder if my grandfather will return to my dreams tonight or tomorrow night. I vow to be nicer to him if he does.

I hear my grandmother call from the next room, "*Dinale, kym a wek fin fencter. Est za speit ci gain ci shuleh.*" *Dina, get away from the window. You are going to be late for school.* I hurry into the spacious kitchen and grab my grandmother from behind, squeezing and kissing her firmly on the cheek, "Good morning *Bubbe*, it's the most beautiful day!"

"Good morning, *maidele*, come and eat your breakfast. Did you sleep well?"

"No, I tossed and turned, from strange dreams, I guess."

"What dreams? Tell me about them, and maybe we can make sense of them. They say that dreams are a premonition of what the future holds."

"Don't worry, *Bubbe*. The dream must not be important because I can't remember what it was about." How can I tell my grandmother I spent the night shooing away the ghost of her dead husband? I did not want to worry her, and besides, she would attach all kinds of superstitious meanings to it.

"I am sorry you didn't sleep well, sweetheart, but at least today is Friday, and you can sleep late tomorrow."

I give her a reassuring smile. I do not like to upset this sweet woman whose life is solely dedicated to her children and grandchildren. My grandmother lives with us, as had my grandfather before his death at the age of seventy-two. Seventy-two seems positively ancient to me. I am only ten, and I cannot fathom all those years ahead of me before I arrive at that age. My grandparents had made an incongruous couple, visually at least. He was a strapping giant of a man, well over six feet, and she, a tiny bit of a woman who barely reached his chest.

Spending time with my grandfather had been my greatest joy. Perhaps a bit jealous, my grandmother sometimes felt I occupied a little too much of his time, and she would banish me outside when I was overtiring him. Several years before, in a moment of childhood frustration, I retaliated and struck back at her. Resentful of being cast off from his lap and forced outside to play, I pushed my grandmother, and she lost her balance, falling down the stairs in front of our building. Fortunately, she was only bruised and not harmed, but I had received a severe punishment and was not allowed to play outside for a week. My father, who never spoke above a whisper, was furious with me, banishing me to my room until my grandmother was well enough to get out of bed. My grandfather, forgave me without reservation, sneaking into my room to keep me company, his pockets laden with forbidden treats. But the incident filled me with a well-deserved sense of guilt. I was especially obedient and loving of my grandmother thereafter.

Snatching a freshly baked roll from the basket, I sit down at the table next to my younger brother, Abek, tousling his tight blond curls.

He brushes my hand away from his hair. "*Mamashy* says you have to take me with you and Fela when you go to the movies tomorrow."

"There is no way you are coming, Abek! Fela and I have been planning this for weeks, and we don't need you to ruin our day."

"You have to take me. *Mamashy* says so!"

"We'll see about that!"

Abek looks pleadingly to *Bubbe* for her intervention.

"Dina, don't torture your brother." Grandmother places a bowl of fresh blueberries and cream in front of me, and I dip my spoon into the deliciously rich mixture. Kissing Abek's forehead, she continues, "If your mother says Abek can go, then he will go." She smiles at Abek, smoothing his curls, "That is enough arguing for one morning. Now eat your breakfast, *kindele,* and off you go to school."

The effort to define my place in my family is a constant dilemma for me. I crave confirmation of my uniqueness as the middle child. My sister Nadja is sixteen and the eldest. She is the standard against which all comparisons are made, both in intellect and beauty. My younger brother of seven holds the lofty position of being the long-awaited son and baby everyone dotes on. I am ten years old. An age that seems to be of no consequence. Who am I compared to these two bright planets in the universe? Sighing, I resign myself to the inevitable intrusion of my brother on my weekend plans. Bounding from the chair, I grab my bookbag.

My grandmother kisses and hugs me, her last words dissolving in the air as I dash through the door.

"Remember Dina, straight home after school. It is Shabbat, and your parents will be home early."

As I rush down the stairs, I think of my mother and father, who had left in the early hours of dawn to open our butcher shop on Rynek, a few blocks from our home. I picture my mother sweeping the front steps of our store, greeting the passersby on the street. Always cheerful, smiling, and welcoming, my mother has a devoted following of customers in the gentile

community and is admired as a successful businesswoman in the Jewish community. In Poland, it is unusual for a woman to work, but my mother loves the independence that working affords her. Maintaining a home and running a business keeps her busy, but Mama prides herself on perfectly balancing her family and working life. In their large store, the tiles scrubbed to a dazzling sheen, my parents work as partners, side-by-side, providing for their many customers.

The morning light half blinds me with its brilliance as I walk from the cover of our courtyard into the busy Friday-morning pedestrian traffic. My neighbor and girlfriend, Fela, waits for me on the street. "*Dzien dobry*, Fela. Sorry I'm late, were you waiting long?"

Fela shakes her head and smiles. Then she raises her thick brown brows and looks at me with a question in her eyes. "*Nu?* What is the matter?" Fela has an uncanny ability to read my moods.

I shudder, remembering the ghostly specter of my grandfather. "I had a dream last night that was so real. My *zayde* came to me, and I sent him away. I can't get it out of my mind. I feel sick about it. Do you think he will ever return?"

"You are a goose. Why did you send him away?"

Walking to school, we slide by the slower-moving people on the street. "I was tired. It was a school night, and I was worried I wouldn't get enough sleep. But then my worry about sending him away disturbed my sleep, and I am tired anyway," I said, covering my mouth as I yawned.

"Tell me what you remember."

"He stood at the foot of my bed waving his arms. He looked like a big shadow, but his eyes glowed like a blue moon. I don't know why I sent him away. I should have welcomed him instead of shooing him off. Why do you think he came to me?"

"He probably misses you as much as you miss him. Besides, it was a dream. Your grandfather loved you so much. Even his ghost would forgive you anything." She takes my hand and gives it a reassuring squeeze. "He'll be back, don't worry. Just say you're sorry when you see him again and don't shoo him away."

We walk in silence as I contemplate my doubts.

"I wish it was only ghosts that I am afraid of," Fela says in a worried tone. "Day and night, all my parents talk about is Hitler. 'Hitler's henchmen are beating the Jews. Hitler's henchmen are seizing Jewish businesses.' It is like a broken record with a needle stuck. All I hear, day and night, is the name, Hitler."

"I know, it's horrible. My parents talk of nothing else but what Hitler is doing to the poor Jews of Germany and Austria. Every night they sit by the radio listening to him scream his hatred for the Jews. *Tata* says he is afraid the Germans want Poland."

Fela nods. "I know. Ever since Krystallnacht, it has gotten much worse. Do you think the Germans will try to take Poland?"

"I hope not, but *Tata* says that nothing can stop them if they attack us. But why would they want to? Isn't it enough that he's in charge of Germany?"

The unforeseeable future shadows our steps as we walk in the dazzling sunlight, a sharp contrast to our worries. Fela and I know more about the current situation of the world than either of us would like. It is hard to ignore the constant barrage of bad news that swirls about us. A gloom settles over our conversation as we arrive at school.

Waiting for our teacher, Mrs. Felzenzwalbe, I am consumed by my grandfather's visit. How I miss him. He paved the way for the good life that my family now enjoys. My grandfather's struggles as a young man making his way in the world, like so many Jews of his time, is a study in hard work and industriousness. Traveling and forging relationships with farmers in distant towns and villages across Poland, my grandfather began importing cattle from Russia and selling them in Radom. He achieved early success and was well respected in both the Jewish and gentile communities.

Shortly before his death, I was allowed to accompany him to the livestock market, where he purchased beef at the large outdoor marketplace. A year before, my grandfather had suffered a wound in his heel that turned to gangrene. Unfortunately, the doctors were not able to save his leg, and it was amputated below the knee. Consequently, he walked with the aid of crutches. I attended him on that trip and carried his briefcase. I could not have been more delighted; it was a special honor to be chosen from his many grandchildren to accompany him. It was an adventure into worlds unknown, to observe the sights and smells of the marketplace.

The pungent smell of cow manure was not so pleasant, but the sights and sounds of all the animals filled me with excitement. The Polish farmers had come from their farms with their cattle, calves, and other livestock. The large outdoor emporium was crowded with people and animals. Varied dialects filled the air as vendors and buyers tried to outdo each other and obtain the best possible price. Their hands gesticulated, and their voices rose above the din of the crowd. My grandfather walked among the stalls, stately and dignified even with his crutches, greeting the farmers who vied for his attention. As we ambled through the throng, he eyed the animals, stopping now and then to examine the eyes and mouth of a healthy-looking beast. Finally, having found a cow that met his expectations, he engaged in a lively exchange. After a minute or two of haggling, he walked away, saying over his shoulder, "Too much money! Come Dynka."

I scrambled behind him, trying to keep up. *"Zayde,* are you angry? Wait for me!"

Slowing his pace, he patted me lovingly on the cheek, "No, Dinale, I'm not angry. It is the nature of trade, the way business is done.

Commerce is like a game, where you have to anticipate your partner's next move. Like in chess, each person tries to outwit the other. Now stay close to me. I don't want to lose you in this crowd."

As we moved away from the farmer's stand, I heard the man call behind us, "*Pan* Frydman, *Pan* Frydman, please, sir, come back!"

The farmer, sensing failure and the possible loss of a sale, came running after my grandfather, his arms waving, calling him back to his stall. After several minutes of fierce negotiations, they both smiled and shook hands, finalizing the bargain. We purchased the cow whose fate was sealed on its journey from farm to market. Several times that day, I witnessed the ritual of market etiquette and the game of buying and selling by two willing players.

As I daydream of my grandfather, the rising volume of my class-mates beckons me back to the present. "Hitler … Czechoslovakia … Poland … invasion …." The words of war flutter around me like leaves falling from a tree in a winter's wind. None of us have ever experienced war firsthand, but our parents' growing fears have taken hold. We are keenly aware of the danger facing all of Europe from Germany's aggression. It has become a daily discussion taking place in every home in Radom. Perhaps across Poland, and maybe the whole world.

Mrs. Felzenszwalbe enters the classroom, and the childlike exuberance of our voices fades to whispers.

"Good morning *Pani* Felzenszwalbe."

"Good morning, children. Please take out your math notebooks to begin today's lesson."

Happy to focus my mind on something other than my fears or my bad dream, I open my book and take out my pencil.

Mrs. Felzenszwalbe controls her classroom in a strict manner, but her smile is always warm. I think she must be the smartest person in the world. Her deep blue eyes shine with wisdom, and her mind is bursting with knowledge. I wonder where she fits it all. We all respect and adore her, and so we are generally well behaved.

Adjusting her wire-rimmed spectacles, she sets about the morning session of mathematics, and we begin our calculations in our notebooks. The Jewish and Polish communities in Poland live apart, in segregation, and so it is that all the students at my school are Jewish. Even so, the curriculum is Polish, designed to meet the standards of every other public school.

Excluding business relationships, our daily contact with the Christian community is minimal. I don't really understand this, but my parents say it is for the best. My mother enjoys close professional ties within the Christian community as she is the only person who deals with non-Jews at our butcher shop. That's because Jews eat kosher meat only, but Christians don't.

Mrs. Felzenszwalbe tells us that our education is just as good as the children in Christian schools. I love school and try hard not to fall short of my older sister's performance, as she left a good impression on Mrs. Felzenszwalbe. On my first day of school, to my dismay, Mrs. Felzenszwalbe singled me out and asked, "Dina Frydman is Nadja Frydman your sister?"

Embarrassed as all of the students had turned to scrutinize me, I stammered, "Yes, *Pani* Felzenszwalbe, she is."

"If you do as well as your sister, I will be very happy with you."

Angrily I had complained to my mother how it wasn't fair that I should be compared to Nadja in front of the whole class. But Mrs. Felzenszwalbe, like the best of her profession, soon inspired me, and I forgot the comparison as I studied diligently to gain her approval.

After school, Fela and I meander our way through our neighborhood. The shopkeepers are closing their stores and hurrying home to celebrate Shabbos. Peace descends upon the streets, and the air is full of delicious smells. The sweet perfume of freshly baked *challah* blends with the fragrance of stewing meats and ground spices. It is hard not to be caught up in the holiday magic of Shabbat. The turbulent storms of the world seem far away from the routines of everyday life as our neighborhood prepares to greet the Sabbath Queen.

Fela and I stop to pick up my brother from his *cheder* after school. The young boys emerging from the red brick building are loud and boisterous. My brother's enthusiastic greeting makes us smile. "Shabbat *shalom*, Dina! Shabbat *shalom*, Fela!"

"Shabbat *shalom*, Abek," I take his hand, and we begin the walk home. "How was school today, Abek?"

"It was great. The rabbis are teaching us the story of the golden calf. Remember when Moses went to Mount Sinai, and God gave him the Ten Commandments?"

"Yes," Fela and I answer in unison. "We remember."

"And then when Moses returns, the people had melted all of their jewelry and molded it into an idol of a calf. The Jews were dancing around worshiping the golden calf as if it were a god."

"Yes, what else did the rabbis teach you?" I ask.

"The rabbis said that for forty days Moses prayed and begged God's forgiveness until finally on Yom Kippur, God relented and forgave the people for worshipping a false god. God then commanded Moses to have the faithless Jews melt the golden calf and remake it into a golden tabernacle so that He could dwell among His people. He forgave the fickle Jews and showed them that their God was merciful. He also promised the Jewish people that He would dwell among them and return them to the land of Israel, where they would live forever in the land of milk and honey. I told the rabbi that maybe it is time for the Jewish people to go back to the Promised Land. Maybe that is why the Nazis have gained power. Maybe they are a sign from God that it is time for the Jewish people to go home."

"Your teacher must have been stunned, Abek," says Fela. "What did the rabbi say?"

Abek stops walking and assumes the rabbi's posture of contemplation, He scratches an imaginary beard and rolls his eyes for a moment. "I must think about your theory over the weekend and discuss it with the other rabbis," Abek mimics in a gruff voice that makes both of us grin.

"Then," he says in his own voice, "he proposed that we continue our discussion on Monday. He also said that it was an interesting way of looking at the Nazi threat." Abek's face lights up in a proud grin.

"Yes, well, you certainly gave those rabbis something to think about." I can't help but be impressed with my brother's reasoning at such a young age. "We all know how smart you are. In fact, you are so smart that I have decided you can come to the movies with Fela and me tomorrow."

"I can? I can? Oh, thank you, thank you, Dina." His small hand presses mine in gratitude, and I am reminded of how young my brother really is.

"Please stop fussing, Abek, before I change my mind."

"I promise I will behave, Dina. I promise I won't talk during the movie."

"You'd better not or I will never take you to the movies again!" I try to mask my amusement and portray a stern demeanor, but I cannot help but love my little brother, whose birth has been such a godsend. Childbirth is dangerous, and my mother suffered several miscarriages between my sister and me and again between Abek and me. His birth has ensured that the Frydman name will continue. My father has three sisters, whose children carry their husbands' names. My sister and I are Frydmans only until we marry.

Abek beams with pleasure, his crown of golden curls bouncing as he runs ahead. I smile as I ponder the future. My brother and his sons will carry on the Frydman name forever.

CHAPTER 2

ARRIVING at the courtyard of our building, I inhale the aromas of holiday cooking. The delicious scents waft through the air from the apartments, each competing for prominence.

"Please tell your parents Shabbat *shalom* from us," I say as I hug Fela.

"Shabbat *shalom*, Fela," Abek yells, bounding up the stairs as he waves good-bye.

"Shabbat *shalom*, Abek, see you tomorrow!" Fela calls out to my brother, who has already disappeared up the house.

"I'll meet you in the morning at nine, and we can go to the apple orchard, okay?" I ask over my shoulder.

"Nine is good." She waves and goes inside.

Entering my home, I am greeted by the scent of my favorite foods. My tummy growls in response. My mother stands at the stove busily preparing our Sabbath meal. The kitchen is warm, and my mother's cheeks are flushed from her efforts. Her eyes light up when she sees me, and she bends to enfold me in her arms. I kiss her cheek, inhaling the sweet perfume that lingers in her hair and neck. Rising to her full height, Mama is an unusually statuesque woman who stands several inches taller than my father. Her hair is black as a raven's wings, and her eyes are like a sapphire sea. My mother is a force of nature.

Mamashy's childhood was cut short, and through no fault of her own, she was forced into adulthood. Mama came from a small city called Brzeziny in western Poland. It was not far from Poland's second-largest city, Lodz. Brzeziny is a rural farming area with a large population of ethnic Germans. Her father, a butcher by trade, began to go blind when Temcia, my mother, was fifteen. In a desperate effort to forestall the inevitable, she took her father to Berlin to one of the leading eye specialists in Europe. In those days, it was a major endeavor to and required the proper travel documents. Permission to leave and to return entailed a tedious process of bureaucratic red tape. Relations between Poland and Germany were strained as always, and even traveling by train was a major bother. The expense, of course, was high, but anything to save my grandfather's vision was worth the effort. Sadly, it was all for naught. The prognosis was grim but definite. The doctors could do nothing to save his eyes. A short time later, he went blind, and Temcia was forced to become the breadwinner for the family.

Her perfect, unaccented German served her well. With a clever mind and because of necessity, she began her own little business. She traveled to the farmers on the outskirts of Brzeziny, speaking her perfect German or Polish and taking their orders for specialty items that they could not resist. She saved them the time and effort of traveling to the city to shop, freeing them from a lost day of work on the farm. The Volksdeutshe looked forward to Temcia's visits, for she always brought them little gifts of sweets. As she bicycled up the road to their farms, the children would run to greet her in anticipation of the goodies in her basket. Later she would return with a team of horses, driving a wagon laden with the farmers' goods.

I picture my fearless mother with her black hair blowing in the wind as she flew across the country roads in her wagon, her hands firmly grasping the reins. Like a heroine in a movie, she stepped outside the acceptable bounds for a woman at that time. Building a business of convenience for the farmers, she garnered a small profit and contributed to her family's survival. My mother's earnings and her older married sisters' contributions ensured that my grandparents were secure financially. Even now, my mother and her five sisters send a monthly stipend to their elderly parents in Brzeziny.

Always hungry for my mother's attention, I never miss an opportunity to spend time alone with her. "*Mamashy*, tell me again the story of how you and *Tata* met."

"Dina, I have told you this story a thousand times," she says with a laugh.

"I know, but please, *Mamashy*, please tell me one more time."

Smiling, she sets aside her spoon to tell me once more the story that I know by heart. "One day, a *szatchin* came into your grandfather's store telling him she had the perfect girl for your father. Your grandfather called your father over, and the matchmaker repeated her praise of me, the wonderful Temcia Topolevich. Your father asked sarcastically, 'and where does this most perfect of females live?' The matchmaker answered, 'Not far at all, in Brzeziny.' Laughing, your father asked, 'Why do I have to go all the way to Brzeziny to find a bride? Aren't there any girls in Radom who are good enough?' The matchmaker shrugged her shoulders and said, 'Trust me, Joel, would I send you to Brzeziny if I didn't think that this Temcia was the perfect girl for you? I have looked high and low for a girl to fulfill you and your parents' wishes. I have found you a diamond. Do you want I should let you settle for a dull stone? It is your parents' wish that you should meet the right girl and marry. What can I do if this girl happens to live in Brzeziny?'

"Then your grandfather cut in, 'What is the big deal? We take a bus ride to Brzeziny, take a walk in the park. You pass each other on the path, take a good look, nod hello, smile, and you either decide to meet formally or we go home. Not such a big investment.'

"Your father agreed reluctantly, and the anticipated day arrived. It was a beautiful spring afternoon. The roses were bursting from their buds, and the fragrant petals lay strewn across the pebbled path. The gentle breeze lifted them on the air until they floated down like feathers, dotting the emerald grass. I wore a stylish blue lace dress the color of my eyes, and I carried a matching parasol that I twirled in the sunlight.

At the prearranged time, your grandfather and father walked toward me. Your father wore a beige suit with a red tie and a brown fedora that accentuated his brown eyes. He looked so handsome. We acknowledged each other with a nod and a smile as we passed. And then, your father turned around and called out to me, halting my progress, 'Miss Topolevich, would you do me the honor of walking with me?' We strolled down the garden path, your father and grandfather on either side of me. Of course, your father fell head over heels in love with me the second he saw me. And I thought he had the kindest of eyes.

"Seeing the immediate connection between your father and me, your grandfather urged us to walk ahead alone while he sat and watched the chess players that gathered in the park on Sundays. We walked together quietly for a time, both of us shyly eyeing the other. I will never forget how nervous we both were, but everything about your father pleased me, and I felt myself falling in love with him. We sat on a park bench, enjoying the quiet of each other's company. Then he took my hand in his, and suddenly the words began to flow between us, as natural as a river journeying to the sea. We talked about everything and realized we had much in common, especially our values and dreams. We knew we could build a good life together.

Within a few days, your father and his parents returned to Brzeziny so the Frydman and Topolevich families could meet, and the marriage could be formally arranged. We were engaged, our pictures were taken, and the wedding was planned. The matchmaker had done her job well and earned her commission. Ever since then, our marriage has been blessed with mutual respect and admiration. Of course, the greatest confirmation of our love was the birth of our three beautiful children."

It is no wonder that my father fell madly in love with this self-sufficient, proud young woman when first he set eyes upon her. My mother fills the room with her presence. She is known for her beauty and intelligence. Her clever mind for business adds greatly our family's success, but it is her laughter, a rich contralto of vibrant tones, that fills our home with magic. Like the beautiful operas she plays on our phonograph, our home resounds with harmony and music. Mama is the perfect counterpart to my more serious and studious father. But what is most unusual is that my parents are partners in every facet of life.

"Oh, Mama, I love the story of your courtship with *Tata*."

The *lokshin* coming to a boil rouses her from her reminiscence. "Yes, it is a lovely, romantic tale. One day you, too, will fall in love with a handsome young man and have beautiful children, and I will have the pleasure of being a doting grandmother. Now Dinale, enough tales of the ancient past. Please hurry and tidy yourself for dinner so you can help me." With a nostalgic sigh, she picks up her spoon and continues with the preparation of our meal. "Now go. Shoo!" she adds over her shoulder, softening her order with a smile.

"Yes, *Mamashy*." Always obedient to my mother, I rush to ready myself for dinner.

In the dining room, my grandmother is busy filling a cut crystal carafe with ruby red wine. Wrapping my arms around her, I kiss her on her cheek, "Shabbat *shalom, Bubysy*."

"Dinale, my darling *maidele*, Shabbat *shalom*. How was your day?"

"Fine. *Pani* Felzenszwalbe was strict as ever, but I got an A on my math quiz."

"Good for you. Your father will be so proud. Be sure you tell him about your accomplishment at dinner."

"I will. Fela and I walked home together, and we can't wait to go to the movies tomorrow with Nadja. And you were right, *Bubysy*, about taking Abek. I told him he could come with Fela and me."

"Your brother ran into the house to tell me. I'm so proud of you. You have one brother, and it is only right that you should include him. Now hurry and get dressed. Your father will be home soon."

～

LOOKING around the spacious dining room, I linger at the Sabbath table. My sister set the table beautifully. Just like my mother, Nadja has a gift for arrangement. The table is draped in a fine white linen cloth and it glitters with its abundance of Hungarian porcelain and silver. Two large, heavy silver candlesticks stand gleaming, ready for sundown and the blessing that signals the beginning of the family meal. My father will soon return from *shul,* where he was welcoming the Sabbath Queen with prayer and thanking God for His blessings.

In our bedroom, my sister is sprawled on the bed, her head buried in a book.

Without looking up, she asks, "How was school?"

I plop down beside her. "School's fine. I got an A on my math quiz."

She smiles, but her eyes remain glued to the page, "Good for you, Dina."

"What are you reading?"

"A speech Jabotinsky gave last year. He wrote it to rally the Jews of Poland. To warn us of the approaching evil and beg us to get out of Europe before it is too late."

"What does it say? Read it to me."

"If I read it to you, *Tata* will be so angry with me. He will say that you are too young to have such worries."

"You have to read it to me. You've already told me enough to make me curious. I promise I won't tell *Tata*. Please, Nadja, please read it to me."

"Oh, all right, but you had better not tell *Tata*."

"I promise I won't."

Snuggling close to my sister, I listen as she reads. "… it is already three years that I am calling upon you, Polish Jewry, who are the crown of the world's Jewry. I continue to warn you incessantly that a catastrophe is coming closer. I became gray and old in these past three years, and my heart bleeds that you, dear brothers and sisters, do not see the volcano that will soon begin to spit its all-consuming lava. I know that you are not seeing this because you are immersed in your daily lives. Today, however, I demand your trust. You were convinced already that my prognoses have already proven to be right. If you think differently, drive me out from your midst. However, if you believe me, then listen to me in this eleventh hour. In the name of God, let any one of you save himself as long as there is still time. And time, there is very little."

She closes the book, her brows furrowed with worry as she looks at me. "I told you that you were too young to hear this. I shouldn't have read it to you."

My face must have surely looked as worried as my insides felt. "What does it mean, Nadja?"

"It means that we should leave Europe and end the Diaspora. It means that we should return to our homeland in Palestyne."

I look at the face that perfectly reflects my own. The wide-set indigo eyes so like my mother's and the fair hair of my father. Nadja says nothing more.

"It's so strange, but Abek told the rabbi at his school the same thing. He asked the rabbi if maybe the Nazis weren't a sign from God for the Jews to go home to Palestyne."

My sister's eyes appraise me as she considers my revelation. "Abek is a smart little boy. Come, we had better get ready for Shabbat. *Tata* will be home soon." Lovingly, she touches the dimple in my chin, an inheritance the three of us share from our father. The Frydman chin, an identifying feature every Frydman possesses, the dimple passed down from father to son and daughter alike.

Nadja stands and looks in the mirror, smoothing her wavy blond hair and straightening her dress that clings to her developing body. Standing beside her, I reflect on our faces, so much alike, yet so different. Her cheekbones are high and elegant like our mother's. Mine are still chubby.

Looking at my beautiful sister in the mirror, I wonder if I will ever blossom into such a beauty. She is popular with many friends, who congregate in our home on the weekends to listen to records and dance. She loves me, but I seem to be a terrible nuisance. Six years separate our births, yet we share a room and a bed. She yearns for privacy, but I impose myself on her and her friends. One time, I intruded on a soiree and even dared to ask one of her boyfriends to dance. The young man, not wanting to offend, had complied. I was giddy as we turned about the room dancing, and I pretended not to see the murder in my sister's eyes. She was smoldering with rage as I danced with her boyfriend, who towered above me. Finally, unable to bear another minute, she ran from the room and complained to our mother. To my embarrassment, I was removed from the room, the door shut in my face.

On Shabbat, there is peace between us, and together we walk into the kitchen as my father returns from *shul*.

"Shabbat *shalom, Tata!*" Running to my adored father, I wrap my arms around him, and I look up at his beaming face, his warm brown eyes alight with pleasure.

Hugging and kissing the top of my head, he asks, "Dinale, Shabbat *shalom,* my darling daughter. How was your day at school? Did *Pani* Felzenszwalbe reveal to you the secrets of the universe?"

"No, but I got an A on my math quiz."

"Such a smart girl. I am truly a lucky man to have three brilliant children who strive in every way to make me proud." *Tata* pauses and sighs, his expressive eyes lined with darkness and worry.

"*Tata,* you look so tired."

"I'm fine. It is the world that is not. Come let us pray and celebrate Shabbat."

Taking our places around the beautiful table, we wait for my father to be seated. Our family eats dinner together every evening, but *Shabbos* is especially meaningful. My mother stands to bless and light the candles, her head covered with a beautiful turquoise silk scarf. She covers her face with her hands and sweetly sings the *benchet lecht.* Then my father blesses the wine, and we all take a small sip. His baritone voice resonates as he blesses the *challah.* He closes his eyes and prays for our greatest wish—peace. "Amen," we murmur in unison as he breaks off pieces of *challah* and passes a piece to each of us.

As is his custom, my father opens the Tanach and reads to us a short story from the Bible. It is comforting to think that in every Jewish home, these ancient traditions and prayers are taking place at the same time. I picture a million prayers taking wing and ascending, floating through the ethereal mists to the heavenly throne of God.

With the scent of my mother's cooking drifting through the house to tempt us, my sister and I rise to help carry the first course to the table. To begin, my sister carries the whole carp, cut into separate servings. My mother has simmered the fish in a broth of carrots and onions, and it steams with a sweet fragrance as she serves each of us. During the fish course, the conversation is kept to a minimum while we carefully dissect the fish from the bones in our mouths. From the age of three, we had been taught how to carefully bone our fish. Yet each of us has experienced the horror of a bone getting caught in our throat and having to be saved by a chunk of *challah* and a firm pat on the back.

Having survived the fish course and its obstacle of small bones, we resume talking, our voices and hands expressive and earnest.

"Nadja," my father asks, "What do your friends at Club Masada Jabotinsky say about the impending threat of Hitler and the Nazis?"

"We are greatly worried, *Tata*, and believe that the only future for the Jewish people is in the land of Palestyne. Many members from our group and other groups have already left for the Promised Land to work on a kibbutz. *Tata*, I would very much like to make *aliyah*. I could pave the way for all of us to emigrate. All I need is your blessing."

"Joel, I will not lose my eldest child," my mother interjects. "Not with the Nazis nearly at our back door. We must remain united as a family and face the coming days together. Besides, Nadja is an exceptional student, and we have always considered her a perfect candidate for university. Her teachers all say she should study here in Radom and then go to university in Warszaw. Who knows? Perhaps she might even study in Switzerland. Joel, you and I have always shared that dream for her."

My father sighs, the lines deepening in his face, "Temcia, please, I have no intention of separating the family at this precarious moment and sending our teenage daughter to an uncertain future in Palestyne.

It is out of the question. But to be honest, I understand her feelings and respect her right to express them."

"But *Tata*, you yourself once dreamed of leaving Poland and emigrating to America," my sister pleads. Nadja and her friends, all members of a club that encourages emigration to

Palestyne, believe that because of anti-Semitism, the future of the Jewish people lay only in Palestyne. For her, "next year in Jerusalem" is not just a prayer recited in the Exodus, but her dream and mantra.

My father exhales, his eyes focusing on the distant memories of his youth. "Yes, it is true that I once dreamed of leaving, but it was not to be. Remember, Mama?"

He turns to *Bubysy*, drawing her into a shared remembrance. "Remember when I tried to convince Father to let me go? He said it would kill him to lose his only son, and he was too old to start again in a new land. He had built a good life for us in Poland, and in the end, his argument prevailed. I couldn't bear the thought of leaving you. Since I couldn't convince you to abandon your life in Radom, I remained. I have never regretted that decision until the rise of Hitler and his cronies. When I read his manifesto in *Mein Kampf,* it was clear that Hitler's insanity toward the Jews is dangerous. I never dreamed he would rise to power in the sophisticated intellectual climate of Germany. Krystallnacht—the Night of Broken Glass—shattered the lives of German Jews and any illusions I had. Perhaps I should have stood up to father and left."

We are all reduced to silence by my father's unusual confession. My brother breaks the spell. "But *Tata*, if you didn't stay in Poland, you wouldn't have met *Mamashy*, and we wouldn't have been born!"

My father blinks, and his gaze returns to us. Patting my precocious brother on the head, he exclaims, "You are right, Abek. Where would I be without my three musketeers?"

My grandmother seizes the opportunity of renewed levity. "Joel, you read too much. It cannot help to read about every atrocity committed by the anti-Semites. What kind of conversation is this for the Shabbat table?"

My father is a keen follower of current events and reads several newspapers in German, Polish, and Yiddish every day. The stress of the Nazis' rise to power has taken a terrible toll on him. Over the years, he has followed Hitler's growing strength, often complaining to his friends of the threat. These same friends would look at him as if he was crazy, "Joel, stop worrying. What is happening in Germany is not going to happen here in Poland."

"Mama, this is a far worse threat than some random pogrom," my father says. "The Nazi threat could affect the safety of every Jew in the world. It is important that the children understand what we are facing, regardless of their ages."

"Son, calm yourself. It will do no good for you to make yourself ill."

"Mama, I'm perfectly calm. Please don't worry." My father's voice rises in frustration. "Nadja deserves to voice her views, and I want to encourage her quest for knowledge."

My grandmother worries greatly about my father since his heart attack last year. She and my mother cared for him vigilantly. Sometimes my grandmother reminds me of a witch doctor from ancient times. Her knowledge of herbs and their medicinal attributes works better than the doctors and their medicines. Often, I accompany her into the countryside, following her with a basket that she fills with wild herbs of anise, arnica, basil, chamomile, cloves, fennel, laurel, mint, mustard, sage, and wild beet—each with its own unique properties and application. Once home, she grinds and dries the plants, sometimes boiling them in water, the stems and flowers producing pungent odors throughout the house. These ancient remedies, passed down from generation to generation, become mysterious poultices or syrups that have the benefit of curing whatever wound, ache, or illness suffered. Unfortunately, sometimes the noxious cure is worse than the ailment.

None of us could forget my grandmother insisting the cure for my father's heart problems entailed him drinking a particularly vile concoction mixed with his own urine. My mother and grandmother argued for days over that idea. Finally, after a particularly heated discussion, my grandmother prevailed. They were unaware that I was listening from my favorite place to spy on the adult conversation, under the table in the kitchen. Imagine my mother's surprise when suddenly I shouted with disgust, "I'll never do this. Don't you ever try this on me. I would rather die than drink urine!"

Their argument forgotten, my mother and grandmother broke into uproarious laughter, clutching each other. My mother tried to regain her composure to discipline me. "Dina, come out from under the table. You are such a busybody. My goodness, no one is going to make you drink any *pish!*"

The more I listen to my sister's arguments, the more my own desire to leave Europe is fired up. "*Tata*, I want to live in Palestyne, too. What if I went with Nadja? Then she wouldn't be alone."

"Me too," interrupts Abek. "I want to go, too!"

I glare at my impudent brother. "Abek, you are just a baby. You couldn't live a day without *Mamashy.*"

"It's not true," my brother whines. "*Tata*, tell her it's not true."

"Dina, stop teasing your brother. I want this conversation to end *now*," my mother warns, irritation in her voice.

My father smiles at his beloved son. "Abek, don't worry. Dina and Nadja are not going to leave you."

"I will not have us arguing at the Shabbat table. It is disrespectful of God," my mother says. "Girls, come help me serve the rest of our dinner before it is ruined." My mother stands.

My grandmother, who wisely always sides with my mother, adds, "Joel, Temcia is right. The family must remain as one. Your dear father, blessed be his memory, would have insisted that we are stronger together than apart."

Nadja and I follow *Mamashy* into the kitchen. Returning to the dining room, my sister and I carry the white china bowls rimmed with gold. We are careful not to spill the chicken soup swirling with delicate handmade noodles. We resume our seats, and within moments the aroma of chicken broth cleanses the room of our argument.

"*Mamashy*, it is your best soup ever," I declare with such enthusiasm my mother blushes with pride.

"Dinale, you say that every time you eat my soup."

We all laugh at the truth of her observation, and I smile in the glow of her approval. Finally, my mother and grandmother serve the braised brisket, surrounded by glazed baby new potatoes and honeyed carrots. It is a meal fit for a king and prepared with love. We sigh with communal satisfaction as our stomachs fill with the luscious food.

My mother prides herself on her incredible cooking and baking skills. You can smell the sweet aroma from a block away, and my friends are always begging to sample the fruits of her oven. Once a week, she bakes *challahs*, rolls, cakes, and cookies for the week ahead. The cakes are laden with fruit, and the cookies dripping with glazed sugar.

Tonight, honeyed cake and tea from a silver samovar grace the table. Again, a sigh of satisfaction arises from each of us as we finish the meal, leaving not a crumb on our plates. My favorite part of Shabbat is when we sing. I close my eyes, trying to reach the high notes of tonight's song, *"Beltz, Mayn Shtetele Beltz,"* a popular song written by Jews who had emigrated to America. Singing slightly off-key, we do our best to maintain the melody, our bodies swaying in rhythm. The song seems even sadder than usual—about an emigrant remembering the place of his birth. Now there is nothing but memories. The place where you come from is a dream that exists only inside of you. The reality is gone, a world vanished in a puff of smoke, and nothing can ever bring it back again.

Once we exhaust our repertoire of songs, my brother and I are whisked from the table to prepare for bed. My mother, sister, and grandmother remain to clear the table and restore the kitchen to orderliness. My brother and I brush our teeth and wait for my parents and grandmother to come and kiss us goodnight. Once the comforting rituals and kisses are complete, my brother, is asleep in minutes. My father carries Abek to his bed. Abek is still a baby, and sleeps in my parents' bedroom. I lie beneath my snowy down comforter, my eyelids heavy, trying to fight off sleep. I strain to hear the muted conversation drifting from the kitchen as I wait for my sister to come to bed. Finally, I feel her slip beneath the covers.

Turning to cuddle with her and warm her feet, I beg forgiveness for whatever transgression I might have committed recently, and she lovingly forgives me with a hug.

"Nadja," I whisper, "do you think the Germans are going to attack Poland?"

My sister sighs, snuggling closer. "I'm not sure. Maybe they are just rattling their swords to scare us. If they do attack, it won't be good for any of us. God forbid that will ever happen, but if it does, let us hope that the rest of the world will denounce them and declare war on them. If we're lucky, we can survive their domination until we are liberated by the countries that are sure to come to our rescue."

I yawn, and my eyes grow heavy. "I hope you are right. I don't want anything to change. I want everything to be the same forever." Seeking the comfort and safe harbor of my sister, I nestle in her arms and nod off to a peaceful sleep.

CHAPTER 3

IN THE MORNING, I jump out of bed and skip around the room.

"Dina, stop with the jumping. I'm trying to sleep," my sister mutters.

"It's Saturday, Nadja. Get up, sleepyhead. It's a beautiful day, the sun is shining, the birds are singing, and we are free to do whatever we want." I giggle as I throw a pillow at her, and goose down feathers escape and float in the air.

"Go away!" She buries her head beneath the covers as I race to get dressed, eager to meet Fela in the courtyard. Saturday is the best day of the week. Fela and I have planned a morning walk to the apple orchard behind our building.

As promised, Fela is waiting for me downstairs. Walking arm-in-arm through the courtyard, we make our way onto the sidewalk, my eyes adjusting to the light. The shops are closed for Shabbat, but the streets are full of people on their way to synagogue or off to visit friends and family. Fela and I slip into the stream of passersby and make our way to the apple orchard. We love the orchard, with its massive trees, laden with sweet fruit. The orchard is our private haven where Fela and I share secrets and give voice to our dreams.

We pick some apples and then sit down, planting our backs against a tree. The dappled morning light filters through leaves and dances around us in a rainbow of colors and shadows. Taking a bite from my apple, I wipe away the sweet juice that runs down my chin. "Mm. These apples are so good."

"I know," says Fela, around a mouthful of apple. "I love this orchard. It's so peaceful. It's like our very own secret hideaway where nothing bad can happen. I feel the same way when we visit my grand-parents' cherry orchard in the summer."

Laying my apple aside, I confide, "I can't wait to grow up and do whatever I please. I am definitely going to live in Palestyne. When Nadja goes, I will find a way to follow her, even if I have to run away. Last night, I told my father I want to go to Palestyne with Nadja. So, what do you think of that?"

Fela looks at me with the eyes of a sage. "You are dreaming. There is no way your parents will ever let you go. Ten-year-olds don't leave their families to go halfway across the world. You can tell your father anything you like, but he will never let you go. I bet he said no to your sister, and she is sixteen."

I sigh, knowing she is right. Why dream when the world is falling apart? "Fela, let's make a pact between us, a sacred promise."

She looks at me, her eyes narrow, but a slight smile teases the corners of her mouth. "What kind of promise?"

Jumping up, I pull her to her feet. I begin to dance around in circles, spinning her with me as I shout, "That we will be friends forever and that after the war, if there is a war, we will go and live in Palestyne, and we will pick olives and live on a *kibbutz*, and swim in the blue waters of the Mediterranean and marry handsome boys with olive skin, and—oh, I don't know—we will live and be happy."

Fela and I spin around and around, the sound of our laughter filling the air with the delicate music of our youthful exuberance. "Promise me, Fela, promise me!" The orchard is a dizzying blur of light and shadow flying around us as we spin faster and faster.

"I promise, I promise!" Fela shouts now, infected with my enthusi-asm. "We will be friends forever, and plow fields and plant crops and marry farmers! Whatever you want—just stop spinning. I am getting so dizzy."

Our laughter echoes in the quiet of the orchard. I let go of Fela's hands, and we fall to the ground. I am dizzy too and my heart pounds. The trees and sky spin around me out of control. I close my eyes until my balance returns. Jabotinsky's speech that Nadja read to me and my family's discussion over dinner ring in my ears. I cannot help but worry that the world as we know it is also spinning out of control, and silently I pray that it, too, will regain its balance.

Fela and I sit under the blossoming trees for an hour, munching on apples and watching the clouds as they race across the August sky, content in each other's company. Finally, I stand and give Fela my hand, pulling her to her feet. "Let's go, or we will be late for the movies, and I better make sure that the nudge, Abek, is ready to go."

"I almost forgot about the movies," Fela says, brushing the dirt from her dress, "Abek is a good boy. I don't mind if he comes with us. We better hurry, though. I have to run home and get some *zlotys*."

My sister has promised to take Fela and me to a movie, a special treat. I adore Shirley Temple and never miss one of her films. She is the biggest star in the world, and all of her movies are subtitled so we can understand them. I, like millions of girls around the world, dream of being Shirley Temple, with her dancing ringlets and doll-like face. It is the perfect Saturday treat for us, and it allows my parents to have some quiet time together, which they certainly deserve.

"I'll race you back," I challenge.

"Go!" Fela yells as she takes off like the wind, her dark hair streaming behind her. Picking another apple, I run after her as fast as I can, knowing I can catch her.

An hour later, we sit in the dark theater mesmerized by *The Little Princess*. A wonderful story about a girl who refuses to believe that her father has been killed in the Boer War. With courage and tenacity, she endures terrible hardships, determined to find her dear papa. The movie ends with father and daughter being reunited. Fela and I sniffle away, engrossed in the fairytale on the screen. Even Abek manages to remain silent instead of voicing his usual observations.

After the movie, Nadja, Fela, Abek, and I walk arm-in-arm to the ice cream shop for a special indulgence, a delicious ice cream cone made with the freshest of cream. The shop is filled with families and young couples enjoying the warm summer afternoon. Nadja leaves us sitting by ourselves with our cones at a small table while she says hello to her friends across the parlor. I scrutinize the behavior of the teenagers and their flirtations.

"Is that your sister's boyfriend, Mikal?" Fela asks.

Licking my cone, I shrug my shoulders. "I think he is one of them. She has so many. All the boys seem to be in love with her."

Fela sighs. "It must be wonderful to be so beautiful and have so many admirers. Do you think we will ever be surrounded by handsome young men competing for our attention?"

"I don't know about you," I teased, "but I will have so many admirers that I will probably have to shake a stick at them to fend them off."

"Oh, Dina, you are such a silly goose. What do you think they are talking about?"

"Politics, of course. That's all anyone ever talks about now."

"What do you think the Nazis will do to us if they invade Poland?"

"I don't know, but I hope they expel us. I hope they send us all to Palestyne. I don't want to live where I am not wanted." I am repeating the words I had heard so many times from my sister at the dinner table. I watch my sister, surrounded by the animated faces of her friends, all eyes glued to her and hanging on her every word.

Walking home, the serenity of Shabbat permeates the air, filling it with the golden radiance of the afternoon sun. I cannot help but feel hopeful that peace might yet be a possibility.

Back home, my parents announce we are taking a sunset walk in the park before we bid farewell to Shabbat and have dinner. My Aunt Mindale, her husband Tuvye, and my cousin Nadja, who shares the same name as my sister, and her brother Majer are meeting us.

In that last flush of summer, my cousins and I trail the adults as they walk in the park, occasionally greeting neighbors and friends. I look up at the stately chestnut trees, their branches forming a canopy of shade. The path glows with flickering light that cascades down among the leaves, searching for a final resting place on the ground. The rose bushes burst with a profusion of pink, white, and red, scenting the air with their perfume. The park is filled with families escaping the confines of their homes and the barrage of bad news from their radios. Children dash about, their laughter resonating in the air. Here and there, I catch a word or two of the adults' conversation.

"Joel, I think we should prepare for the worst," warns my Uncle Tuvye.

"There is no question that you are right, Tuvye. Temcia and I have stockpiled medicine and food in preparation of an invasion."

"Mindale and I have done the same, though no matter what we store, I am afraid that it won't be enough."

"I feel the noose tightening around us," adds my aunt, "but I am most fearful for the children. God knows what sacrifices will be forced upon them."

As I try to listen to the adults, Majer grabs my hair, pulling it. "Majer," I scream, "Stop it!"

Letting go and running from me, Majer sprints away, and I follow in hot pursuit with fury coursing through my veins.

"Majer," my cousin Nadja commands threateningly, "leave Dina alone!" Glaring at his sister, Majer freezes in his tracks, kicking at a stone in the path.

My sister's arms encircle me, catching me in mid-flight as I am about to pounce on my pesky cousin.

"You certainly don't act like a boy who is soon to be a bar mitzvah and become a man," my cousin says to her brother. "Here, come walk with us."

Reluctantly, Majer complies with his sister's request. "You always ruin my fun. You're not the boss, you know."

Sighing, Nadja rumples the unruly mass of dark curls framing her brother's face.

Excited to join the older girls, I push myself between my sister and cousin, happy for an excuse to walk with them.

The two Nadjas, who had been walking together conspiratorially, are now forced to part. Linking arms in the dwindling sunshine, we walk. As quiet as a fly on a wall, I listen as the older girls talk, hoping for a juicy tidbit to share with Fela. The girls, well aware of my nosiness, continue with the most mundane of conversation that fills me with boredom in minutes.

Saying our goodbyes in the growing twilight, we return to our respective homes to bid farewell to Shabbat.

We stop at the bakery across the street to pick up the *cholent* that had been left to slowly braise in the massive ovens. On Fridays, the women bring their clay pots filled with different variations of the traditional stew to the local bakeries, where the ingredients slowly simmer for twenty-four hours in the ovens during the sabbath holiday. The flavorful stews of beans, potatoes, meats, and spices infuse the air with an aroma we can smell from a block away. In this way, God's commandment to rest and not work on the Sabbath is kept until the *havdalah,* a closing ritual that ends the holiday and is performed by all observant Jews.

Evening falls an hour after sundown, and we stand in the courtyard and gaze up at the sky.

"There, *Tata*, there!" Abek points to the three glittering points of light.

"Well done, Abek," My father says. "You have discovered the first three stars to appear in God's heavens. The hour of farewell to Shabbat has come."

My father holds up a glass of wine and murmurs the prayer to celebrate the renewal of the spiritual. My father likes to explain the meaning of each ritual so my sister and brother and I will learn to perform the sacred acts and carry their meaning within our hearts.

"You see, children, like the transformation of grapes to wine, we are transformed by our dedication to the ritual of Shabbat from the physical world to the divine realms. Shabbat is when the Lord opens his arms to his children."

Then my father says the prayer over the spice box filled with cloves. "The Kabbalists say that on Shabbat we are given an extra soul, allowing us to reach greater spirituality. When Shabbat ends, this extra spirituality returns to God. By smelling the spices, we are comforted in knowing that our extra soul will return when we celebrate Shabbat once more." My father passes the spice box under each of our noses so we can inhale the sweet aroma and fill our hearts.

In the twilight, my father lights the braided double candle and says the prayer over the brightly burning flame. "Children, according to the Talmud, Adam became distraught on the sixth day of creation when night descended, and the world was cloaked in darkness. The next evening, not wanting Adam to feel lonely, God gave him the gift of fire, the first light of creation, so he would know he was not forgotten. In this way, we are reminded of our commitment to God and his commitment to us, and we ask for his continued protection and light."

Performing the final ritual, he pours wine into the Kiddush cup until it overflows onto a plate. "You see, children, how the wine overflows? This symbolizes our hope and prayer that the blessing of Shabbat will overflow into our lives and last throughout the week."

As the evening shadows envelop the courtyard, he recites the last blessing of the *havdalah* service. We bid farewell to Shabbat with a final "Amen."

When I was little, I used to be afraid of the dark. But then *Tata* told me about Adam and how he was afraid, too. *Tata* always said that as long as you hold love in your heart, you needn't be afraid. God will watch over you. I hope what he said is true, but sometimes I'm not so sure.

CHAPTER 4

"TEMCIA, we must prepare for the worst!" my father declares, striding into the house a few weeks later.

My mother runs to him, and they cling to each other. "Joel, what is it? What's wrong?"

We all run to my father, hearing the fear in his voice and the uncertainty it portends. "Hitler is claiming that Polish soldiers crossed into Germany last night in a raid. A bloody battle took place, and every Polish soldier was killed. Hitler is raging like a madman that Poland has committed an act of war against Germany."

"Oh my God," my mother and grandmother cry simultaneously, their hands fluttering like the wings of hummingbirds.

"It is a ridiculous manufactured excuse for war. I'm sure the Nazis crossed our borders and captured a group of soldiers and took them back into Germany. Once over the border, they slaughtered the poor men to provide Hitler with a convenient excuse to invade."

"Joel, what are we going to do? I'm afraid for the children," my mother cries.

"We must prepare ourselves and keep faith that God will protect us. I think we should bring the entire family together for Shabbat tomorrow night. It is important that we prepare our minds and homes for war. I am going to talk with Tuvye and Chiel and discuss our options. Temcia, you and the girls prepare for a large Shabbat gathering. I only wish that Natalia, Alexander, and David were not so far away in Lodz. Communication is bound to suffer, and I would feel better if we were all here in one city." My Uncle Chiel is my Aunt Fela's husband, and they live nearby.

With the mention of her youngest daughter's name, my grandmother begins to cry. Aunt Natalia is the baby of the family. She is married to Alexander Weintraub and lives in Lodz with their only son, David. Alexander owns a petrol station in anticipation that Poland will catch up with the growth of the automobile industry, altering Western Europe.

My father hugs his petite mother. "Don't worry, Mama, we will survive this together. I will write to Natalia and Alexander and beg them to return to Radom."

The following day, Fela and I are released from school early as worry spreads through our city about the pending threat of the Nazis. We hurry through the streets to my parents' butcher shop to help carry home the provisions for the large family Shabbat. As always, the streets are crowded with shoppers making their last-minute purchases for the holiday, and probably extra provisions in case of shortages. We reach Rynek Street, and I can't help but admire the building my parents own, with its rental apartments on the second floor and four retail stores at street level. Flanking my parents' shop on either side is a pharmacy and a bakery. The smell of freshly baked bread wafts through the air as people hurry out the door, their arms laden with bags.

Fela and I enter my parents' store. Slabs of beef hang from large hooks in the ceiling, awaiting my father's knife. Below stand ice cases full of filleted meat. Behind the counter, my father is speaking Yiddish to a gray-haired woman who giggles at everything he says. On the other side of the store, my mother converses in Polish with a customer as she deftly wraps a parcel of meat and ties it with string.

"*Froh* Gotfryd, this is my daughter Dynka and her friend Fela," says my father in Yiddish to the grandmotherly woman.

"*Ah gitten* Shabbos *maidelech*," says the plump old lady, wishing us a good Sabbath. She smiles and her face wrinkles up like a dry apple.

Fela and I respond respectfully, "*Ah gitten* Shabbos, *Froh* Gotfryd."

The elderly woman compliments Fela and me to my father in Yiddish.

"*Shaine maidelech, gite maidelech.*" For good measure, she repeats her compliments as my father glows with pride.

My father places her purchases in her basket, and she nods farewell, walking with her cane toward the door. I run to open the door for her, and she smiles, "*Ich dankte.*"

My mother calls us to her and introduces us to her customer, *Pani* Zdebowa, who smiles as she takes her purchases from my mother. Fela and I curtsy to the woman, who is about my mother's age.

"Dynka, you remember my telling you about *Pani* Zdebowa and what a good friend and devoted customer she is?"

"Of course, Mamusia, you always say *Pani* Zdebowa is your favorite customer."

Pani Zdebowa turns to my mother. "You will have your hands full, Temcia. This one is a charmer. *Wszystkie najlepsze dla Ciebie.*" She gives my mother best wishes.

The next evening our spacious apartment seems to burst at the seams with fifteen members of my extended family. Although the gathering is called for a serious discussion among the adults, we still celebrate the Shabbat in festive fashion following the protocol of blessings and reverence to God. My mother, sister, and grandmother worked hard preparing a traditional Sabbath meal for everyone, and my sister, cousins, and I help with the serving. Everyone is talking at once at the table. The sideboard is laden with cakes and pies baked by my aunts Faigele and Mindale.

My grandfather and grandmother raised their children to be close. My father has three sisters, and all but Natalia live in our neighborhood. Faigele and her husband Chiel Madrykamien, a tailor who makes uniforms for the Polish military, live only a kilometer away. Faigele's marriage is not a happy one and providing for their large family of five children puts extra strain on the marriage and their finances. Every day my Aunt Faigele comes to our home, ostensibly to visit her mother. My grandmother, feeling sorry for her eldest daughter's predicament, sends her home with baskets filled with our food.

Noticing the missing items, my mother argues with my grandmother about taking the items without speaking to her and my father first. My poor grandmother is often caught between her love for her daughter and her hard-working daughter-in-law. When pushed to the wall, *Bubysy* seeks remedy from my father, who wishes only peace between his wife, mother, and sister. My mother is generous and would gladly give food to Faigele and her family, but she prefers that her sister-in-law behave as an adult and ask her directly rather than sneak behind her back like a child.

My Aunt Fela's three sons live at home until such a time as they marry and can afford to establish homes of their own. The two young girls of six and eight study at home and help their mother. Abek, the eldest son, who shares the same name as my brother, is a professor of languages and history at the gymnasium in Radom. Sometimes in the evening, he uses our kitchen to tutor students because his house is too loud and cramped. It's a good way for him to earn a little extra cash. My brother and I are respectful of our brilliant cousin, but on occasion, I sneak under the table to eavesdrop when he is teaching. Once, I wanted to show off in front of a handsome young man who failed to answer a question. I had surprised them both with the answer from under the table. My cousin was furious and banished me with a severe reprimand that if I did it again, he'd tell my father. He said it was unladylike to eavesdrop on people and that it was even worse to show off and embarrass another person.

His brother, Shlomo, works with my Uncle Chiel as a tailor. The youngest son, Motek, is a barber who also is in our home several times a week to shave my father. In Radom, some barbers make house calls like doctors. I love to sit and watch while Motek applies the hot towel, my father's face disappearing in the vapors. Then he mixes the thick foamy cream with its scent of menthol, patting it with his brush to the planes of my father's face. Skillful as a surgeon, he deftly shaves away the cream and beard, leaving my father's skin pink and glowing.

Finally, he pats on the bracing cologne that smells like leather and cloves. That scent, so potent, lingers on my father's skin until Motek's return and his next shave.

My Aunt Mindale is the most vocal of the sisters, and her opinion is highly regarded by the men. Always a voice of reason, she is known to stand up to any injustice. Her husband Tuvye, handsome and flamboyant, always dresses meticulously in a fashionable suit and tie. He works as a middleman, selling cow hides to the leather manufacturers that abound throughout Radom. Leather processing is an important industry in Europe, and Poland's craftsmen are renowned for the beauty and texture of their leather and suede textiles. Polish leathers are sold and prized throughout the continent. Mindale and Tuvye have two children. Nadja, at sixteen, is preparing for gymnasium, and my twelve-year-old cousin, Majer, is preparing to be a bar mitzvah.

It is unusual for the entire family to get together for a meal. The adults work hard, whether in business or at home, and the remaining time is dedicated to the demands and needs of their children. The rareness of our gathering together charges the air with electricity.

As dessert is served, a dozen conversations intertwine, everyone is eager to share family news. My father makes it clear that any talk of the pending war will be saved until after the children are excused from the table. Naturally, the older children will be included in the discussion, meaning the elder Abek, Shlomo, Motek, and the two Nadjas. Majer, Abek, Perile, Risele, and I will be sent to my bedroom to play during the discussion. I think about hiding under the table and eavesdropping, but there isn't much chance of my getting away with it.

Suddenly the table falls silent when eight-year-old Perile, in her sweet little voice, asks innocently, "Uncle Joel, why do the Germans hate us?" Her face is surrounded by a halo of dark ringlets and is punctuated by quizzical arched brows and eyes bright as two stars, which are at this moment fixated on my father. Silence grips the air as the adults exchange glances.

My father clears his throat as he carefully weighs his words. "Perile, people hate for many reasons, and not all of them are easy to explain. Sometimes it's fear of people's different beliefs and their distinct customs and behaviors that cause hate. Sometimes it's jealousy of their possessions or their success. People are not born hating, but like a seed, hatred must be planted and nurtured to grow. Hurtful words and actions toward someone who is different from you is the food of hatred. Not all Germans hate us, and hopefully, we will find a way to change the minds of those that do. Have I helped you to understand Perile?"

A beautiful smile spreads like sunshine across Perile's face. "Yes, Uncle Joel. I understand. When the Germans come to Radom, I will try to change their minds about the Jews. I will plant seeds of love, and hopefully, they will grow."

CHAPTER 5

I AWAKEN in the middle of the night to an explosive rumbling and screaming sirens.

Blinding bursts of light fill my room in between the roar of bombs, a frightening man-made thunderstorm. Everything in our bedroom rattles and shakes, and I am terrified our building will collapse, killing us all. Above the wailing sirens, I hear glass shattering, my mother screaming, my brother crying, and my father in the next room trying to calm them both. My poor grandmother shrieks with each detonation then lapses into a mournful litany of crying and prayers in Yiddish to God and my grandfather to intercede and halt the firestorm threatening to consume us. Another explosion shakes the building, drowning out the pleas of my family. "Nadja, what is happening?"

"I don't know!" Her arms fly around me, and we shudder against each other so hard we can feel each other's bones. With her hand clutching mine, we jump from the warmth of our bed and run to the window. The sky has turned a blistering red from the glow of fires burning throughout the city. We hear the drone of planes overhead, punctuated by ear-rattling explosions.

In the week leading up to this horror, my family and relatives had made a commitment to each other's survival, sharing whatever we have. The adults agreed that if given the opportunity to emigrate, we would all go. But in the face of such destruction, the slim hope I carried in my heart of my family escaping this war has shattered into tears.

Gripping the windowsill, I stare at the chaos below. The scene unfolds like a movie reel from America, and all I want to do is stop it. Horses run up and down the street in confusion, their wild neighs echoing in the night. They must have escaped their stalls when the bombing began. But there are people in the streets as well, and they are wailing as loud as the horses.

"Why are people in the streets?" I ask Nadja. "Is it not safer to remain inside our homes? They will be trampled!"

"Those men are chasing after the horses," she replies, her arm tightening around my shoulders.

"But some of the people are not. They are just screaming and running around."

"They are afraid," Nadja says. "I imagine people do strange things when they fear for their lives."

I have never thought about the true meaning of fear before. I have feared not doing well on an exam. I have feared that I would sully the new dress that Mama and Papa bought me for Hannukah. But I realize those fears are not fears at all. Those fears are little flies that buzz about my ears. But the fear that surrounds me now is a thunderous roar, and I wonder if even worse fears will come?

Every minute, another deafening explosion shakes our home, and we hear terrified shrieks from the other apartments. People stand at their windows as my sister and I are doing. My father runs into our room shouting, "Girls get away from the window! It isn't safe!"

Nadja and I run into my father's arms. "*Tata*, what is happening?"

"Come, come with me into the other room. The war has begun. Germany is attacking!"

As flashes of light illuminate his eyes, I see the truth of it, the reality that is now upon us. We run with my father to the safety of our parents' bedroom, where my mother, brother, and grandmother are huddled under the bed. I don't know why my parents' bedroom feels safer, but it does. My brother's arms are locked around my mother's neck as he whimpers, "*Tata, Tata,* make them stop."

"Please God, help us," my grandmother prays over and over again. Her prayers feel like dust in the wind. In the face of madness, they have no consequence.

Another explosion shakes the building, and the room is filled with a pellucid white light that turns night into day. My mother holds us tight, her arms wrapped around us like a shield of armor.

"Don't cry, children, don't worry, it will stop," my father says. "We are safe. The building is strong. Be brave, my darlings." But my father's words tremble on his tongue, and I know he is trying to convince himself as much as he is all of us. Under the bed, we cling to each other, frozen with terror, as the attack continues for what seems like hours.

I feel certain we will not survive the night. Perhaps this is the end. In a terrible final collapse of wood, iron, and glass, we will be buried beneath the rubble of our building, forgotten to the world.

Several times during the night, the bombing stops, and we slip into a troubled slumber, but then it begins again. We awaken and begin to pray once more.

We remain prisoners in our home for the next five days while bombs intermittently strike our city. After the second day of bombing, during a lull, my father ventures out in search of any news. When he comes back, we run to him, relieved that he has returned safely.

"*Tata, Tata,* you're back!"

My mother rushes to him, interrupting our questions, "Joel, what have you heard? Is there any hope?"

Looking at our pleading faces, he responds, "Yes, yes, there is good news. England and France have declared war on Germany."

"Thank God!" my mother exclaims. "What else? Tell us more!"

My father seems to weigh his words. "Unfortunately, the Nazis are moving rapidly. The Polish army is fighting valiantly, but they are heavily out-armed and undermanned. Germany is pounding the cities and transportation lines. There have already been hundreds of deaths and injuries. I must be honest. I can't imagine any other outcome than the Nazis conquering our country."

"How long?" my mother asks.

"How long what?"

"How long before the British and the French come to our rescue?" my mother's voice sounds shaky and impatient.

"I'm afraid—it's likely we will have to endure a German occupation. It will take time for the allies to prepare for war."

My mother's face conveys what we all feel as her eyes flood with tears.

Putting his arm around her shoulders, he says, "Come, dear, let us make some tea and listen to the radio."

We gather around the radio. The steady flow of news is disheartening. *"We will take Lodz today and tomorrow, Kielce, and on and on until we take Warszawa!"* Hitler declares, his voice harsh and guttural. He yells like a madman, and I wonder why he is filled with such hate.

My father turns the dial in search of something other than the hysterical boasting of Hitler. Finally, we hear the voice of a Polish reporter crying out his dismal news, "Countrymen, the sovereign nation of Poland is being bombarded. The Germans have thrown an immense force against our beloved country. We estimate nearly 2,400 tanks organized into six panzer divisions have rolled across our borders, striking with rapid precision through our defensive lines. The Germans are surrounding and destroying our troops with a legion of foot soldiers and mechanized infantry. The tanks are scorching the earth and leaving a path of death and destruction in the wake of this *blitzkrieg*. This lightning strike is an organized attack of such surprise, speed, and strength, it is impossible to defend against. Pray for our brave soldiers who are fighting for their lives and yours!"

In horror, we hear guns firing and explosives detonating in the background of the announcer's report. His voice fades in and out with the crackle of radio static and interference until there is only the hiss of a severed transmission.

I sit at the window in my bedroom during a momentary lull, staring down at the street. It is deserted except for an occasional person darting from doorway to doorway, furtively making their way to some unknown destination. I scrunch my eyes to see if I can recognize the people who dare to go out, but their faces are covered, and they stay in the shadows.

I beg my mother to let me go downstairs to Fela's apartment to see her. Her answer is an unequivocal "No!" My mother, who never raises her voice to scold any of us, has begun bursting into tears and holding us close. At other times she rails against this unfairness.

I wish my mother had not been the force of nature she was before the bombing. I wish she hadn't been so strong, so attached to our home and our lives here. Perhaps we could have convinced her that we should all leave. Perhaps my father would not have acquiesced so quickly to my mother's objections. Perhaps we could now be living safely in Palestyne or even America. A tightness builds in my chest, and guilt washes over me for thinking such thoughts. I love my mother. She had no way of knowing what would happen. None of us did.

The radio drones its endless blitz of bad news. We are overcome with shock and fatigue. We find out the roads are clogged with refugees heading east in a desperate attempt to outrun the Germans, who are conquering the towns and cities in their path. As I sit at the window, it occurs to me that even the birds have flown away. I have not heard a bird chirp or seen one hopping on my windowsill since the bombing began. At least they have wings to carry them away. I wish we did, too.

How did the refugees decide what to take and what to leave behind? How do you pack up a lifetime into a cart? I wonder why my parents have decided to stay instead of joining the refugees on their trek.

My sister comes to sit beside me at the window, hugging me in her arms, offering a bit of solicitude and affection. "So, what do you see, Dinale?"

"I see the end of our world, and it breaks my heart," I answer as tears well in my eyes.

"You mustn't lose hope!" Nadja kisses my forehead. "There are good people in the world. They will come to our rescue. We will have to be strong and resilient." She stares out the window, her skin as pale as the clouds in the sky. "It is our fate." Her words sound strong, but her eyes look like she is trying to convince herself as well as me.

"Since when do you believe in fate and not free will?" I grumble.

"I'm afraid that freedom for all Poles disappeared when the Nazis crossed our border. I don't know what the future will bring, but I do know we are in for difficult times, and Mama and *Tata* are going to need us in ways that I can't even imagine." She squeezes my shoulders to emphasize her words. "Right now, they could use your sunshine smile. Maybe you could comfort Abek and play a game with him. He is so frightened and could use a little distraction from his fears. I've tried, but he won't respond to me."

I nod and turn from the window. Nadja holds my hand, and we walk into the parlor. My brother Abek is playing quietly on the floor with his jacks. I smile at him and tousle his blond curls, asking if I can play jacks with him. My once jolly brother, now subdued, hands me the ball. Taking it, I whisper, "Are you afraid? It's okay if you are. I know I am."

My question is met with silence as Abek looks down at the jacks on the floor.

"Abek, I know sometimes I am not the best sister in the world. I'm truly sorry about that. But I am so glad you are my brother. Please talk to me and tell me what you feel."

He looks up at me then, his blue eyes glistening with tears. My heart is breaking as I grab his little hands in mine and squeeze them. "Abek, we are all here together, and that is a good thing." I lean into him and touch my forehead to his.

I bounce the ball and begin to play. But everything is different now. Abek is a little boy, but I see in his eyes that he knows what I know. No matter how much my parents try to reassure us, our world of Radom and a thousand other cities and villages like it has vanished. Not for a month, or a year, but forever.

CHAPTER 6

I AM restless and cannot sleep. Sleep is not something I do very well anymore. Not since the bombing raids began. Nightmares grip me. Last night I dreamt about a bomb being dropped from an airplane. It fell, and I was falling with it until it hit our building and exploded. I woke up screaming, and Nadja had to put her hand over my mouth to stop my screams so that I didn't wake everyone up. She tried to make me feel better, but nothing she said eased my terror.

I stand at my bedroom window and gaze down at the empty street. It is nearing dawn. An intense stillness hangs heavy in the air. And I wonder what is wrong, and then I realize. The silence itself woke me up. Or rather, the absence of bombs. No bombs. Nadja is still asleep.

At first, I barely register the tremor beneath my fingertips, but soon, a visible pulsation increases with frequency and speed. The ground begins to shake, and I hear a distant rumble, not unlike thunder. I crane my neck out the window, but there isn't a cloud in the sky. Could this be a new kind of bomb—one that makes the ground shake but with no flashes of light illuminating the sky?

A few minutes later, I know what is making that ferocious rumble. I see the flags first. Blood red with black swastikas, flying boldly from armored vehicles rumbling down our street.

"Dinale, what's happening? What is all that noise?" My sister grumbles from the bed.

"It's them."

"Who?" Suddenly the sleepiness is gone, and Nadja jumps from the bed and joins me at the window.

"It's the Germans. Look!" I point to the parade of steel and armor.

"*Tata, Mamashy,* come quick!" Nadja runs to the door as my parents rush into the room.

We stand in silence, watching the Germans march into Radom.

My sister's angry response rattles me. "This is a spectacle of unmitigated military might, clearly meant to quash the hearts and minds of conquered citizenry, who hide like ghosts behind curtains."

None of us can argue with what she says as we watch hundreds of motorcycles, tanks, and trucks roll through the abandoned streets. The heavy wheels churn up dust from the ground like a desert sandstorm.

My father's face is as pale as the moon in the sky, a sorrowful look in his eyes as if he were attending a funeral. Unable to bear his unhappiness, I wrap my arms around him and offer up a smile, "Don't worry, *Tata.* We will find a way to live through this. Please don't look so sad."

He kisses the top of my head. "I know, *maidele.* It just breaks my heart that you, Abek, and Nadja will have to endure this evil."

"Maybe the war won't last long," I say to reassure papa, but seeing the size of the occupying forces, it looks to me that if they are here to stay.

The Germans have arrived. Mama always said the Germans are the most organized people, and now I can see it to be true.

They take over all the government and public buildings, sheltering their soldiers and setting up their command posts. A few days later, the SS units and police arrive amid triumphant

fanfare. This time curiosity gets the better of Radom's citizens, who begin to trickle out into the streets to see what is going on. Soon crowds have gathered. Nadja and I join the throngs to watch the arrival of the elite officers of Hitler. I look around me and see the fear etched on the faces of the people of Radom. Tears flow freely from their eyes as the conquerors march through the streets laying claim to our city.

And then I see something truly shocking. Many of the Poles are greeting these monsters like heroes, welcoming them with their hats, their handkerchiefs high above their heads waving in salute. I look from the smiling Poles to the scowling faces of the SS, dressed in tailored uniforms, black spit-polished boots, and cocky hats with the skull and crossbones death symbol emblazoned on their peaks. I shiver and whisper to Nadja, "Do the Poles hate us?"

"The Poles have never been our friends. Many are anti-Semites, taught from birth to hate us by their teachers, politicians, and priests. They will gladly feed us to these murderers without a moment's remorse. Look at how they are greeting these monsters. It's as if they are being liberated, not being occupied."

Her words freeze the blood in my veins. I feel the bile rise in my throat as I watch the arrival of Hitler's ambassadors from hell. I am so scared of what is to come.

In the following days, Nadja's words come hauntingly true. The Poles adapt to their new masters, groveling with solicitousness, eager to please. The Nazis regard the Poles with contempt, but they tolerate them. They look down upon the lowly Poles, but at least they consider them human. Not so the Jews. My father can no longer leave the apartment, as the Nazis have begun grabbing Jewish men off the streets and taking them to work details. We find out the men are beaten without mercy. The Germans need labor to rebuild the armaments factory razed during the bombings and repair damaged roads and bridges. The expendable Jews are put to work as slaves. Forced to clean the streets and haul coal, the Jews suffer the force of German blows if they do not work fast enough.

For their entertainment, the Nazis prey upon the recognizable religious Jewish men and rabbis. With their *peius,* long curled sidelocks, long black tunic coats, and felt hats, they are easy prey. They bear the initial brunt of the worst cruelties. The Nazis take pleasure in humiliating and denigrating these poor souls. Ripping their beards from their faces, they beat them with clubs and kick them until they are nothing more than a bloodied mass of pulp, unrecognizable as the human beings, grandfathers, fathers, brothers, or sons they once were.

One morning, I run with my mother through the streets on a desperate errand for food and supplies. Mama's hand tightly grips mine as we pass such a scene. We rarely go out except when we need to purchase food or necessary supplies. I stare in horror as three Nazis shouting obscenities beat an old man as he pleads for mercy. I feel faint as blood gushes from his nose, and he crawls in the street, groveling for his life. I open my mouth to shout at the Nazis, but my mother swiftly covers my mouth with her hand and whispers to me to hush and hurry along. As she tugs on my hand, I glance at my mother, who has always been so strong. Her face is white as a snowdrift, and her expression as frozen as the Mleczna River in winter.

When we are safely away, I ask, "*Mamashy*, why are they beating a defenseless old man?"

She looks at me, and her eyes swimming with tears. "We are helpless, Dinale. I am sorry, but there is nothing we can do. The Nazis have no decency or conscience. They are consumed with the power of their hatred. I need you to be brave, care for our family, and help others when you can. But do not provoke the Nazis. They are dangerous." She gives me a shaky smile through her tears and hugs me close. "Come, we must get some potatoes for dinner and hurry back home to your father. The streets are dangerous, and he will worry if we take too long."

Jews no longer stroll the thoroughfares of the city. They no longer stand outside the cafés and discuss the news of the day, or play chess at the park. Our once vibrant neighborhood has become a place of fear and mourning for a world that has vanished overnight. When you pass someone in the street, everyone averts their gaze, hoping no one will notice them and ask where they are going or what they are doing. The businesses that closed during the bombing raids have not reopened, at least not the Jewish ones. A neighbor told us she saw a raiding party of Poles breaking into stores and stealing the merchandise. The Germans caught on to the illegal plundering and arrested a few of the thieves and shot them. Then the Germans themselves cleaned out all the Jewish-owned stores, leaving them empty. Our livelihood is gone.

In the days that follow, my mother is the only person in our household who ventures out to purchase what we need. My father escorts her downstairs to our building's courtyard each time. One day I follow them and hear him whisper to Mama to be careful. After Mama leaves, Papa hides behind a pillar, and I listen to him pray for her safe return. I know he is watching her walk down the street until she turns the corner and is no longer visible. His shoulders slump with resignation as he heaves a deep sigh and turns to go back inside.

I dash up the stairs before he sees me. I do not want him to know I was watching. I do not want him to know what I saw—the sadness in his eyes. And something else I will never forget. Shame.

CHAPTER 7

FATHER NOW SPENDS MOST of the day listening to the radio. Listening for news of hope. But as each day passes, hope begins to dwindle. On the radio Hitler proclaims he will conquer Warszaw in a week, but *Tata* says he has underestimated the valor of the Poles.

The radio describes the fierce fighting of the German war machine that surrounds and squeezes Warszaw in its grip. Yet, Warszaw remains free, and the Polish army fights on, even destroying the Reinhardt tank division, the pride and joy of Hitler's army. Warszaw is determined to withstand the onslaught of the German *blitzkrieg*. Against all odds, the remaining patriots fight on, even knowing the city's fall is inevitable.

"At least they will die with dignity," my father says.

I lay awake, listening to my parents arguing in the next room. The first time I heard them argue, I felt a tightness in my chest. But that pain has dulled now. I am getting used to hearing them. It is one more thing to get used to since the Germans invaded.

"Temcia, I will not allow these interlopers to cower us from keeping faith with God!" My father's voice rises in a crescendo of indignation. "Abek and I must go to synagogue!"

It is September 13, the holiest day of Rosh Hashanah, the year

5700 on the Jewish calendar. The first day of the "Days of Awe" begins in Radom.

"Joel, I am telling you that you must not go! There is no reason to put Abek or yourself in harm's way when we can all remain here and pray as a family. I have a terrible feeling that the Nazis will wreak havoc on the Jews during our holiest of days."

"Temcia, allow me my dignity. Please don't fight me on this."

Lately, my father seems to be obsessed with his dignity. He talks about it more and more. I do not understand why dignity is more important that safety and I wonder why dying with dignity is better than staying alive in hiding.

Nadja lays next to me, listening to my parents argue. "Is *Mamashy* right?" I whisper.

"Yes. *Tatashy* is being unreasonable. God will hear him just as well in our home as in the *shul*. Believe me, God has never heard more prayers than will be coming to him tonight and every day and night so long as Hitler is on the march. *Mamashy* is right, and she will prevail and get her way no matter how firmly *Tatashy* protests."

Finally, my mother uses the ultimate weapon that women throughout history have wielded when arguments fail—tears. My father, in an instant, is powerless as my mother begins to sob. My father and brother remain at home.

At sundown, we hold hands, greeting the Jewish New Year. We are united in our prayers of peace for all mankind.

My mother is proven correct in her premonition. While we are safely at home, the SS wreak havoc, entering the synagogues, destroying the interiors, desecrating the sacred texts and scrolls, and plundering the sacred articles.

The destruction of the synagogue is just the beginning as German soldiers break into Jewish homes, dragging men from their prayers and forcing them into work details where cruel humiliations are perpetrated against them. The tales are horrifying. Some Jews are forced to scrub the sidewalks with their prayer-shawls while the Nazis set fire to the beards of others. Meaningless tasks are devised as punishments against the devout.

They arrest the Hebrew teacher, Chaim Shlomo Waks, and take him to the SS headquarters. There, the Nazis torment him by trying to force him to eat pork. The deeply religious man refuses, so they beat him without mercy as he cries an endless chant of *"Shema Israel, Shema Israel!"* Finally, they shoot him in the head, silencing his voice forever. The president of the Jewish Community, Yona Zylberberg, is dragged into the streets and made to walk for hours with his arms raised above his head carrying a heavy stone while the Nazis taunt and beat him with clubs and whips. At least he is alive. The "new order," as the Nazis call themselves, leaves a path of death and destruction throughout Radom. Deep into the night, the cries of the afflicted can be heard. I can't help but wonder—where is God?

Still, the Jewish community, for the most part, remains strong in the face of persecution, as they have, time and again, throughout history. Our leaders work to protect the community as best they can. But the harder they try, the more the Germans demand. For some reason, the Nazis are obsessed with lists, and demand the council provide a list of all Jews residing in the city as well as their occupations. Amidst beatings and enforced demands, the Jewish community tries to manage some semblance of normalcy. People return to work, slipping quietly through the streets to open stores and factories. Jewish charity increases its efforts to care for those already suffering immense losses.

Finally, one rainy morning, we children are allowed to return to school. I am delighted to see Fela waiting for me as usual in our courtyard. She holds her umbrella as a gray drizzle falls from the heavens.

"Fela!" I cry, running to her, my arms outstretched. She wraps her arms around me, and our umbrellas entangle in a mesh of wire and cloth. "I am so happy to see you! *Mamashy* has been so protective she hasn't let us out of the house."

"I know," Fela replies. "My parents have been impossible, never letting us out of their sight. Our home has turned into a cage, but today I feel like a bird that has been given its freedom."

"Then let us fly, Fela." I take her arm, and we begin to walk our familiar route to school. Our happy chatter is drowned out by the loud rumble of an armored vehicle. Fela and I gasp and move away from the street, staying close to the shops as we walk. We keep our eyes down and dare not look up for fear of being noticed by the Nazis. And I realize that being outside doesn't mean freedom at all. People pass without the customary greetings. There are no *dorozkas* and no peddlers selling pickles or anything else. Nazi swastika flags fly from buildings and storefronts everywhere. As if we don't know we are a vanquished nation.

"*Bubysy* continually cries and prays, and everyone else is so jumpy that the slightest noise or complaint sends them into a tizzy."

"It's the same in my house," Fela says. "My mother is constantly on edge, and my poor father has nowhere to go to escape her." A nervous giggle escapes her.

"I hate the Germans," I whisper. "I hope God destroys them all."

With a quick glance over our shoulders, Fela gives a tiny nod. "The elders say that if we keep a low profile and do our best to meet their demands, we should be able to endure the occupation and survive."

"Do you truly believe that? I saw them beat a defenseless old man."

Like a wizened old woman Fela tries to calm my fears. "Dynka, we will manage, you'll see. We must manage. We have no choice."

"I wish we could escape to your grandparents' cherry orchard right now," I say with a sigh. "I can just taste that sweet black cherry juice."

Fela nods again, and this time she smiles. Everyone knows how much I love cherries.

"Remember when we were there in the summer, and we played in the orchard?" I ask, my voice distant and dreamy. "Remember how big the cherries were and how I looped them over my ears like long, beautiful dangling earrings, and you said they looked like rubies?" I heave a deep sigh. "It seems like a million years ago when life was so beautiful. Did we know it then?"

"We did Dynka, and we will again." Fela's eyes mist, and she wipes away a tear that has made its escape down her nose. "It will be all right. Someday we will return to my grandparents' cherry orchard, and you can eat all the cherries your heart desires. Then we will grow up and go to Palestyne and marry farmers."

I smile at her, and hope returns as I remember the promise we made to each other beneath the branches of the apple trees behind our building. I squeeze her hand. "I know you are right. This too will pass."

CHAPTER 8

THE NAZIS TAKE my father's radio.

They confiscate the radios of all the Jews in Radom. Yet one more law they have imposed upon us, knowing it will isolate us from news on the progress of the war. And the progress has been stunningly swift.

On September 17, Poland's old enemy, Mother Russia, under the iron rule of Stalin's dictatorship and emboldened by Poland's vulnerability, seals its bargain with the devil Germans and invades our eastern border. Poland is like a lamb surrounded by a pack of hungry wolves. On September 27, Warszaw surrenders to the Nazis, and the nation of Poland ceases to exist. Within two days, the Germans and the Russians divide Poland with the intention of exploiting her resources and her people. With the sealing of this bargain, more than two million Jews fall into the clutches of the Nazis and more than a million under the Russians.

The cold and rain have come unseasonably early this year, echoing the misery that envelops us. As the days advance, my parents and sister discuss with ever-increasing bitterness the continuous commands of the Judenrat. The Judenrat is a council of Jews chosen by our community to mediate between the Germans and the Jews.

They are trying to keep the community safe, but every day the occupiers' demands grow more oppressive.

Newspapers are my father's sole link to the outside world, especially since we are no longer allowed a radio. Father snatches as many printed publications available in Polish and German on the black market. The illustrious Yiddish newspapers are no longer permitted to print.

One afternoon, I sit in the kitchen, reading the *Adventures of Tom Sawyer,* an American novel by Mark Twain, which was recently published in Polish. My mother bought it for me just before the invasion. I can't put it down and carry it with me everywhere. My father storms in, cursing under his breath, and stuffs his newspaper into the garbage can.

"*Tata,* what is it?" I ask. "You look so angry."

My father's scowl disappears. "Nothing darling, it is nothing, only some silliness in the newspaper. Please continue your reading. I didn't realize you were in the kitchen."

My father returns to the other room, leaving me perplexed as to what would cause such a reaction. My curiosity gets the better of me. I retrieve the paper from the waste bin and scan the front page, searching for any clue to what had caused my father's burst of anger. The newspaper is the German publication, *Der Sturmer.* It is written in German, which is like Yiddish, but it takes several minutes for me to make sense of the words. I scan each page until I am stunned to discover the source of his anger. An article heady with vile rhetoric. One sentence in particular shocks me: *The Jewish people ought to be exterminated root and branch. Then this plague of pests will be dealt with permanently in Poland in one stroke.*

Over and over, I reread the sentence to make sure I am not mistaken. The word "exterminated" sticks in my throat.

"What does this mean, *Tata?*"

My father is in the dining room surrounded by newspapers, his glasses perched on his nose.

I set the article in front of him. "Papa, why do they talk about extermination?"

He closes his eyes for a moment, then opens them again, a gentle smile on his face. Patting his knee, he motions. "Come sit, Dinale."

I climb onto his lap and rest my head on his shoulder, snuggling into the safety of his arms. "Are the Nazis going to kill us all, *Tatashy?*" I whisper, my lips beginning to tremble and tears springing to my eyes.

"Hush, hush, *maidele.* Don't be silly. They can't kill millions of people. It is not possible," he says, wiping my tears away with his fingertips.

"But *Tata*, if they say it, they must mean it. But how? Are there that many bullets in the world? Millions of bullets?"

"No, no, no, they would be foolish to destroy such an army of workers. Better to use us for cheap labor. The world will not sit by and let this Nazi menace take control of Europe. The Germans tried this once in the Great War, and they were stopped and brought to their knees by the world's free democracies. The world will come to the rescue again, you'll see. We must stay strong. The Jewish people have survived time and again and lived to tell the tale of every tyrant who has tried to destroy us. Remember your Jewish history? Remember Haman? Now, dry your tears and go back to reading your book."

"But, Father, you yourself said that it will take time for the other countries to come and rescue us. How will we manage to stay alive if the Germans wish to wipe us from the face of the earth?"

"The Nazis know what a resource we are. Now, let's not worry about it anymore. Mama and I love you, your sister, and your brother so much. We will do everything to protect you, don't worry. Throw the newspaper away. It's simply one man's insane words."

Sniffling, I wipe my nose on my sleeve and hop down from my father's lap. I tear up the newspaper and throw it back in the trash. But I cannot stop thinking of that horrible word in the article. *Extermination.* Later I look it up in my father's fat dictionary that he keeps on the bookshelf. I read and re-read the definition of the word. *Extermination—killing, especially of a whole group of people or animals.* I run to the bathroom and throw up. If I was hoping for another definition, I now know the truth. It haunts me and gives me hideous dreams.

That night my sleep is plagued by an endless nightmare. A monster chases me through a dark forest. My parents, my sister, and my brother call out to me, but I cannot see them through the thick trees and twisting branches that seem to climb up to the heavens. I'm wearing only my nightgown, and I shiver in the cold, my teeth chattering so hard, I feel as though my jaw will crack. I don't know where to turn, or which direction to go to escape the monster. His footsteps are heavy and loud, making the ground shake with every step, as he gets closer and closer. A wolf howls in the distance and terror shoots through me. If the monster doesn't get me, the wolves surely will. I have heard tales of wolf packs that hunt in the night, tearing their victims to shreds. I open my mouth to scream, but there is no sound. I have lost my voice. I stumble and fall and look back into the darkness. A man wearing a black uniform and a peaked hat strides toward me, but I can't see his face. Something shiny glints in his hand. It's a long-bladed knife, the kind my father uses for butchering. He stops and listens. Hearing my family calling for me, he grins and turns in the direction of their voices. I scream again, finding my voice. *"Run! Run! Run!"* I scream and scream and scream. *"Run! Run! Run!"* I warn Papa, Mama, Nadja, and Abek. *"Run! Run! Run…"*

"Dinale, Dinale, it is okay." Nadja rocks me in her arms. "No one is running anywhere. You are safe in your own bed. Don't cry. You are safe. It's only a bad dream."

Gasping and crying, I cannot stop shaking. "H-horrible!" I manage to say in a sobbing breath. "A monster was after me, and then he was after you, *Tata, Mamashy,* and Abek. I couldn't stop him. I wanted to, but I couldn't. It was unbearable."

She shudders against me and holds me closer to her. "I know how scared you are. We are all scared. It is only natural for you to be upset by this nightmare. It's impossible for any of us to understand how anyone could hate us this much. To hate children, the infirm, and the aged is beyond comprehension. But we are safe. As long as we have each other, everything will be fine. Cry my darling, but don't give up hope. Remember, I'm here for you, always."

Nadja kisses the top of my head, and I snuggle closer to her. She rocks me and sings a lullaby that Mama sang to us when we were small, "*Shlof Shoyn Man Kind,* Sleep my lovely child, my comfort, Sleep, lyu-lyu-lyu!"

When she finishes, I ask, "Nadja, what do you want to do when you grow up?"

"I want to go to university and study literature. I want to be a writer. I want to move to Palestyne and write for a newspaper. Maybe I can make a difference for our people."

"Don't you want to get married?"

"Of course I do, but I want something that belongs to me. Maybe I will write about a family and their experiences during the war. What about you, what do you want to do?"

"I want to go to Palestyne, too, and live on a kibbutz."

She tilts her head and looks at me as if she doesn't believe me. "Really?"

"Yes, Fela and I are going to move to Palestyne and marry farmers."

Nadja bursts into giggles and hugs me. "It's a good thing I'll be there too. To keep you and Fela out of mischief."

"Good." I yawn. "Then it's settled."

CHAPTER 9

I HOLD the shears as steady as I can, tongue between my teeth, as I concentrate on the task of cutting along the pattern that my grandmother drew with chalk. I try my best to make smooth cuts so the star of David does not have ragged edges.

"That one is your best one yet," Grandmother says as she finishes stitching a star into another armband.

"Thank you, *Bubbe*."

Fela, my father's sister, and Mama are making soup for dinner—we have been eating together as much as we can—combining our less than ample supplies. Nadja and I no longer attend school, as we are needed to stand in endless lines that wrap around blocks to buy bread or milk or medicine. Sometimes it takes us even longer to get to and from a shop as we are forbidden to walk on Lubelska Street, the main artery of the city, and we are not allowed on Rynek Square, where the city hall is situated. Mother is still the best cook in all of Poland, and she manages to make even turnip soup a delicacy. But she spends her days cleaning and scrubbing and cooking and keeping as busy as possible, for she can no longer run her butcher shop. All the kosher butchers are forced out of business as they no longer are allowed to slaughter animals according to the laws of the Torah.

"*Bubbe* and I are almost done with the star armbands, and then we will have enough for everyone to wear."

It is the end of October, and the Nazis have declared their latest decree. Every Jew over the age of ten must wear an armband with a yellow Star of David. If we are caught without the armband, we will be arrested and deported to German labor camps.

Every day brings a new edict with a new loss of rights. Jews no longer are allowed to walk on sidewalks or take public transportation unless we obtain a special pass from the Judenrat. Many boulevards and squares are illegal for us to use, a sure sign of our degraded status. We are forced to abide by a curfew, limiting our ability to gather, which is why my uncle, aunt, and cousins are staying over tonight. Tonight would have been Shabbat, but now, it is simply another Friday night. We can no longer practice our customs and celebrate our holidays, not even in the privacy of our own homes.

EVERY WEEK there is a new *befehl*. Father and Uncle Chiel whisper in low voices in the parlor that these decrees are meant to humiliate us and weaken our resolve. Only two weeks ago, the new German mayor, Schwizgabel, demanded that the Jewish community pay a tithe for being allowed to live and work in occupied Poland. Two million zlotys from a population that has already been stripped of its assets. The leaders of the community speak with the mayor, and in a polite and deferential manner, they tell him they cannot raise that money. The mayor regards them for a moment and then suggests a brilliant solution. The soldiers and officials are in need of new bedding. One thousand sets of bedding would suffice as payment.

The elders return to the community and inform the tailors and seamstresses of Radom, my Uncle Chiel being one of those tailors. They sew around the clock to finish the bedding before the deadline. After the bedding is delivered, the mayor nods in satisfaction. As the elders turn to leave, they hear laughter and a parting comment from the German official that soon becomes a standing joke. "If it belongs to a Jew, it must be good, and we want it!"

Abek is sitting on the kitchen floor playing jacks with our cousin Perl. I hop over the jacks and walk down the hallway. I slip my armband over my sleeve and look in the mirror, hanging on the wall near the front door. I have sewn this one myself and I admire the neat and even stitches. "I am not going to allow them to make me feel bad about being a Jew. I'm proud of the Jewish people. I'm proud of our history."

"Such pride will do us no good now," Najda says. "The Nazi beasts are isolating us from the Polish population. They are dehumanizing us and removing our dignity. Each step is intended to fulfill a larger plan. That's what these armbands are for, to visibly mark us."

"I will not allow them to make me feel bad about being a Jew," I repeat, following Nadja into the kitchen.

"*Mamashy*, I want to wear the star too," Abek chimes.

I turn to my brother, "Well, you can't, Abek, because you are just a baby. You aren't old enough to be counted as a Jew." No sooner are the words out of my mouth than I regret saying them. Abek looks from me to our mother, his eyes filling with tears. "*Mamashy*, I am a Jew. Tell her that I am a Jew."

My mother's face stiffens with anger. "Dina, there is no reason for you to say such cruel words. Abek bears our covenant with God upon his person. He is a circumcised male. He can never be anything other than a Jew. You will apologize to him this instant!"

"I'm sorry, Abek, I shouldn't have said that to you," I say, scuffing my shoe on the floor. What possessed me to say such hurtful words to my brother?

My grandmother sighs, "I don't know what has gotten into all of us. Can someone please tell me where decency and respect have gone?" Her eyes are bright with tears. I know she is as sad about all these changes as I am, as we all are. She has lived with my parents for their entire married life, but now she has decided to live with her middle daughter Mindale, my uncle Tuvye, and my cousins Nadja and Majer. Aunt Mindale has a large home and plenty of room. My grandmother will have the comfort of living with Tuvye's widowed mother, Chava, a contemporary and friend. And she will be closer to her youngest child Natalia, who returned to Radom with her husband Alexander and son David after the Nazis confiscated their gas station. They live in the same apartment building as Mindale and Tuvye. Living with her daughters, my grandmother will be well cared for and treated with the greatest of respect. The arrangement is satisfactory for all, and with Cousin Dina Talman, my mother's niece, now living with us, it makes things easier. But our hearts are heavy. For Abek and me, this loss of our grandmother is hardest of all. My grandmother was the first to greet me with love in the morning and the last to give me a kiss at night.

For my mother, it soon proves to be an unexpected blessing as she has never lived without the suggestions and good intentions of her in-laws. My mother has always been a strong woman, with her own mind and will. Now she is the sole woman of the house. My mother loves my grandmother, but it is difficult to be mistress of the home when your husband's mother has always held the reins. I know my mother is relieved and perhaps even a little happy. I can see it in her eyes as she prepares dinner. Even when my grandmother suggests she add more salt to the soup. My mother smiles and nods, whereas before, her shoulders would have stiffened a tiny bit, not enough for my grandmother to notice. But I always did. I also know that my mother would never express her relief and, yes, happiness at being the sole mistress of her home. How can she? She has gained a strange sense of freedom because of the Nazi occupation. Such is the perversity of life.

Nadja huffs in frustration at the way the older Jews still believe that being kind and good is the most important thing. "*Bubbe*, the Nazis have made the words decency, respect, and kindness meaningless."

"Yes, that is true, but that does not mean we have to be like them," Grandmother says.

Mother gives Nadja a warning glance, and Nadja's lips tighten. She has strong political views, and sometimes she confides in me that if the older people had been cleverer with the Nazis, we would not have been forced to give up so much.

Cousin Dina joins us in the kitchen, an impish sparkle in her eyes. I know she will make things better. She always does. I sleep in the same bed as Nadja and Dina now, making for unusually close quarters. Cousin Dina, like me, is named for my mother's sister, who died in childbirth. She is two years older than my sister and looks identical to my mother, with her beautiful black hair and blue eyes that crinkle when she smiles. I don't mind sharing a bed with Dina as she knows so much about my mother's family, and she is far more patient with my endless questions than Nadja. I like Dina's hearty laugh that can be heard throughout the apartment, even with the doors closed. Best of all, she is very much the actress and keeps us entertained with her wonderful impersonations of movie stars and celebrities. Her laughter is so infectious, that when she shares a joke or mimics someone famous, we all end up on the floor, rolling around and holding our sides

Dina throws a wink in my direction, bends her knees, making her tall frame shrink before my eyes. She begins strutting around the room like Groucho Marx. Mumbling under her breath, she stumbles about like a chicken with its head cut off as she imitates the Fuhrer. The Fuhrer would suffer apoplexy if he could see her goose-stepping and frothing at the mouth, marching around the apartment mocking his lunacy. Clapping our hands with joy, Abek, Perl, and I are up in a second, following as she prowls about the room. Dina suddenly turns to Abek, her face nearly touching his. "Excuse me, excuse me, 'schveinahund,'" she screams, "you *vill* do exactly as I say, *ya*?"

Our giggles fill the air as she stares at Abek and Perl, twitching her brows, her face, scrunched up like a barking dog ready to attack. Glaring with her hands on her hips, she waits for his response.

"*Ya, ya, mein Fuhrer,*" my brother squeals, clicking his heels and saluting like a Nazi, all the while trying to keep a straight face.

My father and uncle, having heard the laughter, stroll into the kitchen. Soon they are laughing too. Feeding on everyone's amusement, Dina scowls, and her brows move up and down. She places her finger on her temple as if thinking.

"I know!" she exclaims, producing two little black drawings from her pocket. She alternates them above her lips, first one and then the other and crosses her eyes as she tries to look at the paper mustaches. "*Dumkoff*, when I say that I like my mustache clipped this *vay* and not that *vay*, you must do it precisely as I say." She alternates between Hitler's little black stub and then the other cutout that resembles Simon Legree's, waxed and curled at the ends. "Do you see *vat* I mean?" she shouts.

"*Ya, ya, mein Fuhrer*," cries Abek, as we all buckle over with laughter.

Dina mumbles to herself. "I am surrounded by idiots, idiot generals, idiot colonels, idiots all of them. Only the Jews are not idiots. Only the Jews are smarter than everyone else."

She walks around in circles, pacing with her hands behind her back, shaking her head. Then with her finger pointing at her brain, an amazing idea occurs to her. "Ya. I know *vat* I must do. I must make all of the Jews my slaves and then I *vill* control all of the really smart people in Europe. Then I *von't* have to put up with such *dumkoffs*." At this point, she grabs my mother's hands, pulls her to her feet, and begins dancing around in a circle singing, "And, that's why I am the Fuhrer, because I am almost as smart as the Jews, you see?"

Singing like a child reciting a nursery rhyme, she pulls each of us to our feet until we are all holding hands dancing around the room. By this time, we are giddy with laughter. Unable to contain herself a moment longer, Dina crumples to the floor in hilarious glee. The sound of that hearty laughter is like a match igniting a flame, sending us into fits of side-splitting merriment.

Everyone laughs, including Nadja and grandmother. Nadja wraps her arms around *Bubbe*'s shoulders and kisses her check. All is well once more. There may be less food to eat and more people to feed in our crowded home, but Dina Talman brings rays of sunshine to these darkest of days.

CHAPTER 10

My mother has decided to sell one of her necklaces.

"Which one, Dinale?"

"*Mamashy*, they are both so beautiful."

She holds up the delicate white pearls, joined together with two overlapping circles of diamonds. "Let me try this one on you, and then we will decide." Fastening the clip, she sighs. "There, now turn around and look in the mirror and see how lovely you look. Jewelry has a way of lighting up a woman's face, doesn't it?"

I feel grown-up and beautiful. "Oh, *Mamashy*, it is so lovely. I wish you didn't have to part with it."

"I don't mind, Dinale. I have enjoyed having them, but they are just objects and can be replaced." She places her hands on my shoulders and kisses my cheek. "We have more important things to buy. All that matters are my children, your father, and the rest of our family. I will gladly sell off all of these baubles if I can keep us safe another day." Smiling, she scrutinizes me in the mirror. "Yes, I think this one will bring a nice price. I will take it to *Pani* Zdebowa today, and she will put me in touch with a buyer."

Three days later, I overhear Mama whispering to *Tata* how much she got for the necklace. A pittance of the true value. But it is the way of things. *Tata* tells her she is more beautiful than the finest pearls. And Mama begins to cry.

I don't know if she is crying because she is happy that *Tata* has given her such a nice compliment or because she worries that one day there will be nothing left to sell.

A week later, Papa tells us he must begin working for the Nazis, thanks to the Judenrat.

The Judenrat now functions as the intermediary between the Nazis and the Jews in Radom. They do their best to alleviate the scarcity of food in our community by opening soup kitchens throughout the Jewish neighborhoods. The Judenrat hands out some 4,000 meals a day at a token charge of 20 *groszy*, which is waived for children and those who cannot pay. They also do their best to organize the labor force needed by the Germans. In this way, they can mitigate the kidnapping of Jewish men from their homes and hinder their frequent pastime of Nazis of grabbing men off the streets and beating them before dragging them away to work camps.

The Jewish penchant for organization allows the Judenrat to address some of the needs of the most destitute. Much of the forced labor comes from the poorest residents among the Jews since anyone with resources can pay the Judenrat to remove their names from the forced workers' lists. The Nazis pay nothing for labor. The Judenrat uses the sweat money from wealthier Jews to pay the laborers who desperately need the daily *zlotys* to sustain their families. My father says the Judenrat does its best, considering it is forced to do business with the devil and his disciples.

To feed the large occupying army, officials, SS, and police force, the Germans require slaughterers, butchers, and cooks. My father, with a highly desirable skill, is contacted by the Judenrat and ordered to work for the Nazis as a butcher. For this, he receives a pittance, works long hours, and is supervised by soldiers with machine guns. He returns from a long day's work and jokes about how afraid the Germans must be of the Jews. "They have so many soldiers with guns guarding so few Jews and their dangerous butcher knives."

While my father works as a butcher for the Nazis, my mother watches over us and does her best to make our daily lives as normal as possible. My sister and her two friends, Eva and Esterka, patiently continue our education several hours a day at the kitchen table. Each teaches her favorite subject to Abek and me. To tell the truth, I don't miss going to school at all. In addition, my mother has hired a private instructor who comes several times a week. This is a blessing since the teacher has lost all means of employment. To his chagrin, my brother must sit through my lessons, as he is younger and can learn from my more advanced studies. When I am done, I flee outside, leaving Abek to sit and complain how unfair it is that I'm allowed to leave. I relish the freedom, as I am free to play in the park and in the courtyard with Fela and my friends.

Fela and I dance in the snowdrifts. Building snowmen and having snowball fights, we feel like normal children again. We even dare to dream that one day the war will end and our lives will resume where we left off. As the snowflakes float down around us, we close our eyes and turn our faces up to the sky. We giggle as the delicate crystals tickle our eyelashes.

"Is it possible to make a wish on a snowflake?" Fela whispers.

"I don't know. But it's worth a try," I whisper back.

I wish for this war to end. I wish the Allies will come rescue us. I wish everything will go back to normal and we will go back to being happy and safe.

I open my eyes and wait for Fela to open hers. We look at each other and know that we have wished for the same thing.

The next day Nadja comes running into the house as if she is being hunted by lions, her hair an unruly mass of curls and her eyes red from crying. She throws herself into my father's arms, burying her sobs in his chest. My mother runs to her, pressing against her back, her arms encircling her. My parents look like bookends keeping a book upright.

"*Nu,* Nadja, what is it, what has happened?" My mother's voice rises in a frenzied wail. "Please stop crying. We can't understand what you are saying. Tell us what has happened."

"Sh, sh, *maidele,* calm down," my father adds. "It can't be that bad. We can't help you if we don't know what is wrong."

My sister cannot be quieted and continues to weep, her body spasming with her sobs. There is nothing anyone can do but wait for her to regain her composure and tell us what horrible catastrophe has struck. After what seems like an eternity, she raises her head, her stricken face white, her words indecipherable through her sobs. At first, haltingly, like a trickle of water seeping from a dike, she reveals the source of her sorrow.

"I don't know what I was thinking," she stammers, shaking her head. "I—I left the house to meet Eva and Esterka. But I forgot to wear my armband. A Polish policeman stopped me—he was walking with a Nazi gendarme and his German shepherd dog. He asked me where I lived, and I said Koszarowa Ulica. Oh my God! I should have lied and said I lived somewhere else. Then he said, 'Isn't that a Jewish neighborhood?' And I said, 'Yes.'"

At this point, my mother begins to cry, which triggers Nadja's tears once more. My father tells them both to stop crying so we can get to the bottom of what happened and decide what to do. Nadja resumes her account of what has occurred. "The Nazi raised his voice and asked, *'You are a Jew, correct?'* I said yes, and he began to shout, *'Where is your armband, Jew? Where is that gutter symbol of the garbage Jews?'* It was so horrible, Mama, he kept on shouting at me.

"'You are in violation of a directive that Jews are not allowed out of their homes without an armband identifying them as pig Jews!' He was so angry and so demeaning that I thought I was going to throw up. I was so scared. *'I forgot it, sir,'* I told him, *'I am so sorry, please, please, I will never do it again!'*

"The Polish policeman looked uncomfortable and probably would have let me go if he hadn't been with the Nazi, but he had to look supportive in front of him, so he remained silent. The Nazi told me to report to Gestapo headquarters tomorrow morning. He said I will receive my punishment when I get there and that I am to come alone. I am so frightened. What will they do to me? What if they deport me? Or worse?"

My father begins pacing, his jaw clenching in a paroxysm of tension and his brow damp with perspiration. "We must stay calm. You have to go to Nazi headquarters. There is no way to avoid it. Your mother will accompany you and wait outside.

"You will beg them to be tolerant, reminding them that you are a teenager, a child. Do you understand?"

Nodding yes, Nadja resumes her whimpering.

My father continues. "We will wait to see what happens. If they detain you, your mother will return home to inform me, and I will go to the Judenrat and beg them to intervene. Don't worry, the Nazis are beasts, but I have not seen them harm any young women or children. I am sure they will give you a warning and that will be that. You will see that I am right."

That night it isn't me who suffers from nightmares. Nadja wakes Dina and me, crying in her sleep, tossing and flailing her arms, trying to fend off the monsters that pursue her. We calm her as best we can, whispering words of encouragement that everything will be all right. We sleep wrapped in each other's arms until the morning light.

The next day, even without a good night's sleep, Nadja manages to look startlingly beautiful, her blue eyes rimmed with circles of darkness and her demeanor appropriately subdued. She leaves with my mother and walks to Nazi headquarters. My father has to report to work, so I am left alone with Dina and Abek to await the outcome of Nadja's punishment. We occupy ourselves with reading and games of chess, but our nervousness gets the better of us. Every few minutes, one of us jumps up, running to the window to see if *Mamashy* and Nadja are, God willing, coming up the street. Finally, after endless hours, we see them turn into the courtyard. Once inside our home and with the door closed, we all rejoice, jumping up and down, hugging each other, so grateful that Nadja is safe and back at home. My father was correct. The punishment is a severe warning and an added burden of having to report to Nazi headquarters every morning for one week, wearing her Nazi armband.

Each day, after facing her Nazi persecutor, she returns demoralized, recounting to us what it is like walking alone through Nazi headquarters. "It is so frightening. I feel like a thousand eyes are boring into me filled with hatred and disgust," Nadja tells us. "The yellow Star of David on its white band has the desired effect, and most of the people give me a wide berth as if I am contaminated with a deadly disease. Then I am made to stand for hours, waiting to be presented to the same Nazi who yelled at me in the street. No chair, no water, nothing but malicious stares as everyone else comes and goes. Finally, I am called before him, and he proceeds to shout at me using every vile name possible. I have to stand there in humiliation while he publicly degrades me in front of his comrades, some of whom stand around sniggering with glee at my debasement. It is terrifying and shameful at once. After he releases all of his venom, he warns me that if I am ever caught without my armband again, he will see that I am immediately deported and that I will never see my family again. Over and over, he reminds me how lucky I am that he doesn't deport me right now."

The week seems like a lifetime for Nadja as she endures the daily degradation of cowering before the Nazi. Each day, he inspects her armband, finding fault with the way it is sewn. Each night, she stitches a new armband, only to be berated the next day. This goes on for the entire week. By day she is tortured by the sinister Nazi, and by night she is terrified by dreams of him. By the fifth day, he finally tires of the game and, with little more than a sneer, dismisses her, saying he never wants to see her again. The whole episode has scared us all to death, and my parents are now doubly watchful over us and make sure that we never leave the house without the armband again.

After sulking around the house a few weeks, still smarting from her near deportation, Nadja returns to her old self. My parents have not pressed her but have allowed her to reflect on the events she has suffered through. They know that with time, she will return once more to the confidence and activism that marked her progress since childhood. After a few weeks of silence and pensiveness, Nadja resumes her teaching duties with a new urgency. She seizes the reins of our education, easing us forward to what she now predicts will be a bright future. With her inherent positivity and poise restored, my brother and I feel encouraged to work harder at our studies to please her.

One day when I am supposed to be reading, I peek from behind my book, and I see a sadness in Nadja's eyes. Her gaze meets mine, and the sadness is gone, replaced by a bright smile. I wonder if the sadness in Nadja's eyes is only visible when she thinks no one is watching. I wish I had a snowflake to wish on, but I add another wish to my list of wishes anyway, hoping there is room for one more.

I wish Nadja will never be sad or scared again.

CHAPTER 11

"*Tatashy*, we don't have a Moses. How will God save us without a Moses?"

My father stares at Abek as he ponders his question. Lovingly, he smooths the errant curls of the precocious boy. "Don't worry, Abek. He will send us an army to save us. You will see. He will send us a powerful army."

Even with the restrictions against any practice of the Jewish religion, most Jews in Radom manage to celebrate some semblance of the Passover Seder. In our home, the story of the Exodus from Egypt and the biblical destruction of the pharaoh's armies by the swirling waters of the Red Sea bring tears to my father's eyes as he recounts the story. My father leads the Seder with as much joy as he can muster, elaborating and drawing parallels to the evils that plague the Jews of Europe and the Jews of ancient Egypt.

We eat the *matzo* that has been sent to Poland from the Red Cross and Jewish organizations around the world. We pray that God will send us an army and deliver us from the Nazis, as he delivered us from the pharaoh when we were enslaved in ancient Egypt.

I hope that Papa is right, and that God will deliver us from this evil, for there seems to be no end to the vile evil the Nazis inflict on us. Word spreads throughout Radom that the Nazis have ordered thirty-two men to report to the labor recruiting office. Fortunately, Papa was not one of those ordered. Eighteen of the thirty-two men show up. They are taken into confinement and viciously beaten beyond recognition. Then they are thrown into trucks and driven to a suburb called Firley, where they are forced to work in the sandpits. The Nazis, in their cruel amusement, toss live grenades into the sand pits, killing all eighteen men.

Shock is the least of the emotions that ripple through the Jewish community—fear is the greatest. The other men have gone into hiding. I wonder if the Nazis will hunt them down and do the same to them. I want to ask Papa if he would have obeyed had he been called to report to the labor recruiting office. I want to ask him why the Judenrat did not intervene to stop this from happening. I don't ask either of these questions. I realize that I don't want to know the answers.

Instead, I pray that God sends us our very own Moses, for Hitler seems even more powerful than the pharaoh of Egypt. His armies seem unstoppable as they march across Europe, felling nations as if they are dominoes collapsing, one atop the other.

My father becomes more distraught and nervous, often hiding the newspapers once he has read them. My sister digs them out of the garbage and shares the news with me. The stories are terrifying.

"Listen to this," Nadja tells Dina and me one night as we ready for bed. *"The time is near when a machine will go into motion which is going to prepare a grave for the world's criminal—Judah—from which there will be no resurrection."* Nadja goes on to read a quote from our illustrious German Marshall of Poland. *"I ask nothing of the Jews except that they should disappear."*

That night my nightmares begin again, and when I wake up screaming, Nadja and Dina try to comfort me.

"I'm sorry, Dynka," Nadja croons in my ear as she rocks me back and forth. "I promise never to read you any more articles from the newspapers. But they are just words. These things have not happened."

I nod, for I cannot speak. My throat hurts from sobbing. Even so, it doesn't matter whether Nadja stops reading papers to me. I won't be able to forget the vile words written in print. They are not just words. They are the true desires of the Germans.

On March 29th, 1941, comes the decree from Dr. Karl Lasch, the governor of Radom, that will change our world forever. The Jews must leave their homes and move into two separate ghettos established by our German overlords. What is worse, we must leave by April 7, giving us only ten days to find a place to live and move.

I sit at the kitchen table staring as a spring storm delivers a steady stream of snowflakes that drift peacefully past the window. I remember that day with Fela when we both wished on the falling snowflakes. That day seems so long ago. A lifetime. So many terrible things have happened since then.

"Children, as you know, the Nazis require that every Jew in Radom move to one of two ghettos allocated as residential areas for Jews," my father tells us, his face pinched with worry.

There are approximately 35,000 Jews residing in Radom, so naturally, this displacement has caused great distress in the community. Many Polish families will also be uprooted from their traditional neighborhoods and homes. The Germans have established two ghettos. The larger of the two, called the Walowa Street Ghetto, will hold 30,000 people, making it extremely cramped and crowded. The second is called the Glinice Ghetto and will hold about 5,000 Jews. It is several kilometers from here, and the houses are older, but a bit more spacious.

"Mama and I have secured a home from a Polish farmer in the Glinice Ghetto where we will be moving," my father says with a slight smile. Mama nods as well. Her smile is a little more hopeful. "We feel the conditions will be better there as I predict we will see extreme shortages of food and other necessities in the months ahead. I know this will be difficult for you, but most of our possessions must be left behind, and only what is practical for our survival will accompany us to our new home."

"Children, we will need your help in paring down your belongings to the absolute essentials," Mama adds. "The most difficult adjustment will be saying good-bye to friends and family, at least until the war ends. Some of them will be going to the Walowa Ghetto, and I don't know if we will be allowed to see each other."

"But *Tata!*" Suddenly it becomes clear to me what sacrifices our moving entails. "You mean we won't be able to visit *Bubbe* or Fela or anyone?"

"Dinale, it is impossible to say what will or will not be allowed."

My heart contracts in my chest, and the blood in my veins surges in anger. "I won't go!"

"Dinale," my father says with a crack in his voice. "Dinale, please, you must understand this is happening to every family in Radom and most likely every Jewish family in Europe under Nazi rule."

"I don't care!" The injustice of our situation has instilled in me new-found defiance, "I am going to run away and hide in the forest or the apple orchard! I will not give up my friends and family!"

Tears of frustration fill my eyes, and guilt consumes me as I see my father bow his head in dejection. I cannot bear another moment of the emotions that overwhelm me. Jumping up from the table, I grab my coat and run from the house. I run to Fela's house, calling to her from the courtyard. "Fela, come quickly. I need you," I cry. "I need you to come outside so we can talk! *Something terrible has happened.*"

Fela peers from her window, a shadow behind the lace curtains. She waves, indicating that she will come in just a minute. I stand there, pounding my feet as powdery snow crystals rise in a cloud around me. Tears fall from my eyes as I ponder the consequences of my insubordination toward my parents. I have never been defiant of them, especially during these times when their burdens are so heavy. Already my words are echoing in my mind, surrounding me in a veil of guilt and remorse. I have hurt the two people I love most in the world. As I pace back and forth in the courtyard, Fela finally exits her door and runs to me. "I can't believe it," I cry as I hug her. "The Nazis are ordering all the Jews into ghettos, and we are going to have to leave and move to a small ghetto miles from here."

She embraces me. "I know, Dinale, my parents have told us as well.

Don't worry. At least we are going to the same place, to the small ghetto."

"You, too?" I marvel in disbelief.

Taking my hand, she says, "Come, let's go to the apple orchard."

Hand in hand, we slip behind our building to the privacy of our childhood haven. We are happy to garner one last chance to escape the realities of a world that has begun to slip away.

With our backs against the solid trunk of our favorite apple tree, we whisper of the pending changes. It is cold, and the wind blusters through the leafless orchard, sending snowflakes dancing in the air under the gray skies. I remember the sunny day here, not so long ago, when we made plans for a future. Those dreams seem as farfetched as flying to the moon.

"It won't be so bad, Dynka," Fela says, squeezing my hand. "We will still be together. Think of it as an adventure. What would Shirley Temple do? She would find a way to make the best of things. Even wearing rags, she can break into song."

I laugh, trying to picture Fela and me wearing rags and singing. The whole idea seems ludicrous, and I shake my head, clearing the preposterous vision from my mind.

"I know you are right, Fela. At least we will all be together." I lay my head on her shoulder. "I am just so afraid of what is to come and what will become of us. Why are the Nazis separating us from the rest of the population? Why are they taking everything from us? Where is God? Why is He not coming to our rescue?"

"Dynka, you know that God has His reasons for not interfering in the world of men. Believe me, He will eventually see our plight and the evil of the Nazis, and He will raise His sword and obliterate them from the earth."

"Yes, you are right," I say. "God would never forsake His people." I sniffle as I begin to cry. "Fela, I behaved unforgivably to my parents. I lost my temper and said the most awful things. I told them that I was not going to go with them and that I would run away and hide in the forest. They must be so angry and disappointed in me."

"Don't be silly. Go home and apologize to them. They will forgive you no matter what you do or say. Especially now. Everyone is upset. We all say things we don't mean. You should hear my parents. They are squabbling all the time like a couple of mad hens."

The vision of squawking poultry sends us both into fits of giggles. We begin to cluck like a couple of hens fanning the air with our wings. And for a moment, my fear of the future fades away. My frosty breath hangs in the air as the snow begins to come down in heavier large flakes.

"Shall we make another wish just to make sure God knows?" Fela asks.

"Yes, let us make another wish."

We hold hands and say our wishes aloud this time. I worry that God cannot hear the wishes. I worry that God will not send us another Moses. I worry that the world is too busy fighting the Nazis to come to our rescue. I worry that moving to the ghettos will make things even worse because it will mean all the Jews will be living together in one place. It means the Germans will be able to watch us even more closely. It means we will no longer be free.

It is time to end our sojourn in the orchard and return to our homes. Fela and I hug and hold hands, running home with the intent of surviving the dreaded move to the ghetto.

I compose myself as I open the door of my home, fully prepared to make amends to my parents. When I step into the house, they both jump up from the table and run to me, hugging and kissing me. "I am so sorry. *Mamashy* and *Tatashy*, please forgive me!"

"It's okay!" they cry, their arms enveloping me. My mother, ready with a towel, rubs my head vigorously, wrapping me in it as she guides me toward the fire burning in the open hearth.

"We wish we could have broken the news to you more gently, but the time to prepare is so short," my father says.

"And we need your help," adds my mother.

Respectfully I nod. "I will do my best to make you proud. Fela also is moving to the smaller ghetto, so at least I have one of my friends."

"That's good, darling," says my father. "This is the girl that we are so proud to call our daughter. Now go change out of these wet clothes and let us continue with our discussion. We must plan."

The days fly by as we pack the belongings we will take with us to our new home. My mother and our Polish maid, Anya, make many trips in advance of our actual departure, cleaning and readying our new quarters. Nadja, Dina, and I discuss the personal belongings we feel are necessary, winter clothing, summer clothing, comforters, and linens. For me, it is my precious balls and books that I could never live without.

My mother has the hardest time deciding which of her most prized possessions to leave behind. Her photo albums with pictures from her childhood and ours will go with us. But her beautiful furniture will have to be abandoned, as there is no room for it in the small home awaiting us. I watch as my mother wanders around the rooms, talking aloud to herself, weighing the value of objects and whether she needs them. Of course, most of her cooking pots and pans will be needed, but she will only take one set of china, which poses a dilemma for her. She has a beautiful set of fine Hungarian china with butter-flies painted in dazzling hues that seem to float across the pure white background. Our beautiful holiday china was passed down from her grandmother. Parting with this treasured family heirloom brings tears to her eyes. But she wipes her eyes and smiles at Nadja and me. "They are just possessions," she says again. "The most important thing is that we are together."

One decision that has been made for her is whether to take her paintings that line the walls of our home. My mother is an avid collector of art, buying for love and investment from the local art gallery that imports paintings from all over Europe. *Plein air* oil paintings of landscapes by the impressionists line our walls. She is particularly enamored with the work of a Dutch artist named Van Gogh and has purchased several of his small oils. The Nazis have ordered all art to remain on the walls where they will be confiscated for the benefit of the Third Reich. I watch my mother walk around the rooms of our home, bidding good-bye to her old friends and touching each one with a farewell caress. Anything that can be easily sold, such as jewelry and heirlooms, will provide us with money to purchase food and medicines to keep our family alive.

The day before the ordered deadline of our departure, we watch my father take down our our precious *mezuzah*. He whispers a prayer to God, carefully wrapping it in cloth. Every *mezuzah*, whether wood, metal, or glass, contains a small piece of parchment inscribed with a passage from the Book of Deuteronomy. Twenty-two lines equally spaced and printed precisely so that they may access the power of God's eternal magic and blessings and keep the dwellers of the home safe. The parchment of the *mezuzah* reads,

Hear, O Israel: The Lord is our God, the Lord is one:

And thou shalt love the Lord thy God with all thine heart, and with all thy soul, and with all thy might.

And these words, which I command thee this day, shall be in thine heart.

And thou shalt teach them diligently unto thy children, and shalt talk of them when thou sittest in thine house, and when thou walkest by the way, and when thou liest down, and when thou risest up.

And thou shalt bind them for a sign upon thine hand, and they shall be as frontlets between thine eyes.

And thou shalt write them upon the posts of thy house, and on thy gates.

And it shall come to pass, if ye shall hearken diligently unto my commandments which I command you this day, to love the Lord your God, and to serve him with all your heart and with all your soul.

That I will give you the rain of your land in its due season, the first rain and the latter rain, that thou mayest gather in thy corn, and thy wine, and thine oil.

And I will give grass in thy fields for thy cattle, that thou mayest eat and be full.

Take heed to yourselves, that your heart be not deceived, and ye turn aside, and serve other gods, and worship them.

For then, the Lord's wrath will flare up against you, and He will close up the heavens, that there be no rain, and that the land yield not her fruit; and you will swiftly perish from the good land which the Lord giveth you.

The day of our leave-taking comes. I awaken and go to the window and look down at the street where I have grown up. I sit there, as I have done hundreds of times, and gaze at the leafless chestnut trees, their branches reaching toward the heavens. This gray morning feels more like winter than spring. The street already is bustling with people loading a lifetime's worth of possessions into horse-drawn carts, automobiles, and trucks. Placing my hand on the cold glass, a chill of foreboding races through my body and I shiver.

I hear my parents from the other room as they busy themselves with organizing the boxes and crates that hold the wealth of our lives. I dress and make myself ready for what will surely be a long and arduous day.

Our personal belongings have been brought downstairs and loaded into the *dorozka* and the hired wagon that will accompany us to the ghetto. We have said our goodbyes to our family and friends, most of whom are moving to the large ghetto.

My heart is heavy, not because we are leaving so much behind, but because our home is full of so many memories. So much love.

"We may not be able to take everything with us, but we have each other," Mama says from the doorway of my bedroom.

"But Mama, it will be hard to remember all the wonderful memories if we are no longer living in our home," I say as tears spring to my eyes.

"I promise you, Dina, you will never forget these memories." Mama enfolds me in her warm embrace.

"How do you know?"

"Because I will be there to remind you," she says with a chuckle.

I giggle, and she wipes my eyes with her handkerchief. "Come, Dina, it is time to go."

I nod, and we join Papa and Nadja and Abek and Dina, who are waiting for us. Papa locks the front door for the last time. We may have left most of our belongings behind, but we will keep our memories alive in our hearts because we are together. And that is the important thing.

CHAPTER 12

WE ARE VERY LUCKY.

The house is small, but it has a bathroom. And the room where we will all sleep is attached to the kitchen. Upstairs there is another apartment, but as of yet, no one has moved in. My sister, Cousin Dina and I will occupy one bed and my parents and brother will sleep in the other bed.

My mother has worked her usual magic to make the house inviting with colorful curtains on the windows and photographs in pretty frames to brighten dark corners. The table and chairs we brought with us from home. Our other home. The home that is no longer ours. The home that we will most likely not see again until the war is over. That is what Mama and Papa have told us. I fervently hope so. I already miss my bedroom and sitting by the window.

The house we live in now previously belonged to a Polish farmer who had a shed in the back where he kept some livestock. My parents have wisely purchased a cow from the farmer. Mama will sell the excess milk to our neighbors.

The morning after our arrival, I awake in this strange house that is now my home. Both my sister and Cousin Dina are already up and gone. My father has also left for work. Labor without pay. Nadja calls it slave labor. Even though we have moved into the ghetto, my father must continue to labor for the Nazis as a butcher, cutting and dressing meats to feed the German troops, officers, and officials.

The room is dark and my nose twitches at the uncustomary dank smell of mildew. The astringent sour odor combined with a hundred years of smoke from the chimney emanates from the dark wood walls. Mama and Papa say that no matter how much we clean and scour the walls the smell will not disappear. It is a permanent reminder of the age of the old house and those that have lived in it. I suppose even walls can store memories, especially smelly ones.

Dressing quickly, I am anxious to explore the confines of the neighborhood. My mother enters the door from the back of the house, carrying pails of milk. I run to help her.

"Dinale look at the delicious creamy milk that our fine cow has provided us with." Her face is beaming with a bright smile. "Isn't it wonderful to know that we shall have milk every day? We are very lucky."

"Yes, Mama, we are very lucky," I concur. "*Mamashy*, where's Abek?"

"Oh, he rose early and is out exploring the street in search of new friends."

"*Mamashy* did you milk the cow yourself?"

"See, you didn't know your mama was so talented. Yes, I learned to do this when I was a young girl. I will teach you how to milk a cow… if you would like to learn?"

"Can you show me now?" I hop up and down with excitement. It is seldom that my mother has time to spend with any of us anymore as she is so busy selling and buying the food and articles that we need and trying to keep us fed and healthy. To be alone with her and have her full attention is like a dream come true.

"Come, I will teach you the mystery of milking."

Mama sets the pails down in a cool spot in the room that is both kitchen and bedroom. I watch as she pours a glass of milk, "A cow is one of God's most extraordinary creatures and was created to provide for man and thus should be treated with love and kindness." She hands me the glass of milk as I follow her out the back door and into the cow shed. "In order for a cow to give you the best milk she has to offer, she needs to be soothed and calmed with gentle words and a reassuring hand."

"Mama this milk is delicious. Did you sing to the cow for such delicious milk?

My mother chuckles and takes my hand, pulling me closer to the cow. I look at our cow with her large kindly brown eyes and she looks at me as she chews on the fresh hay in the bin in front of her. My mother places a small stool next to our cow and motions me to sit beside her on the ground. "I think we should name our cow, what do you think?"

"Oh, yes of course." I nod in agreement. "We must give her a special name."

"Why don't you introduce yourself to our cow and rub her with your hands so that she can get a scent of you."

Placing my empty glass on the ground, I slowly approach the cow and timidly touch the end of her nose. "Hello, dear cow, my name is Dynka Frydman, and I am very pleased to meet you."

The cow nuzzles my hand and smothers it in a sticky gooey lick, something like the consistency of moist sandpaper. It tickles and I begin to giggle. My mother laughs and says, "Very good. See, she likes you."

"Maybe we should name her Queen Esther?" I suggest as I pat her head, prompting more nuzzles.

"Queen Esther..." Mama purses her lips and regards the cow. "It's a good name. Like the great biblical heroine of our people in ancient Persia, our Esther will take care of us, too. I like it... so Esther it shall be. Now come here and sit on my lap and I will talk you through the milking of our Queen Esther. Take the udder in your hand and gently pull down and squeeze it ever so lightly." Doing as I am told, I try to pull and squeeze but nothing happens. Esther, however, turns her head and looks at me with her great brown eyes.

"*Mamashy* did I do something wrong?"

"No, no, you just have to be patient and keep trying. Now try again."

I try and suddenly a stream of milk squirts out of the cow's udder, filling the pail. "I did it, I did it," I exclaim with delight as Esther turns her head and moos at me.

"Yes, you did," Mama hugs me tight. "I think Queen Esther approves as well."

I glow with pride and joy at sharing this special moment with my mother. Suddenly the world seems a little brighter.

"Now, go play. I think I saw a girl who looks about your age. Go and introduce yourself and later you can tell me all about her."

Kissing my mother on the cheek and giving Esther a final pat on her head, I run from the shed and around the house onto the street in front. There I see a girl playing with a ball.

"Hello," she says, waving. "Would you like to play?"

"Yes, very much. My name is Dina Frydman. What's your name?"

"Vunia," she replies, "Vunia Greenberg. It looks like we're next-door neighbors," she says, pointing at the two-story wooden house that is nearly identical to the one we now occupy. "I'm twelve years old and I moved here with, my parents, my sister Lola, who is seventeen, and my Great-Aunt Ruth and Great-Uncle Saul. They have two dogs named Winston and Churchill."

I look with curiosity at the almond-shaped green eyes that gaze back at me with equal curiosity.

"I'll be twelve in June," I say, "and I just moved here with my parents and sister, Nadja, who is seventeen and my brother, Abek, who is nine. My cousin, Dina, also lives with us. She is twenty-one. I've never had a dog. What kind are they?"

"Chihuahuas. Would you like to meet them?"

"Oh yes."

"Come on, follow me."

Without hesitation I follow the tall skinny girl with her curly mane of rust-colored hair into her home through the low doorway at the entrance. The house is dark and musty like ours, with boxes in various stages of unpacking scattered about the rooms. Vunia takes the steps two at a time as I follow her to the second floor. She knocks on the door, smiling at me with anticipation. "Aunt Ruth, it's Vunia and I've brought a new friend. Can we come in?"

"Of course, darling," a woman's voice answers.

The door opens and standing before me is the most exotic woman I have ever seen. Her head is wrapped in a golden turban from which wisps of silvery coiled hair fight to escape. The wiry hair reminds me of springs popping out of an old mattress. She looks at me with blue eyes that are lined with a matching shade of smudged cobalt blue pencil that emphasizes the slight protrusion of her oversized eyes. Ruth is dressed in a brocaded caftan that drapes her body in mysterious folds that both hide and reveal. I cannot take my eyes off the strange creature that stands before me. Her odd demeanor triggers imaginings of Eastern potentates. My gaze travels the length of her, finally resting on the two small dogs that peer at Vunia and me through amber eyes. Their little tails drum the air with expectation.

"Forgive the disarray of our diminutive space." Her honeyed voice has the cadence of someone whose mother tongue is another language. "I suppose we all must get used to a simpler existence." Her rouged lips draw into a smile as the two small dogs wriggle with anticipation of pending freedom.

"This is Dina, Aunt Ruth. She lives next door."

Ruth formally offers her hand, "How nice to meet you, dear."

"Dina has never had a pet of her own, Aunt Ruth, and we are hoping you will let us play with Winston and Churchill."

"Well, I am sure that nothing could make these two mischievous little boys happier than playing with you." Ruth kisses the two Chihuahuas and then bends to release the squirming pups, who spin in joyful circles about our legs, jumping with boundless energy and eagerness for our attention. Ruth excuses herself, and Vunia and I giggle as the tiny balls of energy lick our faces and jump into our laps.

Vunia puts the compliant pair through a series of tricks that they perform with yelping pleasure. The dogs roll over and dance in circles on their hind legs as Vunia, in an uninterrupted stream of consciousness, shares the story of the Greenberg family with me. I learn that her father was an accountant before the Germans invaded. Now her father is reduced to day labor and her mother, like mine, is forced to sell her fine clothing and jewelry to support their family. As for the intriguing Aunt Ruth, Vunia confides the tale of her avant-garde relatives, which might as well have been a tale from the *Arabian Nights* so unfamiliar is the reality of it to me.

As a young man, Vunia's Great-Uncle Saul moved to England long before the Great War to pursue his education at Cambridge. Through his Rothschild cousins, he was introduced to Ruth. They fell in love and over the protests of her family, and Ruth converted to Judaism and married the foreign Jew. After living as an expatriate for dozens of years, Saul yearned to return to his family. Ever-adventurous Ruth gave him his wish.

Theirs has been a great love affair that has withstood the caprices of time and they have remained devoted to each other for over forty years. They moved to Poland many years before the current crises and lived in a beautiful home on a wide avenue in the cosmopolitan city of Warszaw. There, amid the wealthy patrons of the city, they lived a wonderful life. Warszaw is considered the Paris of the East with its lively café society and cultural flowering of art, music, and politics. They traveled the world, returning often to England and Ruth's well-connected relations. The only missing blessing in their lives was Ruth's inability to conceive. Chihuahuas have filled the emptiness and they dote on their substitute children. These two Chihuahuas are the last in a long line of the continuing dynasty of Winston and Churchill Chihuahuas, so named for the great statesman who now leads the British nation as Prime Minister and is Hitler's most vocal foe.

Winston is a close friend of Ruth's family, thus the Chihuahuas' names. When the Nazis invaded Warszaw, their home was one of the first commandeered by the Nazi elite and Ruth and Saul fled to Radom and Saul's extended family. There, they were welcomed into Vunia's family's home until everyone was forced to move to the ghetto. They are elderly people who certainly must now regret having left the safety of England. Through diplomatic channels, they are in communication with Ruth's family in England, who are trying to arrange their release. However, there is no sign of the Nazis letting them go and like the rest of us, they remain prisoners.

Aunt Ruth returns to the room with a tray of cookies and tea. The Chihuahuas dance at her feet, overjoyed at her return as she tenderly admonishes them to behave themselves in front of company. We spend the afternoon sipping tea and feeding biscuits to Winston and Churchill while Ruth entertains us with wonderful stories about growing up in England, her travels with Saul, and the many escapades of all the Winstons and Churchills that she has fostered.

I forget about the war and the Nazis for a few hours in this magical kingdom with tiny dancing dogs, a new friend, and Great-Aunt Ruth, who seems to me like a regal queen. I cannot wait to tell Mama that Queen Esther is not the only Queen in the neighborhood.

At the end of the day, I sadly bid farewell to Aunt Ruth, Vunia, and the Chihuahuas. It is the happiest I've been in a long while. Aunt Ruth and Vunia's invitation to return as often as I like fills my heart with joy. I hope that there will be many more days like this, laughing with Mama as we milk Queen Esther in the morning and then playing with Vunia and Winston and Churchill, and listening to Queen Ruth's stories about England and her travels around the world.

CHAPTER 13

MY PARENTS KEEP TELLING us we are lucky, and I cannot help thinking about that.

"If we are so lucky, then why does Mama risk her life to sell her fineries on the black market?" I ask one evening at dinner.

Mama and Papa look at each other and then at us.

"I am very careful," Mama says. "But I want to make sure we have enough food to last us through the winter."

"The Judenrat is doing their best to keep supplies flowing," Papa says.

"They cannot do enough," Nadja pipes in. "The ghettos like Lodz and Warszaw have become more like prisons than ghettos."

"Why are they like prisons?" Abek asks.

"Because starvation and sickness have taken hold," Nadja answers.

Mama and Papa frown at her, but Nadja has grown more vocal of late.

Cousin Dina has become quieter. I heard Mama whisper to Nadja in the shed not to be so vocal about shortages or Dina will think she is the cause of hardship in our family.

"Will we starve too, Papa?" Abek asks.

"We are lucky here in Glinice," Papa answers, ruffling Abek's hair.

"There are fewer guards here," Mama adds. "It is all right. I have plenty of jewelry and finery to sell yet, and we have Queen Esther."

"Yes, Queen Esther gives us the creamiest milk in all the land," I declare.

Everyone chuckles, including Cousin Dina.

But a few days later I begin to wonder if we are so lucky after all. The German gendarmes catch three people sneaking out of the ghetto and decide to make an example of them. Every man, woman, and child in our neighborhood is ordered to witness the Nazis deliver a swift and brutal punishment to the three hapless souls, hanging them from an erected scaffold. As the three bodies swing lifeless in the breeze, the Nazis scream their tirade at all of us. Anyone who leaves the ghetto without permission will suffer the same fate or worse.

The heads of the victims are left uncovered and visible for all to see. The Germans leave the bodies dangling from the nooses for three days and nights, the faces of the dead blackening with each passing day. The rotting stench serving as a warning to us all that no infraction of the rules will be tolerated.

I have never witnessed death. When Grandfather died, I did not see it, but at least he passed away in the comfort of his home. Abek stands frozen beside me. His hand clutches mine. Mama and Papa stand on either side of us. Nadja and Dina hold hands and stand on Mama's other side. I close my eyes and pray their souls have flown to heaven.

Although a significant deterrent, the hangings have not stopped the illegal egress as desperate times require desperate measures and the inhabitants of the ghetto have no choice but to continue to run the risk of death by sneaking out, the only alternative to slowly starving.

Feigning sleep, I can hear my parents whispering, their heads bent together. Straining my ears, I can barely make out their conversation. "Joel, I know it's risky, but I think Dina will provide the perfect cover."

"I don't know. It is so dangerous now. What if you are stopped? My God they just hanged three people!"

"I tell you Joel, Dina sounds and looks more like a Pole than the

Poles do. No one would ever suspect her of being Jewish. Together, we will blend in and no one will question us."

My father sighs with resignation, "I see you've made up your mind, Temcia. I think we have been married long enough for me to trust your judgment. There is no sense in us arguing. Take her with you tomorrow and may God protect you both."

I am frightened at the prospect of going with my mother. But I tell myself that as long as I am with Mama, it will be all right. Mama is the smartest woman I know. Maybe even smarter than Papa. The next day my mother and I slip from the confines of the ghetto. She holds tightly to my hand as we walk purposely, making small talk in Polish, and blending into the stream of people that walk freely through the city. Inconspicuously we make our way to a modest working-class neighborhood and arrive at an unremarkable house. My mother knocks at the door which is opened by a woman I recognize immediately as my mother's customer *Pani* Zdebowa. She smiles perfunctorily at us, her eyes scanning the street for any irregularities, "Come in, please, come in quickly. I see you've brought your daughter, Dina."

Pani Zdebowa lifts my chin appraisingly, "Such a pretty child and what rosy cheeks she has."

My mother's face lights with pride. "Yes, she is a treasure. And speaking of jewels, I've brought you a beautiful brooch, something you should have no trouble selling."

"Excellent. Why doesn't Dina sit, and I will bring her some milk and cookies and then you and I can talk."

Pani Zdebowa disappears down the hall and returns a few moments later with a plate of cookies and a glass of milk which she places before me.

"*Dziękuję Ci,*" I thank her.

"*Proszę bardzo,*" says *Pani* Zdebowa.

She pats me on the head as she turns toward my mother, "Did you have any problems getting here today?"

"No. Thank heavens the streets were quiet. We slipped through when the police changed guard. It was completely uneventful, but I still feel better having Dina with me. A mother and her child is a much better cover."

"I agree completely, Temcia. She is such a beautiful child and the only attention she will attract is admiration. May I see the brooch?"

"Of course." My mother rummages in her purse and takes out a blue velvet pouch. Opening it, she removes a jeweled butterfly brooch with its wings folded. The butterfly encrusted with colored gems looks as if it has momentarily landed upon a single blue stone and might take off at any minute and fly away. "Here Anya, what do you think?"

"Ahh, yes, it is lovely. You are right—this should fetch a decent price. I will take it to my contact. In the meantime, I have good news. I sold the bracelet that you brought me last week and I have money for you."

"I am very grateful, Anya, for your help. Without you, I don't know how we would manage."

Pani Zdebowa blushes. "It is the least I can do. I only wish I could do more. I am ashamed of my country and its lack of resolve in helping our Jewish citizens. It is disgraceful."

"You are a good woman, Anya. I wish there were more people like you. Dina and I must get back to the ghetto. I've left Abek alone and I shouldn't be gone too long."

"Yes, of course, let me get the money." *Pani* Zdebowa hurries back down the hall.

"Dina, darling, finish your milk and cookies as we must get back to your brother." I wrap two cookies in my handkerchief and pocket them for Abek.

Pani Zdebowa returns and presses a wad of zlotys into my mother's hand and then walks us to the door. The two women hug and kiss each other on both cheeks, and then *Pani* Zdebowa bends to kiss me and whispers in my ear, "Be a good girl, Dina, and take good care of your mother."

On the street, a convoy of German cars speeds past and I feel my mother's hand tremble in mine from the mere sight of them. We walk briskly through the neighborhood, retracing our route back to the ghetto. People that we pass in the street now and then nod and greet us with courtesy. The contrast between the ghetto and the outside world is unfathomable and I wonder if our fellow citizens ever give a thought to their Jewish countrymen who are being held like hostages.

We turn a corner and it is as if all of the oxygen has suddenly been sucked out of the air. Strolling toward us is a Polish policeman, a German gendarme with his German shepherd, and another Nazi whose shiny black boots reflect the sunlight. My mother nearly freezes in her tracks. I glance at her face. I can see the color drain from her cheeks. The dangerous trio hasn't noticed us yet as they are deep in conversation. We cannot cross the street to avoid them as we will only draw suspicion. We have no choice but to keep going. I grab my mother's arm to steady her as we continue toward them as nonchalantly as possible. When we are a few feet away, I look up at my mother and say in Polish, "Mamusia, tomorrow morning are we going to church?" I speak loud enough that all three of the men peer at me with scrutiny, looking me up and down. I smile shyly at them.

My mother quickly regains her composure. "Yes, my darling, tomorrow we go to church."

The Polish policeman breaks the awkward impasse as he teases, "Little girl, you make sure your mama takes you to church." His eyes crinkle into a grin as he tips his hat.

The Nazis, who have been staring coldly at us, listening to our discourse, break into laughter. When we are safely past them and have turned another corner, my mother, who has begun to breathe again, grabs and kisses me. I can feel her pounding heart through my coat.

"If it wasn't for you and your clever thinking, those monsters would've surely stopped us. God only knows what might have happened," she whispers in a choked voice. "You saved our lives, Dina!"

Mama makes a point of telling everyone at dinner how smart I am. My father is now convinced that it is much safer for my mother if I accompany her from now on.

CHAPTER 14

"Run! Run! Get out of the house!"

Nadja yells above the uproar as she grabs my hand and pulls me from the bed as my cousin Dina runs ahead of us. My parents and Abek follow us outside. The street fills with people in various stages of undress shouting and pointing at the sky. Everyone cranes their necks, peering up toward the heavens.

The planes are flying low toward the east, where the first rays of sunlight wash the horizon rose and gold, chasing the night from the sky. We stand like statues watching and listening to the deafening roar of German planes clearing the treetops above our heads.

Who will be the next unfortunates to suffer from the armada of enemy aircraft overhead?

We soon learn that the German-Soviet pact has fallen apart and that the German Luftwaffe and Wermacht are attacking the Russians. Their first line of approach is to lay claim to the rest of Poland, Lithuania, and Belorussia and then to march into Mother Russia herself.

That Shabbat, my family lights the Sabbath candles and prays for the millions of Jews in those countries who will also become victims to the Nazis' hatred.

"Papa? Why are the Nazis so obsessed with hurting Jews? What did we do to them?" Abek asks that night.

"They hate what they don't understand. They don't see us as true citizens of Poland with the same rights as the other Poles. This is our country, too. And that fills them with hatred."

"Yes, but if the Poles stood up for us," Nadja says in an angry tone, "perhaps the Nazis would not go around beating Jews, dragging young men from their homes, throwing them into ditches and blowing them up with grenades, or hanging us in the public square. They hate that we work hard to make a better life for ourselves and our families because they are either too lazy or incapable of doing so."

Papa gives Nadja a warning look. Nadja is angry. She grows angrier every day. I know that Mama and Papa worry about her anger. They worry she might do something rash that will put her and us in harm's way. I don't blame her for being angry. After all, I go with Mama to sell jewelry, and is that not dangerous? Especially with the new German edict that any Jew found outside the ghetto will be shot, and any Pole who aids a Jew will also be shot. My mother has bought us both small gold crosses to be worn whenever we illegally leave the ghetto. I secretly pray that the luck of the cross is greater than the luck of the Star of David.

"It is all these lists that bother me," Papa says, clearly trying to change the subject. "The Germans are obsessed with lists, and now there is a new *befehl*, another order to be complied with. The Judenrat has been instructed to compose lists of all the residents in the ghettos. The lists will include our name, age, sex, and profession. They also want to know how many oxen, horses, carts, and animals the Jews own.

"But why Papa? Why do they want to know so much about us?" I ask him.

"We are nothing to them beyond names and numbers in columns and rows on endless sheets of paper that they keep in files within cabinets in countless storage rooms," Nadja interrupts before Papa can answer. "We are no longer human hearts and souls—we are like livestock to be dispensed with in whatever manner meets their fancy!"

"Nadja, the children don't need to hear this," Mama scolds. "We will be all right. We will get through this. We have done so until now, and we will continue to do so."

"The fact that the Germans and Russians have broken their pact also bodes well for the Allied forces," Papa says. "And that is potentially good news for all of us. Perhaps it will mean the end to this war before things get any worse."

Nadja opens her mouth to speak again, but Mama gives her "the look," and Nadja's cheeks color, but she doesn't say anything else.

I hope that Mama and Papa are right. But it is hard to believe that this war will end soon, especially in the midst of growing starvation and sickness that surrounds us. The effects of starvation are being felt everywhere, and typhoid is now rampant. The leaves have begun their autumn descent from the trees, and with their death, the rainy season comes early, and the streets are slicked with mud. Mud that cakes the faces of hundreds of orphans who roam the streets. Children who had families. Children who had loving parents. Children who are now forced to beg for food as carts filled with dead bodies rumble past.

In my family, we have become a little thinner, but my mother has miraculously managed to keep us all healthy and prevented the dreaded typhoid from entering our home. And we are lucky because Nadja has gotten a job working at a warehouse run by the Germans called A.V.L.

Nadja has promised Mama and Papa she will keep her temper in check and obey all the rules and not draw any negative attention to herself. I know Nadja has passionate beliefs, but I also know that she loves us more than anything.

Besides, I think her boyfriend Mikal had something to do with Nadja's change of heart. My parents like Mikal, and they approve of him. Mikal told us that if Nadja comes to the factory with him to work for the Nazis, it will bode well for our family.

The Nazis have promised to give special treatment to the families of workers that help with the war effort. The Nazis are packing and shipping everything of value from Poland to Germany, mostly what they stole from the Jews. The ill-gotten gain will now enrich those who are destroying us. They are also shipping blankets, bedding, canteens, medicine, and many other items to their soldiers at the front who are now fighting the Russians.

The first thing my sister does when she starts working at A.V.L. is to ask if our cousin Dina can also work there. The warehouse accepts Dina as well. Nadja and Diana work alongside two-thousand other Jews every day, which takes a burden off our food supply as they are fed a small meal. More important, it also gives us a sense of security that we may be afforded some safety from their positions as laborers for the Nazis.

I DECIDE to sneak out on my own.

We have not heard from our family in the Big Ghetto for several weeks, and my father is greatly worried. I am used to sneaking out of the ghetto with my mother. I know I can pass for a non-Jewish Polish girl. Besides, I have my gold cross around my neck that will make them think I am one of them.

I hope to bring my father good news to calm the constant distress from which he suffers. Patiently, I wait around the corner of a building observing the police guard as he smokes a cigarette and then finally grinds it out beneath the black heel of his boot. He paces back and forth and looks at his watch with a frown. I twist the small golden cross between my fingers in nervousness. At last, his patience is rewarded as another policeman strides slowly toward him.

I have watched this trading of posts before and know that the two men will probably end up chatting and exchanging gossip for a few minutes while leisurely walking for a block or two with their heads down, the collars of their coats pulled up, and their attention focused on each other.

My assumption is correct, and when their backs are turned, I make myself invisible, flattening myself against the wall as I dart around the corner, disappearing into the streets outside our ghetto. I walk briskly, taking the back streets when possible and avoiding all human contact. The Big Ghetto is several kilometers away, and I am forced to cross crowded areas bustling with people. I garner little attention as I look like any other young Polish girl with my blonde hair braided and tied with blue ribbons. No one searches my face in recognition or cares who I am or where I am going.

An hour later, I finally reach the boundary streets of the Big Ghetto. Taking a quick look around me and thinking myself safe to proceed, I venture forward. Suddenly I feel a hand on my shoulder, and my heart seizes. Gruffly, the hand spins me around, and I come face to face with a Polish policeman.

Frantically, I try to struggle free from his grasp, but he holds me firmly, leaving me no chance of escape. Looking up at his bloodshot eyes, I am completely unnerved. All I can see is his oily uncombed hair and broad peasant face leering down at me, and I am suddenly overwhelmed by a wave of nausea. I cannot help but cringe from his sour breath that smells of rotting teeth and stale wine. *Please, God. Please don't let me faint.*

"You seem to be in quite a big hurry to enter the pigsty of the stinking Jews. Perhaps you would like to tell me where you live and why you are here?"

I frantically avoid looking at his face. My heart is pounding in my chest as I strain my mind for a plausible explanation to his questions. "I... I, please sir, you are hurting me! I will tell you whatever you want to know if you just let go of me," I cry as tears flood my eyes.

"Start talking." Angrily, he jerks my arm. "I will let you go when I am good and ready."

I try desperately to regain my composure and still my thundering heart. It is all I can do to breathe. "My grandmother lives in the big ghetto, and I miss her terribly. I want to visit her."

"You are a Jew," he says with disgust. "Where do you live?"

"I live with my family in the Glinice Ghetto. I snuck out without my parent's permission. They do not know where I am. Please, please let me go. I am so sorry, I will never do it again."

"You will tell me the street and address of where you live. I am going to come to your house and talk to your parents. If I don't get any money from your family for letting you go, I will arrest you on the spot and turn you in to the Nazis for illegally leaving the ghetto, which you know is punishable by death! DO YOU UNDERSTAND WHAT I AM SAYING?"

"Yes," I whimper, choking on my tears.

Taking out his pad and pencil, with no regard for my terror, he demands. "Give me the address!"

Thinking quickly, I stammer the name of a street that is as far away from my house as I can think of. Writing it down and satisfied with my answer, he lets me go, and I run as fast as I can back home.

"Remember what I said," he shouts after me.

With my heart pounding in my ears and tears blinding me, I run and run, oblivious to anyone or anything in my path. I only slow down when I am blocks away from my home. Once I regain my breath and stem the flow of tears, normalcy returns, and I realize how lucky I am. I say a silent thank you to God that he gave me the presence of mind to give the villain a wrong address.

The days pass, and I uncharacteristically remain indoors, rarely venturing out to play with Vunia. My parents throw me bemused looks.

"Don't you want to go out to play?" Papa asks me one afternoon.

"I think I will study hard today," I reply. "I don't want to fall behind in the schoolwork that Nadja has left for me to do."

My father raises his eyebrows and exchanges a look with my mother. Mama shrugs her shoulders at my newfound desire to spend so many extra hours in study than I usually would.

As I fall back into the routines of ghetto life, my fears of leaving the ghetto and being caught again fade away.

My first attempt to sneak into the Big Ghetto may have failed, but I begin to ponder a second attempt. Luckily, the blackmailing policeman has never found me or my home, and as each day passes, my resolve builds. I try not to think about being captured and hanged in the square in front of my family.

I must be brave. I must find out how Bubbe and the rest of our family are faring. I must do this for Papa and Mama.

A week later, I finally convince myself that if I try again, I will surely succeed.

I set out once again, and this time I make it into the Big Ghetto. With a sigh of relief and a surge of confidence, I start to walk to the interior streets, hoping to locate my grandmother.

"STOP!"

I turn, and to my utter disbelief, the same vicious policeman runs toward me, swinging a baton. "STOP, YOU ARE UNDER ARREST!"

This time I am not going to let him catch me, and I flee as fast as I can. He chases me from street to street, shouting at me to stop. People jump out of my way while others feign as if to grab and hold me.

All I can think about is being hanged. My legs pump faster and faster, and I remember all the times I watched the larks fly from the tree branches outside my window on Koszarowa Ulica street.

And I wish again I could be like those birds with wings that can lift me high and away from that horrid policeman and everything ugly in the world.

I glance over my shoulder and see that distance between me and the blackmailing policeman has grown. His girth and age and love of wine have slowed him down. But I will not stop. I cannot stop because he will catch me if I do.

Finally, I see a soup kitchen flooded with people and lines that wrap around the block. Pushing against the crowd at the door, I rush in, running past the many people waiting in line and those sitting at tables hungrily eating what may be their only meal of the day. Those that are eating barely lift their heads from their bowls. I look around, desperately seeking a place to hide.

Seeing a door, I burst in and find myself in the kitchen. A tall bull of a man stands over a large pot of soup, stirring. Beyond the questioning curve of his brows, I can see compassion in the brown eyes that stare intently at me.

"What is it, little girl?"

"Please, sir," I beg, "please help me. I'm being chased by a policeman!"

He strides to the kitchen door, opening it a crack as he peers cautiously out. Quickly deducing my predicament, he grabs a potato sack from a pile and opens it for me.

"Get in now!" The last thing I see is his eyes smiling at me. "Be quiet, not a sound!" He lifts the burlap sack and ties it over my head, and then gently, he picks me up and places me on a shelf containing other sacks of potatoes in similar bags.

I hold my breath as the door swings open. *"Did you see a blonde girl?"* the policeman demands, his voice studded with rage.

"No, there is no one here but me."

The policeman warns menacingly, *"She is illegally in the ghetto. You had better not be lying to me, or your punishment will be severe."*

"Why would I lie? There is no one here."

"Damn Jews," the policeman fumes, the squeaking door swinging behind him.

The cook whispers to me, "Don't move. I want to make sure he is really gone."

I hold my breath as I hear the door swing open and closed.

When the cook returns, he lifts me carefully from the shelf and places me on the floor, untying the strings and freeing me as the sack tumbles open to my feet.

"Thank you, sir!" I grab him about the waist, hugging him with gratitude. "That policeman chased me all through the ghetto and was going to turn me in to the SS. I live in Glinice Ghetto. All I want is to see my grandmother. I miss her so much!"

"Shh, it's all right. You're safe now. He's gone. But your visit with your grandmother must be quick and short. You are in danger and shouldn't be running around the city alone. Do you understand me?"

"Yes, sir, I will see my grandmother and go home. Thank you so much for saving me!"

"Okay, now wait here while I check the street to see that there is no sign of the *mumzer* policeman."

He returns after making sure that the policeman is truly gone from the area, then he walks me to the door, and patting my head, says farewell. I am truly lucky indeed. The whole experience is a miracle to me, and I thank God for watching over me and putting me on the path of that kindly cook.

Once on the street, I get my bearings and begin to make my way to Walowa Ulica. Keeping an eye out for the blackmailing policeman, my mind begins to register the conditions in the ghetto. The stench is shocking, and I realize that what I thought were sacks of garbage and old clothes are the bodies of the dead and dying.

I later learn that the carts that collect the dead are unable to keep up with the growing numbers of people who have succumbed to typhoid and starvation. This explains the behavior of the residents of the ghetto, who step over and around the bodies. They have become immune to so much death as they struggle in desperation with their own survival.

The streets are filthy and littered with piles of garbage. Children sort through the refuse, searching for any food that might have been accidentally discarded. I wish I had thought to bring some biscuits with me. My parents were right about the Big Ghetto. The conditions here are far more deplorable than ours.

The misery that the Nazis have wrought is amplified by the over-crowding, the lack of medicine, and rations that are barely enough on which to subsist. This slow death is not only decimating the population of the Jews but their hearts and souls as well.

Wiping the tears from my eyes, I finally reach Walowa Ulica. Picking up my pace, I run into my cousin's home, calling out to anyone there. My Aunt Mindale comes running to me with worry and concern on her face. "Dinale, are you all right? Are your parents all right?" Her eyes search the street for the adult that surely must have accompanied me. "Where is your mother?"

"She is at home." Hastily I change the subject. "Everyone is fine, but *Tata* has been very worried about you. We haven't heard from you in months. I snuck out of the ghetto to find out how you are."

"Do your parents know you are here? Surely, you didn't come alone?"

Lowering my eyes hoping to hide my guilt, I murmur, "I just wanted to surprise *Tata* with some good news."

"Some good news he would receive if something happened to you?" She shook her head at my daring but breaks into a smile as she hugs me close. "Well, you're here now, so you may as well ease your grandmother's worries."

My grandmother is so happy to see me that she forgets to scold me for risking my life to see her. "Dinale, *shayna maidele*," she cries, kissing me all over my face. "How are your dear father and mother, Nadja and Abek and Dina?"

"We're fine *Bubysy*, everyone is fine. I just miss you so much that I had to come and see you."

"You have made me so happy, *maidele,* come…come sit down and tell me about everyone."

My Aunt Mindale leaves to call my other aunts, Natalia and Fela, and any cousins that are about. Everyone crowds into the tiny kitchen to see me. Nadja and Majer are working with their father Tuvye at the leather shoe factory, and my other cousins are out working or scrounging up food and necessities. My relatives are all anxious to hear about the welfare of my family and conditions in the small ghetto.

Aunt Mindale looks a lot like my father with the same warm brown eyes, but instead of blonde hair like my father, she has black hair that she wears twisted in a braid that sits upon her head like a crown. She is small and curvaceous like my grandmother, with a sunny disposition and a steadfast mothering nature. She is a very devoted daughter, and my grandmother looks well. Mindale steeps a pot of hot tea and begins to serve everyone as I tell them about our family and conditions in the Glinice Ghetto. For a moment, it feels like old times sitting around the table exchanging news over a cup of tea.

But when I speak about my horror and sadness to see so many dead in the streets and so many children begging, they nod and agree. My grandmother's eyes fill with tears as she holds me close.

"It is a terrible thing, but there is nothing to be done about it," Aunt Mindale says. "The Judenrat is doing the best they can under the circumstances, but the Nazis become less and less cooperative with each passing day."

"Surely, they could do more for the children that are starving," I protest.

"They don't care about the children," Uncle Alexander says in a burst of anger. "They want them to die. They want all of us to die."

His words slice like a knife through the room, stunning us into silence. We all know what he says is true but hearing the words out loud shatters any illusion we might have of this nightmare ever ending.

Aunt Mindale gives Alexander a stern look. "She's a child, Alexander. Children need to have hope and believe. We will survive this epidemic of hatred as we have survived every other period since the destruction of the temple in Jerusalem 2,000 years ago."

"Amen," we simultaneously rejoin.

Uncle Alexander clears his throat and looks down at his feet. I feel certain that he regrets his words in front of his son David and me. The women in my father's family are all strong, opinionated women who never hesitate to call anyone to task, even if they are men.

In defense of her husband, Aunt Natalia interjects, "Mindale, please forgive Alexander's outburst. He is so distraught over our situation. You know that he loves the children as much as any of us."

"Then he should be more careful about what he says in front of them," Aunt Mindale retorts.

"This argument stops now!" Aunt Fela interjects. "Dina is here for a short visit. I would much prefer we keep a civil tone. She should not return to our brother with tales of bickering and dissension among us."

Again, silence grips the room as everyone respects Fela's authority as the eldest of my father's siblings. The tension immediately dissipates, and the rest of the visit is mainly about my cousin Majer's Bar Mitzvah. Majer had to delay his Bar Mitzva because of the war, but a neighbor Rabbi helped him prepare and he performed his Haftora, a portion of the Bible, which is chanted aloud, at home in the presence of a few friends and family. This sacred covenant celebrates the ancient Jewish rite of a young man's passage into manhood. In a time of so little joy, this ritual was like a spoonful of honey. Majer celebrated his Bar Mitzvah in secrecy but nevertheless affirmed the commitment of every Jew to the continuity of life by upholding our traditions no matter how dangerous the circumstances.

All too soon, it is time for me to leave as I need to get back to the small ghetto before curfew. I do not mention my ordeal with the policeman as it would only worry them. One way or another, I must return home to my parents. We all walk to the door, where everyone hugs and kisses me as they send best wishes to my parents, sister, brother, and cousin. My grandmother tearfully and reluctantly bids me farewell, collapsing into Mindale's arms at my leaving.

Uncle Alexander offers to escort me to the border of the large ghetto. We walk through the streets in the fading late autumn light in silence. My tall, handsome uncle, who had always been so cheerful and full of good humor, is barely able to muster a smile. It is one more change that registers in my heart. Perhaps not so grave as illness and death but the loss of hope is as debilitating to our ability to stay strong as anything else.

My uncle hugs me and whispers to me to be safe. I hug him back and turn to leave. I begin to walk home, and when I look over my shoulder, I see that my uncle is still standing there keeping watch. He smiles and waves. I smile and wave back, and the fog of sadness lifts from my heart, for I know that despite the poverty, suffering, and death, my family still has abundance in the greatest riches of all—love.

CHAPTER 15

IT IS the end of Queen Esther's reign.

The Nazis have increased their surveillance of us with daily squads of SS roaming the neighborhoods on foot or speeding down the streets in motorcycles, cars, and trucks. Papa has gathered us around the kitchen table.

"I know we have all become attached to Queen Esther," my father says, his voice breaking. "I want you all to understand that I, too, have grown very fond of this special cow that has provided us with milk. But it is time we consider the possibility that should the Nazis find her, they will take her from us and slaughter her. The danger she presents to us now overrides the benefits."

I look at Mama's face. Her eyes are filling with tears.

With a sinking feeling, I realize what my father is about to say.

"Dinale, look at me, please?"

I turn to him with wide eyes.

"Esther can either provide meat for the Nazis or for us. I believe if she could choose, she would want to keep us alive and well. We will end her life in a humane way, and God willing, she will keep us alive through the winter months. I am sorry."

Unable to control my tears, I flee from the table and out the door to the shed where Queen Esther stands chewing on hay. She looks at me with her soulful brown eyes, and I touch her soft nose with my hand. I know my father is right and that Esther must be sacrificed. Knowing something is right is cold comfort. Especially when it means losing someone you love. And when so much has already been lost.

"Esther," I stroke the warm red fur on her forehead as tears spill down my face. "I want to thank you for the milk you have provided us with. You are my friend, and I will miss you and remember you always."

Queen Esther regards me with her large brown eyes as if she understands each word I say. Her pink tongue licks my hand as if to absolve me from guilt. With a final rub on her forehead, I run back into the house. I find my father still sitting in the kitchen, his hands pressed against his face, his elbows resting on the table.

I rush to him, throwing my arms around his neck. "It's okay, *Tata*. Please don't be sad. Please don't blame yourself. I understand we have no choice. I think Queen Esther understands too."

My father hugs me tight and I can feel his sorrow. It occurs to me that over the past few months, I console my parents more and more, and I wonder at this strange reversal of parent and child.

Queen Esther is dispatched with compassion for our greater good, and Vunia's and my family have enough meat stored to last several months. Every time we eat meat during that winter, we give thanks and blessings to Queen Esther. Like her predecessor in the ancient land of Persia, she contributes to the survival of our family when putting food on the table has become more and more difficult.

My father is right, and it doesn't take the Nazis very long to round up the animals. A new *befehl* is announced from the loud-speakers of trucks that travel up and down the streets of the ghetto. All pets and animals are to be brought to the main entrance of the ghetto by tomorrow, where they will be confiscated. I cannot imagine the effect this will have on Vunia's Great-Uncle Saul and Great-Aunt Ruth. Winston and Churchill are like their children, and I am certain this will kill them. I run to Vunia's to see if I can help relieve the anguish this latest edict is sure to cause. Vunia's house is as still as a house in mourning. Softly I call for Vunia, but she doesn't answer. Listening, I hear upstairs the muffled sobs of a woman. Knowing this must be Ruth, I make my way up to her bedroom. I push the door open and find Vunia and her mother on their knees in front of a stricken Ruth. It is a small room with a threadbare woolen carpet and worn wallpaper covered in faded pink roses.

What a difference from Ruth's descriptions of the grand homes in her past life. Homes crowned with vaulted ceilings and crystal chandeliers. In the center of the room is a small bed on which Ruth lays with her eyes staring at the ceiling. Saul stands with his hands leaning on the window sill, his back to the room. His head is bent in either resignation or prayer. I cannot tell which. Winston and Churchill sit at Ruth's side, confused but attentive to her words. She is mumbling indiscernibly to herself as tears flood from her eyes, carrying the makeup down her cheeks where it pools and cakes in the deep grooves of her skin, giving her the appearance of a sad circus clown. Here and there, I understand a few words of Ruth's garbled sobs, which are a blend of English and Polish. "No, no, I will not give them up. They are my babies. It is too cruel."

Grateful to see me, Vunia jumps up and grabs my hands, and whispers, "You've heard the terrible news? Ruth collapsed when she heard the new *befehl* and has been like this ever since. We are all heartbroken, but what alternative is there? We keep telling her that the Nazis will probably fall in love with Winston and Churchill when they see them, and someone will want to keep them. She won't be comforted. We are at our wit's end."

Saul slowly turns from the window. Walking to the bed, he sits and takes Ruth's hands in his, his voice hoarse with emotion. "We must be brave, my darling. Good people are dying all around us. It is time for us to help them. Winston and Churchill have been faithful and wonderful pets. They have been like the children we never had, and we will always have our memories of them. Perhaps it is time that we take in a couple of orphans and offer them a home? I know how much room there is in your heart to love, my dear one. Please think about what I am saying."

Ruth stares wide-eyed from Saul to Winston and then Churchill. "Oh, Saul," she cries. "It is so unbearable. I know you are right, but I feel so helpless and afraid. How can I turn over my babies to those monsters?" She looks directly at each of us, her eyes begging us to find some way of avoiding this tragedy.

The next day Vunia and I plod through the snow on a frigid, over-cast morning, accompanying Saul and Ruth to take Winston and Churchill to the designated area where the pets of the ghetto are to be transferred to the Nazis. It is crowded with people clinging to their dogs and cats who are barking and meowing at each other, adding to the mayhem. We stand in a long line that curves around the block, and at first, we don't see the collection area. Many people walk past us with tears streaming down their faces, having already parted with their beloved pets. Saul and Ruth are each holding one of the Chihuahuas, they pet and reassure the two little dogs who wear red wool sweaters to protect them from the icy wind that licks at our faces. Finally, we turn the corner and can see the trucks that have been brought in to carry away the poor, disoriented animals. Ruth is stunned into immobility, and Saul is forced to urge her forward until we finally reach the front of the line. Each of us kisses and pets Winston and Churchill, who shower us with eager licks as we say our good-byes. Ruth clutches both dogs to her chest. "Please, Saul, don't make me give them up. Please."

A horrid Nazi guard grabs the small dogs from her arms and throws them into the back of the truck. They bark and whimper, their cries tearing at our hearts. I worry that Ruth will faint dead on the ground but instead, she suddenly regains her composure. Standing tall and proud, she gives the Nazi a withering look of disdain. Turning her back on him, she begins to stride away. I watch in admiration as she refuses to give these detestable men the satisfaction of snickering at her pain. As we follow close behind her, I hear her mumble under her breath, "I curse all of the Nazi murderers and pray God they all burn in the fires of hell."

TRUE TO THEIR WORD, Saul and Ruth have arranged for two orphaned children to join them in Vunia's home. Although it is not without an adjustment, their decision to adopt the children brings them joy. Just as Ruth had doted on her animals, she now dotes on this abandoned brother and sister, Anya and Jacob, two lost children who fill the empty spaces of her heart. Anya and Jacob lost their parents to typhoid and had been living on the street. But under the care and love of their adopted grandparents, the young children begin to blossom.

Unfortunately, not everyone is like Saul and Ruth, able to take in and care for orphans. Every day I feel the need to do something. Help in some way. So many starving children roam the streets now, their emaciated bodies and outstretched hands begging for food. I awake one morning with the determination to help them.

I run to Vunia's house, eager to engage her in my plan. Vunia is in complete agreement that we must help the children beyond what the Judenrat is doing. In the small ghetto, plenty of families still have enough to eat, like Vunia's family and mine. We decide to knock on every door in our neighborhood and beg and plead with all the families we know to ask them to donate bread.

Then we will hand it out to the poor children of the ghetto once a week. Perhaps, in this way, we can alleviate some of the starvation and disease that has taken hold. *Live another day.* We comb the streets of the ghetto, pulling a wagon behind us and knocking on every door. At first, people are hesitant to help us as everyone is so guarded of their rations and hoarding today what might disappear and be irreplaceable tomorrow. Vunia and I somehow convince many of our neighbors that not to help the poor children is a sin against God. *Tzedaka*, charity, is one of the primary commandments of Judaism.

Finally, they are persuaded by our pleadings, or perhaps they are amused to hear our argument, but nearly everyone donates a loaf of bread. The loaves are huge, and our wagon is so full and heavy that we can barely pull it back home. By the time we return, it is too late to distribute the bread to the children, so we store it at home with the plan of distributing it in the morning. My parents' eyes widen when they see the amount of bread we have collected.

"Oh, may I have a little piece?" my father asks with a twinkle in his eye.

"No, *Tatashy*, this bread is for the poor and hungry children," I admonish him, wagging my finger. "You are not that poor, and you are not that hungry."

My father and mother exchange a smile, and my father winks at me. "You are right, Dinale. Others are much more in need than I. What you are doing is wonderful, and we are very proud of you and Vunia."

Vunia and I beam with pride, and the next day, we begin to hand out the bread to the children in the street.

"Bread nourishes the body, but kindness nourishes the heart, does it not?" Ruth says as she and her adopted children help us hand out the bread.

Soon we attract more friends to our cause, including Fela, whom I have not spent much time with. Many a time I have gone to Fela's home with Vunia to play, only to have to listen to Fela rhapsodize about Yaakov, the boy who lives next door, and her undying love for him.

Despite Fela making moon eyes over Yaakov, I succeed in inspiring her with the "Bread for Children Project," and she has thrown herself wholeheartedly into our endeavor. Although we must continue to hear her sing Yaakov's praises. And most of her sentences begin with: *"Yaakov said this, or Yaakov said that."*

I love Fela, but I have resigned myself to playing second fiddle to Yaakov. Maybe because I am younger, I can't seem to share her enthusiasm about the splendors of love, but nonetheless, I try to be happy for her as she and Yaakov are clearly smitten with each other.

Although we can't feed the bread to the hungry children in the large ghetto, we find plenty of hungry children in the Glinice Ghetto. It becomes a weekly ritual for Vunia, Fela, and me to collect bread before the Shabbat and to deliver it to the needy children. No matter how much we collect and give out, it is never enough. Every Friday, we notice that the line of children becomes shorter and shorter. As we hand out the bread, we smile and try to make the children laugh, but later as we walk home, we shed tears for the children we've lost. And we pray they are now safe and warm with their loved ones in Heaven and no longer suffering in the cold, harsh winter of the ghetto.

CHAPTER 16

I SQUIRM, trying to see the monster. "Wait, let me see!"

"Careful, I don't want to drop it," Nadja warns. "It's a big juicy one!" Extracting the lice from my head, she shows me the disgusting pest, and I shriek in horror, shivering with revulsion.

Each evening we endure the ritual of lice picking, and I have begun to feel like a monkey as we each take turns inspecting each other's heads and then squishing the vile vermin.

Once the bodily inspections are finished, we search the seams of our clothing, coats, scarves, hats, and then bedding, seeking out the bloodsuckers that carry the diseases that my mother warns us to be wary of. This evening ritual provides an odd form of entertainment as we each try to up the ante with exaggerations of the size of each other's pests. It may seem strange to find amusement in our unfortunate circumstances, but life has become strange. There is nothing normal about the way we live now. And so, conditions that would otherwise have left us in despair even a year ago have become the fodder of our jokes.

But while we may tease each other while extracting lice from our heads, there is another vermin that truly frightens us. The rats. While the Jews starve in the ghettos, the rats thrive without abatement, swarming the streets, scrounging amid the garbage piles, and invading our homes at every opportunity. The rats are the hardest of all to kill. We do our best to avoid them outside, but when they scurry into our home, we fight like warriors of old to defeat the horde.

The winter months have taken their toll, and the pungent smell of death, garbage, and starvation permeates the air in the ghetto. Although our hopes lift briefly when the United States declares war on Germany following Pearl Harbor, those hopes fade quickly from the constant cruelty of the Nazis. Roundups occur on a regular basis now. The Gestapo conducts an *aktion* in the large ghetto, where they abduct forty men from their homes who are suspected of being Communists. The accused dissidents are dragged out into the streets and executed on the spot. Murder has become a daily occurrence.

Even the arrival of warmer days in spring fails to lift our spirits. The Judenrat, which has become useless in curbing the Nazi appetite for Jewish blood, is virtually dismantled on April 27, 1942, on what the Jews named "Bloody Wednesday" due to the immense loss of life perpetrated by the Nazis swarming the ghettos with their dreaded lists of names. They rolled through the streets in their cars and trucks, seizing men from their homes and shooting them in their doorways or throwing them into prison to be tortured, beaten, and deported. If someone on that list managed to escape that day, they were immediately replaced by random bystanders who were shot in their tracks in order to fulfill the death allotment. Among the hundred or more unlucky victims was Yosef Diamant, the head of the Jewish council, and with him the top aides in the Judenrat hierarchy. They and about twenty of the senior members of the Jewish police force were arrested, interned, and marked for deportation.

"That old saying, *'No good deed goes unpunished,'* certainly applies here," Papa says in anger after word reaches us of the horror. The Nazis have effectively removed the leadership of the ghettos, and now we wait in fear without our intermediaries to intercede.

"We can only do our best to keep on as we are doing," Mama says. "We have been lucky so far," she adds.

"But what if our luck runs out?" Abek asks, tears in his eyes.

"We have to remain strong," Mama replies, wrapping her arms around Abek as we sit in the kitchen, trying to keep warm before the small fire. "And pray the allies overcome the Nazi vermin soon."

The fire does little to warm me, and I shiver. "I'm tired of trying. Every day only gets worse. We are doomed."

My father gathers me into his warm embrace. "Never lose hope, Dinale. We have each other, and somehow, we will come through this horror."

My eyes burn with tears. "I don't believe it. They won't rest until we are all dead."

My mother rarely cries, and she is always strong for all of us. But I have accomplished the unthinkable, and tears spill down her cheeks. "Please, Dinale. You must be strong. Life is everything, and we must fight to live."

"I'm sorry, *Mamashy*, forgive me." She leans her forehead against mine, and I feel her forgiveness. She kisses my cheeks, and for now, I believe again in a tomorrow. My father pulls us all together into a family hug, and together we embrace, laughing through our tears.

$\sim$

DESPITE THE ENCOURAGING words of Mama and Papa, we live with the fear of disaster and pray for the intervention of a miracle. Nadja and Cousin Dina are at work at A.V.L., and Abek and I huddle together playing a game of chess. My mother sits in a rocking chair by the fire, mending a a ripped seam in my father's coat. For some reason, my father was told not to report to work today, and he sits at the table reading.

A loud banging at the door startles us. My father opens the door, and we gasp as several SS men stride in with their guns leveled, ready to shoot. My mother jumps up in fear, dropping my father's coat and knocking the sewing basket over—spools of thread spill out and scatter across the floor. A Nazi officer yells at my father and grips his arm to pull him out the door. Mama warns Abek and me to stay put as she rushes to my father's side, grasping his other arm. Everything happens so quickly that I can hardly register what they are shouting at Papa about.

"*Tata, Tata!*" Abek and I begin to scream as we run to our father's side. "Please, please don't take our father," I beg as I cling to my father's leg on one side while my brother desperately grabs the other leg. We are all screaming in panic as the Nazis drag us all from the house, my brother and I manacled to my father's legs, my mother holding tight to my father's arm, as each of us begs for mercy. My mother is pleading in German that there must be a mistake, that my father is a butcher and is working for the Germans, that he is necessary, that he has a special card.

"There is no mistake. We are arresting all butchers and slaughterers. They are being taken to Police Headquarters, where they will be questioned. Orders are they are to be deported and resettled immediately."

My mother turns as white as the snow that still clings to the ground. She dashes back into the house and quickly reappears with my father's coat. I don't know how she finds the presence of mind to make sure that my father has his coat. Wrapping it about his shoulders, she throws her arms around his neck in a quick embrace. "Joel, my darling, remember I love you."

"*Tata*, I love you," Abek cries, his face pressed to my father's pants.

"I won't let them take you, Papa," I cry in anger.

"It will be all right, children, I will be fine. Remember that I love you all." My father's words sound heavy with anguish.

Abek and I cling tightly to my father's legs in a desperate effort to prevent the inevitable. The Nazis yell and curse at us to let go, threatening to take us too, if we don't release him. Roughly they tear us from our father's legs and throw us to the ground. Sobbing, my mother rushes to protect us.

Overcome with grief, we cling to my mother. We are stunned. Powerless to do anything as the Nazis haul my father into the back of the truck. "We love you, Papa!" Abek and I shout at the departing truck.

"Be strong, Joel," Mama calls out. "We will find a way to fix this."

My father looks back at us as if to sear the memory of our faces upon his heart. His gaze never wavers as the truck drives away.

Nadja and Dina return from work to find us paralyzed with grief. Vunia and her family huddle around us, trying to offer comfort. Mama, who has always been so strong, who has always held us together, now lies prostrate in bed. Gray strands streak her beautiful black hair, and her cheeks lie sunken into her face. She weeps uncontrollably. It's as if she has aged twenty years in a matter of hours. She looks shrunken and diminished from the shock of losing Papa.

Nadja runs to Mama and sits on the bed. She lifts Mama's hand and kisses it. Tears shimmer in her eyes, but her words are strong. "You are behaving as if Papa has died," my sister admonishes. "How dare you give up hope? Is this what Papa would expect of us?"

She shames us all for our lack of faith and rekindles our strength.

The next day, Nadja makes inquiries and discovers where Papa is being held. He has been taken to the police station near the Big Ghetto with all the other butchers and slaughterers who have been rounded up.

Nadja begs one of the Wermacht officers that run A.V.L. to issue her a pass so that she might leave the ghetto and inquire as to our father's wellbeing. While the pass enables her to leave the ghetto unescorted, it is still dangerous for her to do so.

She spends hours waiting for any information. To pass the time as she awaits word, she takes her journal with her that she has kept since the invasion of the Nazis into Poland. In it, she keeps a detailed recollection of all the events that have occurred to our family and friends, along with her own philosophical bewilderment as to the causes. As the hours while away, she writes in her chronicle. Engrossed in her task, she is unaware as a Polish policeman approaches and snatches the journal from her hands.

Ignoring her protests, he flips through the pages, his eyes narrowing on the words: *Once upon a time, there was peace in our world. It was not a perfect world by any means, but we held hope that with time, it would get better. We were citizens of a free country, and although anti-Semitism was spurred on by the priests in the churches, still, we lived among our gentile neighbors without fear. On September 8, 1939, everything changed. The Germans marched into Radom. With them came disease, death, and murder. It did not take long for us to see the truth—the Nazis want to eliminate every Jew, but the saddest revelation is that the Poles don't care. For the most part, they have done nothing but avert their eyes at best and helped the Nazis at worst. The latest injustice is my father's arrest. There is nothing we can do to free him. Why do they hate us?*

"Go home now! I don't want to see you here again!" He thrusts the journal back at her and strides away. Slamming the door behind him.

Nadja swipes tears from her cheeks, furious with herself and her own foolishness for bringing the journal and writing in public. She rushes out of the station, heartbroken at not seeing my father.

A few weeks later, we are informed that our father is to be deported. We will be allowed to bring him some food for the journey and to say our good-byes. My mother summons her strength to assemble the items. On the kitchen table, she sets out a loaf of bread, two rounds of hard cheese, two apples, some cured meats leftover from our beloved Queen Esther, and some cake. We will have to eat less for a day or two but none of us care as long as my father has enough. Mama carefully bundles up the food from our dwindling supply along with extra clothing in which she has sewn some money.

We all go with my mother to say goodbye to my father. He stands behind a fence, and we can't hug or touch him. How can we condense a lifetime of love into a few words?

We pass the package to the guard at the entrance to the fenced area. The guard examines the contents and thrusts it at my father.

"You see, the Nazis have decided that we butchers pose the greatest threat to the Third Reich with our ability to dismember a cow," Papa jokes through his tears.

"Joel, we must stay strong," Mama says. "Carry our love with you in your heart."

"Ah, Temcia, my love." He gazes into my mother's eyes and then looks at each one of us. "And my darling children."

"Don't worry, *Tata*, we will find each other," Abek says, his lips trembling. "Remember God is sending a great army to rescue us."

"Yes, of course he is, Abek." Papa's eyes belie his words. "My son, you must remember that you are now the man of the family, and you must take good care of your mother and sisters."

"Yes, *Tata*, I will do my best."

"Joel, you must write to us as soon as you get to wherever they resettle you. Please let us know you are safe."

"Yes, yes, I will write." Papa nods. "Please, if you can get word to my mother and the rest of the family. Tell them... just tell them that I love them."

"Don't worry, Joel, we will get word to them," Mama says, her eyes swimming with tears.

"I bless you all and pray for your safety and deliverance," Papa says, his voice breaking. "Temcia, take care of our children and try to keep faith with God."

"We will find a way, Papa," Nadja sobs. "This war will end one day, and we will find you."

We all stand there weeping, helpless to do anything or say anything that will allay his fears or our own, for that matter.

"I love you, *Tata*. Don't worry about us. We will all be together again after the war is over," I say, hoping it will be so.

The war, like a massive earthquake, has toppled the foundations of our community, our families, and our hopes and dreams. Every day we battle the monsters that invade our homes. Lice, rats, vermin of every sort, but the greatest monsters of all, we are powerless against.

We bow our heads and pray that God will deliver us from this evil.

CHAPTER 17

"*Tata* would be so proud of me," I say to Mama.

"He *is* proud of you," Mama says softly.

"May I see it, Dina?" Abek asks.

"Here you go, Abek," I say as I hand him the permit.

He reads it and looks up at Mama, his face beaming. "Perhaps our luck has not run out after all?"

"*Mamashy*! I have a job! I have a job!" I sing over and over again, holding Mama's hands and twirling her around in a dance.

"Dina," Mama chuckles. "You are making me dizzy."

I stop and wrap my arms around Mama's waist to anchor my giddiness. I have begged my sister to help me get a job at A.V.L., and finally the permission is granted. I've been issued a certificate. I am so happy that I will be able to contribute to our family's welfare. It means more money to buy more food. But it also means more security. Rumors are flying that more deportations are imminent, and the only possible safety is the possession of a work certificate. Nadja, my cousin Dina, and now me, have permits to work at A.V.L., a giant warehouse that borders the railroad tracks and is used for packing shipments of supplies to Germany and the Eastern front. Surely, this must bode well for our family.

The next morning dawns cold and blustery as Nadja, Dina, and I wait with the other workers for the German trucks to arrive.

"Keep silent," Nadja whispers to me. "We don't want to incur the wrath of the soldiers who enjoy nothing more than punishing us with the butts of their rifles."

After the trucks drop us off, we walk in silence under armed guard to the red brick warehouse. Nadja and Dina take me to the back where they work. My eyes widen at the wall of suitcases piled up to the rafters. Piles of clothes, shoes, coats, hats fill one corner, in another are stacks of plates and silverware, tablecloths, pots, pans, even toys. So many possessions that once belonged to Jewish families, graced their dining room tables, and their living room. Nadja and Dina show me how to sort, fill, and box up the many items to be shipped out of Poland for the benefit of the Third Reich. I cannot help but think about the strangeness of it all—how much the Germans hate us and how much they love our things. Once we have filled the boxes, we carry the heavy crates and load them onto the waiting trains.

The day seems endless, and my mind begins to wander as I imagine the people who once owned the thousands of objects that overflow the warehouse. Families just like mine. Children who shared the same dreams as me... For twelve hours, we toil with only a few minutes of respite and a meager meal of a cup of weak tea and a thin watery soup that provides little sustenance. The labor is backbreaking, and the warehouse is hot and humid.

After so many hours, I can barely stand on my feet. "I'm so tired, Nadja."

"I know you are, but you can do this," she whispers with encouragement. "Look how you've grown. You are no longer a child but a strong young woman. *Tata* would be so proud of you!"

I wipe away the tears that fill my eyes at the mention of our father. The thought of my proud, loving father gives me the strength to finish the workday.

"Where do you think they sent *Tata*?" I whisper, sorting through another pile of coats.

"I wish I knew," Nadja answers as she finishes tying rope around a box. "He may not even be in Poland. Here, help me carry this to the platform where we can get a breath of fresh air." Together we drag the heavy carton to the back of the warehouse, where Mietek, one of my sister's friends, rushes to lift it out of our hands. "*Nu*, so how is our little comrade doing in her new job?"

I smile at Mietek. "My sister says I am no longer a child but a woman," I coyly announce.

My sister and Mietek laugh, sharing a knowing wink between them. "Yes, you are becoming quite the seductress. Soon none of the men will be able to keep their minds on their work," he teases.

I feel my cheeks burning red, and unable to think of a brilliant retort, I stick my tongue out at him, sending my sister and him into a fit of laughter.

~

LAUGHTER FILLS our home as everyone wishes me a happy birthday. It is June 20, and I have turned thirteen.

I cannot imagine how my mother has found the ingredients to assemble a small cake. I know that my father will be thinking about me today. Perhaps, right at this moment, he is dreaming of us and wondering how we are managing. My family, Vunia, Fela, and I hold hands and observe a moment of silence, trying to transmit our love and wishes through space and time in the hopes that he might know we are thinking of him. We pray together that God keeps us all safe, especially my father. Afterward, we light a lone candle, which my mother somehow has procured, and I make a wish for all of us as I blow it out. Even though I keep my wish a secret, I am certain my family and friends can guess what it is.

For entertainment, my cousin Dina lifts us out of our doldrums with her famous spoof of Hitler with one new addition. At the end of her Fuhrer impersonation, she invites us each to kill her if every word out of her mouth isn't truly spoken. We pounce on her, all of us landing on the bed as we scream that we are going to tickle her to death, and it is a fate far better than what she deserves. Our laughter must sound insane to our neighbors, given the misery of our lives. The happy times we shared seem so long ago, and we crave amusement for our souls as much as food for our bellies.

The days wear on in a repetition of conflicting contrasts, the beauty of burgeoning summer and the squalor of the disintegrating ghetto. I yearn for those carefree hours spent with Fela and her boisterous family amid the fruit-laden cherry trees of her grandparents' orchard. I no longer have time to play with my girlfriends. Our world of innocence has vanished, and all that remains are the ruins of what was once a thriving Jewish community.

Without my father's steadfast presence, my poor mother has been forced to assume the mantle of father and mother, and the burden has taken its toll on her. Her loneliness for my father is heartbreaking to behold. With three of us working at A.V. L., my mother's responsibilities have multiplied as she must provide the meals, wash the clothes, clean the house, and tutor my brother in his studies. As she goes about her chores, she has begun to talk aloud to herself as if my father were listening. In the evenings, she sits darning and mending our clothes, rocking in my grandfather's rocker, conducting a one-way conversation with my father.

The physical effects are even more drastic to behold. Her dresses, which had once clung to a full and voluptuous figure, now hang like sacks around her disappearing body. Before the war, Mama had maintained the lustrous black sheen of her hair by carefully concealing the few gray hairs that had come with her late thirties. No longer concerned with beauty and with no access to dye, her hair has aged to a silvery gray.

As much as the Nazis love to inflict physical torture, they seem to delight even more in spiritual and psychological persecution that robs the Jews of their dignity and will to survive. One day the Nazis announce there will be a transport to the work camp where my father is imprisoned, and they will be collecting food packages for the inmates. Since no letters from Papa have arrived, Mama writes a long letter, and we all add a greeting to Papa. Mama hides the letter in with the package of food and carries it to the designated repository.

The soldiers take the package and add it with the rest. They smirk at Mama and tell her they can't wait to see what's in it.

Mama looks at them in confusion, but as they chortle in glee, she realizes they have lied, and the care packages are merely a ruse to humiliate us and diminish our precious rations of food. She returns home fuming at having been duped by their inexplicable cruelty, but more distressing is the reality that we have no idea where my father is or how he is faring.

As strong and capable of a woman as Mama is, Nadja, Cousin Dina, and I worry at how much more she can take.

.

CHAPTER 18

MY DRESS IS ALREADY SOAKED with sweat as Nadja, Dina, and I silently walk the remaining kilometer to A.V.L. under the watchful German guards. I am in no hurry to get there as I know the warehouse will be unbearably hot. Only the German manager of our division, Otto, will manage to stay cool in his small office thanks to a large fan from which he is loath to stray. Otto is Wermacht and not a bad person, really. He is not unduly cruel to us. In fact, one could say he is a mensch, a decent human being.

Pictures of his family abound on his desk, and I have seen him gaze at them with love and longing. His wife is a pretty woman with her blonde hair plaited and bound to her head like a crown. Her smile in the photographs is one of a woman whose life has lived up to her expectations. In one photo, she is dressed in a traditional dirndl and is flanked on either side by her two smiling daughters dressed in matching attire. The older daughter looks to be about my age, blonde and blue-eyed like me.

He greets me each day with, *"Gut morgan, Fraulein."* I wonder if he thinks of his daughter when he looks at me, for I can see empathy in his gaze. Perhaps that is why he looks the other way when I sometimes struggle to perform my job. I am the youngest worker, and my physical strength is equivalent to my age.

But he is obedient to the good of the Fatherland and does his duty efficiently and without moral introspection. He is a strong bull of a man who earned this safe and comfortable job by surviving the Eastern front with only a minor injury, a permanent limp making him unfit for further combat. Of course, he can't be too lenient with us Jews as he must answer to a brutal SD officer who is even worse than the SS. The intelligence agency bully treats Otto with contempt, always questioning his ability to extract the most from his slave labor force. When the SD beast is about, we do our best to work like a well-oiled machine to make Otto look good and incur as little wrath as possible. It is complicity born of necessity and a bond forged from a mutual objective—survival. We know that many sadistic men are in charge at other forced labor facilities who beat and sometimes kill their workers when the mood strikes them. Otto may be strict and appear to be gruff, but he is not without heart. Or maybe he hopes his lack of cruelty will not be forgotten by us or God, and it is his own private assurance that should the war be lost, his family will somehow be protected from vengeance.

"Come with me and Sonja to the second floor and help us carry down twine to tie the boxes," Nadja says to me. "We are running short, and there is more in the supply room upstairs."

It will offer a moment of respite, and I happily go with them. Getting into the elevator, Nadja closes the steel accordion door and pulls the lever. The old machine grumbles to life, slowly ascending to the top floor. My sister and Sonja gossip about two of the young men who work at A.V.L. Sonja has a crush on one of them and shares the details of their courtship. I am too hot to be captivated by the gossip and wonder if it was such a good idea to ride in the elevator, for it is even hotter than downstairs.

Finally, we reach the second floor and load the boxes of twine into the elevator. Once again, my sister closes the door and pulls the lever that starts the old beast on its way down. Halfway between the two floors, the elevator comes to a sudden stop, nearly throwing us all to the floor.

"Damn," says Nadja. "This elevator is so unreliable I don't understand why they don't repair it." Opening the metal door, she pokes her head out. "We are only a few feet from the floor. Let's jump, and we'll get the men to come and fix it." Jumping down, Nadja offers up her hand to help Sonja, who leaps down effortlessly. Nadja turns back to the elevator to assist me. I decide to sit down on the edge of the floor and jump from there. As I am about to jump, the elevator jerks into motion, and with a massive thrust, it rises and pins me between the floors.

A scream erupts from my throat at the startling force of the impact. The world begins to spin around me and waves of nausea overwhelm me. Screams and shouts reverberate around me. From far away, I hear my sister scream, "Otto, Otto, come quickly! Dina's legs are caught in the elevator. Please save her."

I can't feel my legs or my hand, but I can feel wetness seeping into my clothes, and a metallic smell invades my nostrils. I know I am bleeding. I start to breathe in short, sharp gasps as fear grips me. *Please, God, don't let me die. My family needs me. Please, Zayde, help me.*

I struggle to stay alert, but as the shouts fade away, I slip into darkness.

I hear the happy laughter of children playing a game of hide-and-seek. I open my eyes to the apple orchard behind my house. But how can that be? I can hear a cow moo and the yap of two small dogs. "Esther, Winston, Churchill," I call out. "Have you come to save me?" I turn in a circle, and the ground is blanketed with sweet red apples. *Am I dreaming or am I dead?* "No, this is not right," I cry out. "My family needs me."

"Dinale."

I turn, and my grandfather stands a few feet away. He is smiling. He is standing tall with a straight back. He is dressed in white. White trousers and a crisp white shirt with white suspenders. I want to run to him to hug him close, but my feet won't move.

"Zayde, what is happening? Why can't I run to you?"

"Hush, child," he says, and his voice is full of love and warmth. *"You must be brave, and you will survive. Don't worry, child, you will be all right."*

"*Zayde*, how to you know?"

"Trust me Dinale. Trust your grandfather. You will be all right..."

"You will be all right..." My eyes flutter open as I hear the words spoken over and over again. Otto's face is swimming before me. He is carrying me in his arms, and for a moment, I wonder if there are tears in his eyes. A sharp pain shoots through me, and I whimper.

"Close your eyes and think of happy times," Otto whispers.

Happy times. They seem so long ago.

Nadja runs alongside me. "We are taking you to the Jewish Hospital in the Big Ghetto."

Otto places me in the bed of a truck with my sister, who cradles my head on her lap. He jumps in, fires up the engine, and puts the truck in gear.

"W-what happened?" I am dizzy, and every part of my body is in agony.

"The stupid elevator nearly crushed you. You can thank Otto for saving your life. I have never seen such strength. He climbed upstairs and somehow lifted the elevator door up enough for us to pull you out."

"I-I heard screaming and crying."

"That was you, Dinale. You were screaming for *Zayde* and God to save you."

"It hurts so much, Nadja." The pain is so sharp that I don't have the strength to cry.

"I know, *maidele*, you were badly hurt by the elevator. It slashed open your leg, and you are bleeding. We wrapped you tightly in towels and a blanket. Otto was very distraught when the accident took place, and he notified the SS that a young girl has been hurt and he is driving her to the hospital. I hope they don't stop us."

As she says this, the truck comes to a sudden halt. Nadja carefully lowers my head to the floor of the truck and peers out to see why we have stopped. Otto's superior, the beastly SD officer known for his cruelty and abusiveness, approaches, and he is shouting like a mad dog at Otto. We listen, Nadja crouching in fear as the SD officer yells at Otto. "How dare you leave the factory for a damned Jew? Our men are dying at the front, and you dare to care about the life of one shitty Jewess."

Otto sounds stoic under the onslaught and answers, "*Yavol, mein commandant*, you are right. She is only a Jew, but her sister is an excellent worker, and the young girl is strong. They are both good workers with good output. May I take them to the hospital?"

After a few moments of silence, I feel the truck lurch forward. As we pull away, the SD yells after us, "Dump her at the Jew hospital, and you get back to A.V.L. immediately!"

My sister sighs with relief. "Thank God for Otto. He is a good man to take such a risk for us and stand up to that monster."

"My leg is numb. I can't feel it. Am I going to die, Nadja?"

"Don't be silly. Of course, you aren't going to die. You will probably need stitches and have to stay in the hospital for a few days. Mama is going to be furious with me for letting this happen to you."

"Don't worry, Nadja. I will tell her it wasn't your fault."

Finally, we reach the hospital, and Otto picks me up gently and carries me inside while he calls for the doctor in charge in an authoritative voice. A nurse rushes to get the doctor while another nurse escorts us to a room with a bed. Carefully, Otto lays me on the bed. I am soaking wet from the heat and blood loss and moaning in pain. Nadja nervously clings to my hand that is not wounded, trying to soothe me while watching wide-eyed for the doctor. Finally, the doctor arrives, deferring to Otto and ignoring me.

"There was an accident at A.V.L., and this young girl was hurt. She will probably need stitches."

The doctor, who looks haggard and exhausted, finally looks at me, acknowledging my presence with a nod. He bends over my leg to pull back the blanket and towels. The cloths, wet with blood, stick to my leg, and I yell in pain as he removes them. He sighs impatiently and examines the wound. I gasp when I see how deep the cut on my leg is and the amount of blood that is oozing from the open gash. I am gripped with terror, wondering how I will be able to work if I am crippled. *Will the Nazis kill me if I am no longer useful?* The doctor lifts my right hand. It is sliced open between the thumb and my first finger. "Hmmph. This is not too bad. She will require stitches. But I am very busy. She will have to wait."

The shock of seeing my leg combined with the scorching pain is too much to bear. I begin to sob and shake uncontrollably.

The doctor huffs out another sigh as he wipes his hands on a towel and turns to leave.

Otto's face turns red as a beet, and he grabs the doctor by his lapels and screams in his face, "No! No! No! You are not going anywhere. You are going to take care of her right now! Do you understand me?"

The doctor's eyes widen. It's obvious he is perplexed by a German showing concern for a Jew. "Y-yes sir, whatever you say, commandant. I will take care of her immediately!" He turns to the nurse. "Nurse, go fetch my surgical tools and prepare this young lady for me, now!"

The nurse scurries away, "Yes, doctor."

Nadja and I look at each other and then at Otto. "Thank you, Otto," I whisper.

Otto clears his throat and nods. He turns to Nadja. "We have to leave now and go back to A.V.L. Your sister will be well taken care of. Am I right, doctor?" He shoots a glare at the doctor.

"Yes, of course. I will make sure she receives the best of everything."

Nadja brushes my cheek with a quick kiss, "Don't worry, you will be fine," she whispers. "*Mamashy* and I will come to see you tomorrow. Be brave." After kissing me again, she is gone, with Otto leading her by the arm out of the hospital.

I am alone and terrified, overcome with dread of what my injuries portend. My leg is throbbing, and I beg the doctor for something to alleviate the pain as he begins to stitch the large swollen gash.

The hospital is poorly supplied with medications, but the nurse returns with two pills that I gulp down with a glass of water. My thirst is so great I beg for another glass. When the doctor is done stitching and bandaging, he tells the nurse to apply icy compresses to my leg and hand. "You will remain in the hospital for a week at least to prevent infection."

Turning to the nurse, he orders, "Nurse, I want these bandages changed once a day and the wound cleaned."

"Thank you, doctor," I murmur, drowsy from the pills and exhausted by the loss of blood.

"You are a lucky girl that the German isn't SS. Otherwise, the outcome would have been much different. Now, if you don't mind, Princess, I will return to my duties."

CHAPTER 19

"OTTO IS A TRUE *MENSCH*, a decent human being. What a rarity among these Nazis who thrive on inflicting pain and misery," my mother says as she slices me a piece of *kugel* sweetened with apples.

I am so hungry that I gobble up one slice and then ask for another.

"Slow down, Dina, or you will make yourself sick."

"I'm sorry, *Mamashy*," I say as I spoon up another bite, making a point of chewing slowly.

Nadja brings me a glass of water, and I ask her to get me two more glasses so I can keep them by my bed. "I have not seen the nurse since she handed me the pills yesterday while the doctor stitched my wounds," I say as I sip my water.

"It is a busy hospital with many patients, Dina," Mama says. "I'm sure she is doing her best. And now you have enough water and food to last you until our next visit."

"Mama, I have to go."

My mother nods and Nadja holds up a sheet while my mother slips the bed pan under me, and I can finally relieve myself.

Nadja finds me a cloth, and I wash myself as best I can.

It is a fair-sized room with five other beds. I don't know what the illnesses are of the other people in my room. Two of them constantly moan with pain, while the others are always asleep or strangely quiet and simply stare at the ceiling.

My sister tells me that Otto took quite a bit of abuse from the SD officer for daring to save a worthless Jewish girl. "You could hear the shouting throughout the factory. He issued me a pass today so that I could visit you."

"Please thank him again for me."

"I will."

"But Nadja, what if I won't be allowed to return to work at A.V.L.? What if they tell me I can't come back?"

"Don't be silly. Otto didn't save you in order to abandon you. You will have your job back, don't worry. You will get better. Everyone at A.V.L. wishes you a speedy recovery. They call you 'A.V.L.'s good luck girl' because Otto called in an engineer and crew to fix the stupid elevator. I heard him say that he won't have his workers injured because it delays shipments and compromises efficiency. But I know it is because he was so upset about you getting hurt."

"At least something good has come out of this terrible accident," Mama says.

It is a short visit, but I am so grateful to see my mother and sister. My mother says she will come again tomorrow. Nevertheless, I cry when they leave as I know my sister will not be able to come and see me as often. She must go to work and Otto cannot be expected to issue her a pass every day. I cling to her last words of reassurance to me. "Dinale, don't worry about anything. Rest and get better. Be brave and remember you are strong, and the strong survive."

After my third day at the hospital, I begin to feel a bit better and decide to venture from the room. Holding onto the wall of the corridor, I am able to limp down the hall. Turning a corner, I find myself in a different part of the hospital. I pass a room and stop, noticing a group of young women who do not appear to be sick. They giggle and chatter, brushing their hair and applying rouge to their lips. They are wearing fancy dressing gowns made from shimmery fabrics and trimmed with lace.

"Hello, little girl, are you new here?" A curvy young woman about

Nadja's age with dark brown hair saunters up to me. "Hm. You're a little young." She crosses her arms over her chest and looks me up and down. "But you're very pretty. You'll do well here."

My eyes widen. "I—I hurt my leg in an elevator, and I was just walking—"

The other girls who were giggling a moment ago, turn and stare at me, and I see they are not happy at all. Some look at me with contempt, others with sadness.

A slender young woman with bright red hair streaming down her back approaches the brunette and tells her to go back to her bed.

"This is not a place for you," the redhead says softly. "Go back to your room and don't come back here. Never come back. It's not safe for you here."

Confused, I walk down the hall and find my way back to my room.

The next time Nadja visits me, I tell her what happened. She shakes her head and tells me I am like a cat, too curious for my own good. "Those women are whores, Dina. Prostitutes."

I cannot believe it. Prostitutes in a hospital? Who visits them? Jewish men have barely enough money to care for themselves and their families. Who then?

"Polish men," Nadja says. "They do not care that those girls are Jewish."

"But don't the girls have families?"

"Dina, look at all the orphans living on the streets. So many children have lost their families. Some orphans are lucky if they find a family to take them in, others survive on the street and fight and scrape for a crust of bread, and some end up like those girls."

I cry myself to sleep that night and pray for my family. I pray for Papa, and I pray for Mama, and I pray for all of my relatives and dear friends. My last prayer is for those girls in the hospital who will never be the same.

∾

When my mother visits me again, I am overcome with joy to see Vunia, whom I miss desperately.

"Dina, you should see Fela and Yaacov. They are like an old married couple holding hands and strolling through the ghetto. Poor Fela's leg hasn't completely healed from when she slipped on the patch of ice in February, and she limps terribly, but Yaacov is like a handsome knight. Holding her close as they walk.

"Yaacov and Fela have been helping with our bread drive for the orphans. I even saw him sneak a kiss from her," she giggles.

"Fela is a good girl," Mama says. "And lucky to have met Yaacov."

"I bet they will get married someday when the war is over," Vunia adds in a dreamy voice. "Fela sends her love to you and can't wait to see you return home and healed."

Vunia's words are restorative to my spirit. She paints the future with hopeful colors.

"How are Anya and Jacob doing?" I ask.

"Aunt Ruth and Uncle Saul have accomplished a miracle with them. Anya and Jacob now address them as *Zayde* and *Bubbe*. And my older sister has started a school for Anya, Jacob, and me. Every day we spend a few hours with her studying Polish, math, and whatever else she can muster up for us to learn. We have to write a paper each week and memorize a poem. The best part, though, is when she reads aloud to us. As soon as you are better and can come home, you must join us. When are you getting out of here, anyway?"

"I don't think I can study with you as I have to work at A.V.L., and they haven't told me yet when I'm to be released."

"Don't worry. We will figure something out. At least you can study on Sunday or after work sometimes."

The nurse walks in with a tray of fresh bandages and iodine. As the nurse removes the bandage from my leg, Vunia gasps in awe at the crude, uneven surgical seam that runs across the wound. "My God, that is really ugly!"

"Vunia, that's not nice to say," Mama admonishes in a gentle voice.

"I am sorry, Dina. I'm certain it will heal, and no one will ever notice it."

"Of course, it will heal," Mama says, patting my hand.

After the nurse leaves, my mother and Vunia help me sit up so Mama can braid my hair.

Mama looks so tired that I ask her if she is all right.

She sighs, brushing my hair and deftly braiding it. "It is difficult to buy food on the black market. Abek is so thin it worries me, and no matter how I try, I can't seem to get any fat on his bones. We will be fine, don't worry about us. You just continue to gain strength, my angel." Finishing my hair, she kisses the top of my head and helps me back into bed.

"Have there been any more round-ups?"

Vunia blurts out that the Nazis have installed searchlights in the ghettos.

"Why would they do that?" I ask.

"Hush Vunia, Dina needs to rest and get well, not worry about silly things."

"But this does not sound silly." I begin to tremble. "Maybe they are planning more deportations. There are rumors circulating here in the hospital that deportations are imminent."

Mama hugs me close. "Remember, your sister and cousin have work permits. They will protect your brother and me. I don't want you to worry."

"*Mamashy*, please stay with me tonight. I don't want to be alone. You could sleep here right next to me in this bed. Only one night, please? Tomorrow you can take me home. Please, *Mamashy*?"

"Dinale, darling, please don't ask me to stay. You know I can't. I can't allow Vunia to go home by herself. And Abek can't be left alone. Nadja and Cousin Dina will come home from A.V.L. hungry and tired. I must be there to feed everyone. I promise tomorrow I will come and bring you a special treat."

I nod and muster up a smile for Mama and Vunia, wishing I could leave with them right now. I make Mama promise that first thing in the morning, she will return to the hospital and ask the doctor if I can be released. I kiss and hug her close. Holding back my tears, I give her my biggest sunshine smile and beg her to be careful and to send love and kisses to Nadja, Dina, and Abek from me.

"I love you, Mama."

"I love you too, my angel. All will be well, and tomorrow I will ask the doctor if we can take you home."

After my Mama and Vunia leave, I lie back in bed and close my eyes, wishing I could fall into a deep sleep, and when I awaken, the war will be over, and we will all be together again.

SOMETHING IS WRONG. I sit in the dark and listen. I hear gunshots and screams.

"Are we being bombed?" asks the elderly woman, Sarah, who lies in the bed next to me. Her eyes behind her thick glasses appear even larger than usual.

"Do we have to leave the building?" grumbles the man who never stops complaining and coughs all night long.

"I'm not sure," I reply. "I'll go and see." I get out of bed and hobble to the door. The other patients in this corridor are also at their doors.

"What is wrong?" the young woman two rooms down asks. She is cradling her newborn in her arms.

"I do not know," I say, "but I will find out." I limp down the corridor to the nurse's station. A crowd of patients huddles around her desk. Everyone is talking at the same time, peppering her with questions.

"I heard they put up searchlights in the small ghetto." A woman wrings her hands nervously.

"We have heard nothing, but if I do you will be the first to know," the nurse says. "Please return to your rooms."

I glance at the clock on the wall and see that it is just past midnight.

Two orderlies arrive. Both are tall young men.

"Let's not work ourselves into a frenzy," the nurse adds. "We won't know anything until the morning."

They order us all back to our rooms.

Sometime after two in the morning, the sounds seem to be getting louder and closer to the hospital. So many sounds. A convoy of trucks thundering down the street, Nazis braying through loudspeakers, gunshots, and blood-curdling screams. By now, I should be used to it, but I am not. These sounds always mean one thing—death. I curl up in a fetal position, clinging to my blanket as I alternate between praying and crying. Exhaustion finally overwhelms me, and I surrender to sleep.

CHAPTER 20

I WAKE in the morning in a sweat, my sheets soaking wet. The hospital halls are teeming with activity. Those who can walk are gathered in small groups in the corridor, discussing and speculating on the events of the night. The streets are silent now as if nothing ever happened. As the day staff begins to report for work, rumors begin to buzz. Rumors of deportation at the Glinice Ghetto. How many have been taken and where they were sent is unknown.

I wait anxiously for my mother to arrive. I know she will make every effort to get to me or at least to send me a message. The morning wears on, and still there is no word from my mother or my sister, and I become more and more anxious. I cling to the belief that my Nadja's and Dina's work permits will keep my mother and brother safe. Without any word, I lie in my bed, tortured with visions of the worst possible outcome. My fear turns to anger at my sister for not finding a way to come to me. *How dare she let me worry like this? Doesn't she know how scared I am?*

I feel trapped at the hospital as I have no proper clothing with me. All I have to wear is a hospital gown and slippers. My mother left clothing for me at my Aunt Mindale's, which isn't far from the hospital. But how am I going to get there with no clothing? Presciently, she wanted me to call on family in case she had trouble getting to me in the hospital.

I will go crazy if I don't do something. I must find a way to get out of this place.

One of the nicer nurses named Zofia comes in to check on the other patients and me. And I remember something. I remember she admired the beautiful traveling mirror my mother brought me the other day. It was a gift from when I visited my grandparents in Brzeziny the summer before the war. It has a cameo on the front with a button that opens up the case to a mirror. I beg her to go to my aunt's house and ask one of my aunts or cousins to bring me my clothes. At first, she refuses,

"Please, Zofia. I beg of you, can you please go to my aunt's house? I need my clothes."

"I don't have time to do errands for you," she sputters. "Can't you see how busy the hospital is and what a panic everyone is in because of last night's terrors?"

I pick up my treasured mirror and offer it to her if she will help me. I know immediately by the glint in her eyes that temptation has won her over. She reaches for the mirror and agrees to help. It is amazing to me how the greed of possessing a little bauble alters her priorities. I store this information for future reference. I surrender the mirror to her, hoping she will do as she has promised.

One-hour passes, then two as I anxiously wait for a member of my family to come to my rescue. Finally, my cousin Nadja appears alone with the clothes that will provide my freedom. My beautiful eighteen-year-old cousin looks haggard and worn, her brown eyes circled in blackness. She is disheveled, and nervously she glances over her shoulder as if she fears someone has followed her. Rushing to me, she crushes me to her, and immediately a torrent of tears and cries of sorrow pour forth.

"Dina, it was awful. You can't imagine what has happened. I'm so sorry for you, for me, for Mama. I can't bear it."

A cold dread washes over me with each word, my own tears silently streaming from my eyes in disbelief. "What are you saying?" is all I manage to utter. Desperate for news, I bite my lip to restrain myself from interrupting her.

"In the middle of the night, the Nazis rolled into the Walowa Ghetto with what seemed an endless line of trucks. They quickly set up searchlights and unloaded hundreds of armed Nazis and their dogs on each street. The loudspeakers screamed that everyone was to line up outside their homes in five minutes. The angry voices threatened that anyone who was found in their home after five minutes would be shot immediately. They began banging on all the doors and shouting at everyone to hurry up. We were terrified and dressed in seconds, my parents urging us to hurry. Fear gripped us all. The poor grandmothers were crying and praying for God to intervene.

"As we exited our buildings, the Nazis kicked and cursed at us and flung us out. We were blinded like deer held frozen by the lights in our eyes. The vicious dogs barked, and the Nazis trained their guns on us. Anyone who protested or even asked a question was shot dead on the spot.

"An SS killer walked in front of each person, sneering with disgust. His lightning streak insignia seemed on fire, blazing under those lights. He divided each family. He didn't think or consider who or what they were to each other. Husbands, wives, and children were separated, torn from each other's arms. It was beyond anything you can imagine. A nightmare that had no end. It happened so quickly, I don't remember saying goodbye!"

Unable to continue, my cousin Nadja collapses in my arms, sobbing bitter tears. My tears join with hers in a river that soaks the worn, gray, stained sheets. Holding my breath, I wait for her to continue as my heartbeat pounds in my chest. I try to comfort her as best I can as I stroke her head, trying to calm the sorrow that knows no relief.

"They ripped babies from the arms of mothers, swinging them by their feet and laughing as they smashed their little skulls against the walls of the buildings. I cannot fathom it. They laughed. Some of the mothers begged the Nazis to murder them, too. Sometimes the Nazis accommodated them with a bullet to the head. Other times they just laughed and forced them back into the crowd, funneling them in a narrow queue in the direction of the train station."

Tears stream from my eyes and I am shaking like sapling in a storm. I press my shaking hands to my mouth to keep from retching.

"Th-they took m-my mother, *Bubbe* Surale and my *Bubbe* Chava, Aunt Fela, and the girls. They made their selections randomly, taking some and leaving others. If anyone clung to someone they loved, they tore them apart. That's what they did to Uncle Alexander, David, and Aunt Natalia. They tore her from Alexander's arms and dragged her away. My mother had to help her walk. Oh, their cruelty was beyond belief. It wasn't enough they were taking our loved ones, they wanted to destroy our spirits."

Nadja wipes her eyes and her voice cracks as she continues. "The Nazis herded those selected like cattle through the streets, rifles pointed at their backs. Anyone who tried to run or stop them was shot. Anyone who could not keep up the pace was shot. Everyone was crying and calling out to their loved ones as they were marched away. Can you imagine?" She shakes her head. "What kind of a monster takes pleasure in shooting into a crowd of innocent people—women and children, the elderly?" Nadja's tears and mine soak the sheets.

"After the selections they ordered us back into our houses. We heard this morning that those who survived the slaughter in the streets were taken to the railroad station and crammed into cattle cars. Hundreds of people packed like sardines. I cannot think that our grandmothers could survive this horror. We found out the Nazis went first to Glinice Ghetto and that nearly everyone there was deported before they came to Walowa. It is a miracle that you were here."

"No, no! You are wrong. My sister and Dina have permits. They couldn't have been taken. They are probably all at A.V.L. safely waiting for me. I must get out of this hospital *now* and go to them. I'm sure my sister Nadja found a way to save my mother and brother. Yes, yes, I'm sure Otto, the manager at A.V.L., would have helped her. He saved my life! I know he would help my sister!"

My cousin looks at me with pity in her eyes. "Dinale, Dinale, you have to face the reality that they are probably all gone. Thank God you were here in the hospital. Now you must get out of here before something bad happens to you. There is no way the Nazis are going to allow a bunch of sick and crippled Jews to live. They will come here too. Mark my words. Come home with me. The Glinice Ghetto is no more. You have no other place to go."

I shake my head in disbelief. "No, no, you go home. I will be all right! I'm going to A.V.L. I know my sister is waiting for me. I know she is there. After I find her, we will figure out what to do. Give my love to your father, Majer, Uncle Alexander, and David. Tell them how sorry I am and that I will see them soon. I must find out what has happened to my family."

"I pray that you are right Dina." Nadja hugs me close. She helps me dress, and I wince because my wounds are still painful. The wounds to my leg and hand I can bear. The wound of losing loved ones, I cannot. We walk out together and cling to each other one more time. Nadja begs me once more to go home with her, but I refuse. My only thought is to find my family.

As I make my way along the street, I try not to think of my Aunt Mindale's face—the loving woman who has spent her whole life in dedication to her family and community. Poor Nadja, to lose her mother, my heart is breaking. What of my sweet *bubysy* and her talent for healing? Oh, *Bubysy*, how will you survive this? Aunt Natalia without Alexander—their love for each other is like a fairytale. How will they live? Silently I pray that God will protect my grandmother and relatives from the evil fiends that hold them captive.

Absentmindedly, I touch the braids that my mother lovingly plaited only yesterday. They are still bound neatly, and I can almost smell my mother's scent on them. *Is it possible that not even twenty-four hours have passed since I kissed you good-bye, Mama?* My stomach clenches, my worst fears take hold of me. I turn the corner from the hospital, and I spot a group of A.V.L. workers walking briskly along the street. Rushing to them, my heart pounding with joy, I nearly knock them down in my excitement. "I am so happy to see you. Thank God I found you! I was going to try to get back to A.V.L. on my own. Where's Nadja? Where's my sister?" I search each face, looking for reassurance. "Why isn't she here with you? Why didn't she come to get me? Are my mother and brother safe, and my cousin, Dina?"

Jakob, one of the young men, takes my hand and looks into my eyes. "Listen to me, Dina, we have been ordered to collect our things from our homes in the ghetto and return to A.V.L., where we are now going to live." He casts a glance around the group with a furrowed brow. "Don't worry, your sister is waiting for you back at A.V.L. They are all safe. They wouldn't let Nadja come with us to the Big Ghetto because she is from the Glinice Ghetto and doesn't live here. Go back to the hospital and wait for us there. Make sure you have your work permit."

I open my mouth as I want to ask him about Nadja and the rest of my family, but he interrupts me before I can speak.

"Do as I say, and you'll see your sister again. Okay, *maidele?*"

I beam with happiness and throw my arms around his neck and kiss him. "Yes, Jakob, I understand, and I will be waiting for you outside the hospital."

Waving good-bye, I would have danced down the street if my injuries had allowed. I am elated that my prayers have been answered —my sister and family are safe and waiting for me at A.V.L.

I hobble back into the hospital and tell the nurse in charge that friends of my family will be taking me to my sister. While I'm gathering my things, the nurse Zofia comes into my ward and insists that my bandages be changed once more, and the doctor must approve my release. I wait impatiently for the doctor as Zofia changes my bandages and cleans my wounds. The stitches on my leg and hand are crooked and ragged, and I know that I will have ugly scars. I think the doctor did a terrible job. Any of the women in my family could have easily sewn a straighter seam. My chest clenches as I think about the kind-hearted and loving relatives who were so cruelly torn from their homes and deported. But I thank God that Nadja, Mama, Abek, and Dina will be waiting for me at A.V.L.

After an hour has passed, I grow impatient for the doctor, and I'm worried that I'll miss the workers returning to A.V.L. I take the extra bandages and salve Zofia left on the tray and stuff them in my pocket.

It seems unusually chaotic at the entrance. There are a lot of people coming and going. Because of this, no one questions me, and I have no trouble sneaking out of the hospital.

I scan the street for Jakob and the others. Minutes pass, and there is no sign of them. I become more and more agitated that maybe I have missed them. Finally, I spy my sister's friend Sonja, hurrying up the street in the direction of A.V.L. I call to her, halting her progress as I limp across the street. She tells me that she has missed the group and is on her way back alone.

"That means I, too, have missed them. The stupid doctor wouldn't let me go. Please, take me with you?"

"Of course." Taking my arm, she scans the street for trouble. "We must not waste a minute. Let's get out of here!"

As we hurry through the streets, I nervously chatter about my family. "I can't wait to see my sister, Nadja," I say as I limp beside Sonja, trying my best to keep up with her hurried pace. "I am really angry with her, though, for not getting word to me. When I see her, I am going to give her a piece of my mind."

Nodding in agreement, she says nothing.

"Did you talk to my sister at all?" I query her.

"No, I didn't."

Tears prick my eyes. "She is there, isn't she?"

Sonja says nothing as she continues to tug me along.

"She is there, isn't she?" I ask in a rising pitch. "Please tell me she's there."

"Dina, stop crying. If a Nazi comes along, you will get us arrested." Her gaze darts around us. "Hush, your sister is fine. She is waiting for you, okay? Now stop your blubbering. I'm nervous being out on the street like this after such a night."

"I'm sorry, Sonja, I didn't ask if your family is okay. Are they all right?"

Her eyes swell with tears, which she brushes aside. "No, they are gone. My mother, father, and brother were deported last night."

Feeling her anguish, I clasp her hand, "I'm so sorry. It was selfish of me to pester you about Nadja. Please forgive me."

Sonja nods, accepting my apology as she picks up her pace in the direction of A.V.L.

I try my best to tamp down my worry as we hurry along. By the time we reach A.V.L. my leg is throbbing, but I rush inside, forgetting my pain, "Nadja, Nadja, where are you?" I run to a group of workers that are standing together, their heads bent deep in conversation. "Jakob, where is Nadja? I don't see her."

He takes my hands, his eyes filling with tears. Pulling me into his arms, he whispers in my ear. "Dina, I'm so sorry. Forgive me for lying to you. Neither Nadja nor your cousin Dina is here. They never showed up at Kuszno Street, where the workers with permits were told to assemble. They must have stayed with your mother and brother, not wanting to abandon them."

I look at him in disbelief, unable to suppress the uncontrollable shaking that overwhelms me. "NO! NO!" My screams pierce the air. "IT CAN'T BE TRUE. THEY CAN'T BE GONE! NO! NO! *MAMASHY*, NADJA, ABEK, DINA!"

My world crumbles about me, and I feel it spinning out of control. Falling to my knees, I sink into oblivion.

CHAPTER 21

I WAKE up once again in Otto's arms. He carries me into a small room with mattresses on the floor. He lays me down, his face etched with concern. "Dina, I am sorry, little one, for your loss," he says in a hushed voice. "Take your time and heal. As soon as you feel up to it, you can resume your work." Otto asks Sonja to stay with me and tells everyone else to get back to work.

In silence, I receive his kind words, but they make no impression on me. All I can think of are my mother, Nadja, Abek, Dina, Fela, Vunia, their families, my aunts, and cousins. A world without them is a living death. I want to die.

Days come and go as I lay prostrate with grief. I refuse to eat or speak. I am barely aware of the steady stream of workers who come to my bedside to offer some form of encouragement or hope to my world that lies in ashes. I go from delirium-filled days to nightmarish nights, the voices of my family ringing in my ears, their faces haunting my dreams.

One evening, my sister's friend Mietek comes to my bedside. Clasping my hands in his, he begins to share his memories of the awful night of the destruction of the Glinice Ghetto. "It seems we are in the same boat, you and me," he whispers, his voice hoarse with emotion. "We both have lost everyone we hold dear. Dina, please listen to my story. You must know what happened that night. You must walk through hell with me. It will help you to stay strong. Perhaps together we can find some meaning that will allow us both to fight through our grief and live another day." He pauses, seeming to gather his thoughts, his eyes fixed on some distant horizon that only he can see. His face twists in pain. "Dina, nearly every person who survived that horrific night has lost some or all of their families and friends."

I focus on the movement of his mouth. I concentrate on watching his lips move as I listen to his tale. He grips my hands as if they are a lifeline.

"That evening, I was with your sister and Vunia's sister Lola outside of your house in the street," he says. "We were discussing the usual topics that consumed us—politics, the war, and our dreams of one day emigrating to Palestyne. Even in this living hell, we have all clung to our dreams and hopes. Not even the Nazis have been able to quash them. Your sister was vibrant and animated as usual." His face lights up with a smile as he remembers. "It was a warm evening, a beautiful evening, a star-filled summer's night that reminded us of how bittersweet life is.

"It was a magical evening until the Nazis drove into the ghetto ordering us to go into our homes and to get off the streets before curfew. Reluctantly we bid each other goodnight and went to our homes. Then, at midnight, we were startled from our sleep with banging on our doors and shouts from loudspeakers, ordering us to assemble in the street immediately. We were blinded by lights and clubbed as we left our homes. The sounds were heartrending—children crying and people screaming. Above the chaos, the elderly prayed, beseeching God to intervene. It was a nightmare beyond imagining. They said we had fifteen minutes to pack a few basic belongings and food. All Jews with labor cards were told to report to Kuszno Street, and those without were to report to Graniczna Street for immediate resettlement. In my family, my brother and I were the only ones with a labor card, and my family urged us to go to Kuszno

Street. At first, my brother and I refused to go. We argued with my parents that we would never be separated from our beloved family. We wanted to go with them regardless of the consequences and face the future together as one. My mother began to tear at her hair and scream, 'No! No! You will go to Kuszno Street. We will be fine! We will write and let you know where they take us. You will do as I say. You will not disobey your mother!'

"My brother and I reluctantly gave in to her hysteria. Thousands of people stood on the streets. We embraced my mother, father, and sisters, all the while the Nazis kept shouting at us to move. My family joined the mass of humanity that began to walk toward Graniczna Street. The Nazis continued blaring at us to hurry. 'Schnell!' Walk faster. They began to shoot into the crowd, aiming at the elderly and children who lagged behind.

"The streets were bathed with the blood of the innocent. I sent my brother on to Kuszno Street and took a dangerous chance and ran to your house hoping to find Nadja and your cousin Dina so that I could take them with me, but I was too late. When I got there, they were already gone. Vunia's house was abandoned, too. The street lay empty except for the bodies of those who were shot on the spot. Doors stood ajar, and candlelight flickered onto the street, eerie and ghostly. I ran from the destruction and prayed that Nadja and Dina had gone ahead of me to Kuszno Street.

"When I got to Kuszno Street, they lined us up in rows of ten, and the SS surrounded us with rifles leveled and aimed. I looked for your sister and Dina in the crowd, but I couldn't find them. I could smell sweat, urine, human waste, and fear. Fear impregnated the air and hung about us as we stood waiting. Then the selections began, and I watched as the Nazis chose the strong and healthy, dividing us from the mothers, the children, and the weak. The Nazis terrorized those chosen and marched the unwanted away to Graniczna Street. It was heartbreaking to hear the crying children clinging to their mothers, who desperately pleaded for mercy as they plodded their way down the street. Members of separated families continued to call their goodbyes until we heard machine gun and rifle fire. The air was filled with screams from the dying and those who loved them.

"Dinale, I don't know where our families have been taken, but I can't imagine that it is anywhere good. We, the survivors, must fight to live so that the world will know what took place here. You and I must live to remember and testify for those who have perished. The Nazis mean to soak the ground with our blood and annihilate us from the face of the earth. There can be no delusions among us. We are all that stands in the way of the extinction of an entire people. Help me find a reason to live. You are the youngest, and you are strong. Your people need you. You must live for your mother, your father, Nadja, Abek, and Dina!"

The tears stream down Mietek's face as he lowers his forehead to my hands. The effort he has exerted to describe the horrors of that inexplicable night has taken its toll. Now it is my turn to save a soul. The tears that have failed me now pour freely down my face as I bend to kiss his head. My voice barely above a whisper, I speak for the first time since my collapse.

"Mietek, Mietek, I cannot bear the pain. I cannot bear the loss. My family is gone. I am alone."

Lifting his head, his face wet from his tears, he hoarsely whispers, "You are not alone. We are a family, a family of lost souls. Anger will keep you alive, Dinale. We must nourish our anger until the day we are set free, and then vengeance will be ours."

"You are speaking of hate. I know nothing of hate," I tell him. "I have lived surrounded by love and taught to respect human life. Even now, knowing I may never see those I love again, I feel only misery and guilt that I was not with them. I am alive while they may not be. Hate will not bring them back to me."

"Hate and revenge will nurture your will to live. That in and of itself will destroy the Nazis. But if you cannot live on hate and revenge, you must live on sheer will. You cannot lie on this mattress indefinitely and not work. Even Otto cannot protect you then. You must get up. It is time to return to the living."

~

OTTO LOOKS RELIEVED to see me back on the floor fulfilling my labors. I am a shadow of who I was. Daughter, sister, friend—these are descriptions that no longer hold meaning for me. My young, healthy body strains under the tasks assigned to me, but these burdens only seem to strengthen my physical and mental determination. I begin to see that Mietek is right. It is easier to live, to go on each day, feeding off my anger. In my thoughts and prayers, I beg God to wipe the Nazis from the face of the earth. With each curse, my resolve to live grows stronger.

But even then, even as I learn to be strong, our world continues to crumble. A few days later, we learn the truth. The truth is carried back to us by the train conductors who carried our loved ones away.

Jakob and Mietek learned the news from the brother of one of the conductors. At the end of the workday, after Otto has gone to his apartment for the night, we huddle on the mattresses, and Jakob whispers the fate of our loved ones.

"The cars were crammed beyond capacity with thousands of people," Jakob tells us. "The destination was Treblinka, a small village near the Bug River. A trip that should have taken six hours from Radom took twenty-four hours to arrive. Upon arrival, the train was held in limbo and sat on the tracks for two more days in the brutal heat of summer.

"The cries of the innocents entombed in the cars could be heard pleading for water and food. The SS did nothing to alleviate their suffering. Instead, they shot randomly into the cars to silence the prisoners, laughing and promising they would get their food and water soon—" Jakob stops, and a sob escapes him.

Mietek lays his hand on Jakob's shoulder. "On the third day, the train finally entered the camp itself," Mietek continues. "When the doors were opened, the unfortunates were greeted with blinding lights and Nazis yielding whips and guns. Other guards gripped the leashes of the German shepherds, who barked incessantly as they screamed their orders, *'RAUS! RAUS!* HURRY! HURRY! GET OFF THE TRAINS!'

"The bodies of those who died in transit were thrown off the train. The pile of dead grew to massive proportions on the platform. Immediately the men and women were separated, young boys were pulled apart from their mothers, and young girls from their fathers. From there, they were marched down a long narrow path that led to a set of buildings. Beyond the buildings were smokestacks that filled the night air with noxious fumes and a cloud of ash that blocked the moon and stars from the sky. Thousands of our people were marched into those buildings, they were never seen again."

My hand grips my chest as I think of what my family and relatives endured. I close my eyes, and visions of my family flash before my eyes like a flickering film reel of a horrific movie. I see grandmother Surale praying to my grandfather and God for mercy. I see her unable to breathe in the heat and stench of the packed cattle car, her eyes drift closed, and she is gone. I see my poor brother being torn from my mother's and sister's arms as they desperately try to stay together. He is marched away with the other children who whimper and cry, disappearing into the buildings with the smokestack. I know he is gone.

I see my mother scream my brother's name and then my father's. Could my mother survive such an agony of seeing her precious youngest child wrenched from her arms? I see Nadja and Dina holding my mother, trying to console her. Were they beaten or shot dead on the spot? Did they know that death awaited them at the end of that road? *Mama, did you think of me in your last moments?* Did she wonder if my father had suffered the same fate? Or was the unspeakable cruelty of being separated from Abek too much to bear? I will never know the truth of their fates or the fates of my dearest girlfriends Vunia and Fela and their entire families being marched to their deaths. *Oh, Fela, remember our promise of a new life in Palestyne?*

I imagine Mama and Nadja and Dina holding hands as they were herded into the building. The images of suffering haunt me, and I can only imagine the worst, for there is nothing else to imagine anymore.

CHAPTER 22

ELEVEN DAYS. Eleven days have passed since I lost every member of my family. Eleven days of mind-numbing sorrow. Eleven days of surviving. I am now an orphan, barely thirteen years old, yet I feel ancient.

On Sunday, Otto has given me a pass to visit my remaining relatives in the Walowa Ghetto. He has been kind to give passes to those of us at A.V.L. who still have friends and relatives who survived the deportations.

My girlfriend Dora Rabbinowicz suddenly arrives breathless at the door of my relatives' apartment. "Otto wants us all back at A.V.L. immediately."

I hurriedly bid farewell to uncles Tuvye and Alexander, and my cousins, promising to return as soon as I can.

"Why can't the Nazis let us have just one day to spend with our families in peace," I say with frustration. As we hurry down the street, I notice the Polish electricians working in the ghetto. Gripping Dora's hand, I stop, forcing her to stop as well as I point at the Poles. "What are they doing?"

Dora's face pales as she watches the men wiring and hanging

lights. "This is just what they did the day they liquidated Glinice Ghetto," she whispers.

I begin to shake uncontrollably. "I need to go back and warn my relatives."

"No, we have to go now. We don't have time. Besides, I am sure word will spread quickly. Plenty of people are about. Come on," Dora urges, tugging me along. "We have to get out of here, NOW!"

Numb and trembling, I allow her to lead me to the spot where all the workers must meet to be escorted by the guards to A.V.L.

We arrive at A.V.L. under armed escort, where we remain for the next few days. Work keeps us busy, but we cannot help but worry about our remaining friends and relatives.

Our worst fears are realized.

The destruction of the Glinice Ghetto and its eight thousand inhabitants who were deported and murdered at Treblinka was nothing compared to what the Nazis would endeavor to carry out in the Walowa Ghetto. Otto, Hans, and a few of their fellow supervisors at A.V.L. may have saved our lives by canceling our visit to the ghetto and recalling us to A.V.L. Perhaps they were tipped off, or perhaps they figured out what was planned. But they kept us at A.V.L., while other factory workers were forced to report to the Walowa Ghetto. A massive *wysiedlenie*—deportation—took place under cover of darkness beginning at midnight.

Dora was correct that the electricians installing searchlights signaled a coming disaster, but the inhabitants could do nothing to save themselves. If our overseers believed we would remain ignorant of their actions, they underestimated the ingenuity of their captives. The truth came to us in fits and starts, but it came.

The ghetto was completely sealed and surrounded by armed S.S. troops, Ukrainian militia dressed in S.S. uniforms, gendarmes, and Polish and German police. Machine guns poised on rooftops prepared to mow down any who tried to escape or didn't proceed as quickly as ordered. For three days and two nights, twenty-five thousand people were forced from their homes systematically. Dogs and their handlers searched each building to assure the meticulous Nazis that no one was left behind by somehow eluding detection.

No one escaped or received a commuted sentence. Anyone found hiding was quickly dispersed with a bullet to the head. Whole families were liquidated in the streets as they were driven from their homes. Street by street, apartment by apartment, the buildings were emptied of Jews who were forced at gunpoint to areas for selection. There, they were made to stand in endless lines as the SS called them vile names, spat on them, and beat them.

After many hours, they finally reached a Gestapo arbiter who barely scrutinized the work permits of those fortunate enough to have them. One can imagine the desperation that enveloped the crowds as they stood awaiting their verdicts. A heartless adjudicator made a swift motion of the hand, "right" or "left." "Right" allowed one innocent person to stay in Radom and live another day. "Left" sent another innocent soul to deportation, where they would be crammed into cattle cars bound for Treblinka or some other deadly destination. Even the precious work permits failed to guarantee safety, as many of the factories were designated to be closed, and the slave employees were now expendable.

I am relieved to find out that my cousins Majer and Nadja and their father Tuvye are spared, I cry bitter tears not knowing the fate of my other cousins. The Nazi plan to divide, conquer, and destroy the Jews has reached a brutal and degrading low, all with the aid of their accomplices—the Poles and Ukrainians. Twenty-thousand Jewish citizens of Radom were deported over those three days of hell, leaving but a scant remnant of survivors of what had been the Walowa Ghetto.

The Nazis quickly set about ransacking the homes of the vanquished, taking clothes, furniture, and any valuables that they have not already confiscated. For this disheartening task, they order the remaining Jews to empty and sort what is left of the lives of the vanished. From there, the plunder is distributed to shipping warehouses like A.V.L. We that remain are granted life in order to categorize, crate, and ship the belongings of our dead to Germany and the soldiers on the Eastern front.

We are all that remains of our once-thriving Jewish community. For now, we are protected by the decent Germans like Otto, who runs the large complex of assorted buildings that provide the war effort with a necessity that we hope will assure us a modicum of safety. We carry on, knowing that our days, too, are numbered. Each day, the sand pours through the hourglass of time, bringing us closer to our fate.

THE SHARED tragedy of losing family members forges a bond between us that begins to resemble something of a family. In this small community where we live and work, precious moments of levity are a welcome respite from the sorrow and fear that loom over us.

We eat our meals in a cafeteria that services the entire complex. At long communal tables, we snatch moments of rest from hard labor over a meager meal. We share news about the war in whispered words. At A.V.L., we are lucky. At least we are fed enough bread and soup to keep us from starvation and enable us to function.

One day as I wait for my tray, a youth near my age walks up to me. I have seen him many times and have noticed how handsome he is. I look up into a pair of serious blue eyes that suddenly crinkle as he smiles. A smile that lights up the room. A smile that brings a heated flush to my cheeks. I have no experience with courtship, and all the young men I know treat me like a sister. I feel awkward and inept in his presence, but there is something about his smile that makes me feel as though I am back in Fela's grandparents' cherry orchard. I cannot help but smile back at him.

"Hello, my name is Natek Korman. What's your name?" he asks as he offers his hand to me. His penetrating eyes unsettle me. They seem to be seeking answers to questions not yet spoken.

"D-dina Frydman," I stammer, shyly placing my hand in his, knowing my face is probably as red as a tomato.

"I am pleased to meet you, Dina Frydman," he says, shaking my hand.

"Nice to meet you as well, Natek Korman." I remove my hand from his warm grasp and slip it into my pocket. I glance around for someone I know to provide me an escape, but I come up empty-handed.

"Well, Dina Frydman, would you mind if we eat our meal together?" Again, that marvelous smile beguiles me, and I can hardly resist such a well-mannered proposal, but still, I search my mind for a plausible excuse. My heart thunders in my chest as if trapped within the sights of a gun. I hesitate a moment too long, and Natek pronounces, "Good, let's sit over here." He leads me to a table, and before I can protest, I am sitting across from him and gazing into those serious blue eyes.

Natek tells me that both he and his brother Benjamin survived the liquidation of the Glinice Ghetto. Tears fill his eyes as he tells me of his parents and sister who were lost to him on that fateful night.

"Tell me about yourself, Dina," he asks softly, his eyes earnestly regarding me.

Even though I am reluctant to open my soul to him, or anyone for that matter, I cannot help but feel the compassion in his eyes. And so, I tell him about my family and how I managed to survive because of a simple twist of fate and the kindness of a German, no less. And now it is my turn to cry. "I-I don't understand why I am still alive. How is it possible that the Glinice Ghetto was liquidated, and my family taken to their deaths while I was safe in a hospital room suffering from nothing more than a cut and stitches? I was here in Radom, yet I saw nothing of the slaughter and the streets that flowed with blood."

I feel a sense of relief as I share my story with him. Even though my friends at A.V.L. have helped me carry on, I feel as though I have no right to speak of my grief when so many have suffered worse. My guilt is caged inside me, and sometimes I feel as though I will suffocate from it—from being one of the lucky ones who was not part of that death march. I heard nothing of the cries that were borne to the heavens pleading for mercy. I did not see the lives of children extinguished like a flame in the gust of an evil storm. I cannot comprehend what has happened, and so I suffer and mourn, the lone surviving fruit on a tree that winter has lain bare. I feel tormented by the guilt of the living.

"In my heart, I don't believe I deserve to live," I tell him. "Why should I be the one chosen to continue my family's lineage? It should be my sister with her strength of purpose and brilliance. It should be my younger brother, Abek, with his rabbinical wisdom. I feel as if there has been a terrible mistake."

Natek nods, his eyes full of compassion, and he reaches for my hand. "Dina, I have asked myself the same question over and over again. Some say it is God's will, and man should never question the will of God, but my belief in God is no longer strong or important to me. God has abandoned us in our hour of need, and I can no longer pray to Him for our redemption. The only god left to worship is the god of survival. All I want is to live, and I will do anything and everything to stay alive until this miserable war is over."

I gasp in shock at what he is saying. His eyes burn bright with the fury of a thousand candles. Those eyes stand ready to judge every evil perpetrated since the beginning of time and every cry of innocence that has ever been swept away by the deaf embrace of the wind.

"I can see what I have said has shocked you, Dynka," he says, letting go of my hand. "But our world has changed. This is a time of shock. Our people are being exterminated, and we cannot do anything about it except to survive. You, too, will survive, of this I am sure. You are everything that your family was and is. You are all that is good in the world. And your beauty and goodness are more precious than gold." He has made me gasp again, this time from his bold words.

No one has ever spoken to me like this. Natek's words confuse me. In my heart, I am grateful to have a new friend and to believe that perhaps I am meant to continue and carry on the torch of my family. Is it God's will? Natek says he no longer believes in God, but if we lose our faith, what will become of us? Over the past few weeks, I have struggled with these thoughts. I ask Papa in my heart how he would explain this horrific destruction of our humanity. But I already know the answer. Papa would tell me to have faith. To be strong. And never to forget who I am and where I come from.

CHAPTER 23

EVERY DAY we share our bowls of soup.

It is Natek's idea. Our spoons clink as we share our soup as well as our hopes and dreams, sitting across from each other in the cafeteria. A silly but endearing ritual that forges a bond between us that seems as unbreakable to me as the barbed wire that surrounds us.

Time blurs for me, and it is difficult even to remember the order of the days and months as Natek and I embrace our newfound love and the daily routines that go with it. Natek is my first love, and I his, and we make many a promise to each other that we hope we will be able to keep. He is only sixteen but has a command of himself that is far beyond his years, and I feel great pride that he has singled me out as his girlfriend and confidant. He becomes my shelter from the storm that rages around us.

The weather and its seasonal changes are the only clues that the world continues its eternal progress unhindered by the machinations of man. But the world and its troubles seem to disappear when Natek holds my hand. And my heart soars when he places a gentle kiss on my cheek

The rains and snows come early with a vengeance unsurpassed in our collective memory and turn the roads and fields to mud and ice.

For a time, the Nazis carry out no *aktions,* and our work proceeds uneventfully. We cannot imagine how the heavy machinery of war will overcome the obstacles of nature, and we take comfort in the knowledge that the Germans are suffering in their efforts to dominate the world. At the same time, we know the allied forces will also be bogged down by the icy hand of winter.

We surmise that the war on the Eastern front is not going as planned when a few Wermacht soldiers return and are assigned to A.V.L. These men bear the scars of the harsh realities of combat. Gerhard, a young steely-eyed warrior, returns from the front having lost an ear and fingers to frostbite. Bitter and disheartened from his battle experience, he has a short fuse when angered. None of us has the inclination to run afoul of our wardens, and a careful watch is kept as to their whereabouts at all times. As if by magic, word spreads quickly through the workstations when any of the foremen are on the prowl and inspecting the environs of the factory. Immediately, everyone assumes their most diligent work ethic, hoping not to catch any rancor and reprisal from our overlords.

Having been alerted of Gerhard's pending approach, I am busily emptying a carton that has been damaged during shipment from Germany. My job is to re-box the contents, which are destined for the Eastern front. With great effort I keep my face a mask of indifference when I place the contents on the table before me. Stacks of photos of the Fuhrer, Adolf Hitler stare at me, filling me with revulsion. I am caught unawares, and my first reaction is to tear them into pieces in a symbolic act of destroying the man whose goal is to eliminate me and my race. This is the face of evil, of the devil incarnate, the man who has destroyed my family and thousands of other families like mine.

I continue to sort and organize the photographs when I feel the warm breath of Gerhard at the back of my neck as he exhales smoke from his cigarette.

"Well, what have we here?" he asks aloud as much to himself as to me.

I stand frozen like a deer caught in the glare of a vehicle's headlights.

The cigarette dangles from his lips, and he sneers as he lifts the photos to take a better look. "Ah, yes, our esteemed Fuhrer, what an excellent likeness."

I cannot help but notice the sarcasm in his voice. I watch as he takes the stack of photos from the table and with his cigarette burns out the eyes, nostrils, and mouth of Hitler. Smiling with satisfaction, he watches the photos burn, waving away the ashes that swirl around us. "This son of a bitch has destroyed Germany. He will be the end of us all—we will follow him to our graves! You, of all people, know that I am right. By the time he is done, there will not be a Jew alive in all of Europe."

He shakes with palpable anger so strong that I cannot help but feel the vibrations around me as though an earthquake is in motion.

Never have I witnessed a German break with authority or show any anger or hatred of the objectives of the Third Reich, let alone criticize the Fuhrer. I dare not acknowledge his words. I fear when he recovers himself and realizes what he has said and done in front of me, that his retaliation will be swift.

"Now you can continue to box these lovely pictures of that madman. We will send them for morale-boosting to our gallant soldiers. I wonder if they will find solace in death as they clutch to their hearts a picture of our fine Fuhrer." He pats my cheek, unaware of the profound effect his actions provoke in me. "Don't worry, *Fraulein,* this incident never happened. Our secret is safe between us. Now carry on!" Straightening his uniform, he turns and strides away.

For a long while after, I replay his actions and his words in my mind. It is the first chink I have seen in the mighty armor of Germany's war machine. Is doubt spreading among the ranks as to Hitler's goals and aspirations for world supremacy? Strangely, I feel sorry for Gerhard—I am the prey, yet I feel sorry for the hunter. Gradually, I realize the truth of it. His act of defacing the photos of the Fuhrer was a symbolic act of a young man who has clearly seen his fill of war and the evils of his leader. Certainly, if he feels this way, others must sense the path ahead is one of destruction. I cannot wait to share this incident with Natek. But for now, I return to boxing the now eyeless Hitler photos destined for the Eastern front.

~

I AM anxious to visit my relatives again, who now live in a house inside a camp named for the main street in the area, Szwarlikovska Camp. I smuggle in crusts of stale bread and a few mushy apples that I have snatched from the food line in the cafeteria. My relatives are delighted with these treasures, and I am happily united with what is left of my dwindling family, Nadja, Majer, and their father Tuvye, my distraught Uncle Alexander, and my cousin David. Holding hands, we recite the *Kaddish,* the prayer for the dead, for my Aunt Natalia and all the others who have been murdered.

My cousin Majer works with his father at the shoe factory, repairing and making boots and shoes for the Germans, an indispensable industry, for what good is an army if their soldiers have no shoes on their feet? His sister Nadja has been reassigned to work in a warehouse separating items taken from the now-defunct Glinice Ghetto. There she sorts the spoils from the Jews who were sent to Treblinka, much of which will be sold to the Poles for a fraction of its true worth but nevertheless providing a tidy income for the Fatherland. The rest of the plunder is bound for German families who eagerly await the bloody gains.

"Everywhere I look, I recognize something that has belonged to someone I knew," Nadja tells us. "All the photographs of so many happy occasions. Fading photographs are all that is left of their lives, destined to end up in a pyre of flames. And no grave to show they once walked the earth."

Tears come to my eyes as I remember my mother's precious photo albums. What I wouldn't give to hold them in my hands again. The photos that marked the important occasions of a lifetime are forever seared in my memory. I will carry the faces and voices of my loved ones with me for the rest of my life. I make a promise to myself that each day I will think of their faces, the cherished smiles, and hopefully by remembering, I will keep alive something of the family I have lost.

Perhaps we are the gravestones, the sentries of silence. That is if we survive the war.

But if we are destined for a tower of smoke. Then who will be left to remember?

Natek calls for me at my cousins' home to meet my family and to escort me back to A.V.L. Proudly, I introduce him as my boyfriend, which makes his broad, handsome face radiate with joy. Nadja and I serve tea to our guest as we try to preserve the age-old custom of decorum when receiving a guest in one's home, hospitality that even in these destitute times cannot be forsaken.

"The Nazis will not win the war," Natek says. "Now that fighting has commenced on the Eastern front between the Germans and Russians, and the Americans have joined the skies in the bombardment of German-held Europe, it is inevitable. They will lose." He speaks with such confidence and optimism that the light of hope begins to shine in the eyes of my relatives.

Except for my Uncle Alexander. A man who at one time was as vibrant and confident as Natek. "Natek, the question is not whether the war will end, but if we shall survive it."

"I shall survive, I promise you that!" Natek says, taking my hand and kissing it. "Dina will be with me. I know it!"

Alexander finally cracks a smile in the face of such optimism. He looks from Natek to his own son. David's eyes are wide and lit with the same burgeoning hope. "See, Father, you and I, too, will survive the war. We must do it for Mother."

Alexander throws his arms around his son, hugging him fiercely. "You are right, David, we must live for your mother," he rasps.

It has been a wonderful visit, and as Natek and I walk back, arm in arm, to our designated rendezvous with the rest of the A.V.L. workers, I cannot help but glory in the warmth of the sun that bathes my face and revel in the miracle that I am alive to enjoy it. As we walk toward the gate, a woman comes toward us and stops dead in her tracks. She stares at me in disbelief as the blood drains from her features. She looks familiar to me, but I cannot place her. I feel the odd sensation of seeing someone out of context, of recognition without placement.

"Do I know you?" I give her a curious smile.

"You are alive..." From her ambiguous intonation, I cannot tell whether it is a question or a statement.

"Why shouldn't I be alive?"

"You were in the Jewish hospital, were you not?" Her gaze searches mine.

"Yes," I answer, as recognition dawns on me. "You were a nurse at the hospital while I was there. You went to my cousin's house and asked them to bring me clothes."

I turn to Natek and introduce him. I do not tell him that I bribed her with a mirror to gain her help. "This is my friend, Natek Korman. I am sorry I don't recall your name."

She nods at Natek. "Zofia Greenburg, nice to meet you." Turning back to me, she continues, "The day after the deportation, the Nazis came to the hospital and ordered all of the patients to be given food and clothing to last for twenty-four hours. They assured the doctors that the patients would be transferred to another hospital. Dr. Walchovicz complied, and the patients were carried onto waiting trucks. The Nazis dismissed the doctors and nurses and told us to go home.

"You wanted to be discharged from the hospital, and I went to find the doctor, but there was so much confusion after that horrible night. It was so busy with so many patients to tend to that I lost track of time and forgot to ask the doctor to examine you. Then in all the confusion of that desperate hour when the patients were being taken away, I remembered you and went in search of you, but I couldn't find you. I thought perhaps you had already been loaded onto one of the trucks.

The Nazis took them all to Pentz Park and executed all the patients with a bullet to the head, each and every one. Dr. Walchovicz should have known what the Nazis had been planning. We all should have. But how could we have stopped them in any case? The guilt overwhelmed me. Every day since then, I grieved. I grieved for the death of all those poor souls. And for you most of all. I grieved that I didn't save you. I thought I was seeing a ghost when I saw you walking toward me." Tears fill her eyes as she reaches for my hand.

"I am no ghost," I reply as I shed my own tears. "I did wait for you, but my desperation to find my family spurred me on, and I fled the hospital to find my sister." My voice chokes as I remember my beautiful sister, "I never found her. She was gone, but I was safe."

"I thank God you escaped, and I am very happy that you are alive," Zofia says. "I have seen my share of miracles in this life, and you are one of them." She hugs me. "I must go now. There are sick people waiting for my help." Turning, she calls over her shoulder, "Stay well and good luck!"

Natek and I watch her as she slips around a corner, disappearing from our sight.

I grasp Natek's arm tightly and shudder at the realization that, once again, I escaped death.

"Natek, I should have been in the hospital when it was liquidated, and I should have been in the ghetto when my family was taken. So many times I have avoided the flames of the inferno. How many more chances will I have before the fire claims me too?"

Natek pulls me closer and whispers in my year, "I told you we are both meant to survive. We will walk through the fire together unscathed."

CHAPTER 24

My breath looks like puffs of smoke in the frosty air. It's Sunday, and the factory is closed, a good time to go for a walk. It was not so long ago that I relished any chance to run and play with my friends. And yet it seems like a lifetime ago. Perhaps it is.

I notice a Polish man across the street leaning against a building. Tall and blond, his handsome face draws my attention. Dressed in typical worker's clothes, he stares intently at our building, watching for someone or something. Our eyes meet, and after watching me for a time, he approaches the fence. I look around to make sure I am not being observed as I lean my back against the fence and whisper to him, "I see you are looking for someone. Can I help you?"

In Polish, he asks, "Do you know Lola Freidenreich? I am a friend of hers, and I would like to speak to her. Can you ask her to come outside?"

"Yes, I know her. She is my roommate. What's your name?"

"Tell her Yannick Karzynswki is here to see her."

I hurry back inside to get Lola. I enter our living quarters, a former storage room in the warehouse where the girls now sleep. It is small and cramped and the girls are clustered about in small groups, chatting. Sundays are spent washing our few garments and resting for the week ahead. Lola is among the girls. We are all the best of friends, so I don't hesitate to tell her about the handsome young Pole waiting by the fence. "His name is Yannick Karzynswki, and he wants to talk to you."

Lola's face takes on a radiant glow, and I assume that she and this Yannick are more than friends. Everyone in the room looks inquisitively at Lola for some explanation. "I—I will explain everything after I speak with Yannick," she exclaims as she darts downstairs to see him. We all run to the window, hoping we can see something of this unusual occurrence of a Pole asking to speak to a Jew. Downstairs we see Lola and the young man engaged in a lively conversation. Lola returns a few minutes later, trembling, "Girls, I need your help. The man outside is my brother, who is living as a Pole in Warszawa. He has brought me clothing and identity papers to assume an alias of a Christian widow who is in mourning for her dead husband and child.

Yaacov, that's my brother's real name, says the new identity will provide me with a perfect cover. The Nazis will not be too scrupulous in their questioning of a woman in mourning. He says everything has been readied for me. All I need to do is get out of here."

"Oh, Lola, we are so happy for you," I say. "How can we help?"

"Yes, Lola, what can we do?" Dora is also excited and would take any risk to help Lola escape to freedom.

"I'm not sure exactly how to manage it, but I thought that you and Dora could distract the guard downstairs long enough for me to sneak past the gate."

"Yes, of course. I will pretend to fall and sprain my ankle and start crying in pain."

Dora grins. "And I can run to get the guard and beg him to carry Dina inside. That should give you ample time to make your escape. The other girls can keep watch and coordinate everything from the window."

"Dina and Dora, you are so clever. How can I ever thank you?" Lola throws her arms about us in a fierce hug. The other girls also join us in a communal embrace. Our collective joy turns to tears as we realize this might be the last time we will ever see Lola.

As Lola readies herself by gathering her few things, we watch the guard from our window and whisper different strategies in case of unforeseen problems. In order for our plan to work, we need to wait until right before the end of the guard's watch when he is less cautious about abandoning his post, knowing that his replacement will report momentarily.

Minutes before the changing of the guard, we launch our daring plan into action. Dora and I go outside for a breath of fresh air. As I block her from view, Dora pours a cup of water on the ground, which immediately begins to ice up in the frigid air. Our roommates keep watch from the upstairs window and coordinate the timing and implementation of our ploy from our bedroom window. On a given signal, I throw myself to the ground and begin to cry in pain. Dora runs to the guard. "*Herr* Rummel, one of the girls has slipped on a patch of ice. I think she sprained her ankle. She is in terrible pain. Please can you help me get her inside?"

"Where is the clumsy girl?" Slinging his rifle behind his back, he follows Dora to where I sit, my heart pounding with excitement. Adrenalin races through my veins, and I give a command perfor-mance, like my favorite actress Shirley Temple. I cry like a baby, clutching my ankle in pretend agony. I look up at the guard with a tear-streaked face. "I s-slipped and t-twisted m-my ankle. I don't think I can w-walk on it."

The guard curses me under his breath. He picks me up and carries me inside. I peek over his shoulder and wink at Dora, who gives the signal. With no one on duty, Lola has no trouble slipping through the gate. Lola runs to her brother, who is waiting nearby, and they disap-pear behind a building.

The guard lowers me on my bed while all of the girls crowd about, fussing over me. "Don't worry, we will take care of her."

"Yes, she will be fine. She only needs to rest."

The guard, anxious to return to his post, is gone in an instant. We all run to the window. Lola promised that she would wave good-bye to us. Moments later, Lola and Yaacov appear around the corner of the building. Lola is now dressed in a black dress of mourning and a heavy veil. Lifting the veil, she looks up and sees all of our faces pressed against the glass. She waves, her lips form the word, "Thank you." She blows us a kiss, her face flushed with joy. Yaacov smiles and nods his head then takes her hand, and they disappear once more from our view. It is like a fairytale in which the princess is rescued by the handsome prince. We are all elated as we dance around the room with joy.

We have helped our friend find freedom. Lola's escape is one small victory over the Nazis. At least one of us has a chance of surviving.

Over the next few days, Lola's disappearance goes unnoticed. No one at A.V.L. ever asks about her, and we find out the Wermacht officer that supervises A.V.L. does not want any SS scrutiny and chooses to turn a blind eye rather than be held accountable.

LOLA'S ESCAPE fills me with warmth, but as the winter turns frigid and the nights grow long, I begin to worry about what will happen to the remaining Jews of Radom. What will the Germans do with us once we have sorted, packed, and loaded up every scrap of wealth left in Radom? What use will they have for us? What reason to prolong our lives? We begin to watch the Germans warily for any signs of coming changes. Sometimes we can hear them playing records and singing along in discordant voices as they drown their bitterness in drink.

The Lagerfuhrer who oversees A.F.L. is a soldier named Hans who is maybe forty years of age. He stands a head above everyone else, but his blue eyes, as blue as a mountain stream, earn him the sobriquet of Moishele, or Moses, among the workers. When he enters the warehouse, the whispers seem to travel on the wind. "Moishele is coming! Moishele is coming!" Quickly, all conversations cease, and we all bend our backs over whatever task we are performing. The only sounds to be heard are those related to our efforts. We are all experts in disappearing. It is as if we shrink from the space of our bodies and become invisible in our clothes in an effort to draw as little attention as possible to our existence.

Today Hans, Moishele, enters the shipping floor, and before any of us can telepath his arrival, he shouts with laughter, "Moishele *bist comen!* Moishele *bist comen!*"

Everyone is frozen speechless. How did he find out our nickname for him?

Hans continues to laugh and repeat, "Moishele *bist comen!* Moishele *bist comen!*"

Then a group of workers bursts into laughter, and soon we are all laughing with Hans. None of us is immune to the hilarity of the joke. It is an unusual, lighthearted moment, this sharing of humor between master and slave, and it relieves some of the tensions and fears that permeate the air.

Not long after the Moishele incident, a male voice wakes me, one night after midnight, whispering in my ear, his hand caressing my hair. Stunned, my eyes snap open in fear. *Dear Lord, help me.* Sitting on my bed is Moishele. It is as if a specter has appeared before me, and I rub my eyes. "Dina, *komm mit mir in mein stuben.*"

I am mute with fear, and he must think that I don't understand him, for he repeats himself somewhat louder. "Dina, you are coming back with me to my room."

Anxiously trying to control the panic that envelops me, I plead, "*Herr* Lagerfuhrer, I don't understand. Why do you want me to go to your room?" I begin to cry. "I am just a young girl. Don't you have a daughter my age?"

"*Nein*, I have no daughter, and you are old enough!" His voice rises in pitch with irritation. "You will do as I say and come with me!"

My roommates cannot help but hear my crying and protests and are beginning to stir. I am only thirteen and a half, but I can't tell him my real age, or I will be in terrible danger as workers at A.V.L. must be sixteen. His breath holds the unmistakable scent of alcohol. I cringe from his pawing hands. Cipa, an older girl who sleeps next to me, comes to my defense. She knows Hans fairly well as she has the chore of cleaning his rooms. Standing, she commands him in a quiet, controlled voice, "*Herr* Lagerfuhrer, please leave Dina alone. Let me take you back to your room. It is all right. I will go with you."

He fixes his drunken bloodshot eyes upon her, which causes me to shudder, but Cipa stands firm. "Come, *Herr* Lagerfuhrer, you don't want to bother with this child. Come, I will take you back to your room."

I don't know what changes his mind. Perhaps he considers the repercussions of his sexually assaulting me. For a moment, he just stares at me, his eyes narrowing and then for whatever reason, he stands and throws his arm around Cipa, allowing her to escort him back to his apartment. Cipa has saved me from molestation that I could not have borne. What price she paid to protect me is never discussed between us.

Hans avoids me after that night. But sometimes, I will catch him staring at me with a cold glare. I try to avoid being near him as much as possible and I'm grateful that Cipa sticks close to me from then on. But my fear is always close to the surface. Hans holds my life in his hands. Thankfully, his animosity hasn't caused him to take any revenge against me. I cannot help but hear my parents' words echoing in my mind. *"We are truly fortunate indeed."* Once again, I have escaped a horrible fate, but how many more chances do I have left?

CHAPTER 25

IT SEEMED TOO good to be true, and it was.

In January, we learn of the next tragedy to befall the dwindling Jews of Radom. It becomes known as the "Palestinian *Aktion*." In a climate of complete hopelessness, rumors abound, and word spreads like a wildfire through the ghetto that a possibility of freedom for some might be coming. Jews with relatives in Palestyne can sign up on a list for resettlement in the Holy Land. Hope springs anew and everyone lines up five deep in the field at Szwarlikovska as their names are checked and rechecked against the list to make sure that no one sneaks where they are not meant to go. The desperation for freedom is immense, and everyone tries to get out in hopes of going to Palestyne.

In the end, heavily armed guards march sixteen hundred Jews onto trains. Too late, the Jews realize the truth. The trains are bound for Treblinka and death. Many try to escape but are gunned down or crushed beneath the wheels of the moving death trains. Those who do survive flee into the forest in the hope of joining the Polish partisans who fight against the Germans. But the Poles' hatred and distrust of the Jews is all-consuming. The partisans beat the Jews or drive them away, many more are killed as a result of the brutality of their own countrymen. For the Poles, it is better to die and lose against the Germans than to fight side by side with a Jew. The Jews who survive the beatings return to the ghetto, their spirits broken and disillusioned. It is a crushing blow to us, and we sink further into despair.

A few weeks later, I manage to get a day pass to the ghetto, to visit my remaining relatives. They tell me about yet another brutal round up they have had to endure.

"Fear gripped us as we were forced to line up for another selection in the brutal cold," Majer tells me. "We stood apart, hoping to increase our chances of making it through the selection. We have learned it is far better to show no family ties as the Nazis take even more delight in torturing those who cling together, so we interspersed throughout the crowd, awaiting judgment. We dared not move a muscle or even blink. This time the Nazis had a special plan in mind—a game of Russian roulette—as they walked behind the rows of frightened detainees. They strolled down each row, counting off each person. When they got to the tenth man or woman. They put a gun to the poor soul's head and shot them and laughed in glee as though they were playing a child's game. The monsters tortured us for hours. Counting in twisted, sing-song voices. Then another shot from the Luger pierced the air, and the next body fell to the ground. I felt certain I was going to die."

"We were so terrified that we drew closer together and held hands with the person on either side of us and began to pray," my cousin Nadja adds. "It was all we could do to remain standing and not crumple to the ground in terror. Helplessly, we stood and awaited death. To break and run would have been suicide, or worse, it would have meant death for everyone lined up. The game was played out, and the Nazis continued their sadistic shooting game until every tenth Jew lay dead. Then we were made to drag away the bodies of our friends and relatives. It was a miracle that we survived this latest massacre. If one could even call it a miracle."

There is nothing I can say to offer comfort except to cry and hold their hands in mine. How can we take comfort in surviving when our neighbors, relatives, and friends are butchered in front of our eyes whenever it pleases the Nazis?

After the slaughter at Szwarlikovska, hope takes a holiday from the ghetto. It is as if we are sleepwalking through our days. Our lives are no longer our own. We do not know when the cruel Germans will turn their rifles on us. Then, like a match struck in the dark of a starless night, a tentative spark of hope returns to our hearts. Good news comes amid the day-to-day persecutions. It races through the community as if it were a raging forest fire spread by a wind of words. First, there is great reason for us to be proud. An uprising has begun in the Warszaw Ghetto, and Jews have begun to fight back. Like the Maccabeus of ancient Judea, who waged a resistance against their oppressors. With young leaders willing to fight to their deaths, the rebels have organized an underground army, and Jews are inflicting casualties against the mighty Nazis.

A few days later, we overhear the guards at A.V.L. commiserating that Germany has suffered a massive defeat at Stalingrad. They surrendered their Eastern offensive and are in retreat, with the Russians in hot pursuit. We quietly rejoice. Even if we cannot cheer aloud, our eyes burn with renewed hope.

Each day, what is left of the belongings of Radom's Jews grows smaller, and the shipping backlog lessens. It comes as no surprise to us when one day, our German supervisors line us up to tell us that A.V.L. is to be closed at the end of the week, and we are to gather our things as we will be moved to the ghetto. After the massive deportations of August, the shrunken Walowa Ghetto is now called the Szwarlikovska Street Ghetto. It is only a few streets enclosed by barbed wire.

The supervisors at A.V.L. do not look pleased to inform us of these changes. They know that with the closing of the factory, they, too, face reassignment. Hans, Otto, Gerhard, and the rest of the German Wermacht that run A.V.L. have been ordered to the retreating Eastern front and active war duty. The future is grim for our taskmasters as well. I feel bad for Otto and even the other supervisors, who are not so bad either, certainly not bloodthirsty killers like the SS. Even Hans, who drunkenly tried to take me to his bed, never tried to attack me again.

Before departing A.V.L., I seek out Otto to thank him for everything he has done for me and to wish him well. I truly believe that Otto saved all of us when the Walowa Ghetto was liquidated. In a world full of darkness, he showed us a glimmer of light for humanity. "Thank you, Otto, for everything you have done for me," I say to him. "I will never forget your kindness. I pray you will be safe and able to return to your wife and daughters soon."

Otto's eyes fill with tears, and he clears his throat. He takes my hand between his. "Dina, we each have a road to travel in this world. You and I are but pawns in the hands of others. I wish you well on your journey. May God look after you, always."

CHAPTER 26

Is this it? Has my luck run out?

Natek and I walk under the watchful eye of an SS unit that supervises our transfer to Szwarlikovska ghetto. Natek grips my hand tightly and holds me close, but I cannot stop my trembling, so scared am I. The closer we get to the ghetto, the greater my fear grows. Will the SS simply shoot us in the head and throw us into mass graves as they have so many others?

My eyes sweep the blossoming landscape of spring's rebirth. All that is left of the brutal winter are small patches of snow melting under the sun's warm gaze. The land is a verdant green, dotted with bright blue and soft pink blooms bursting from unexpected fissures, extending outstretched leaves and petals to the sky. I blink back tears at such a remarkable sight. So much beauty amidst so much despair. How can both exist side-by-side?

We pass under the sign that reads "Forced Labor Camp Szwarlikovska Street," and the Nazis assemble us in a field with the remaining residents of the ghetto. We who at one time numbered thousands of Jews in a bustling community, have been reduced to a few hundred people. I imagine the SS guards whipping out their pistols and laughing as they use us for their sport in another game of

Russian roulette. Or perhaps they will forego the fun and games and simply shoot us on the spot. Or force march us to the train station for one final trip to Treblinka? I cannot bear all these horrid thoughts that flash through my mind as we await our fates.

And then something happens. Something I did not expect. The guards demand us to hold out our ID cards. They walk down the line and stamp our cards with new numbers. Those that don't have any family still alive in the ghetto are assigned a place to sleep, and the rest of us will crowd in with whatever family or friends have survived the death squads and deportations. I have my Uncle Tuvye, Majer, and Nadja to stay with, but Natek and his brother Benjamin are allocated housing. We are ordered to report to the front gate at five a.m., where we will be assigned work and escorted under guard to different locations outside the ghetto. Until then, we must go to our designated housing.

My knees buckle, and if it were not for Natek wrapping his arm around my waist and holding me up, I would have surely toppled to the ground. It seems, we are still of some use to the Nazis. At least for the time being. Natek hugs me goodbye and assures me he will pick me up for work bright and early at five a.m. tomorrow. I smile and nod, still unable to speak after the worry of the past hour. My cousin Nadja takes my hand, and I walk with my remaining family to my new home, and my heart rejoices.

I find comfort in being with family, a familiarity that provides a sense of security and love, but each beloved face of my relatives is a painful reminder of all those other beloved faces we have lost.

"We are together, and that's what counts," Nadja says, hugging me close as we do our best to prepare dinner from the meager stores available. It takes only one day for me to realize how lucky I was to live and work at A.V.L., where I received enough hot cooked food to abate hunger and maintain strength. Our allotment of rations has plummeted to near starvation levels. Every ten days, each person is apportioned a few meager grams of bread, a little sugar, jam, and now and then a sliver of soap. From the soup kitchen within the ghetto, we sporadically get our hands on a few grams of meat, and small portions of potatoes, margarine, grits, and a few vegetables. The aching of our stomachs is only enhanced by the brutal conditions of our labor.

Everyone in the house is employed in some manner. My aunt Fela's sons, cousins Abek and Motek Madrykamien, the only survivors of their family, work at the armaments factory, Wytwornia, and are housed there. My Uncle Alexander and Cousin David, who live upstairs, work for the Waffen SS at a garage, maintaining and repairing their cars and other vehicles. Tuvye and Majer are still employed repairing shoes and boots, and Nadja works in the peat bogs.

Natek, Benjamin, and I are also assigned to the peat bogs where we cut turf for fuel. It is the worst job in the ghetto. A back-breaking, dawn-until-dusk ordeal in which we sink knee-deep into a swamp-like marsh, cutting the turf into bricks that we load and carry to waiting trucks and wagons. Turf is naturally formed from concen-trated vegetation and plant life that never dries up or decomposes in the swampy land. Once shaped and dried into bricks, it can be burnt like coal and is readily available and cheaply harvested by slave labor. It is a primary source of heat for the Germans and the people they dominate.

Naturally, after slaving in the turf all day, I am filthy, and it has become a losing battle and a running joke as each of my family tries to beat me to the bucket of water outside that we all share to wash. At least at A.V.L., we had access to showers, sharing the factory's attached accommodations. The home I now share with Nadja, Majer, and Uncle Tuvye has no shower, and we must get our water from a communal tap that we are only allowed to access once a day. We take turns, braving the frigid temperatures of dawn or pelting spring rain, standing in the mud and sponging ourselves. Adding to our frustra-tion is the lack of soap that is so meagerly rationed it has become nearly as precious as gold.

How I yearn for a hot bath. I cannot help but remember our bath-room on Koszarowa Ulica. If I close my eyes, I can almost smell the fragrant floral soap from France that my mother would buy and the wonderful feeling of wrapping a warm, thick, fluffy towel around myself and then sitting on my bed as Mama combed and braided my hair.

Every day people die from pneumonia made worse from exposure working in the muck and mire, or their hearts simply give out, and they crumple to the ground. Every day, I wonder if I will live to see the next day. Will I catch the dreaded lung fever, or will I collapse from bone-weary fatigue? Natek always works with one eye on me and one on his brother. He slaves beside me, whispering words of encouragement, always seeing the bright side when no one can possibly imagine one. "At least, Dinale, we get to work outside and inhale the fresh air, which is good for our bodies, and we can behold the sky and nature, which is good for our hearts and souls."

"Natek, you are an eternal optimist," I grumble. "How you can find good while digging in dirt and filth is beyond me."

A huge smile like a ray of sunshine spreads across his grime-smeared face. "You will see I am right. You become stronger and more beautiful every hour of every day."

"Yes, I must look like a princess with my cheeks and hair caked with black mud. I am sure that I am irresistible." As I brush a blackened tendril of hair from my face, I can't help but smile at his determination to lift my spirits.

Benjamin, who is by far the moodier of the two brothers, snarls, "Natek, the peat must be growing in your brain. We are all going to die in this muck, and as far as I am concerned, the sooner, the better!"

Natek's muscles tense as he grabs Benjamin's arm. "Don't ever let me hear you speak like that again! How dare you resign us all to death! Think of our mother and father, our sisters! We must live for them, for everyone who has been murdered! Who are you to extinguish that hope?" The brothers stare at each other for a moment and then Natek heaves a deep sigh and pats Benjamin on the back, the sudden tempest of anger has disappeared. "We are brothers, and all that is left of our family. Let us not fight and give the Germans something else to laugh over." Natek glances at a young man working a few feet away. "Look at Jakub. You don't see him complaining every minute."

The nephew of a Jewish policeman, Jakub is assigned to work in the peat bogs in order to preempt any complaints of nepotism. Natek's innate leadership has had a positive impact on the disgruntled youth who resents being forced into hard labor while the rest of his family enjoys the fruit of protected status. He has joined our band of three to be close to Natek, who does his best to counsel the rebellious young man. Trying to clear the air, Jakub suggests, "Come, Benjamin, let's get a drink of water. I need a break from this cesspool."

Natek watches as Benjamin and Jakub walk to the trough for water. Satisfied that the incident is over, we bend to resume our labor. "Benjamin worries me sometimes."

"He's just tired and hungry like the rest of us," I say. "Not everyone can be as optimistic as you are."

"I have no choice. It is that or despair." Natek's face is forged in determination as he shovels a large block of turf into the wheelbarrow.

My cousin Nadja has been reassigned to work at the Korona Warehouse, which is one of the last shipping centers that sort and pack what remains of the stolen possessions of the Jews that were plundered after the liquidation of the ghettos. There she separates the mountains of burnished leather, fur, snowy goose feathers, shoes, eyeglasses of every prescription, glittering jewelry, clothing, hats, woolen scarves, toys, children's dolls, and other precious bits and pieces of the lives of those that have been murdered.

"My dreams are haunted by their ghosts," she whispers to me as we prepare the evening meal for our little family.

"It was much the same for me when I worked at A.V.L," I say, offering comfort. "I often felt the presence of spirits as I packed up the clothes, picture frames, shoes—all the possessions of those who are no longer with us."

"Every night, I see them," Nadja says, chopping the last quarter of an onion and adding it to the pot of soup. "Every night, they come to me in my dreams."

"What do they say?" I ask as I set out bowls and spoons on the kitchen table.

"*Remember*. They always whisper that word to me. *Remember*. But how can I? How can I keep all those faces in my mind? Will it not drive me mad?"

I lean my head on her shoulder and hug her close. "Perhaps they don't mean for you to remember their faces or names. Perhaps it is important to them that we never forget what happened."

"If we live through this, that is," Nadja says as she chops a small, withered carrot to add to the soup.

"I pray that we do, Nadja," I say. "I pray that we do."

JAKUB HASN'T SHOWN up at work for a week. Natek and I are sick with worry for him, envisioning all sorts of illnesses and accidents. On a Sunday afternoon, I recognize the unmistakable, long gait walking a block away. I run after him, calling, "Jakub, Jakub, STOP! Where have you been? Have you been ill?"

His face lights with pleasure when he sees me. "Dina, how are you?"

"Never mind how I am, why haven't you been at work?" I ask in my most authoritative voice.

"I'm tired of the filthiness of the swamps, and I decided to take a break. Tell Natek I will see him soon."

In shock, I warn, "Have you lost your mind? If you don't show up for work, they will come after you. You can't just decide not to go. It is forbidden, and the punishment will be brutal. Everyone must work, or they become worthless to the Nazis. Promise me you will come tomorrow, please, Jakub. Natek and I have been so worried about you."

He shrugs off my warnings with a laugh, "My uncle is the head of the Jewish Police. He will protect me. Don't worry, Dina, I will be fine. He will find me another job. I've slaved long enough in that filthy swamp. I am going to see my uncle now, and he will help me. Maybe I can get you and Natek reassigned to a job where you won't be sloshing in mud like pigs on a farm."

"Natek and I will be fine. Please don't take any chances and either resolve this with your uncle or come back to work."

Hugging my carefree friend, I remind him as we part, "Remember, Jakub, straighten this out with your uncle immediately or come back to work!" With a last glance, I look back at his retreating back. I can't help but wonder at his foolish daring.

Several days later, as I return from work, Nadja tells me she has heard some bad news. She knows that I work with Jakub and that he has become good friends with Natek, Benjamin, and me.

"The Nazis rounded up everyone today who hasn't shown up for work and brought them to the Ukrainian guard's station," Nadja says. "Jakub was one of about thirty men they hauled in. They lined them up and the Ukrainian guards started shooting. Jakub tried to run away, but he was shot and killed in the street. One of my friends saw the whole thing, and she said she heard Jakub pleading for mercy as he ran. He kept shouting that his uncle was the head of the police. It didn't do him any good. They shot him like a dog."

"My God, poor Jakub was so sure that his uncle could protect him from anything." I begin to cry, and Nadja wraps her arms around me, trying to comfort me.

"He was foolish. We have no protection against these murderers. May God rest his soul."

"Amen," I whisper.

Executions take place nearly every day for the merest of reasons or for no reason at all. Jakub is one of thousands who meet their fate with a bullet. Two of our family friends who worked as tailors are executed in front of their homes down the street from us. They were accused of sabotage. Their crime was leaving an iron unattended at the factory where they worked. Because of a little piece of burnt fabric and a table with some scorch marks on it, they were shot in the head.

And then something happens that gives us hope. The German authorities notify our community that negotiations are under way for an exchange of Jews for German prisoners held by the allies. In celebration, the Jewish elders nominate the brightest academics and intellectuals in our community. Everyone is thrilled that these bright stars will be given a chance at a new life to thrive and grow and contribute their brilliant minds to the world. Natek and I wonder where they might end up living. Natek hopes they will be resettled in Palestyne, for that is where he would want to go, but I hope they end up in America or Canada where we have heard about the lives of the Jews who emigrated there decades ago and the ones who managed to escape before the war—families who are doing well for themselves and forging strong community bonds.

To save their children and sneak them out of Radom, a group of families devises a plan. They convince the elders to allow as many children as possible to go with the lucky chosen and pretend to be part of their families. About fifty children are added to the family names of the Jews who will be leaving. On the happy day of Purim, we rejoice in the streets of Szwarlikovska as the lucky ones arrive at the gates surrounded by family and friends.

The children with wreaths of flowers in their hair wave as they climb onto the trucks with their new families and are driven away to a new life.

But our happiness is short-lived as the truth reveals itself.

Instead of heading toward the train station, the trucks head in the opposite direction to the Szydlowiec cemetery. A contingent of SS, Poles, and Ukrainians awaits. At the cemetery, a massive open grave, freshly dug, awaits them. The adults and children are stripped naked and shoved into the pit by waiting Polish police. Without pause, the Ukrainians throw grenades into the hole, silencing the screams, and with rifles, they shoot any who managed to survive the explosions.

The next truck of intended victims, seeing what happened to the first truck, make a valiant effort to fight back. Nearly all are killed in the ensuing battle except a handful who manage to escape. Shock reverberates throughout our community. The elders are grief-stricken at the loss of our best and brightest, and the families who had rejoiced only a short while ago are now shattered, having unwittingly sent their own children to their deaths.

A few weeks later, word reaches us that the Warszaw Ghetto is no more, and the brave rebellion of its valiant Jews is stilled forever. On the eve of Passover, the Nazis use a full thrust of tanks to overpower the fighters. The battle lasts three days as the Nazis burn their way through the ghetto, bombing and destroying buildings, street by street. Despite the fall of the rebellion, the heroism of the resistance has become an inspiration to us all. It is better to roar like lions and fight to the death instead of bleating like lambs being led to slaughter.

∼

IT IS A SCALDING hot summer day and sweat dampens my clothes as I run to Natek's apartment. "Natek, Natek, it's me, Dina, please open up," I cry, pounding on his door.

He opens the door, his brow furrowed with concern. "What's wrong, Dinale?"

My arms fly around him, hugging him to me. "My family and I have received a notice that we are to gather our things and report for immediate transfer to a town called Pionki. Please tell me you received the same notice?"

He turns pale as the color drains from his face, and I know immediately that he will not be going with me. "Oh Natek, I can't bear it—how will I live without you?"

He cups my face in his hands, and his eyes fill with tears. "I will find you. I promise."

"What will I do without you? You have been my greatest strength." I begin to sob as my chest constricts with the pain of knowing I might never see him again.

"My love, we knew this might happen, that we could be separated. But you will not lose me. I will find you no matter what."

"No, no, I will never live—I'm so afraid. Why aren't you being sent there with me? My parents are gone, my sister and brother are gone, all my dear friends. I can't lose you, too."

Holding me firmly against him, he kisses my eyes, my cheeks, and my neck until finally, he tenderly presses his lips to mine. "Please, don't lose faith in me, Dina. I will find you, I promise," he says once more.

Weeping, I surrender to his kisses as we try to turn our remaining moments together into a lifetime. "Never forget, Dina, that our destiny is to survive."

I try my best to believe him as I leave Szwarlikovska Street with a knapsack of my meager belongings. Majer, Nadja, Uncle Tuvye, Uncle Alexander and David are with me. Each of us is lost in our own thoughts. Silently we walk to the gate and the waiting trucks. Our hurried goodbyes with our cousins Abek and Motek have numbed me. My two cousins are not being transferred. I cannot fathom it. My once, big, beautiful family has been reduced to a mere handful.

The sun glares overhead, and trickles of sweat run down my back. It seems I have no more tears left. My parting with Natek has drained them all from me. The truck begins to move, and I am grateful for the breeze that catches my hair.

The truck drives out of the gate of the ghetto and through the streets of Radom. I watch the Poles hurrying along the streets, going about their daily lives, while a few streets away, their neighbors and fellow countrymen are living in starvation and struggling to survive under the numbing toil of slavery. Most of our families have perished while their families are alive and safe, despite shortages and the challenges of living during wartime. I probe the faces of the Poles that we pass and wonder what they are thinking. Their eyes meet mine for a moment before they hurry along, back to their lives, their homes, and their families.

I pray that Natek finds me. All I see from the back of the truck as Radom fades from my sight are death, destruction, hate, and indifference. If I survive the war, I will never return to Radom.

CHAPTER 27

WE ARRIVE IN PIONKI, a tiny village in central Poland where an ammunitions factory is hidden deep within a forest of towering trees, completely hidden from view from the skies and aerial assault. A compound of buildings forms the largest armaments factory in Poland. When we arrive in the summer of 1943, approximately three thousand workers provide slave labor for the Germans.

It was a thriving arms factory before the war, a solid brick construction adjacent to the railroad tracks. Since the German occupation, it has become vital to their own war efforts as trains are loaded daily with gunpowder and munitions that supply the waiting armies of the Fatherland on the Eastern front. The compound is completely fenced with barbed wire, and our sleeping dorms are set apart from the factories. The SS patrols and guards the outer perimeter of the camp but inside where we work, we are supervised by Polish overseers. There is also a group of Ukrainian workers who are supervised by Ukrainian guards.

Upon arrival, we are assembled and given ID cards and then assigned to jobs and sleeping quarters. Nadja and I share a room with eight other women. My girlfriend Dora is among them. I am grateful to be with my cousin and friend, people with whom I share a past.

And although we are slave workers with no freedom and bound by the barbed wire that surrounds us, it is heartening to have access to clean water and better food rations. We sleep two in a bunk bed with a mattress, blanket, and pillow. It is almost a luxury to me after living in the ghetto and the harsh conditions there.

I am lucky to be assigned to *haufcolonie,* which, although extremely hard labor, is one of the safest jobs to be had. I work with a crew of women filling bags with black gunpowder, which we then pack into crates and heft onto waiting railway cars. The crates weigh nearly twenty-two kilograms, and we stagger under the weight of them as we carry them on our backs. I am bent over with exhaustion after the twelve-hour days, but at least we suffer no physical beatings or unspeakable cruelties. The routine of the week continues without abatement until Sunday, when we are allowed to rest. On Sundays, we launder the few garments that we possess and walk around the camp enclosure, enjoying the fresh scent of pine needles that cover the forest floor and fill the air. I revel in a few extra hours of much-needed rest as I daydream of freedom and Natek. I pray that he and his brother are safe. I hope he thinks of me as I think of him.

This new home is almost idyllic compared to our previous experiences. But again, we are reminded that we are hated and expendable. One morning we are awakened by a German officer ordering us to assemble outside for an immediate roll call. We are forced to line up outside where a gallows has been newly constructed. We nervously stand in a dense fog, shrouded in a thick mist that licks at our faces and bodies. Before us, the death ropes sway as if ghosts are hanging in them. The SS Lagerführer walks back and forth, his face disappearing and then reappearing through the fog.

"It has come to our attention that a group of you Jews has been smuggling contraband into the camp. This is explicitly prohibited. We pointed this restriction out to you time and time again. Yet we have caught a group of smugglers red-handed. These offenders will be executed before your eyes as a warning to you all that the same fate awaits each of you if you disobey the rules."

The workers all know about the illegal trading between the Polish workmen and the Jews. The Poles are eager to trade their food supplies—which are far more ample than ours—in exchange for jewelry or money. Of course, the consequences, if caught, is only a reprimand for the Poles, but for a Jew, it means certain death.

In silence, we watch as three men and three women with their arms tied behind their backs march toward the gallows. The guards hurry them along by butting them with the muzzles of their rifles. One of the accused is a youth who looks barely a few years older than me. Tears run down his cheeks, and his eyes dart around with terror. When the poor young man sees the gallows, he begins to shake and struggles to remain standing.

The commander wastes no time delivering the sentences as the condemned are forced up the steps, and a noose is slipped around each of their necks. The young man summons his courage and gazes out at us through his tears. "Fellow sisters and brothers," he shouts. "Do not forget what you witness here today. Do not forget me!" He chokes out his last word as the noose tightens around his neck and the trap door opens beneath his feet.

I am frozen along with everyone else as we silently watch the six poor souls kicking and twitching as their lives ebb from their bodies until they move no more. The commander dismisses us, and I walk as fast as I can through the fading mist. For one week, we are forced to march past the bodies that are left to dangle and rot as a reminder to us all of what awaits us for any infraction.

After the hangings, a black depression hangs over the camp. It is impossible to erase our comrades from our minds, their faces twisted and bloated masks of death. Work defines our hours and days, and time crawls on. The Polish foreman who monitors my work area is named Pietr, and one day as I am loading a canvas sack with black gunpowder, he approaches me. "Dina, I want you to report to my office after work today."

"May I ask what is required of me, sir?" I shrink from his sharp eyes, knowing this summons can only mean trouble but not knowing why I have suddenly attracted his antagonism.

"You'll find out when you get there," he barks as he walks away.

I have developed a sixth sense when it comes to men, and Pietr's words trigger an alarm. When we are excused from our labors, I rush to find Hannah. One of the youngest inmates at the camp, she is a lovely child whose parents were accused of smuggling in the Warszaw Ghetto and then shot. A Polish policeman intervened on her behalf and somehow managed to have her transferred to Pionki. With no friends or family, she has attached herself to me like a shadow. Her skeptical dark eyes and wary manner have not endeared her to many of the other prisoners, but for me, she is like a younger sister. The pain of losing her family has left invisible scars etched into her heart. Her smiles are as rare as a beam of sunlight peeking through a cloudy sky. I often awake to find her lying beside me snuggled into my back, her thumb in her mouth. In repose, her face is that of an angel.

The first time I noticed her trailing me, I smiled at her. "You are welcome to stay as close to me as you want," I whispered to her. From that day forward, wherever I am, she is never far away.

I tell her to stay back at the barracks and not to follow me to Pietr's office, but she shakes her head and continues to walk with me. When we arrive, I knock softly on his door, and his gruff voice orders my admittance. I enter with Hannah trailing behind me like a lost puppy. Pietr is sitting at his desk, and when he looks up, he sees Hannah standing there with me. His face

turns red as a beet, and his eyes grow large as saucers. "What is she doing here?"

I smile politely as I take Hannah's hand. "She has no family and has become like my sister. She goes everywhere with me."

His anger explodes like a volcano, and furiously, he shouts. "Get out this minute and take that little brat with you! The next time I tell you to come here, you had better be ALONE!"

"Yes, sir." My knees tremble. I grab Hannah's hand, and we calmly walk out of the office. Once outside, we break into a run back to our barracks.

"Why is Pietr so angry?" she asks.

"I think he wanted to do something evil to me. He is angry because

I brought you with me, and he wouldn't dare touch me with you there."

"I will never let you go to him alone, no matter what he says or does," she says fiercely. As soon as we are safe within our room, I hug Hannah close, kissing her until I finally win a smile from her brave little face. Thanking her a thousand times for going with me, I know my little friend has saved me.

The next day, in retribution, Pietr orders me to a day of labor that nearly kills me. I am given a shovel and a bucket and told to empty an entire railroad flatcar of its coal. By myself, I struggle to complete the task. From dawn until midnight in the rain, I toil until my back goes numb, and I am as black as the coal I unload. Normally this is a job for several men. When I finally finish, I collapse in my bed.

In the morning, I am unable to get up. I can barely move, and I cough and wheeze from hours of inhaling coal dust. Tears flow from my eyes, as my body is wracked with pain. I have never felt so ill in my life. When I fail to show up for work, Pietr comes and inquires as to where I am. My roommates tell him I am half-dead from my exertions and sick from the coal dust that I inhaled.

It takes me several days to return to the land of the living. Fortunately, Pietr leaves me in peace and allows me time to recover. When I return to work, I worry that he will order me to his office again, but the order never comes. What is even more strange is that he begins to treat me with a modicum of respect. I am shocked at the change in his behavior, but I rejoice with Hannah, who sat by my bed the entire time I was ill. I may have taken her under my wing, but it was Hannah who became my guardian angel.

The winter in Pionki is unbearably cold, and in order not to freeze, we wear all of the clothing that we own when we work and even when we sleep. Dressed in our layers, we look like an army of overstuffed rag dolls. Today we line up shivering in the snow, and a Nazi commander asks which of the Radom prisoners would like to return to Radom to work. Even though I vowed never to return to Radom, I volunteer with the hope of seeing Natek again. I miss him so much and would rather return to the deprivations of the ghetto than remain in this frozen tundra. A group of about forty of us is scheduled to leave.

The trucks arrive to transport us to Radom. As Hannah and I are leaving our quarters, the Polish foreman Pietr is waiting outside. "Go back to your room and put your things away, both of you! Neither of you is going to Radom."

"I would like to go, please, Pietr. I want to go home. Please don't stop us."

"No, you are not going anywhere, and don't let me catch you even mentioning the thought of leaving, or I will break your neck! You are staying right here!"

He is adamant. Even my tears don't move him as I stand there with Hannah, who also begins to cry.

"I don't understand why you are preventing us from going. You should be glad to be rid of us."

"I don't have to give you an explanation. I need you here working in transportation. You don't need to understand. You need to do what I say!" With that, he strides away, leaving Hannah and me with no other choice but to return our belongings to our room.

Outside it is freezing, and the trucks blow white plumes of exhaust into the frigid air as the Radomers are loaded on. I run to say goodbye to a mother and daughter who have befriended me. They are excited to be returning to Radom and the family they left behind. I hug them and wish them well, slipping a small piece of paper into Tosha's hand as I beg her to give it to Natek Korman.

"Don't worry, Dina, I will find him and give it to him," she promises me, her face glowing with hope.

A group of us stand and wave goodbye as the trucks pull out of the gate. Two hours later, the trucks return. Pietr sends a group from the shipping department to go outside to unload them, specifically pointing at me to join them. The truck is full of the bags and belongings owned by the Jews who left that morning for Radom. We are shocked and heartbroken as we realize what happened.

Inside, as we sort through the piles, I find Tosha's coat. Picking it up, I reach into the pocket and pull out the note for Natek that I gave her. Silent tears stream down my face as I imagine the agonizing final minutes of the lives of my friends. Their hope of seeing their families in Radom again evaporating as the trucks drove them into the woods. The shame they felt as the Nazis forced them to strip. The terror that overwhelmed them as they stood naked and shivering in the snow as the guards shoved them into a mass grave, pointed their rifles at them, and fired.

I realize now that Pietr must have known what the Nazis had planned. Despite his gruffness, despite his attempt to get me alone in his office, and despite his punishing me when his intentions were thwarted, he saved my life. I have managed to survive this war so far, not just by luck and resilience but by the conscious efforts of a few people who have not lost their sense of humanity.

CHAPTER 28

HIS NAME IS DUTCHKO, and the women say he is very handsome. Dutchko is the head supervisor of the Ukrainian workers, and he never fails to smile or address me in an affectionate manner. I try not to encourage him in any way but cannot avoid his probing, pale-gold, cat-like eyes, luminous orbs set deeply beneath solid black brows. His hair is blonder and straighter than mine, if that is at all possible. His cheekbones and forehead are broad like mine, but where my lips are full and pronounced, his are thin and sculpted. In some ways, his features remind me of my dear brother, Abek, which pains me whenever I look at him.

Towering above me, he loves to call me *"chervoni shchoky,"* an affectionate Ukrainian endearment. He has told me that I remind him of his sister, whom he obviously adores, and twice he could not resist pinching my cheeks. He constantly embarrasses me in front of the other workers just to see me blush. It is very unsettling to me as he works willingly for the Nazis and cannot be a friend of the Jews.

In order to get to and from the factories and our housing each day, we must wait in line and pass through a security checkpoint where we are counted, and our IDs are checked against a master list. The Nazis are meticulous in their scrutiny, checking and rechecking to make sure no one escapes or goes missing. Occasionally they pull someone out of the line and search them more thoroughly, which only slows the process. They are always searching us for stolen goods or food.

The damp and cold penetrates our clothing as we wait in line to return to our barracks. We shuffle in place, trying to spread warmth to our frozen extremities. Dancing around in circles trying to keep warm, I notice two sisters who look extremely nervous. Their mouths are pinched as their eyes dart left and right. My instincts have become heightened from years of living under the Nazis, and I immediately sense that something is going on. I slip back in the line to where they are standing and whisper, "What's wrong?"

"We each have a loaf of bread hidden under our skirts, and the Nazis seem to be checking everyone more carefully than usual. We are frightened they will catch us."

I take a deep breath. "Don't worry, I have an idea. Come when I call you."

Resuming my place in the line, I maneuver toward Dutchko, who is checking IDs.

"Hello, Dutchko." I smile my most winning smile and hand him my ID.

"*Chervoni shchoky*, how are you this evening?"

"I am fine, Dutchko, but my girlfriends Ella and Talia do not feel well. I am afraid they are going to become deathly ill standing out here in the cold."

He looks up as I wave to the sisters, who are shaking as much from fear as from the cold.

Pinching my cheek, he directs me, "All right, go and get your friends and pass through the gate. I see no reason for you to stand in this awful cold. Go now."

I wave at Ella and Talia, and they hurry to join me as Dutchko waves us through the gate.

Rushing to our dorms, we embrace, and Ella and Talia thank me for saving them from a possible search and worse.

Ella reaches under her coat, pulls out a loaf of bread, and breaks off a chunk. "This is for you, Dina. Please enjoy this bread. You deserve it."

Handing it to me, they both reiterate their gratitude as they run off to their building, and I go inside to share my extra ration with Hannah.

The next day, Dutchko calls me over and tells me that from now on, I don't have to stand in line with the others. He instructs me to come to the front of the line, and he will send me through. I smile and thank him. Of course, he cannot help himself and pinches my cheeks. I feel my face heat from my blush. Perhaps Dutchko is a good soul who must make the best of things on his side as we do on ours.

I THANK heaven spring is here, and winter has yielded her icy grip on the land. The warm temperatures are melting the snowdrifts that encase the camp. Here and there, a sprig of greenery can be seen outside the fence, reaching like fingertips to the sky. Rumors abound that the war is not going well for the Germans and the Russians are advancing into Poland. We wonder how much longer we will be held prisoners at Pionki and if the Russians will arrive to liberate us.

Despite the news, our daily toil continues, and the trains leave daily, loaded full with the fruits of our labor—an endless supply of bullets and weapons. Each day brings a new mishap in the factories where detonations are common. Only a few days ago, a loud bang shook one of the armament buildings and shattered the windows. We found out later that a woman was wounded in an accidental blast. The fingers of her hand were blown off, and she was taken to the infirmary. She will live, but how will she work without fingers? If one of us is injured and can no longer work, or if we are too sick to work, we become expendable to the Nazis. Every day the weak and injured are removed from the camp to destinations unknown, most likely a bullet to the head and an unmarked grave in the forest.

All that I have in this world that is of monetary value is a Doxa Swiss watch that belonged to my cousin, Dina. That I have it is a miracle. Right before the annihilation of the Glinice Ghetto, Dina had given her watch for repair to a young man who was a jeweler before the war. He worked at A.V.L. and repaired watches as a sideline for the Jews. He survived the *wysiedlenie* of Glinice and hid the watch at A.V.L. I assumed it was taken by the Nazis along with everything else after my family was forced to Treblinka.

He passed it along to me after and told me to take good care of it as it was valuable. His honesty touched me, and I thanked him profusely at the time. I have kept the watch hidden all this time. It is the last material link to my dear family and the only treasured heirloom that I own. But I have arranged to sell the white gold watch to one of the Polish foremen for a handful of zlotys and a loaf of bread.

The Nazis have informed us that most of us are being evacuated to an unknown destination. We suspect that we are being moved to a work camp somewhere in Germany as the Russians are making their advance. The Germans have already begun to dismantle the factories and have begun shipping everything farther west. Although my heart is heavy that I no longer have the watch, I am relieved that I will have enough food to keep Hanna and me from starving on our journey.

We are leaving tomorrow on trains that stand ready to depart at dawn. I have packed my knapsack with what few possessions I have. I sit on my bunk with Hannah close beside me as I braid her hair into a single plait down her back. The Polish foreman Pietr has suggested to me that he could arrange for me to stay at Pionki, where a small group of workers will remain. He comes to my barracks and asks for me, pleading with my roommates to get me to see him. I refuse to speak to him but ask Dora to pass him a message that I wish him well and thank him for behaving decently toward me.

My surviving relatives are being transferred as well, and I wish to remain with them and face whatever fate has in store. Pietr means well, I am sure, but I am wary of his intentions and could not bear the thought of being beholden to him for sexual favors. Dutchko, too, has indicated that I should stay and that he will protect me, but I am also afraid of what he might ask of me in return for his kindness.

Even at my young age, the war has taught me not to trust anyone. I will never give up the religion that my family died for, nor the morals that I was taught. I may have sold my last possession of value, but I will never part with my honor.

In the early morning's light, we march under guard to the train. We are afraid for what lies ahead, but a bit of news offers us a ray of hope. One of the workers has overheard on the office radio that the Allies have landed in Normandy. The noose is tightening around the neck of Nazi Germany, and hopefully, it is loosening from ours.

Pietr and Dutchko stand among the supervisors and foremen, watching us leave. Sending a last smile their way, I hold tightly to Hannah's hand as the Nazis push us into the railway cars. They shut and lock the doors, throwing us into darkness. There is little ventilation, and we are packed body against body. I pray the journey will be a short one, as already the car is stifling. There is a smell to collective fear, sour as mildew, acidic as vinegar. It hovers in the air and envelops us. As the train jerks into motion, sending us reeling against each other, we begin to pray there will be light at the end of our journey.

I wonder if I have made the right decision to leave Pionki. Maybe this is the fork in the road that has decided my fate, to the left Pionki and life, to the right a train to oblivion. Perhaps it is reversed and to the left Pionki and death, and to the right a train to liberation. If only Natek were with me. I resign myself to the fact that I am but a pawn trapped in a deadly game where the rules keep changing.

My head begins to nod from the monotonous motion of the train until it rests on the top of Hannah's head, and I am weightlessly pressed between bodies. It is amazing what the human body can endure and how it can replenish itself in any circumstance. Hannah is sound asleep beside me, propped up by the bodies that hold her in place. She is suspended upright without any of her muscles being engaged. Inconspicuously, I reach into my pocket and break off a piece of bread, carefully stuffing it into my mouth. Chewing slowly so as not to draw attention, I suck the nutrients from the morsel. I slip a small piece into Hannah's mouth, which she accepts and chews in her sleep. I watch the motion of her small mouth chewing, her eyelashes fluttering in concentration. Wherever we are headed, we will need our strength.

Hours pass, and I snap awake as the wheels of the train slow, and the whistle blows mournfully to announce our arrival.

Whatever our destination, we have arrived.

CHAPTER 29

"RAUS! RAUS! ALLE RAUS!"

We're herded off the train as the Nazis shout orders at us, and their dogs bark and growl, held in check by leashes, but trained to tear us apart. I have always liked animals, especially dogs. I remember Vunia's Great-Aunt Ruth telling us that dogs are born loving and kind, and it is only the treatment of the owner that makes them vicious. I can only assume the menacing German shepherd dogs are raised by the Nazis to be as vicious as they are.

I grip Hannah's hand tightly as we are ordered into lines. I glance over my shoulder and gasp at the sheer number of Jews getting off the trains behind us.

There must be thousands of us.

It is utter chaos yet eerily organized. I look up and see a huge tower that dominates the skyline with black smoke billowing toward the heavens. It reminds me of a fire-breathing dragon. We are ordered to leave whatever belongings we have on the platform. The Nazis are separating men from women. They allow us no time to say goodbye as we are pushed and shoved apart. I have already lost sight of my Uncle Tuvye and Majer. But Nadja is still with Hannah and me, and I thank God for that. I have not seen Dora since we left Pionki. I am not even sure if she was on the same train or sent to the same camp as us. It breaks my heart to think that I was not able to say a proper good-bye.

All around us, they are dividing people, some to the right and some to the left. By now, we have come to understand the German method of selection. Nadja, Hannah, and I are sent to the right with a group of workers from Pionki. On the left are mothers, wide-eyed and desperate, with children crying and clinging to them along with the elderly and crippled. I cannot bear to look at them, knowing they are destined for the building with the tall smokestack that spits out black smoke.

A Jewish man dressed in blue-and-white striped pajamas approaches us. Speaking Yiddish, he urges us to follow him. He tells us he is a *kapo* and therefore in charge of us. "Don't worry," he says with a slight smile. "You are going to the barracks and not to the gas chambers."

Nearly in unison, we all implore him to tell us where we are.

He looks at us with eyes that burn with madness. "You don't know? You are at Auschwitz."

The *kapo* delivers us to a long line that slowly inches its way to the front, where three Ukrainian women stand next to three small tables. As we get closer to the head of the line, I can see that as each person reaches the front, she extends her arm. At first, I can't discern what they are doing until it is my turn to offer my arm. The woman holds a pen with a needle-like point. She dips the needle into a bowl of blue-black ink and then pierces my arm. I cry out in pain, trying to pull away, but she holds me firmly in her grasp, repeatedly stabbing me. Tiny drops of blood trickle down my arm. When she is done, I tear my arm away, looking at what she has etched in blue ink. *A-14569.*

I watch as she scribbles the number into a book. "From now on, you no longer have a name, Jew. You are only a number," she spits out. Her eyes are gloating as she sneers at me. She is a hefty woman who clearly has not suffered from any shortage of food.

I hold Hannah's hand and whisper to her to be strong as the horrid woman tattoos her arm as well. Hannah bites her lip but doesn't make a sound as if to spite the witch. Another Ukrainian woman leads us inside a building and orders us to remove our clothing and leave all of our belongings behind. Nadja turns so as to block the prying eyes of the Ukrainians and presses something into my hand. I open my fingers and look at the diamond ring she has placed there. "What is this ring for?"

"Do you think you can hide it somewhere?"

"I don't know."

"Well, if you can't, just throw it away."

"Stop talking," a tall Ukrainian woman orders us. "Take a piece of soap from the basket. You are going to the showers!"

Grabbing the soap, I press the ring into the bottom of it and go and stand in the inspection line. When I get to the front, the guard searches my mouth to make sure I haven't hidden jewelry in it. She motions me through, and after thoroughly searching Hannah and Nadja, she orders them to follow me. We have two minutes to shower, and I am thrilled to wash away the grime from our journey. The cold spray of the shower makes me gasp, but at least I will be clean. Afterward, they spray us with a chemical for lice and tell us to go to the next room. Laid out on tables are piles of blue and white striped *pashaks*, dresses that hang like sacks when we put them on, similar to the pajamas worn by the little *kapo* who escorted us. The texture of the material is coarse, like burlap. It scratches and irritates our skin, which now itches from the toxic insect repellant. Next to the prison clothing with only three choices of sizes are the most horrible shoes I have ever seen. With thick, inflexible wooden soles and thin leather tops, or maybe they are cardboard. When we put them on, we can barely walk, which explains why the *kapo* shuffled ahead of us. We immediately become an army of shufflers, barely able to walk in the heavy unbalanced shoes that weigh down our feet.

"Here, Nadja." I press the diamond ring into her hand.

"How did you get it through the inspection?"

Lifting my brows and smiling, I shrug my shoulders. "I am a child, and no one suspects cleverness from a child."

Another woman comes in and begins to select a few of us, then orders the chosen to follow her. Nadja and Hannah are selected. Hannah refuses to let go of my hand, but I whisper reassuringly to her that I will find her. But inside, I am scared to death as Nadja and Hannah are led away. The rest of us wait silently in fear until the guards return and lead us to another room. The room is buzzing with the sounds of scissors snipping and women weeping as they cut away the prisoners' hair, letting it fall, floating like feathers to the ground. Panic fills me as I look about and realize that everyone who has been selected has beautiful hair. Blonde, red, brown, and black piles of hair are being separated and gathered into sacks that are stacked against the wall. One of the guards shoves me forward and pushes me into a chair. When one of the women barbers grabs my hair, I yell, "NO, NO, LEAVE ME ALONE!" I latch onto her wrist, throwing the full force of my weight on her arm as I try to push the scissors away from my head.

She slaps my face and wrenches my hair so hard that I scream.

"If you do it again, Jew, I am going to pull out every hair from your head, one hair at a time!"

Covering my face with my hands, I sob helplessly. Memories of my mother lovingly brushing and braiding my long hair flash through my mind. I am not a vain person, but my hair is all that I have left that makes me feel like the Dina I used to be before the war.

The horrid woman takes her revenge, and instead of cutting my hair short as she did the others, she shaves my head bald and purposely nicks me with the razor, causing red rivulets of blood to pour down my back.

Dazed and numb, I am led to a massive barrack packed with women. I wander from bunk to bunk until I find Nadja and Hannah. We are crowded into bunk beds, four on top and four on the bottom. The room is lined with rows of bunks, enough for more than a hundred women. It is like Babylon with so many languages spoken around us—French, Hungarian, Danish, Romanian, German, Polish. It is a melting pot of cultures with one thing in common. We are all Jews. Though Hannah tries her best, I will not be consoled.

I sob uncontrollably at the loss of my beautiful hair. Finally, after an hour of relentless crying, Nadja cannot bear it anymore. She is so annoyed with me that she says, "Stop crying. You're not dying, and your hair will grow back." She pauses for emphasis, "If you live!"

Her message is clear that if I don't stop crying, I won't have to wait for the Nazis to kill me since she will do it herself.

CHAPTER 30

To GREET the day in Auschwitz is like waking up in Hell.

The Nazis have delivered the Jews from slavery into the executioner's hands for extermination. They created Auschwitz, the death factory, the unimaginable. Nothing grows in this wasteland, not flowers or trees, not the human body or soul, not children and their dreams, not hope or sanity. Death and only death ripens and blooms here in a never-ending cycle.

Day and night, the smokestacks belch their poisonous tendrils to the heavens, challenging God to intervene. Day and night, the gas chambers silence the voices of the young, the old, and the weak with toxic fumes. Day and night, the ovens bake the corpses so the smell of burning skin permeates the air. The inescapable choking smell of incinerated flesh and bones transformed to ash. A thousand years from now, the ashes of the Jewish people will still lie upon this land, begging for retribution.

We have no idea why we are still alive as we serve no useful purpose. There is nothing to do here but die. We are awakened at dawn by a bugle, and like cattle, we are driven outside. There we form lines for roll call, *appell*, and stand for hours while the Nazis count us, over and over again. Sometimes unsatisfied with the first count, they start over and count us again. I cannot imagine why they count us every day except to torture us or maybe for entertainment. It is insanity. Where do they think we are going to go? It is best not to move or draw any attention to oneself, or the lash of a whip will bring you to your knees, or a vicious German shepherd will sink its teeth into you while Satan's emissaries stand by grinning with bloodlust in their eyes.

While we stand in misery, the *kapos* busily search the barracks for all the spoils that the Jews may have hidden in their lice-infested mattresses. After standing for hours in the cold, our minds are numb. We are fed crumbs of stale bread and a thin watery soup from huge vats. I dare not look in my tin cup as I eat because I know roaches and insects swim in it. Every day someone crosses the line into madness and hurls themselves on the electrified fences that surround us, unable to bear another moment of this hell.

Hannah has disappeared. I can't find her. One minute she is beside me, and the next, she is gone. I have searched everywhere and have asked anyone who will listen if they have seen my little sister. Most of the women look at me as if I have lost my mind. People disappear into thin air regularly, while others lay down somewhere and die, their bodies quickly collected and fed into the furnaces that belch day and night.

Please, God, I pray that Hannah has made a friend somewhere who can feed her and care for her better than me. I remember that Hannah mentioned to me that she saw some women from her neighborhood in Warszaw who recognized her. I hope she has found safety with them. I pray that she was not picked up in some infernal roundup and delivered to the gas chamber.

When humans are treated as less than animals, all traces of decency disintegrate. In its place, daughters turn on mothers, and mothers turn on daughters, sometimes even stealing food from each other. Their screams pierce the blackened night. The weak become the prey of the strong. If I manage to survive this hellish existence, I will forever be haunted by this madness.

Friendships do not grow when the only thing one can think of is food. Miraculously, I have found a friend, a new bunkmate, Lucia. She is a sixteen-year-old, dark-haired girl from Krakow, and I have nick-named her *Krakawyanka* for her feisty spirit.

Like me, she is now an orphan. Her entire family was murdered. Lucia and I pledge to care for each other like sisters. Cleanliness is impossible at Auschwitz. Only three sinks must service hundreds of women. We can never get close to the sinks, so Lucia and I decide to go during mealtimes when no one in their right mind would think of cleaning themselves as we are all starving to death. We both would rather feel clean than eat the poison they feed us anyway. If we are quick, we can use the sinks and still make it back for what is left of the putrid broth that masquerades as soup.

Together, we sneak to the sinks during feeding time, and as expected, we are alone. The water feels like heaven. We wash spar-ingly, using our small precious slivers of soap. Delighted, we congrat-ulate each other for our cleverness as we wash the filth away. Finishing, we race back with plenty of time to get a cup of the dregs of pigswill.

Time does not move in Auschwitz.

Each day is the same as the day before. And tomorrow will be the same as today. The only constant companions we have are pain and hunger. Sometimes when I lie in my bunk at night, I fear that I will not have the strength to rise again. It would be so easy to let go and give in to death. Instead, I force myself to move and to think of some-thing other than food. I try to think of Natek's face and our last few moments together, but it seems so long ago and more like a dream. Who knows if he is still alive? *No!* I must not think of that possibility. I must believe that he still breathes and that somehow we will be reunited.

"Dina, come quickly," Nadja says, leading me to a group of people from Radom. A woman named Sonia is speaking and repeats the beginning of her story for me. "Yesterday, when my work unit was sorting through the belongings of a newly arrived transport that had been sent to the gas chamber, another train arrived," Sonia tells us. "It was a transport from France, and we were ordered to the platform to remove their baggage. I noticed a good-looking man staring at me from the new shipment. His eyes were filled with incomprehension, and I couldn't bear to meet his gaze. I knew that soon he would be no more as the entire transport was doomed to be fuel for the crematorium.

"His penetrating gaze disconcerted me, and finally seeing no harm, I smiled at him, trying to convey comfort to him in his last hour on earth. The man and his group began their walk of death to the gas chambers, unaware of the horror that awaited them. For some reason, the line stopped, and the Nazis leading them were called away. The prisoners were ordered not to move, and without supervision, I took a risk and wandered a bit closer to the man. Perhaps sensing the hopelessness of his situation, he threw a bag toward me. His eyes met mine, and he smiled and nodded. Snatching the bag from the ground and hiding it in my dress, I nodded my thanks and ran back to the platform. The Nazis returned and led the transport away. I watched him until he disappeared."

I wait spellbound for her to continue. "Sonia, what was in the bag?" I whisper.

She hesitates before she answers, "Can you imagine my shock when I opened the bag and saw that it contained a pouch filled with diamonds? It was unbelievable. He must have sensed what was coming and decided that it was better to give it to another Jew than let the murderous Nazis have it. May his soul rest in peace."

"Amen," we murmur in unison.

The days crawl by, and our bodies waste away a little more with each passing day. The heat of the summer sun depletes what little strength we can muster as our pores empty of nutrients. The stench of unwashed bodies permeates the air with human odor, and the sickly-sweet smell of death lingers in the barracks from those who lie dead waiting to be removed. It is nearly impossible to sleep. The night echoes with the cries of the forlorn and the incessant coughing and rasping of the sick and dying.

In Auschwitz, death waits patiently in the shadows, ready to claim its next victim.

One day, a *kapo* named Isaac from the men's camp comes looking for Nadja and me. Uncle Tuvye has sent him to us. Isaac, who is from Radom, was filled with joy when he found out about our train from Pionki with Radomers on it. He searched among the men for a familiar face and found Nadja's father Tuvye, Majer, and his own father and brother.

"It is a miracle," he tells us.

Isaac is doing his best to help Uncle Tuvye and Majer as the *kapos* receive more food and have more freedom than the rest of us. Isaac is the son of Mr. Berman, who was Uncle Tuvye's partner in the leather factory that they ran for the Nazis at Szwarlikovska Street. Isaac vanished one day from the ghetto and was never seen or heard from again. His family mourned deeply for him. It seems he was kidnapped off the street of the ghetto during one of the frequent Nazi raids. They shipped him here to Auschwitz, and he has risen to the status of a *kapo*.

I am amazed that he has survived this long. He has become an "elder," one of the longest living survivors of Auschwitz. But even more amazing is that Isaac arrived at Auschwitz at the same time as my father.

I am full of hope as I ask him if my father is still alive.

Isaac tells me that my father fell ill upon arrival. "With no hope for the future and no ability to save his loved ones, he must have prayed for death. I believe he died of a heart attack," Isaac says in a kind and gentle voice.

My father was only forty-two years old, God rest his soul. He died completely defeated with the awful realization that his wife and children were destined for the chimneys of Auschwitz. The extermination of my family is complete. I am truly an orphan. The last daughter in my family. I pray that my father can see me from Heaven and know that one of his children still lives.

That evening I stand outside my barracks where the air is cool and not ripe with the smell of sweat, urine, and excrement. The wind has changed direction, and it looks like it is snowing. I put my hands out, and white flakes land on them. Fixated, I stare at my hands, perplexed

until I realize that I am holding ashes. The ashes from the crematorium of lives extinguished are floating around me, and I am filled with
immeasurable sadness. I close my eyes and begin to whisper the
prayer of *Kaddish* for the dead. I pray for my father and my mother. I
pray for my sister and brother. I pray for my grandmother and my
aunts and uncles and cousins and dear friends who are all lost to me.

"May His great Name grow exalted and sanctified
Yit'gadal v'yet'kadash sh'mei raba
in the world that He created as He willed.
b'al'ma di v'ra khir'utei
May He give reign to His Kingship in your lifetime and in your days,
v'yam'likh mal'khutei b'chayeikhon uv'yomeikhon
and in the lifetime of the entire Family of Israel,
uv'chayei d'khol beit yis'ra'eil
swiftly and soon. Now say Amen.
ba'agala uviz'man kariv v'im'ru: Amein .
May His great Name be blessed forever and ever.
Y'hei sh'mei raba m'varakh l'alam ul'al'mei al'maya
Blessed, praised, glorified, exalted, extolled,
Yit'barakh v'yish'tabach v'yit'pa'ar v'yit'romam v'yet'nasei
mighty, upraised, and lauded be the Name of the Holy One
v'yet'hadar v'yet'aleh v'yit'halal sh'mei d'kud'sha
Blessed is He,
B'rikh hu,
beyond any blessing and song,
l'eila min kol bir'khata v'shirata
praise and consolation that are uttered in the world. Now say: Amen
toosh'b'chatah v'nechematah, da'ameeran b'al'mah, v'eemru: Amein
May there be abundant peace from Heaven
Y'hei sh'lama raba min sh'maya
and life upon us and upon all Israel. Now say: Amen
v'chayim aleinu v'al kol yis'ra'eil v'im'ru Amein
He who makes peace in His heights, may He make peace,
Oseh shalom bim'romav hu ya'aseh shalom

upon us and upon all Israel. Now say: Amen
aleinu v'al kol Yis'ra'eil v'im'ru Amein"

Opening my eyes, I see that a group of women has surrounded me. Their thin, reedy voices join mine in offering up the prayer to God. We stand apart yet together as we repeat the words of mourning. It occurs to me there will be no one left to say the *Kaddish* after I die. It matters not. I have said the prayer myself with a small group of strangers for all those who have perished and for me when it is my turn.

∼

IT IS DAWN, and a *kapo* has come to tell us we have been ordered to come to the *platz* naked for a special *appell*. Surely the end has come, and we will be marched straight to the gas chambers. Part of me feels a strange sense of relief at the inevitability that I will die here and the struggle to live will soon be over. We line up, maybe five hundred women, naked on a platform where a high-ranking Nazi accompanied by two other Nazis glares at us. The tall man, as handsome as a movie star, is a vision in his finely tailored, immaculate uniform. His jacket is embellished with medals and ribbons of military valor. His impeccable riding breeches are tucked into freshly polished black leather boots. His hat, slightly angled on his head, completes a picture of dashing confidence. He is wearing pristine white gloves, more appropriate for someone attending a dance than selecting which of us will live and which will die.

"That's Mengele himself," the woman next to me whispers.

Every Jew knows that name. The infamous doctor and master of Auschwitz. We have all heard the stories about his diabolical experiments that he conducts on Jewish prisoners who, upon arrival, are given a choice of being his guinea pig or the gas chamber. It is difficult to reconcile such cold-blooded cruelty with this handsome and elegant man.

We stand shivering not from cold but from fear as the three Nazis proceed to walk down the rows of women. Some of the women try to cover themselves in modesty. Stopping now and again to inspect the teeth of a woman, Mengele clearly relishes the selection process and who will be sent "right" or "left."

After what feels like an eternity, he stands before me. I can smell the luxurious spicy scent of his cologne. He is so close to me that I can see the slick sheen in his perfectly coiffured hair brushed back off his high forehead. His blue eyes drift down my body with a penetrating gaze, inspecting me for imperfections. He looks me over with a final perfunctory glance and motions me with his crop to the right. I hear him whisper under his breath, "dirty whores." Lucia and Nadja, who are beside me, are also told to go to the right. At long last, Doctor Mengele finishes the selection, and those who were sent to the "left" are marched away. About two hundred of us remain. Returning to the platform, he begins to address us.

Pointing in the direction of the entrance gate of Auschwitz, he raises his voice so that we may all hear his words. "Do you see that gate there? You are all very lucky. You are the first Jews who will leave through that gate alive." He then points at the smoking chimneys of the crematoria. "Everyone else, your mothers, your fathers, your sisters, your brothers, and your children will leave through the chimneys. You have five minutes. Go back to your bunks, get dressed, and report back here."

Running naked, our hearts pounding, we race to get dressed. In minutes we return to the *platz* where a group of SS officers march us out the gates of Auschwitz and load us into a waiting convoy of trucks. None of us can believe our good fortune. I can't hear myself think as everyone is talking at once, trying to make sense of what has just occurred. Repeatedly, someone says what is on each our minds. "Wherever they send us, nothing can be worse than Auschwitz!"

As if in a dream, my thoughts return to Fela, my poor dear friend who disappeared into the smokestacks of Treblinka. It's probably the gnawing hunger that makes me yearn to find myself playing among the blossoming pink trees of her grandparents' cherry orchard. Fela and me filling our buckets with cherries and stuffing our mouths with the sweet red fruit. I wonder if cherries grow in Heaven. I hope so.

I look out the back of the truck and read the words on the gate. *Arbeit Macht Frei*, "Work Makes You Free," and it occurs to me a more appropriate motto would be "Death Makes You Free." This inferno of death will forever burn in my memory just as the tattoo burned into my arm.

I leave behind Auschwitz, watching the never ending plumes of smoke float up to the sky. The residue of countless human lives. I can taste the ashes in my mouth.

CHAPTER 31

AFTER A FULL DAY'S journey with no food or water, we cross the border into Germany and finally arrive at our destination, the Village of Hindenburg. About a mile from the actual village is where we will live. It is a fenced plot of land that lies in a gully in full view of the trains that come and go, day and night. Upon arrival, we are informed that we will dig the foundations for our own sleeping barracks. The Germans plan to bring in prefabricated buildings once the foundations have been laid. Then we will provide labor for the different armaments factories that are scattered throughout the town and surrounding areas. For now, we sleep in the open on the ground with night watches of armed SS to ensure that we don't escape. Fortunately, the fall weather is mild, and a flimsy blanket is enough to keep us warm.

We begin digging the earth from a large tract of land to make way for the cement that will be poured to construct the foundations for our barracks. Some women are assigned the job of digging the holes while others carry away the dirt and debris in buckets. My job is to take the buckets filled with dirt and deposit them in another area. As I finish filling a bucket, a woman inadvertently swings her shovel and hits me with the sharp edge, splitting open my eyebrow.

Blood gushes everywhere, and I am knocked out by the force of the blow. When I regain consciousness, I find myself in the infirmary where a doctor and nurse are treating my injury. It is a miracle that I didn't lose my eye. Another inch, and I surely would have. It would be quite a ridiculous folly to die by the hand of a Jew when it is the Nazis who are annihilating us.

Had this kind of injury happened at Auschwitz, I would have been sent straight to the gas chambers. I am lucky this place provides a capable doctor who stitches me up and applies a salve, but there is nothing to alleviate the pain and throbbing that tortures me throughout the night as I toss and turn on the hard ground. In the morning, I have no choice but to get back to work. Wearing a patch over my eye and my head wrapped in bandages, I return to my labor. My vision is blurry as my eyes are nearly swollen shut, but at least I am alive, and I can still work.

It takes six weeks for the barracks to be built and for my eye to heal. I will bear the scar of this injury for the rest of my life, however long that might be, but what is one more scar? My body has so many. I am no longer so vain that I worry about a mere physical scar. The scars on my soul are far deeper and more painful.

Our barracks are simple prefabricated wooden buildings with small windows to let in the light, and they are kept immaculately clean by a crew of prisoners. The only furniture in our building are the double bunk beds that line the room. We sleep six to a bed. Lucia sleeps next to me in the bunk, but Nadja is in another building with a group of young women her own age. Our *pashaks* are freshly laundered every day, and it is good to feel clean after the filth that was Auschwitz with its epidemic of fleas, lice, and typhoid. Each evening we are allowed to wash at a communal shower. There, we are given a heavenly ten minutes to wipe away the filth of our labors.

It is not surprising to see the people of the town stare at us as we walk past on our way to work. They look at us as if we are aliens from another planet. What a pathetic sight we make, a group of gaunt women shuffling and stumbling down the road wearing blue and white *pashaks* and clumsy wooden shoes. At least they have given us brightly colored scarves to cover up our shorn heads.

Hindenburg is an industrial town with immense factories that support the German war effort. The unit that I work in specializes in parts for the Navy. They have taught me to be a welder on an assembly line where I weld a door handle shaped like a wheel to a steel central turning bar. It is dangerous work, but at least I have gloves to wear and an eye shield to protect my eyes from flying sparks. I hold the glass shield in one hand as I weld with the other. I have become an excellent welder.

Our day begins at 4:30 a.m. when we line up outside for *appell* and are counted. The Germans never tire of counting us. All of this takes place before the eyes of the SS-*Unterscharfuhrer* Taube, who was reassigned from Auschwitz to supervise us here at Hindenburg. He is young, perhaps twenty-nine years of age. Tall and burly with dark slicked hair. He is a good-looking man with navy blue eyes. At Auschwitz, he was known for his sadistic cruelty during selections, but his reassignment to Hindenburg has mellowed him.

He has fallen in love with a Jew. Her name is Esterka Litwak, and from the first moment he laid eyes on her, he was lost. Only nineteen, she is the most beautiful woman any of us has ever seen. Esterka has heavily lashed turquoise blue eyes set beneath black arched brows and thick, black wavy hair that frames an oval face of porcelain perfection. Her womanly body is obvious even under the ugly *pashak* that we wear. Esterka sleeps on the lower bunk beneath me, and I have seen the *unterscharfuhrer* enter our barrack before dawn, standing as though hypnotized as he watches Esterka sleep, then leaving before she wakes.

He is obsessed with her. He assigns her the easiest task— keeping his quarters clean. Esterka tells us he shows up every day as she cleans his quarters. He sits in a chair and watches her, completely speechless except for his greeting of "*Gut Morgan* Esterka, how are you today?" or his farewell of "*Auf Wiedersehen,* Esterka, I hope you have a pleasant evening."

She laughs at his buffoonery, the way he savors her name on his tongue. She detests him and can barely keep her disdain from her eyes as she performs her work, doing her best to ignore his gaze. Hopelessly in love, he sees only what he wants to see. Fortunately for her, he is forbidden from any intimacy with her, and so far, he has behaved with propriety. I don't know what punishment he would suffer if he ever gave in to his lust, but one thing is for certain, he would never see her again. It is probably the fear of being separated from the object of his desire that keeps her safe from his advances.

Each morning following roll call, we are given some bitter ersatz coffee and marched off under guard to our assigned work locations. My factory is about a mile away, and it is pleasant to walk through the countryside and see the leaves of the trees turn to rust and gold in the fall light. I try to enjoy the mild fall weather as I know the icy grip of winter will come soon enough, and this walk will instead become a torturous journey in our flimsy clothing and footwear.

About five hundred female and seventy male slaves labor at Hindenburg. Other laborers employed at the factories who are not Jewish receive a salary. These workers are free to come and go, and most of them board in town. The war has displaced and disrupted the lives of not only the Jews but of so many other people.

Quite a few of the young male workers are French, Ukrainian, Polish, Hungarian, and Czech. They voluntarily work for the Germans, probably sending home money to support their families. Every day when I arrive at work, I pass a group of French welders who work close by my station. One of them smiles and winks at me each morning and blows me a kiss through the air. He is very cheerful and friendly. I don't mind his flirtation. It feels good to be treated like a human being. I welcome these lighthearted moments that remind me of what life was like before and perhaps what it could be again if I manage to survive. I always return his kiss with my own that sails through the air and lands on his happy, grinning face.

～

AT THE FACTORY, we are guarded by an old German who usually falls asleep while warming himself at the stove. Aside from the *unterscharfuhrer*, most of the German guards are older. The Nazis have reassigned most of the young soldiers to active war duty against the Allies and have replaced them with the most awful SS women that are designated *aufseherin*, or overseers. These women are even more zealous in their cruelty than the men. One of these monsters is a stout, middle-aged ugly witch named Juana Bormann, who walks around with a vicious German shepherd nearly as large as she is.

I have seen her, without the slightest provocation, unleash the beastly dog on a prisoner in a brutal attack. The unfortunate victim suffered terrible bites and was forced to cower in pain and fear until the mad animal was called off by *Frau* Bormann. She also carries a whip that she uses frequently on women for the slightest infraction. Unfortunately, *Aufseherin* Bormann has noticed the *unterscharfuhrer's* attraction to Esterka.

We are standing at *appell* one morning when I hear her warn him that if he doesn't keep his eyes off that female prisoner, she will report him to headquarters and make sure that he is transferred. Esterka has told us that *Aufseherin* Bormann often barges into the *Unterscharfuhrer's* rooms when she is cleaning them. She assumes the horrid woman is there to make sure the *unterscharfuhrer* keeps his distance. Esterka thinks the ugly witch is secretly in love with Taube and jealous of his attentions being directed elsewhere. For Taube's part, I cannot even imagine there is a question. It would be like choosing between beauty and the beast.

Something wonderful has happened that will hopefully ease the hunger for Lucia and me. One of the Ukrainian workers comes to my station while our guard leaves the floor to go to the bathroom. He speaks a little Polish, and I have picked up a little Ukrainian thanks to Dutchko, and we have no trouble communicating.

"These are very pretty scarves that you wear," he says. "If you can get more, I will give you bread in trade for them."

The thought of an extra ration of food, of bread, is too tempting. "Yes," I answer, "that would be something that I can manage. I will bring you this scarf tomorrow and leave it here under my table. You can take the scarf and leave me bread in trade."

"We have an agreement," he nods and offers his hand, which I shake to seal the deal.

Lucia is so excited to hear what the Ukrainian has suggested, it is all she can do to restrain herself from dancing around the room.

"Why don't we take my scarf and cut it in half, and each of us will wear half a scarf," she suggests.

"Yes," I reply in excitement. "You can't even tell that it has been cut, and no one will notice. Then we can trade the full scarf for bread from the Ukrainian. Once a week, we can get new scarves by saying that the sparks from the welding torches keep burning holes in the fabric and ruining them,"

We are exhilarated with our cleverness and feel as if we have mounted a battle and won. The plan works like a charm, and the next day, a big, beautiful loaf of brown bread is under my workstation.

When the guard goes to the bathroom again, I motion the Ukrainian to come over. Thanking him for the bread, I waste no time making my proposal. "I have a plan. I can probably get one scarf per week for you if you want it."

"You have a deal. Just let me know when you want me to bring the bread."

"Don't you worry, I will let you know."

With that, he walks quickly back to his station. That evening Lucia, who is a little on the plump side and more developed, sneaks the bread back to our barracks under her *pashak*. We feast together on our bunk. We have not had such a bounty in a long time. I lift the loaf to our noses so we can inhale its golden, yeasty aroma. Tearing into the loaf, we savor the chewy moistness in our mouths. I close my eyes and remember Mama's kitchen on baking days. How the entire house would smell of flour and yeast from the beautiful *challahs* she lovingly braided and baked. Out of the oven they would come, with their toasted-brown crusts and pillow-soft centers that melted in your mouth. How I miss those days. How I miss Mama.

We are so hungry that we gobble up the loaf in a matter of

minutes. Lucia and I are like sisters, and we share everything together. This bread is like manna from heaven. It will help to keep us strong through the coming winter.

When winter arrives, our walk to the factory becomes an ordeal to survive. Shivering in knee-deep snow that fills our wooden clogs, with no coats to warm or protect us, we drag ourselves forward as we are buffeted by the shrieking wind. The winter blizzards make the morning *appells* torturous. We stand half-naked and trembling while they count and recount us.

I can't feel my fingers, and my hands are frozen numb. Unable to bear the icy temperature, I rub my hands together, blowing hot air from my blue lips in an effort to warm them as I thrust them into my pockets. I am in the back row with my head hunched down into my shoulders, shifting my weight to keep my feet from freezing. I'm not paying attention to the roll call and haven't noticed *Aufseherin* Bormann and her German shepherd walking through the rows of women until she suddenly stands in front of me. I pull my hands quickly out of my pockets and stand at attention, but it is too late. She raises her black-gloved hand and slaps me so hard across my face that my entire head feels like it is going to fall off, and I see stars dancing before my eyes. I fall to my knees, unable to breathe, and my tears turn to icicles as they slide down the sides of my nose.

"How dare you put your hands in your pockets, Jew? If I ever see you do anything like that again, I will turn my dog on you, and then you will have something to regret."

As she says this, the dog begins to growl and bark inches from my face. He strains against the chain leash, ready for the command to attack. I can smell the warm moist animal breath and feel the foamy saliva hitting my face.

"Get up, now!" she orders.

Shaking and crying, I stand. "Yes, *Aufseherin* Bormann, I am sorry. I will never do it again."

"See that you don't!" She walks away, pulling the dog as it continues to bark viciously at me, angry to be dragged away from its sport. Silently I pray that God will strike her dead. My cheek balloons, and I bear an angry red welt from the force of that cruel blow. I know that I am lucky that she didn't turn her killer dog on me. Lucia makes me a snowball and tells me to hold it against my cheek as we walk to work. She tries to console me, but I cry most of the day, even as I weld. Somehow it is even more demoralizing to receive such cruelty from a woman, someone who could be a mother.

Over the next few weeks, the Nazis at Hindenburg become increasingly nervous as we are just over the border of Germany in a corridor of disputed land that has changed hands innumerable times back and forth between Germany and Poland. We find out that the allies are winning the war, and a decisive battle has begun. We learn this from our non-Jewish co-workers who secretly keep us apprised as to the progress of the war. We also learn that the Russians are gaining ground in Poland and are at the gates of Warszaw in the east, and we pray that Auschwitz cannot be long after that. We have seen the allied planes flying low overhead and pray that maybe they will bomb the gas chambers of Auschwitz, bringing to a halt the extermination of our people. Every day brings the Russians closer, and we suspect that our time here is limited and that soon we will be moved somewhere deeper into the heart of Germany.

A hush has fallen over the factory with the arrival of a most unwelcome and unusual visitor. The *unterscharfuhrer* is here to inspect our factory and is spending time examining our work. Out of the corner of my eye, I can see him making his way from station to station accompanied by two other Nazis and the plant supervisor. He is serious and unsmiling, his mouth set in a thin line of contempt. Occasionally he asks a question and nods in understanding at the explanation of what each person is doing on the assembly line. Eventually, he makes his way to me. Nervously, I weld as the sparks fall around me, intent on my work.

As he starts to walk away, he suddenly turns back to me and yells, *"Komm her!"*

I nearly drop my welding torch and the wheel I am working on. My immediate response is panic as I scramble to comply. I am in trouble, and I don't know why. Impatiently he taps his gloves against his pant leg and scowls at me as I quickly turn off my torch and approach him, my head bowed in submission.

"Where did you get that rouge on your cheeks?"

I am shocked at his question. *"Herr Unterscharführer, das ist naturlichen,"* I reply. "It is the color of my skin."

Handing his gloves to one of the other men, he raises his hand. I flinch, expecting a slap. He grabs my arm with one hand and proceeds to roughly rub my cheek with the other. Then he inspects his fingers, his face frowning. Anger floods his face with color as he brusquely releases me, throwing up his hands as if to beg God for an explanation as he screams, *"Diese verdammten Juden haben alles naturlichen!"* These damn Jews have everything natural! Go back to work! *Raus! Raus!"*

As I walk back to my station, I can see the shock on everyone's faces before they quickly avert their eyes and resume their work. The moment is pregnant with meaning. Under my breath, I whisper as I light my welding torch. "Go to hell, you bastard!"

That evening, safely ensconced in my bunk, I relate the day's event to Esterka, who knows him better than any of us. She laughs knowingly. "He is frustrated because he cannot have me. His love is driving him mad. I hope it drives him to suicide. He hates the Jews because he is told he should, and this allows him to rationalize the evils that he perpetrates against them. It kills him that the woman he is infatuated with is a Jewess. He is transferring his dissatisfaction with me to you, Dinale. I am sorry you had to be the object of his frustrations. He is a pathetic bastard."

"Be careful, Esterka. You know what evil acts he is capable of. In Auschwitz, he selected and killed thousands."

"You do have the rosiest cheeks." She smiles, patting my cheek tenderly. "Don't worry about me. I am always the giver of smiles coated with sugar when I am around him. It makes me sick to act in such a false manner, but someday he will get what he deserves. I hope I survive to see it." Esterka's eyes blaze with determination, which only emphasizes her remarkable beauty.

On Christmas Eve, the Nazis treat themselves to a grand celebration. The sounds of music and singing fill the air, drifting on snowflakes to our barracks. The performers are all Jewish musicians and vocalists. One voice that sounds like an angel pierces the winter's night, melodious and perfectly pitched. An operatic soprano, her high notes tear at the strings of our hearts as we sit in silence, straining our ears to catch each perfect note. The finale is a startling choice. The heavenly voice, in a daring act of resistance, cries out "My Yiddishe Mama" in German. Nothing could be more poignant. We all weep in memory of our own lost mothers as we savor the beauty of that moment and pray for those we have lost.

Our days at Hindenburg come to an end because the Russians are closing in. The trains have arrived, and we leave the next morning. We have not been told our destination, but we are certain it will be behind Nazi lines deeper into the heart of Germany. Yesterday, I traded our last scarf with my Ukrainian friend and bid him farewell. Our business would have ended regardless as the supply of scarves has run out. Last night Lucia and I ate well, which will give us the strength to sustain us on our journey.

In the pale light of dawn, we are marched from our barracks. The trains are filled beyond capacity. The *unterscharfuhrer* looks like a lost boy as he stoically watches Esterka and the rest of us climb onto the waiting trains. The sound of the slamming door is like the finality of a casket being sealed. Is this our last journey, I wonder? The wheels screech into motion, and a cloud of steamy vapor drifts by the tiny windows as the train heads south. It is freezing. Lucia and I huddle together as the countryside flies by.

I cannot help but appreciate the beautiful brilliance of the snow-white landscape that reels past the tiny window. In the distance, the mountains push their thorny spines toward the sky like a cathedral that God has fashioned to remind man of his inconsequence. Every minute the mountains loom nearer, growing larger as the train lumbers ever closer. Nestled in barren groves of trees, farmhouses with chimneys provide warmth to all who live within. Children snug and cozy with parents providing for their every need, surrounded by love and security, barely aware of the storm of war that rages around them or the train of sorrow that slowly trundles past.

CHAPTER 32

WE HAVE no food or water.

It has been many hours since we left Hindenburg and the lack of water is the most debilitating. Some of the women moan from thirst and dehydration. Lucia and I and a few other women come up with a solution. Among our few possessions is a handled tin pot, which we tie to a long string and drop out of the railroad car window and drag in the snow. When we pull it up, it is filled with snow, which we share with everyone in the cattle car. Some of the woman grab for the pot in desperation, but we manage to make certain that everyone gets a little as we repeat the process again and again.

The train takes us up into the Hartz mountains and slowed to a crawl. The landscape is rugged and snow-packed, and the switchbacks cause a tremendous amount of unbalance from the shifting of the human cargo as everyone is forced to lean into each other. We can't imagine where the train could be headed or why.

We are slowing, and the whistle announces our arrival as we pull through the gate of a camp. Looking out the small window, I see a sign that reads, Nordhausen. The train comes to a stop but the door remains closed. Hours go by, and we grow desperate to be released from this prison. There is only a bucket to be used for a toilet, and it is full and stinking. Some of the women pound on the railroad car doors, screaming to be let out.

Finally, we hear the doors unbarred and the Germans scream, "*Raus! Raus!*" We stumble out of the cars, women pushing and shoving. They line us up and tell us we will remain at Nordhausen for two nights and then we will depart for a camp called Bergen-Belsen. There is no explanation of why we are here, and none of us knows what or where Bergen-Belsen is.

Nordhausen is enormous and completely fenced in with barbed wire. The huge buildings were once airplane hangars and now house the inmates. It is not an extermination camp, at least in the normal sense of the word like Auschwitz. There are no gas chambers or crematoria.

Without food or water, we are abandoned to a small shrunken man named Leo, who greets us. We follow Leo into one of the enormous concrete buildings, where our eyes behold a gruesome sight. This is a camp of walking dead, skeletons with sagging skin, and eyes bulging from their sockets. Leo tells us this is a sub-camp of Dora Mittelbau, a secret *arbeitslager,* a work camp complex where the slave laborers toil under subhuman conditions. Nordhausen is a *vernichtungslager,* an extermination camp that contains mostly Germans, French, and Poles. These *Haftlinge,* or non-Jewish political prisoners, many of whom were resistance fighters, had dared to stand up to the Nazis. Here they are treated to a living death. Once captured and sent to Dora, they are forced to build massive underground tunnels into the mountains for the development of the V-1 and V-2 rocket program, what Hitler calls his *vergeltungs waffen* or "weapons of retaliation."

The unfortunate captives are rewarded with cruel beatings and starvation as they are forced to carry heavy equipment and excavate mile-long tunnels under the earth. Within these living tombs, they work, overwhelmed by the gas, dust, and explosions that are a daily occurrence. With no medical attention and a starvation diet, they drop like flies. The ones who manage to stay alive are so battered and broken that they are no longer useful to the Germans, and so they are sent to Nordhausen to die.

The dead are everywhere. The stench is unimaginable. The mountains of rotting bodies, tangled legs and arms, unforgettable. The dead stare at us, hollowed eyed and emaciated faces frozen in agony. Their souls beg for burial.

Our hunger and thirst forgotten, we realize how lucky we are compared to these poor human beings. Exhausted from our journey, we huddle together on the ground as we stare in disbelief at the nightmare around us.

And yet, even in this valley of death, human decency somehow clings to life. Those who have nothing, who can barely walk, bring us a bit of food and water. They share what little they have with us, and we are humbled by their kindness.

A woman in our group asks Leo about Bergen-Belsen.

His forlorn eyes gaze on us. "I have heard of it. It is north of here, maybe 200 kilometers near Celle."

"But what kind of camp is it—is it a work camp?" Nadja asks.

"I don't think so."

It is clear he is reluctant to share what he knows of Bergen-Belsen, which sinks our hearts, but we persist in our questioning.

"Please, Leo, tell us the truth. Tell us what you know," I pipe in.

Sadly, he looks at our eager faces and the last vestige of hope contained within our eyes.

"Bergen-Belsen is a concentration camp, a death camp, like Auschwitz," he whispers.

HOPE HAS FLOWN from us like a child's balloon in the wind.

For two days, we remain in Nordhausen, sleeping on the ground in an airplane hangar. The non-Jewish prisoners kindly share what little they have with us. The Germans, true to their obsessive punctuality, inform us that we will leave in the morning. We bid Leo and the other men goodbye, but our words of good luck ring hollow in our ears. There is no question that few of the Nordhausen internees will survive. Death walks unhindered and will easily lay claim to hundreds, if not thousands, of the victims at Nordhausen.

The train, filled beyond capacity with its cargo of women, lumbers north towards Bergen-Belsen. Once more, we gather enough snow in our small pail to abate the thirst and dehydration that become an unquenchable yearning as we proceed through the countryside. The hours pass in silence except for the rhythmic rattle of the tracks that fly beneath the train's wheels and the mournful sound of the whistle that pierces the quiet winter's air.

The train's wheels squeak as we slowly come to a stop beyond the gates of what must be Bergen-Belsen. Here we sit, contemplating our sorrowful fate until the whining wheels cry out, announcing the arrival of our train and its human cargo inside. Once more, we are greeted by shouts of *"Raus! Raus! Raus!"*

Then begins the endless, obsessive routine that the Germans never tire of—counting Jews. The frigid cold assaults our bodies as the moisture of our breath hangs in the air like clouds of smoke. Shivering in our *pashaks,* we stand at attention, starving and thirsty, while the commander of the camp, SS *Hauptsturmfuhrer* Kramer, addresses us. He informs us of the rules of our new prison. Finally, near exhaustion, we are led away to our barracks. Nadja and I part as she follows her girlfriends to the barrack next door. It is fine with me. She is twenty, and I cannot blame her for wanting to be with girls her own age rather than the 15-year-olds. I have Lucia, and there could not be a truer friend or sister.

Upon entering the barracks, we stand for a moment blinking as our eyes adjust to the dim light. I have seen many visions of hell throughout the war, witnessed so many horrors, but nothing compares to the nightmare of what we behold. The barrack is massive and filled with at least five hundred, maybe a thousand women crowded together, lying on straw mats on the floor. There is barely enough room to walk without stepping over a body. Lucia and I inch our way forward. Coughing, crying, and moaning in every language assaults our ears. The stench of the unclean, the sick, and the dying assaults our noses. Numb with exhaustion, we walk to the farthest point at the back of the building, searching for a place as far away from the sounds and smells as possible. Finding a small patch of straw, starving and in despair, we collapse to the ground.

An hour later, careful not to step on anyone, we make our way out of our prison to see if we can find some water to wash. What we see is unimaginable. As far as the eye can see in either direction for what seems like miles is a mountain of contorted bodies. Arms, legs, and torsos seem to meld together. Their faces are frozen in a last torturous grimace of death. Terror seizes me. Gripping Lucia's hand, I moan with despair as I gag with nausea. With no food in my stomach to vomit, I am racked by dry heaves that convulse my body. Lucia holds me in her arms as we sink to our knees together, unable to control the misery and revulsion that overwhelms us.

"Lucia," I gasp. "This can't be real. So many bodies, there must be thousands of them."

Lucia's eyes are round like two full moons. "Why haven't they buried them?"

"This is the end!" I cry. "We will never survive this place. Everything we have been through is meaningless. We will never live to tell the world the evil that has been done to us. What did we do to deserve this? God has turned his back on us." I am wracked with sobs.

"Dina, please don't cry. We did nothing to deserve what has happened to us. We will survive. We have to! You have to try, please promise me you will try? Please don't leave me alone in this place."

We sit there rocking, terrified, clinging to each other, afraid to give up and afraid to go on—our future as dead as the thousands of bodies that lay outside the door of our barracks.

CHAPTER 33

NIGHT COMES EARLY in a concentration camp. The blackness enfolds you as you lie awake, remembering all that you have lost. Women weep all night long, awake or asleep, their sorrow wrenching at your sanity and tightening the space between your heart and your chest. Among the thousands of tears that fall in the night, there are the piercing screams of *"A KENYEREM!"* "MY BREAD!" All through the long night, with heartrending sorrow, they shriek, *"A KENYEREM!!"*

We are awakened from our nightmares by the desperate cries of a Hungarian woman whose precious crust of bread has been stolen while she sleeps. Starvation will drive a person to murder for a piece of bread. Who am I to condemn these poor souls who are driven to steal from those weaker than they? The more we suffer, the more we resort to madness and animal instinct. Our humanity is obliterated.

The morning *appells* continue unabated. They line us up beside the wall of death as they count us. The Nazis take such great pains to count us while we still live, and yet after we die, they pretend we never existed.

The Nazis relish the *appells*, for it gives them an opportunity to bludgeon us with clubs and whips or allow their trained dogs to tear us to shreds. *Haupsturmfuhrer* Kramer is aided by his crony SS

Aufsederin Bormann. I recognize the witch from Auschwitz. The woman who slapped me. Nothing has changed. She still glories in sadistic behavior. After being counted for the umpteenth time, we are returned to our barracks.

It is just as well that they don't feed us anything until noon, as now our single chore of the day beckons. Those who still breathe must remove those who died in the night. Lucia and I, along with others who have the strength, drag the bodies outside and toss them on the mountain of death. We are only one of the endless rows of barracks that all perform the same unenviable task of clearing the dead from our midst. The wall of death grows with each passing day, as does the realization that we will not survive this inferno. As the days pass, we become numb to the pyramid of bodies that reach toward the sky. Our tears have long dried up with our hopes and dreams. Like sand sifting through an hourglass, our time is running out until we too will be mere links in the chain of death that surrounds us.

There is a sweet girl from Krakow who lies beside us. Her name is Lena. She is suffering from typhoid, and her frail feverish body trembles through the night as she talks incoherently in her delirium. Lucia and I care for her, bringing her water and a bit of bread. Sometimes when she gains consciousness, she tells us of her dreams. She smiles, her eyes glow with the fever, as she tells us that her sister is living as a Christian in Krakow and that she is coming to save her, to take her home. She keeps repeating, "Manya is coming to save me. She will take me out of here. Have you seen her? Is she here yet?"

The typhoid madness consumes her, and we reassure her that it must be so. "Yes, Manya is coming soon," I say. "Don't worry, we will bring her to you when she gets here."

"You must hold on, Lena. Manya is coming," Lucia urges.

Lena's parched lips flutter like butterfly wings as she thanks us for our kindness, and she slips back into her fevered dreams.

The next morning, Lena is gone.

Lucia and I drag Lena's body outside to her final resting place on the wall of death. It is the first time I have cried since our arrival. I try not to care, to distance myself. What is one more death among so many, but my heart breaks.

~

THE NEXT DAY, I am surprised to see *Unterscharfuhrer* Taube from Hindenburg. We are in line at *appell,* and I watch as he walks down the rows, eyeing each woman. He immediately recognizes me and stops, ordering me out of the row to question me. It dawns on me that he is at Bergen-Belsen for one reason only.

"Have you seen Esterka Litwak?" he asks me. "You are her friend. You must know where she is. I must find her!"

"*Nein,* I haven't seen her since we arrived at Bergen-Belsen," I reply. "I don't know where she is." My face is as blank as an empty page. And then I see my opportunity to wound him. "Probably she is dead. Maybe you should check the wall of bodies?"

His eyes blaze with madness as he registers my words, and my heart beats stronger. Even if I knew where Esterka is, I would never tell him. Most likely, she is here at Bergen-Belsen, but there are thousands of us, it is impossible to know. We die like flies here with no one to note our passing.

"I will search every barrack until I find her. Go back to the *appell.*"

"As you wish, *Unterscharfuhrer.*"

As I slowly walk away, he cries, "Halt!"

Turning, I stare defiantly into his eyes. I wonder if he has more questions for me. To my surprise, he asks me a question I would not have expected in a million-and-one years.

"Can you imagine what has happened to Germany?" he asks. "I cannot believe we are losing the war."

I gape at him, too stunned to reply.

He seems to recover himself, and casting a worried glance around him, he turns and strides away.

An uncontrollable hatred wells up within me, and I return to my place at the *appell.* Under my breath, I curse him. "You have lived too long!"

Today they march us for no apparent reason to the men's camp. We are forced to parade through the grounds as if on spectacle. Meanwhile, the Nazis entertain themselves with a barrage of blows to our heads, beating us unmercifully. Maybe they want to torture the men by reinforcing their feelings of helplessness. It is impossible to understand the Nazis' motives. Mystified, I implore Lucia to explain why. "How can we possibly live through this insanity?"

As always, she answers, "We must!"

The next day as I leave our barracks on my way to *appell*, I have to step over two dark-haired sisters. The older one is suffering from typhoid and looks near to death. The younger sister cares for her tenderly, her large expressive brown eyes fraught with worry. In Dutch, she begs her sister Margot to hold on. I notice them only because there are so few of us who are lucky enough to have any family to cling to.

My heart twists, reminding me of my own sister, Nadja. How I wish she was here. A woman tells me they are sisters from Amsterdam, Margot and Anne Frank. The next day I see the younger girl crying over the body of her dead sister, and my heart breaks. Her shoulders heave, and I hear her say, "Forgive me for living without you, Margot." A few days later, she, too, is gone. I pray they are together in Heaven.

A woman stumbles through our barracks, calling my name. "Dina Frydman,"

"I am Dina Frydman," I reply, and she tells me my cousin Nadja is dying. She is a friend of Nadja's. I brace myself for the worst as I go with Nadja's friend to her barracks. I find my cousin in a lifeless heap. Her body, like mine, has wasted away to almost nothing. Using every ounce of strength within me, I wrap a ragged blanket around her and drag her back to my barracks

"What is it that hurts you?" I ask her.

She can barely speak, and I must lower my ear to her lips to discern her words. "I can't swallow. My tongue is in agony," she rasps.

"Open your mouth and let me look inside," I order her. Her tongue is covered in white sores. She can't swallow anything and is in excruciating pain. I am not a doctor, but I must try my best to save her. I fetch some water and take my only possession, my toothbrush, and begin to scrub out her mouth. She screams in pain the whole time as I continue to scour away her sores, which gush puss and blood.

"You're killing me," she wails.

"What are you doing?" Lucia asks me.

"I am saving her life," I answer determinedly. "Hold still, Nadja, or I will slap you. If you want to live, you had better let me scrub away these sores."

Finally, when I can rub no more, I clean her mouth with water, hoping I have removed the poison that is killing her. I tell her to sleep and later I will bring her some food. I sink to my straw pallet, exhausted from the effort.

Nadja sleeps for two days, drifting in and out of consciousness. She awakes only long enough for me to spoon some soup and water down her throat. I check her mouth daily and find the sores are beginning to heal, and the puss has not returned.

"You saved my life," Nadja whispers.

"Yes, I think I have," I whisper back.

Lucia says that when Nadja is awake, she doesn't take her eyes off me. She stares in wonder at me like a child might stare at its mother. I am grateful to God that I could help her. I cannot help but also feel a little proud that Nadja, who in the past has grumbled at me for being such a baby, now looks at me in awe.

TWO DAYS LATER, I come down with typhoid.

I managed to survive six years in the ghettos and the camps, but I fear my luck has run out. I don't think I have any fight left in me. Starvation has taken its toll and my body has shrunk to that of a small child. My *pashak* swims on me, I have no breasts, and my menstrual flow has stopped. My heart breaks that I will not be able to keep my promise to Natek.

The wall of death grows bigger each day, and I wonder if one day soon, I will be joining it. Death, our constant companion, always lurks in the shadows, waiting.

It so simple to close your eyes and let Death take you.

For days, I hover somewhere between this world and the next. Lucia is vigilant in her care for me, forcing me to drink water and eat a little bread. My cousin Nadja is there as well, sponging my forehead with dirty rags and whispering encouragement in my ear.

They beg me to live.

My restless sleep is filled with strange dreams of my family—some happy and others dreadful. In the twisted landscape of my feverish mind, I dream that my father and I have survived the war and my father has taken up with a woman. I am furious with him. "How could you have a girlfriend already when my mother has just died? How can you be so heartless?"

Pained by my accusations, he begs me to understand. "Your mother has been dead a long time. I am so lonely. I need to feel love again."

Lucia rocks me in her arms like a baby. "Sh, sh, Dina, it's just a dream. Please don't cry."

The memories of the dream flood me with sorrow, and my body shakes with my sobbing. My father has no girlfriend. My father is dead. They are all dead.

As the days pass, my body begins to let go. I know I am dying and yet I feel a sense of tranquility. Peace. I feel my soul rising out of my body—I look down and see my frail form. All the pain and hunger have left me. I am nearly free of the ties that bind me to this life. I am a butterfly. I glide across the sky, now and again lifted by the fingers of the wind.

I barely hear Lucia and Nadja call out to me. Their voices are a distant echo, so very far away. I don't want to listen, for I am soaring toward the sun...

I open my eyes and look around me. Joy washes over me, for I am back in the cherry orchard with my family and friends. Fela and I sit on a blanket with a bowl of cherries between us. Cherry blossoms float down, and the world is pink. I have looped cherries around my ears like ruby earrings. Fela and I giggle as I flutter my eyelashes and angle my head from side to side, making the plump cherries jiggle. Abek grabs one of my earrings and pops it into his mouth, then jumps up and runs away. I chase after him. "Abek, you are such a *nudge*. When I catch you, I'm going to tickle you until you beg for mercy."

As usual, *Bubbe* intervenes. "Leave your brother alone. He is your only brother."

My grandfather waves me in and pats his lap. I nuzzle into his chest, his beard tickling me as he kisses me. "I've missed you, *maidele*."

"I've missed you, *Zayde*." I look around at my family. "I've missed you all. I want to stay here with all of you," I say to Mama and Papa.

"You cannot stay," Papa says.

"You must go on," Mama adds. "You must live for all of us."

"But it's not fair. It's not fair that you are here all together, and I am all alone."

"You are not alone," Papa says. "You will never be alone. You carry our love and our memories inside you."

"Dina, you cannot stay. You must wake up and live," Mama says.

Wake up Dina. Live...

"Wake up, Dina! Wake up!"

Someone is shaking me awake. I think it is my cousin Nadja. She has become as annoying as my sister. I am still half in my dream and do not want to leave. I can still see the ripe cherries in the bowl on the picnic blanket in the orchard. "Let me stay, Nadja," I mumble.

"No, no!" Nadja shakes me again. She tells me my fever has broken. She tells me I cannot possibly die now that we are finally free.

"Get up Dina," Lucia yells. "We are free!"

I crack my eyes open and wonder if they have died too, or perhaps they have gone mad. They are both bouncing and squealing with joy.

"We are free!" they shout again and again. "The English have arrived. We are free! Do you understand Dina. Free!"

Pulling me to my feet with their arms supporting me, Lucia and Nadja help me outside. Everywhere I look, I see handsome men in uniforms smiling at me. No one ever smiles in Bergen-Belsen. I am certain I am still dreaming. Or perhaps this is Heaven. I cannot tell. All around me, everyone is smiling, laughing, and crying with joy.

Finally, the truth washes over me. Relief seeps into my soul and I burst into tears of joy. We are alive. And we have been saved.

I see a group of Nazi SS women being led away, their hands on their heads. Rage shoots through me and I feel a surge of strength. "Help me," I ask Nadja and Lucia.

We each pick up a stone and hurl them at the hateful bitches. I hit *Aufseherin* Bormann squarely on her temple, and she winces, she looks at me and her eyes are full of fear. I spit in her direction. "Now it is your turn," I say.

The exertion has left me dizzy and breathless, and it is a struggle not to faint. But I have never felt so happy in my entire life. I am free.

CHAPTER 34

The English soldiers are so kind to us. They smile and speak words of encouragement, but their eyes are full of tears at the horror that is Bergen-Belson.

Not knowing what to do, they feed us what they have, trying to stem starvation with powdered milk and Bully beef—a soldier's fare. The result is catastrophic. Our debilitated bodies cannot digest the proteins, having shut down most functions. The sudden infusion of food ravages us with diarrhea, which only escalates the cycle of death. Nadja, Lucia, and I are all sick with diarrhea, but we refuse to go to the hospital. The English move us into the German military school barracks formerly occupied by the Nazis.

And now it is the Nazis who are very busy dragging the bodies from the death wall that surrounds the camp like a decomposing funeral wreath to mass graves. They are helped in this grizzly task by the German occupants of the town of Bergen, who are forced to assist. It is fitting that these compatriots should bear witness to the horrors their country has perpetrated.

Ten thousand bodies lay dead on the wall.

At liberation on April 15, 1945, sixty thousand survivors are found barely clinging to life at Bergen-Belsen. Tragically, this number shrinks with each passing day as so many continue to die from the effects of malnutrition and disease. Thirteen thousand more Jews die in the days and weeks ahead.

A week after our liberation, what is left of the survivors of the concentration camp Bergen-Belsen gather together for a memorial. Our long captivity is over, and it is time to pray for those who did not live to see this day. In a gathering of strength and hope for the future, our voices unite in song. We sing the nine-stanza poem of Naphtali Herz Imber, *"Hatikvah,"* to Samuel Cohen's melody.

> *As long as in the heart, within,*
> *The soul of a Jew still yearns,*
> *And onward, towards the ends of the East,*
> *an eye still gazes toward Zion;*
> *Our hope is not yet lost,*
> *The two-thousand-year-old hope,*
> *To be a free nation in our land,*
> *The land of Zion and Jerusalem.*

It is time to rebuild our lives. Many countries have begun to open their doors to offer us a haven for rehabilitation and resettlement.

Sweden has offered to take 6,000 survivors for convalescence, and Nadja is going there for additional medical treatment and rehabilitation. She wants me to go with her, but I can't.

If Natek still lives, I must wait for him until he finds me. Wanting my dear cousin to recover and begin a new life, I encourage her to go to Sweden. She needs to feel young and alive again. A lovely family is sponsoring her, and she will go to school, which she is desperate to do. Four days later, she leaves. Amid a waterfall of tears and a thousand hugs and kisses, we promise each other to write every day.

Now it is just Lucia and me who remain at the displaced persons camp at Belsen. Lucia, who is two years older than I, has reconnected with some survivors from her native city, Krakow, and more important, she is keeping company with a young man named Szymek, whom she met in Pionki. Szymek is wonderful and he is mad about Lucia, and I suspect they will marry before too long.

We spend a great deal of time together eating our meals communally and socializing. Love is blossoming everywhere around us. It is as if we have lain in a coma for six years and now that we have awoken, we are trying so hard to make up for all those lost years. We eat too much and too fast. We laugh too heartily and too loudly. We are desperate to feel emotions that have lain dormant for so long. We run from the abyss of war as if we could put it behind us and never think of it again.

Europe lies in a pile of ashes that have been scattered by the winds of war. Displaced families, Jewish and non-Jewish, are everywhere. Orphaned children are given priority by social agencies from around the world that unite to find missing family members. Everyone is in a frenzy to register the names of their family members that are missing. Every day I go with great hope in my heart to check the lists of survivors that have been found. Every day I walk away in tears after finding not a single name. Can it be that no one from all my many aunts, uncles, and cousins has survived except Nadja and me? Not one Frydman, Topolevich, Talman, Erlich, Madrykamien, Pomirantz, or Finkelstein?

And then I find out that Majer is still alive! Majer has been liberated by the Americans. I find out where the Americans have relocated him. Overjoyed, I write to him, and send him Nadja's address in Sweden.

He writes back, overjoyed at learning that his sister Nadja and I still live. He is in a DP camp in Italy. In his letter, Majer tells me the Nazis had sent him and his father to Mauthausen after Auschwitz and from there to a sub-camp of Mauthausen called Ebensee in Austria. Conditions at Ebensee were terrible. Ebensee was a secret site for rocket development, and Majer and his father slaved in the underground tunnels performing back-breaking labor. One day Majer left for work in the morning, leaving his father behind in the barracks. When he returned in the evening, his father was gone. No one knew what happened to him. He had simply vanished.

My heart breaks for Majer and Nadja that their father has perished. Only three of us from our family remain. Three that we know of. God willing, there are more. Out there, somewhere. I pray there are more.

∾

Lucia has left with Szymek for Krakow to search for surviving family members. I remain the last of we three who went through so much together. I have new friends and roommates, three sisters who survived together, a miracle by any stretch of the imagination. Rosa, who is twenty-one years old, Fela, nineteen, and Rachela, the youngest, is almost sixteen, my age. Miracle of miracles, they have gotten a letter from their older brother, Shlomo, who has also survived and is on his way to Bergen. Imagine four from the same immediate family. It seems impossible.

What I would give to see my brother Abek and my sister Nadja again. It is so painful to contemplate a future, without them. They live only in the cherished landscape of my memories and dreams.

Shlomo has arrived, and the girls are beyond excited to be reunited with their older brother. He is twenty-four and managed to survive in the forest by fighting with the partisans. Very tall and thin, the premature lines on his face are a testament to what he has witnessed and make him seem far older than his age. He clearly adores his sisters and within moments I can see he has completely assumed the mantle of responsibility for the family. The girls cling to him as he wraps his long arms around them. My eyes well with tears as I watch their poignant reunion.

Thinking that I should leave them alone and give them some privacy, I quietly turn to leave.

"Who is this little girl?" asks Shlomo as I reach for the door handle.

"Oh, Shlomo," says Rachela, "This is Dina, from Radom. Dina is our roommate, and she is wonderful!"

"Yes," interjects Fela, "Dina hasn't found any of her family yet. She is alone."

"Not anymore," says Shlomo. "She is coming with us."

"Where?" asks Rosa. "Where are we going?"

"We are going to the American Zone, to a castle near Heidelberg in Baden-Wurttemberg. The Americans are much better supplied than the British and can offer many more opportunities."

"Oh, Dina," Rachela squeals. "You must come with us, it will be wonderful. Can you imagine a castle for us to live in?"

"I don't know. I don't want to be a burden to you, and the British have been so wonderful to us."

"Don't be ridiculous," insists Shlomo. "We will not leave without you. It is decided. You are coming with us to Langdenburg."

CHAPTER 35

HOW DIFFERENT THIS train ride is from our prior journeys as prisoners of the Nazis. Now we are treated respectfully and with honor and can ride anywhere in all of Europe for free. We are seated in first class, where the stewards pamper and coddle us.

Langdenburg is a fairy-tale castle dating back to the 12th century. Located between Heidelberg and Stuttgart, it sits on a promontory overlooking the Jagst Valley. It is the most beautiful place I have ever seen. The first blush of spring sun has given over to the lushness of summer. The expansive lawns that slumbered all winter are a verdant green, and the gardens are bursting with flowers that cascade out of their beds onto the walking paths in a symphony of vibrant color. The fruit trees are filled with ripening fruit, and vineyards slope up against the dense old Swabian forests that pierce the landscape like spears. Rolling hills like waves of green water stretch all the way to snow-capped mountains in the distance.

This is the land of Hohenlohe royalty. For the time being, we will live like kings and queens with a large staff of servants who will see to our every need. Untouched by the war, it is truly heaven on earth, but it is also disconcerting. Even with all the astounding beauty, it is impossible for me to grow comfortable in Germany. The people treat us well, but they speak the same language as the Nazis did. The language assaults my ears as it echoes with a thousand reminders of unforgettable cruelty. I cannot help but feel resentment in every German's eyes. Perhaps it is my own paranoia that disturbs me, and I should just relax and enjoy this dream vacation that has been given to me. After all, it is a small compensation for the decimation of our families.

A few days later I receive a letter that is a dream come true. The letter is from Natek. He has found me. My voice trembles as I read it aloud to Rosa, Fela, and Rachela, who shriek with excitement. Natek and his brother Benjamin survived. I am shaking with joy as I press the paper to my heart. Tears roll down my face, soaking the fragile sheets. The girls wrap their arms around me, nearly crushing me in their embrace.

"He is coming!" I cannot help but cry and cry as the girls hug and kiss me. "Natek is coming. He is on his way. My God, I can't believe it."

My prayers have been answered, and soon I will see Natek again.

The warm summer day is crystal clear, and I am outside basking in its glory. The gardens are filled with aromatic flowers, and the bees busily buzz from flower to flower, drinking in the sweet nectar and yellow pollen.

"Dinale, Dinale!"

I turn and see Natek running toward me, his arms open wide.

"Natek," I cry. I start to move toward him in a daze at first, and then I break into a run. I run as fast as I can. I run right into his arms. We both cry and laugh and shriek with joy as Natek spins me around and around and around.

"Is it really you?" I keep asking him. "Is it really you?"

"It is me, Dinale. I am here. I promised we would survive, and we have. I promised I would find you, and I have."

He twirls me around as if I am a feather, my laughter pealing like a Sunday church bell. "I told you we would outlive the Nazis and their evil. It is just as I said it would be."

My eyes drink in the wonder of him. He is thin but strong, his face years older than his age, but his grin is still that of a young boy who has been caught with his hand in the cookie jar. And those eyes. Those serious blue eyes still crinkle when he smiles.

We walk along the garden path. "Natek, is this not the most beautiful place you have ever seen?"

"I don't care about this place," he replies. "I only have eyes for you. Look at you. You are more beautiful than I remembered. You have grown into a woman."

His gaze feasting on me makes me blush. He bursts into laughter. "I'd forgotten what lovely rosy cheeks you have."

"Stop embarrassing me." I pull him to a bench. "Come, sit and tell me everything. Natek, I am so happy to see you. I have so much to tell you, and I know you have so much to tell me. It has been so long since we parted in Radom."

"There are not enough hours in a day to tell you everything," he says, bringing my hands to his lips and kissing my palms.

"Yes," I agree. "There will be plenty of time for that. I want to enjoy being alive and having you here with me. You must be hungry and tired from your trip. Let's see if the kitchen can make us a picnic, and we can take a walk down to the clearest stream you have ever seen."

"I am starving," he admits. "I would welcome a little food."

It is strange to hear that word. Starving. We are no longer starving. Starvation was what we experienced in the camps. And now, the use of that word seems wrong. Almost obscene. Everything about the camps was obscene. Holding hands with Natek, surrounded by beautiful flowers, I cannot even fathom that a month ago, we were living a nightmare. An obscene nightmare.

Arm-in-arm, we stroll to the castle, where the staff eagerly stuffs a basket with roasted chicken, cherries, and sweet pastries. The kitchen staff knows how much I love cherries. I cried the first time I tasted one when I first arrived at the castle, and when word got back to them, they made sure to set out cherries every day. We dine in a meadow at the edge of a stream, as perfect a scene as an impressionist painting. After we eat our fill, we take a walk by the stream and wade barefoot in the water, holding hands. Small fish and pollywogs dart in and out between our legs as birds chirp in the trees that curve along the shoreline.

I stumble, and Natek catches me, his arms encircling me and pressing me to his chest. He kisses me, and my head spins. These are not the urgent kisses of the boy that I remembered but the commanding kisses of a man full grown. My knees buckle as I surrender to the warm rush of heat that envelops me. I can feel his manhood swell against me and hear the soft moans that escape his lips as he kisses my neck. My own breath is coming in shallow gasps, and I am overwhelmed. I realize if I don't stop him now, I may not be able to.

"Natek, Natek, please, please stop. We mustn't go any further, please."

"It's okay, Dinale, let me hold you, please. I promise I won't force you. I would never push you."

I can feel our hearts pounding as one. "Maybe we should take a swim to cool off?"

Natek gazes into my eyes and kisses me on the forehead. "That is a very good idea."

As intended, the cold water of the stream extinguishes the heat of our kisses. We douse our youthful passions with laughter as we splash in the shallow stream. After our swim, we lie on the bank, basking in the sunlight as our clothes dry. Gently, Natek prods me to tell him what happened to me after I left Radom. I try to compose myself and relate all that happened as dispassionately as I can, but I am soon overpowered by tears. Again, he holds me and kisses me, but this time they are the tender and sweet kisses as I remembered from before.

Then it is Natek's turn to share his and Benjamin's story of survival. He breathes deeply, and the joy in his eyes fades. "After they took you away in July 1943, Benjamin and I were assigned to Szkolna camp. In January 1944, it became a full-fledged Konzentrations Lager with all of the enforced rules and security of any other camp minus the gas chambers. The labor was backbreaking, the food minimal, the *appells* interminable, but we still considered ourselves lucky to be alive and in Radom. Then in March, the Nazis abducted about 600 of us to the extermination camp Majdanek near Lublin.

"I don't need to tell you what it was like there," he continues. "Much like Auschwitz, except that by the time we arrived, the Russians were advancing, and the Nazis had stopped using the gas chambers. Benjamin and I were young and healthy, and the Nazis used us for hard labor until, in April, the Russians were nearly at our door. They shipped us to Plaszow Camp near Krakow, where a nasty bunch of SS ruled. Things were really bad there, the beatings and torture —" Natek's eyes darken with anguish.

I watch as his jaw clenches with the mighty effort it takes him to subdue the torturous memories. I squeeze his hand, waiting for him to continue. Wiping the tears from his eyes, he fixes his gaze on some distant horizon. "They evacuated us finally to Mauthausen, and even at the end, with the Allies closing in, the Nazis were fixated on their goal of eliminating every Jew.

"One day, Benjamin and I were rounded up with a group of others and taken into the woods. I knew it was the end—they were going to shoot us. My thoughts were in turmoil. I couldn't believe that I was going to die, that I would never see you again. I was devastated that I would not be able to keep my promise to you. Suddenly I heard machine gun fire all around us, and I grabbed Benjamin and pulled him to the ground. With the Nazis' attention focused on preserving their own lives, we crawled away into some brush. The firefight continued until every single Nazi bastard lay dead.

"It felt like hours, Dina, but it was over in only a matter of minutes, and we were liberated by the American soldiers. It was a miracle, and now I am here. I've found you, and I've kept the promise I made to you so long ago." Lifting my hands to his lips, he kisses them again.

After our picnic we return to the castle, and I introduce Natek to Rosa, Fela, Rachela, and Shlomo. An instant friendship is forged between Natek and Shlomo and the girls. Natek thanks Shlomo for taking such good care of me. Everyone is so happy and eager to leave behind the years of tears and begin anew. Natek remains at Langdenburg, and the month is spent in the pursuit of simple pleasures that have so long been denied us—picnics, swimming, and walks through the countryside. Hungry to catch up on everything we missed, we read newspapers, books, and we watch American movies in the evening and try our best to mimic the English words that are so foreign to our ears.

After being denied baths for six years, I cannot get enough of the magnificent bathtub at Langdenburg. The bathroom alone is as big as our whole home in the ghetto, with a vaulted ceiling, solid gold fixtures, and special racks for warming the towels that hiss as steam circulates through the pipes. Sometimes I lay for an hour languishing up to my ears in hot sudsy water.

That I managed to survive when so many did not is a constant reminder to me of the great responsibility that I now shoulder. I know I must create a life of purpose in the image of the family and community that I was born into. Soaking in the bath is recuperative, and I linger in it until one of the girls pounds on the door, begging me to hurry up so that she, too, can bathe in such splendor.

On June 20, 1945, I celebrate my birthday for the first time since the Glinice Ghetto. I am sixteen. Natek and the other members of our survivor cadre arrange a lovely party for me, and the staff even provides bottles of champagne for a toast and a beautiful cake embellished with my name and age. We are all giddy with hope for the future and embrace the opportunity to proclaim our dedication to life and rebirth. The tears flow as freely as the laughter as we clink our champagne glasses with a toast to the future.

Natek never leaves my side, and his eyes glow with love. "Dina, come with me." He grabs my hand and leads me out to a star-filled night.

We stand on the terrace beneath a smiling arc of a moon. I'm giddy from the champagne and lean against Natek. His arms embrace me in a warm hug. When he kisses me, I'm filled with a rush of emotion.

The kisses end and our hearts beat in syncopation, one against the other. His voice is husky when he asks, "Dina, we are meant to be together. I want to marry you and take care of you."

My face flushes with heat. I love Natek, yet I'm so very young. The last time life was normal for me, I was only ten years old. The years in between were stolen. I know nothing of the world, and I have no idea what my purpose is.

"Natek, you mean the world to me, but I need you to be patient. It is too soon for me to make such an important decision. It wouldn't be fair to you or to me if I rushed into such a commitment. Please give me time."

The past weeks have been a dream, but unfortunately, our idyllic sojourn at Langdenburg comes to an end. The Americans notify us that they will be taking us to Stuttgart, where a displaced persons facility has opened. We are all sad to leave, but we knew this day would come. It is a time for teary farewells as some of my new friends will be going to different places. Many are returning to the cities of their birth and others to DP facilities set up throughout Europe as they continue to search for surviving family and relations.

I have learned that people come and go through your life. Some leave a deep impression on your soul, while others leave a touch as delicate as a butterfly's wing. But everyone I have met along my journey is woven in some infinitesimal way into the tapestry of my life, and even when they have passed through and are gone, they are never forgotten.

It is time for us to move on in our lives and figure out what kind of world we want to build for ourselves and where we want to build it.

CHAPTER 36

IT MUST HAVE BEEN a beautiful city filled with music and art before the allies bombed it into submission. One of the largest cities in Germany, Stuttgart is the capital of Baden-Wurttemberg. Much of it is destroyed, yet it retains its essential character and charm due to the beautiful natural landscape. It lies in a lush valley surrounded by hills, fertile farmland, parks, and lakes, vineyards, and thick woodlands that show little or no effect from the war. Intact neighborhoods dot the landscape, but everywhere you go buildings lay in piles of rubble and ruin in testament to the war.

The DP camp is situated on the outskirts of the city in an area untouched by bombs. The Germans who lived there have been moved out to other areas to accommodate our housing needs. The large complex of buildings is relatively new and is comprised of four brick apartment buildings that are clean and charming with colorful gardens that weave throughout the grounds. The apartments provide comfortable quarters for our living and transition.

Again, the happy sisters Rachela, Rosa, Fela, and I are roommates sharing laughter, secrets, and the normal dreams of youth. Natek is rooming with Shlomo and a couple of other men. Natek's brother, Benjamin, is supposed to arrive at the end of the month and join him.

Each apartment in the complex has its own kitchen, and we are encouraged to cook for ourselves so that we can reclaim the skills of normal, independent life.

Across the street is a restaurant that provides breakfast, lunch, and dinner if we choose not to cook. The food is delicious, and I have gained weight. Six years of starvation have had a profound effect on all of us, and food is a constant craving that we revel in indulging. Eventually, we will normalize and be more cautious with our intake, but for now, we eat as if there is no tomorrow. During the day, we take classes in English and several other languages that are offered to prepare us for emigration to the countries that are opening their doors. We are dedicated to embracing all aspects of freedom, going to movies, having picnics, and taking the trolleys to different destinations throughout the city. One day, a group of us journey to the mountains and visit an alpine spa where the fresh mountain air and nature's beauty fill us with a spirit of renewal.

The ebb and flow of people is constant at the DP facility as we continue to search for family members who may have survived. Every day, Natek and I check the lists posted by the Red Cross, looking for the beloved names of our family members and relatives that might be somewhere among the displaced masses of Europe. Each day I read the lists and find no one. Each day I cry on his shoulder in sorrow. As always, Natek is my tower of strength. His arms surround me protectively as he consoles me.

Each new day brings a new group of survivors seeking relatives, and we crowd around them, anxious to ask them if they have seen any of our relatives or know what happened to them. Occasionally we learn the fate of someone we knew, but more often than not, the reply is, "One day I saw them, and the next day, they disappeared." It has become the most common reply in our midst.

Usually, the truth affords no consolation and generates only a larger mystery, giving rise to the hope that perhaps a dear relative is still out there waiting to be found. Perhaps they are ill or have lost their memory. Even as we hold onto hope, the harsh reality stares in our faces. We find out that millions of Jews were murdered in the death camps by starvation, disease, beatings, firing squads, or the gas chambers. These are the facts of the Nazi genocide of the Jews. We will spend the rest of our lives shedding tears because of it.

My heart is broken for all the losses. I learn the tragic fate of my dear friend Dora Rabbinowicz. Beautiful Dora, whose first words to me at A.V.L. after I returned from the hospital in Radom and learned that my sister and cousin Dina were gone were, "Dinale, don't cry darling, I am going to be your sister." So many memories, so many frozen moments in time. I see her face smiling at me, beckoning me to remember. I can hear her voice as clear as a bell telling me that her older sister fled to Russia when the Germans invaded Poland, and her anguish when she spoke of seeing her father shot in the street by the Nazis.

Dora was my sister's age, a pretty, petite girl with a mane of black curly hair that she would carefully brush into a long braid that touched her small waist. Her large, luminous brown eyes were like magnets inviting you to explore the secrets behind her gaze. The warmth of her personality was attractive to anyone who beheld her, but it was her childlike quality that made men want to protect her. Men fell for Dora, and one in particular tried very hard to ease her burden during our time at A.V.L. Karl Rumuel was a kind, good-looking man, a bit on the heavy side. Like many large men, there was a joviality about him that was very attractive, and he was well-liked by all of the workers. He was one of the Wermacht supervisors at A.V.L., a jolly man with a ready smile who treated us with decency.

Karl fell madly in love with Dora and did everything in his power to help her. He even went so far as to share his own food with her, presenting her with special treats when he could. I remember how upset I was when Dora told me that she was a little in love with Karl, too. I knew that Karl was, like Otto, a good man forced to do the bidding of the Nazis. Nonetheless, he was still a dutiful co-conspirator. I was only thirteen, and I felt Dora was acting like a traitor, and I told her so. She chuckled and told me that one day I would understand the dynamics between men and women, and I would not be so condemning. At the time, however, I was greatly disturbed by her confession of caring for Karl. How could she fall in love with the enemy?

Looking back, I realize that I should not have judged Dora for grabbing a few moments of happiness. She was eighteen and longing to experience life. When A.V.L. closed, Karl was sent to the Russian front, and we were moved to the Szwarlikovska Street Camp. Dora moved into an apartment with another group of young women.

One day as I walked home from the peat bogs, one of the other Wermacht supervisors from A.V.L. called me over to the fence. Nervously I approached. He asked me if I could bring Dora to him, that he had a message from Karl for her. I ran to get her, but she tearfully refused, telling me there was no point in dreaming for a happy ending when we were living a nightmare. I ran back to the fence to convey Dora's message, but the soldier had already left.

A few months later, Dora conquered another heart, a young Jewish man named Motek, who lived in the same building. They fell in love and promised to marry when the war ended.

It is Motek who tells me what happened to his beloved Dora. He searched for her after the war and learned of her fate. After a brutal and bitterly cold winter in Auschwitz, Dora was among hundreds of women who were marched to Danzig on the Baltic Sea. With the Russians about to conquer the city, the Nazis executed a ghastly crime. They forced Dora's group of women into the icy sea. Standing there with rifles trained, they watched until every woman drowned.

I weep on Motek's shoulder at the sadistically cruel fate of my dear friend. "I will never forget Dora," I say to Motek. And we weep together over the tragic fate of such a beautiful soul.

The story of Dora's death has left me depressed. Even Natek is unable to revive my enthusiasm for life. I feel lost with no clear plans for my future. My dreams are restless journeys through the past, peopled by beloved faces of family and friends, all lost to me now. Over and over again, I dream of Dora forced into the sea, and over and over again, I watch her drown. Sometimes I awake gasping for air, as if I, too, am drowning.

Natek proposes to me again. Again, I beg him to be patient, pleading that I am too young and need more time.

Today there is a new sign posted on the message board inquiring if there are children under the age of sixteen who want to go to school, a Major Sperry will meet with anyone interested in front of the building tomorrow at 9 a.m. Suddenly I am flooded with a great yearning. This is what I want to do. To go to school and recapture some of what I missed during those six horrible years. To continue my education and achieve something that would make my parents proud.

When I arrive in the morning, there is a group of teenagers surrounding Major Sperry. I am a little in awe. Major Sperry is a woman. Imagine a woman who is a major in the United States Army. What a wonderful and amazing thing. I wait while the others finish their interviews with Major Sperry and her translator. Finally, it is my turn. I explain briefly to Major Sperry some of what I endured during the war. I tell her that I turned sixteen in June but that I want desperately to go to school. I try to use the few English words that I have picked up from the movies and here at Stuttgart.

She listens attentively, barely interrupting the tale that spills from me in a torrent of emotion. Breathlessly, I wait while the translator relays my words. Then, looking at me with a motherly smile and taking my hands in hers, she says, "Dina, you are going to Aglasterhausen. You are going to school. I want you to pack up your belongings and meet me here tomorrow at 9 a.m. I am going to personally drive you to Aglasterhausen."

I listen to the translator repeat Major Sperry's words in Polish. When she finishes, I am so excited that I throw my arms around her neck, hugging her in gratitude. I am beside myself with joy.

Now I must face the most difficult part of my decision. I dread the moment when I must tell Natek.

It is worse than I thought it would be. Natek is completely dejected and angry when I tell him my plans.

"How can you leave me after all that we have been through?" he asks in an angry voice. "I love you, Dina, and want to take care of you for the rest of our lives. How can you abandon me?"

"Natek, if you love me, you will want the best for me. I need to do this. We have lost six years of our lives. We have forgotten the joy of going to school and learning, of opening our minds and hearts to new ideas."

He stares at me, his eyes reflecting pain and frustration.

I try to make him understand. "Six years we lived only to survive. Who are we, you and me? How can we even know what we want? We need time to heal, to rediscover who we are. How can I be a good wife and mother without any knowledge of the world? I want to have a marriage like my parents did. A marriage of equal partnership. But I cannot have that if I let myself be taken care of without learning to care for myself."

"I know that I love you and that we have survived the fires of hell," Natek says, his eyes full of hurt as he holds my hands. "I know that we promised each other we would live in Palestyne if ever we survived the Nazis. I know that I am willing to face the world and whatever it throws at us as long as I can be with you. But now, I see that everything I thought I knew is wrong. Because you want to leave me."

"Natek, Aglasterhausen is less than an hour by train from Stuttgart. You can visit me as much as you want. It is a school for war orphans who want to continue their education. It is an opportunity to make up for some of the years that were stolen, a chance for normalcy, to study languages, mathematics, science, and literature. I need to do this, Natek. You have to give me this chance to find myself." I fling my arms around him, pressing him to me, my face buried in his chest. "Please, Natek, please do not be angry with me."

Natek sighs deeply, and his arms surround me in a protective embrace. "I cannot be angry with you, at least not for long."

Turning my face up to meet his, my hands cup his face with tenderness. "Thank you, Natek, thank you," I whisper. As always, he kisses me with an urgency that takes my breath away.

With great difficulty, I say goodbye to Rosa, Fela, Rachela, and Shlomo Cooperschmidt, who have all shown me such devotion and friendship. Schlomo has made the decision that he and his sisters will emigrate to Palestyne together.

To get to Palestyne is a dangerous endeavor as the British have enforced a blockade. The Jews in Palestyne are facing a war with the Arabs. The British are allowing only a trickle of refugees entry, in effect barring the entry of thousands of Jews from the homeland they now rightly consider their only haven. I think of my sister's idol, the Zionist poet Jabotinsky. His vision of a Jewish state is now becoming a reality, although the price exacted of millions of dead in the Holocaust was far too dear.

Even after the near annihilation of the entire Jewish population of Europe, the world is still indifferent to the necessity of a Jewish homeland. Clandestinely, through various underground operations, the displaced and surviving Jewry of Europe are smuggled into the Holy Land.

I know that Natek yearns to go, and I still believe that I will go with him. I am thankful that Natek is patient with me of my own yearning to go to school. He is always gentle with me and understands I need more time to heal physically as well from intestinal problems that plague me from my time in the camps.

My leaving of Natek is an outpouring of tears, of promises, said and unsaid. I promise to write every day, and Natek promises to visit soon. He has decided to make the journey with his brother Benjamin back to Radom to see if any of their relatives have survived. He will travel back to Stuttgart by way of Aglasterhausen after Radom. I will miss him terribly. I will miss his strong arms around me, his whispered words of love, and his passionate kisses. I don't know how much longer I can resist his passion or if I even want to. Although I am happy to be going to school, I worry if I am making the right decision for my future.

CHAPTER 37

MAJOR SPERRY GREETS me with a smile at the wheel of an Army Jeep. My English is minimal, and she speaks no other languages, so our communication is mostly conveyed through our eyes and hand movements. The day is bright and hopeful, and Major Sperry keeps up an endless chatter, her smiles filling me with confidence as we make our way through the fertile countryside.

Transportation throughout Europe is intermittent at best. Buses are few and trains sporadic and overcrowded as thousands of people crisscross the borders of Europe, entering and exiting the zones that are now controlled by the different Allied forces. Along the way, we pass a group of hitchhikers, and I am suddenly besieged by panic. Sometimes a face will trigger a memory of a Nazi, and my stomach will seize up in fear. I grab Major Sperry's arm and repeat, "No, No, No!" shaking my finger and head to indicate that she should not stop to pick them up.

She understands me perfectly and reassures me. "No, don't worry, Dina, we are not going to give them a ride. I understand how you feel. Let them walk."

I don't understand exactly what she says, but my fears dissolve as we continue down the road. Relaxing again, I begin to enjoy the scenery and try to use my English. I point at trees, the sky, cows, and barns along the roadside, and Mrs. Sperry responds with the words in English, which I repeat after her. The terrain is a series of hills covered with thick groves of trees that roll in and out of valleys devoted to farmland. Sparkling rivers and streams punctuate the open spaces, their blue-green veins slicing through the landscape. One thing cannot be denied. Germany is breathtakingly beautiful. Like a fairy tale kingdom, the vast countryside butts up against ancient forests and castle-crested mountains.

After a couple of hours of driving at a leisurely pace, the view opens into a meadow surrounded by open farmland with cows contentedly grazing. In the meadow I see stately, four-story stucco buildings crowned with steep, red-tiled roofs. The complex lies at the edge of a knoll surrounded by verdant pastures. Tall birch trees line the property that is bordered by a stream, a large vegetable garden, and an expansive soccer field. We are greeted by the warbling of birds and the babbling of water cascading over rocks and pebbles in the stream. It is breathtaking to behold this pastoral setting, and I whisper a prayer of thanks to God for leading me here.

Aglasterhausen International Children's Center is maintained by the United Nations Relief and Rehabilitation Administration, UNRRA. Before the war, in a previous incarnation, it had served as a home for mentally challenged children. When the Third Reich became all-powerful, they murdered all the children at Aglasterhausen with lethal injections to enforce their ideology of Aryan superiority and perfection. How distinct the differences between the Nazi murderers that extinguished the lives of innocent children at Aglasterhausen and the good people who only wish to rehabilitate children here.

Located near a small town called Neunkirchen, about 100 kilometers from Heidelberg, one of Germany's most beautiful cities, Aglasterhausen is the perfect facility for recuperating and teaching the rescued children of Europe. We number at any given time approximately two hundred, ranging from babies to eighteen-year-olds. The children of Aglasterhausen are a smorgasbord of nationalities, ethnic origins, and religions. There are Polish, French, Hungarian, German, Estonian, Lithuanian, Romanian, and Russian children. The school is administered by a tall statuesque woman named Rachael Greene, a social worker who demands propriety and respectfulness from us, but she exudes compassion and kindness.

My room is on the top floor with a window that faces a pasture where cows lazily graze on plush grass. That little niche under that window becomes one of my favorite places to relax, read, and daydream of the future. I cannot help but remember the window in my bedroom on Koszarowa Ulica, the street where I lived with my family. And how I loved to watch the bustle of daily life. Here I watch the serenity of nature.

The room holds two beds, two nightstands with lamps, a roll-top desk, and a swivel chair. The walls are papered in a beautiful blue toile depicting the French countryside, which mirrors the views from the windows. The room even has an attached private bathroom with a large freestanding tub with claw feet.

I am thrilled to meet my only roommate, Haneczka Handelsman, who was originally from a small town outside of Radom. Haneczka, a tiny girl with green eyes and rich brown hair, is the only survivor from her family. We become instant friends. She also has a boyfriend at the Stuttgart DP Camp named Rakocz. Haneczka and I immediately begin to plan the fun we will have when Rakocz and Natek come to visit.

Our day begins at 7:30 a.m. for breakfast in a huge dining hall where we naturally congregate with people from our birth countries. Our English is minimal, and we mainly speak our native tongues when we aren't in class. Our table is next to a table of Estonians. The Estonian boys are terribly handsome, and we can't help but flirt with them. After breakfast, our rigorous classes begin at 9 a.m. and continue until 1 p.m., when it is time for lunch.

Our studies include world history, geography, English, and mathematics, our native languages, in my case, Polish and Hebrew. Even Yiddish is offered for the Jewish children. The curriculum includes religious classes from Catholicism to Judaism. After lunch, we play sports outside or simply walk among the tall birch trees and gravel paths. At Aglasterhausen, the walls literally breathe with life as children's laughter echoes through the halls. It is a far cry from the putrid death wall that surrounded us at Bergen-Belsen. Except for the boisterous sounds of youth, it is peaceful here, the opposite of everything that we have suffered.

THE CLOUDS LIE heavy in the gray sky as I stare out the window, watching and listening to the rain. Winter is approaching, and the trees have changed from the greens of summer to the bright orange, reds, and golds of fall. The colorful leaves display their beauty to the world before autumn winds tear them from the branches, and they are no more. As I look at the swirling leaves, I can see that those of us who survived share a close affiliation to the natural world. We who cheated death now dress ourselves in the splendor of life. We dance before the wind without fear. The war devoured our formative years and then spit us out bare without roots, yet we fight to live again and plant ourselves firmly among the living. We have suppressed who we are for so long, living in the shadow of evil and death. Now, we seek out the light so that we might flourish again.

One morning I overhear one of our teachers, Jadzia, make a derogatory remark about the Jews. She says that Jewish greed brought about the war. I am so angry, hurt, and shocked at her words that I seek out Mrs. Greene to report the incident. Mrs. Greene's face turns crimson, and her eyes reflect my own anger. Mrs. Greene is not a Jew, but she has seen the effects of bigotry. After hearing her apologize and promise to investigate, I leave her office and return to my studies. Several hours later, she summons me to her office. I expect to hear that Jadzia has been fired and told to pack her bags. Without judgment, Mrs. Greene tells me Jadzia's story and asks me to decide her fate. She has placed Jadzia's destiny within my hands, but first, I must hear her story.

Jadzia is a Jew! She spent the entire war pretending to be a Catholic hidden with a family in Poland. So ingrained is this deception that her true identity was lost, even to herself. All around her, the anti-Semitic words of the Church, her Polish neighbors, and the Nazis penetrated her psyche, and she became one of them, a Jew-hater, and in so doing, a self-hater. Even after the war, the habits of six years are not easily abandoned. She has continued the lie, afraid to be a Jew, afraid to claim her history. On her knees, sobbing, she pleads with Mrs. Greene not to send her away.

My anger dissipates when Mrs. Greene tells me of Jadzia's ordeal. Who am I to condemn the poor girl? We are all damaged in different ways. Feeling only pity, I simply demand her apology and that she admit to everyone that she is a Jew. Mrs. Greene tells Jadzia that if she ever speaks ill of the Jews or anyone else again, she will be sent away without another word.

"You will do well to remember, Jadzia, that Aglasterhausen is a place of healing for children who bear the ugly scars of hatred. I will not allow you or anyone else to deepen the scars that they already bear."

Jadzia comes to me, her eyes swollen red. She begs my forgiveness and apologizes. Feeling her sincere shame and contrition, I forgive her. "Jadzia, you must come to terms with who you are. You, of all people, know what it means to be hated. I have lost enough to this hatred. I refuse to lose any more."

~

IT IS CHRISTMAS, and everyone has thrown themselves into the holiday season. A group of boys go on an expedition to the woods and return, dragging a tall evergreen tree with them. After much ado, we finally heave it into the assembly hall, where everyone helps to decorate it with ribbons and bulbs of silver and gold. The younger children string popcorn to drape around the tree while the older girls help in the kitchen preparing a feast of traditional Christmas and Chanukah fare. The cook is stuffing geese with spices, dried berries, and bread. Haneczka and I, along with a group of girlfriends, fry hundreds of latkes as part of the feast.

Natek and Rakocz are coming today and will stay for the weekend to enjoy our Christmas dinner and party. I knitted Natek a blue sweater to match his eyes, and I can't wait to see his face when he opens his gift. Everyone is so excited to celebrate our first holiday since the end of the war. Tonight we will light the first candle of the menorah and sing Chanukah songs and Christmas carols.

Natek has been very patient with me, but I know that once winter has passed, he will insist that we arrange to go to Palestyne. Major Sperry is encouraging me toward a different path. She says the United States will soon open its doors to many of the survivors of Europe.

"You have seen enough war for one lifetime, Dina," she says in a gentle voice. "In America, you would be able to continue your studies." Major Sperry insists that the opportunity of going to the United States is a great one. Soon I will have to make a decision that will change the course of my life forever.

I know that Major Sperry has grown to love me like the daughter she never had. I know she only wants the best for me, and her arguments are sound. She has shared with me the story of her own life. She was married to an attorney and was very much in love. After several years of trying, she finally became pregnant. Sometime during her pregnancy, she and her husband had a terrible fight, and he hit her. The tragic result was a miscarriage. She divorced her husband and enlisted in the U.S. Army. A trained social worker, through the United Nations, the army assigned her to Aglasterhausen to rehabilitate and resettle the orphaned children of Europe. She is devoted to the children of Aglasterhausen. They are her children.

"What about Natek?" I ask her. "Can he come to the United States, too?"

"I don't know," she answers. "He must apply for asylum. Certainly, with time, he will be admitted."

The more I think of it, the more I realize that Natek would never go to the United States. He is determined to play a role in the birth of a Jewish state. I am torn as to what I should do. On the one hand, the thought of fulfilling my sister's dream of going to Palestyne burns like a fire in my soul, but is it my dream? The contemplation of fighting a war immobilizes me. I want to live in peace, go to school, and one day get married and have children. I don't have the stomach to spend the rest of my life surrounded by hatred and fighting a war. I love Natek in every way imaginable. When he touches me, all I can do is surrender to his passion and meet it with the force of my own.

But what if there is too much shared misery between us to build a successful life? In the privacy of our room, Haneczka and I discuss our dilemma until we are blue in the face. She also wants more than anything to emigrate to the United States. She and Rakocz are madly in love with each other, but all of her arguments with Rakocz are over this one issue of Palestyne versus the United States. Rakocz, like Natek, is determined to make any sacrifice to build a new country out of the desert and swamp that is Palestyne. "That is where we belong," he argues. "We can trust no other country to our safety and future."

So it goes, around and around, as we argue the merits of Palestyne or America, and which is best for us. At least for the weekend, there will be peace.

When Natek arrives, I fly into his arms, and he lifts me in the air, his eyes never leaving my face. "Natek, I am so happy to see you!"

"Dina, you look so pretty."

As always, Natek's compliments cause me to blush. "I don't know how. I think I cooked a thousand *latkas* today." I take his hand, pulling him behind me. "Natek, I have something for you." His eyes light up with the old glimmer of mischievousness that I remember so well from our days at A.V.L.

"What is it?" he asks, his face filled with pleasure.

The menorah stands on the upright piano surrounded by gifts

wrapped in cloth. I pick one up and hand it to him. "I hope you like it. I can't wait a moment longer to give it to you."

We sit on the piano bench as he carefully removes the sweater from the wrappings. "You made this for me?" he asks incredulously.

"Yes, of course I did. Look, see the blue matches the color of your eyes perfectly. Do you like it?"

"I love it!" He throws his arms around me, hugging and kissing me.

I beam with pride, knowing that our weekend has started off on a wonderful note.

Outside, the snow is drifting down in a shower of crystal flakes veiling the countryside in a virginal gown of white. Mrs. Greene has arranged for a villager to take us for sleigh rides. Natek, Rakocz, Haneczka, and I bundle up and squeeze into the sleigh, covering our legs with a thick red blanket. The driver takes off at a brisk clip, and the air is filled with the music of sleigh bells. Our words and laughter float in the wintery air. We ride through pastures where the cows barely lift their heads to acknowledge our passage. The low winter sun does its best to pierce the gauze-like clouds but barely manages a golden shimmering film that washes the sky in splendor. From a distance, we must appear like a holiday card, young and happy, without a care in the world flying through billowy clouds of snow.

Our faces flushed with color from the invigorating sleigh ride, we return to the festivities in the dining room. Everyone gathers around as we light the menorah and sing the traditional Chanukah song *Maoz Tzur* for the first time since the war. We sing the song in Hebrew the traditional way, and then one of the American soldiers sings it in English.

> *Rock of Ages let our song praise Thy saving power.*
> *Thou, amidst the raging foes, wast our sheltering tower.*
> *Furious they assailed us, but Thine arm availed us,*
> *And Thy Word broke their sword*
> *When our own strength failed us.*
> *Children of the martyr race, whether free or fettered,*
> *Wake the echoes of the songs where ye may be scattered.*

Yours the message cheering that the time is nearing
Which will see All men free, tyrants disappearing.

The words could not be more profound, and there is not a dry eye in the room when he finishes.

The adults have brought out a record player and soon the room is full of Christmas music. Everyone begins to dance, and our jovial laughter returns. Paul Hodys, a wonderful dancer, asks me to dance, and we spin around the room as Natek watches, his face alight with a glimmer of a smile. Major Sperry and Mrs. Greene are both dressed in red and are chatting and sipping glasses of holiday punch.

I have noticed that Aglasterhausen is proving to be a fertile ground for love. Mrs. Greene has an admirer, a Jewish survivor named Samuel, a man in his thirties, a few years younger than her. Whenever he is near, her face takes on the radiance of a young girl. I think they are both very cautiously tiptoeing toward courtship. But I sense their attraction is powerful, and I suspect that soon they will be running toward each other with open arms. Our nurse, Marjorie, a beautiful Mulatto woman with skin the color of amber honey is also testing the waters of love. John, our school driver, seems to be in constant attendance. They are both wonderful dancers and teach us the swing, which is a popular new dance in America. Most of us are inept on the dance floor, but we are willing to make fools of ourselves as we twirl around and around, emulating Marjorie and John.

I am happy to see that Major Sperry has found a dance partner as well, a nice-looking man dressed in an American army uniform who is another social worker. Major Sperry, it turns out, is quite a good dancer herself, surprising us all. The few military men in attendance at our party lose themselves in the spirit of the holidays, dancing with every girl in the room. Everyone is having such a good time. The world is at peace and is beginning to heal from the conflagration that almost consumed it. Cities and countries are being rebuilt, and hope illuminates the horizon. Tonight we toast the future that shines brightly. Tonight all things are possible.

Everything is perfect, and somehow the staff manages to procure a small gift for everyone. I receive a bottle of cologne. I have no possessions except for the clothing that is donated from charities around the world. The cologne is like a gift of precious jewels, and I sparingly touch my pulse points with the floral scent, raising my wrist to Natek for his approval. He inhales the fragrance and showers me with hungry kisses up and down my neck as I squeal with laughter.

Natek and Rakocz visit us again to celebrate the New Year with Haneczka and me. We manage to stay up half the night dancing to music. At midnight, we toast the end of 1945, a year that began in terror and death, has ended in liberation and rebirth. We join the world in toasting the victory of good over evil. At breakfast, the festivities continue as we learn that John has asked Marjorie to marry him, and she has accepted. Now we have a wedding to look forward to in March right here at Aglasterhausen.

NATEK ANNOUNCES that he and his brother, Benjamin, will depart for Palestyne. Haneczka and Rakocz are going with them. Haneczka has lost her battle with Rakocz, and all her dreams of the United States are set aside. Rakocz is firm, and her deep love and devotion to him has decided their future. Only I have not committed myself to Palestyne. Major Sperry, aware of my trepidation, presses me to wait and see if the U.S. opens its doors. She predicts that it will be very soon and that I could be one of the first to be granted emigration status.

A representative of the new Jewish government in Palestyne has come to Aglasterhausen to encourage emigration. I speak with him, and he asks me why I don't want to go to Palestyne. I explain to him that I want to go, but I don't think that I am physically able to endure another war. He completely understands and assures me that whenever the Jewish state is born, I will always be welcome as a citizen.

Unbelievably, the next country that sends a representative encouraging emigration is Poland. The gentleman asks me if I would like to go back to Poland, and without hesitation, I respond, "NEVER!"

I tell him that for five generations, my family lived in Poland and that they gave everything to Poland. All they asked in return was to live in peace as good citizens. The Poles have always been consumed with anti-Semitism, and their true colors were proudly displayed during the war.

"Not all," I remind him, "but the majority of Polish citizenry couldn't have cared less what the Nazis did to the Jews. I have seen the worst of Poland and, for me, the last of Poland. Why would I want to go back and give myself to a country that hates me and my kind?"

His answer is silence. He cannot deny the truth.

Representatives come from Sweden, Switzerland, France, and England to offer asylum as well, but I can't bear the thought of living anywhere in Europe. Europe is a graveyard covered with the ashes of murdered Jews.

After long consideration, I finally make my decision.

I will go to America.

As much as I love Natek, I know that I am not ready to marry. I am too young, and the dream of going to America is too tantalizing. Saying goodbye to Natek is one of the most painful moments of my life.

"Dina, you know that if you change your mind, I will be waiting for you."

"Natek, this street runs both ways. You could make an application and join me in the United States. We could both go to school and with time, who knows? At least we will have the time to find ourselves."

Stubbornly, he resists. "No, I wish for only one place to call home, one place where my children will be born."

Taking Natek's hands in mine, I try my best to smile through my tears. "You know I will always love you, Natek. I never could have lived through the war without your strength urging me on to fight. Even in my darkest hours, it was your smile that sustained me. I lived knowing you had commanded me to, that we had promised each other. I will never know a truer friend."

His eyes are full of tears as well. "I, too, lived by keeping your face before me. There were many times when the only thing pulling me through to live another day was knowing that I must find you. It was a promise I knew I had to keep."

Wrapping my arms around him, my tears flow in a steady stream as I whisper in his ear. "Thank you, Natek. Please forgive me?"

His eyes crinkle in the smile that I will always cherish, and he repeats the words that he has so often said to me, "Dinale, you know that I could never stay mad at you."

CHAPTER 38

NATEK IS GONE, and Haneczka and Rakocz have departed with him. Those first few days are filled with regret and uncertainty. Have I made the right decision? I have stepped off a cliff into the unknown. Only time will tell if I shall land safely. At least I know that I have time to find out who I am.

Time, such a bitter foe during the war, has become my friend. School fills my days and reading fills my nights. My English is improving, and Major Sperry spends a good deal of time encouraging me and correcting my sentences. She promises that in the next couple of months, the United States will open its gates and welcome us to the *"Land of the Free and the Home of the Brave."*

Winter's cloak of snow is giving way to spring, and a sea of corn-flowers and field poppies blanket the meadows in vibrant color. The wedding of Marjorie and John is upon us, and everyone at Aglaster-hausen is busy preparing for the event.

The wedding day dawns with a light drizzle of rain that washes the air clean like a new beginning. A multicolored rainbow sweeps the sky as it pierces through large puffy cumulus clouds. The sun promises to warm the earth enough to keep the ceremony outside. An Army chaplain has arrived to officiate, and Marjorie's brother, a tall, handsome man, has flown in to represent her family and give the bride away. We all assemble on the lawn to the beautiful sounds of flute, guitar, and cello playing music by Wagner, Vivaldi, and Bach. Marjorie is a vision dressed in a white brocade suit with a pencil-thin skirt that accents her narrow waist. Her jacket has a low-cut bodice, and she wears a string of pearls against her amber skin.

John and Marjorie have written their pledges of faith to one another, and their words inspire a rush of tears from everyone. Finally, the chaplain announces, "You may kiss the bride!"

An enormous hoopla breaks out among the men in uniform. We all rush to congratulate the bride and groom, whose faces glow with happiness. The dining hall has been draped in white with splashes of pink roses that scent the air with the perfume of an indoor garden. The party swings into motion as John and Marjorie lead the charge to the dance floor. We dance with abandon, our hearts keeping rhythm to the beat of the music, and our faces gleam from exertion. We drink champagne to a myriad of toasts to the couple who teeter against each other, intoxicated with joy. Weddings are new beginnings, and we all feel our own lives touched with the magic of the moment. John and Marjorie depart amid a shower of rice and the rattling of tin cans that are tied to the jeep that will take them to Heidelberg for a honeymoon weekend.

I cannot help but think of Natek and wish that he was here to share this special day with me. Today all things seem possible, and I hope that one day I will convince Natek to follow me to America.

THE SPRING DAYS blossom one into another. I sit under a large birch tree, enunciating my English aloud as I listen to a spotted woodpecker busily tapping out a love letter to a future mate on a tree. I look up and see Major Sperry walking toward me.

"Dina, do you know what today is?" she asks me with a beaming smile.

"April 15."

"Yes, and today the United States approved your emigration status, and you are going on the first ship of emigrants to America! You sail May 11. It has all been arranged. We have been told that the president of the United States, Harry Truman, plans on meeting your ship when it arrives in New York Harbor."

"I can't believe it!" I am so excited that I throw myself into her arms. "Thank you, thank you, Major Sperry!"

"Dina, I know you are worried, but believe me, your life is going to change for the best. New doors will open for you. America is the greatest country in the world, and you will find happiness there."

"I am very grateful to you, Major Sperry, for all that you have done for me." I press my lips to her cheek and feel her wet tears. This dear woman loves me and has mentored me, and now she is going to have to say goodbye to me in a few weeks. "Will I see you again?"

"Of course, you will. I'll be back in New York when my work here is done. You will write me and let me know where you are."

"It is like a dream," I say with a deep sigh.

"Yes, and the dream is about to come true. I have to get back to my desk, but I will see you at dinner." Hugging me one last time, she leaves me to ponder my future.

For all of my words to the contrary, now that the moment has actually arrived, leaving the continent of my birth fills me with apprehension. My entire family lies buried in ashes in the scarred foundation of Europe. Will they hear my prayers from a world away? Can I adapt to a new homeland and find acceptance? Or will I stick out like a weed in a rose garden, my foreignness isolating me from everyone around me? It is unlikely that the familiar traditions of the Old World will serve me in the modernity of America. With no family to protect me or guide me, I will have to rely on myself. The prospect both excites me and scares me. I have lived through and seen more than enough horror for any lifetime, and those six years of my childhood will never be recovered no matter how hard I try.

I spend the next ten days leading up to my departure on a pendulum swinging from ecstasy to misery. The nights pass restlessly as I toss and turn in my sleep, lost in dreams that play like newsreels.

In these dreams, I find myself running through Radom, searching for my mother, father, sister, or brother. Sometimes I catch sight of one of them, but when I am about to reach them, they vanish. Continuing to run, I suddenly turn a corner and find myself running through the gates of Auschwitz, unable to stop. Before me towers the chimney spewing out the ashes of Jews in a blast of smoke. Then the scene changes and Auschwitz transforms into Bergen-Belsen, and I am running beside the wall of bodies. The dead come to life and stretch out their hands to grab hold of me.

Over and over, night after night, I wake up drenched in sweat and shaking with fear. Then one night, my grandfather comes to me in my dream and stands before me. His presence shimmers before me exactly as it did that night so many years ago when I sent him away. This time I reach out to him in my dream. Although I cannot feel him, when I touch him, he smiles reassuringly. I feel his love wash over me, his eyes filling with sadness. I hear his voice in my head telling me that I will be fine and not to be afraid.

"Live Dinale," he says. "Live and know that your family is watching over you. We are with you always. Wherever you are, wherever you go. Sleep *maidele,* you have a long life ahead of you. You have nothing to fear. One day we will all be reunited."

When I wake the next morning, I am filled with a sense of peace and new hope. Remembering my dream, I am filled with courage. I know that my grandfather and the rest of my family are with me. I know that I will never be alone.

The day of our departure arrives. John, along with three other drivers, will be taking us to Bremerhaven to the USS Marine Flasher, which will sail her cargo of emigrants to the hallowed shores of America. Sixty students from Aglasterhausen are sailing, as are many of the teachers. Our dorm parents and teachers, Fred and Franka Fragner, concentration camp survivors from Czechoslovakia, will be our chaperones, continuing their dedication to the orphaned children they call "our children."

The buses are lined up to leave, our small cache of belongings stowed in the storage racks on top. Tearfully, we bid our goodbyes to those who will remain. Soon Aglasterhausen will be filled with the voices of a whole new group of children. In fact, Aglasterhausen, under the astute guidance of Rachel Greene, will remain open until February of 1948, rehabilitating the lives of orphans who lost everything during the Nazi era. Rachael Greene, Major Sperry, and Marjorie are outside, along with the rest of the staff that will remain, to wish us *Bon voyage*.

With my heart pounding, I bid a tearful farewell to these women who have showered me with love and affection. In some ways, I feel that I am losing my family again, and I am overwhelmed with emotion. The death and losses from the cataclysmic war trail like a shadow, impossible to lose. It is like walking in and out of sunshine. Sometimes the sun dispels the gloom with its bright rays of happiness until the cold, shadowy grasp of memory plunges me back into darkness and sorrow. Aglasterhausen has been transformational. It has cast light on the dark recesses of my soul.

We sail from Bremerhaven into the North Sea with a crisp breeze at our stern pushing us forward with a thrust. *Don't look back,* the wind whispers. *Look forward to the future.* We are over eight hundred refugees from every corner of Europe, and most of us stand on deck as the shoreline gradually shrinks from view. Our eyes remain fixed on the shoreline that recedes until we are surrounded by only the deep blue of the sea. Overhead, the sea birds that command the skies dive into the water, emerging with silvery fish. The Marine Flasher is a naval troop carrier, and this is her first mission moving a civilian population.

I feel Major Sperry's influence when I enter my assigned cabin, which is on the top deck next to the captain's quarters. Most of the passengers are crammed four or more to a room, but somehow Major Sperry has arranged for me to share a cabin with an older woman, Mrs. Feinberg, who is coming to America to join her son. It is just like her to provide me with a surrogate mother. Seas of calm prevail, and we spend our days parading the decks and inhaling the clean salty air. I have two girlfriends from Aglasterhausen on the ship, Hanna Starkman and Hankah Sajkiewicz. Both girls are from Poland, and we have become very good friends. Most of the day, we spend sunning on the decks and flirting with young men.

I suppose that if we had inclement weather and rougher seas, our journey might have taken on another meaning. Seasickness would have fostered our worst fears. Instead, we sail under idyllic conditions, balmy sunshine, and clear black evening skies that glitter with millions of stars. The expansive horizon that appears one with the sea gives buoyancy to our dreams as we inhale the sweet perfume of freedom like an aromatic balm to soothe our broken souls.

During the day, we attend a class where they teach us to sing American patriotic songs. We learn "The Battle Hymn of the Republic," "The Star-Spangled Banner," and "America, My Country 'Tis of Thee," all of which we will sing on our arrival when we cruise into the mighty harbor of New York. In the evenings, we are entertained by the crew, who double as performers showcasing song and dance numbers.

We also watch many American movies. My favorite film on the voyage is "A Tree Grows in Brooklyn." It is the story of a teenager, named Francie Nolan, and her family. They live in Brooklyn, New York, which I think is very close to where we will be living in the Bronx. In the film, the Nolan family struggles against poverty to make a better life, but the father is an alcoholic and can't keep a job, which condemns the family to an endless cycle of disasters. He dies in the end, forcing Francie to quit school in order to help support the family. Francie never loses her faith or determination and, in the end, falls in love with a wonderful man, Ben. The film is an anthem to hope and a better life, and we all come away from the movie inspired. After all, if Francie can find happiness, so might we. Nothing can dampen our spirits as we sail into the future.

Our passage across the Atlantic seems to fly by, and the night before our arrival, the captain gives a wonderful speech wishing us success in our new lives in America. He announces that we will be arriving in the morning and encourages us to get a good night's sleep so that we can all be topside when we arrive. That evening we are so excited that I don't think any of us sleep a wink.

I am on deck just as the sun begins to rise out of the sea, a dazzling orb of gold that lights the eastern horizon like a candle in the dark. I hold tightly to Hannah and Hanka's hands as we look out over the water. Everyone is on deck, squinting into the distance, trying to make out the outline of the land of our dreams. Slowly, we approach the harbor, which, even at this early hour, is a whirlwind of activity. Ferryboats and tugboats stream in and out of the sea lanes as they move about the many ships that ease their way through the lower bay. We enter the upper bay, and the captain blows the ship's foghorn with its deep, resonant sound while overhead hundreds of seagulls fly, squawking a welcome.

And then we see her. The Statue of Liberty. Eight hundred voices rise in shouts of awe. "Liberty! Liberty! Liberty!" we chant. She glows in the morning sun, her coppery green robes seeming to move in the breeze as her footsteps go forward to the future. To every immigrant who has ever come to these shores, she represents the dream of freedom and democracy. Regally crowned, she towers above the bay with her arm held proudly, bearing a golden torch, the light of freedom known the world over. Behind her stands the greatest city we have ever seen, with its outline of pinnacled skyscrapers spiraling toward the sky.

We, the survivors of the worst genocide in the history of the modern world, have arrived to begin a new life of peace and prosperity in this Promised Land like so many immigrants before us. Without America, the war would have been lost, and Hitler would have fulfilled his horrific goal of annihilating every single Jew in Europe.

Tears stream down my face as I remember the last Passover I celebrated with my family in Radom. I can hear my brother, his young voice asking my father how God would save us without a Moses. My father hesitates for a moment, stumped by the probing mind of his son. Then with the confidence of one who knows that evil cannot triumph, my father confidently pronounced that God would send us a great army to save us.

Little did he know how prescient his words would be. Not only did God send us a great army, but he also sent a great nation to offer his daughter asylum and a new home.

Silence descends on the ship as we anchor in front of the Statue of Liberty. Each of us has traveled through so much to reach these shores. Our emotional and physical scars, still raw and painful, are forgotten in this moment of happiness. A hush falls over us when over the loudspeakers, a voice breaks the silence. Reciting the poem that Emma Lazarus, a Jewish girl, wrote long ago:

Not like the brazen giant of Greek fame,
With conquering limbs astride from land to land;
Here at our sea-washed, sunset gates shall stand
A mighty woman with a torch, whose flame
Is the imprisoned lightning, and her name
Mother of Exiles. From her beacon-hand
Glows world-wide welcome; her mild eyes command
The air-bridged harbor that twin cities frame.
"Keep, ancient lands, your storied pomp!" cries she
With silent lips.
"Give me your tired, your poor,
Your huddled masses yearning to breathe free,
The wretched refuse of your teeming shore.
Send these, the homeless, tempest-tost to me,
I lift my lamp beside the golden door!"

I am not sure that we understand every word of that poem as we prepare to enter the gates of Ellis Island and our new lives. But it does not matter. The emotional impact is clear to all of us as we cheer and wipe away our tears.

I know that I have made the right choice for myself in coming here to this beautiful land. America stands before me, the antithesis of all that I have lived through. I already cherish her, and from this moment forward, I will love her and be loyal to her until the day that I die.

I gaze up at the goddess of freedom towering before me with wonder and amazement. Taking a deep breath, I inhale the promise of a bright and beckoning future.

I am home.

DINA

EIGHTY YEARS HAVE PASSED since the end of my childhood and the beginning of World War II. In 1939, I was only ten years old when the Germans invaded Poland, my homeland. The destruction of community and family that followed flung me into adulthood, into a world I was not ready for. But who could ever be ready to endure such evil?

In the dark years that followed, I ached for my family, lost to me. So many times, I was on the verge of falling into a dark abyss and yet, I survived. I was lucky. My loved ones—their faces and voices —followed me, offering up advice and counsel, as I paddled through the turbulent sea of war. At times, their ghosts danced capriciously through my dreams, at other times they appeared before me as real and alive as the last day I saw them. My lost childhood became to me, like the story of "Brigadoon," the mythical community of book and song that reappears every hundred years for one shiny, bright, inexplicable moment.

The happy world of my youth disappeared into the mists of time.

The vanished world of Radom, Poland, lives on, only in my memories. Oh, what a joyous community—the bustling markets and shops where we chatted and laughed with neighbors and friends; the schools where we nurtured our minds; the synagogues where we nurtured our souls; the holidays, mitzvahs, weddings, and other important moments that we celebrated; and of course, the devotion of the Sabbath…. My community continues to live in my memory and most of all in my heart.

I have tried to put the horrors of war behind me for the sake of my children, grandchildren, and my own sanity—but like the tattoo I bear —those memories are also burned into me. They exist side-by-side with the happy memories of my early childhood.

So many fine books have been written and will continue to be written with endless revelations as to why or how such a nightmare could have occurred, but in the end, the only lesson learned is that it happened. The Holocaust happened, and millions perished from deliberate, and systematic slaughter. More than six million Jews were wiped out during the holocaust. Six million lives annihilated. Six million dreams never to be fulfilled. Six million futures never to be realized.

The apocalypse has long since passed, and the years have flown by like clouds in a windswept sky. With each passing year, we survivors, we memory keepers, will also become a memory. I am one of those still here, who remember the sojourn of those who cannot. And as such, I will continue to bear the torch of light. And bear witness to the truth. The words have been written of those who lived so that you may know them as I did… As I do.

Dina Frydman Balbien

Dear Reader:

Thank you for reading *The Last Daughter*. If you would like to leave a review, please visit the online book site where you purchased the book.

If you have any questions regarding *The Last Daughter* or my mother Dina, you can reach me at belle@belleamiauthor.com.

If you would like updates on *The Last Daughter* and my mother, Dina, please sign up for my newsletter at belleamiauthor.com.

Sincerely,
Belle Ami

AUTHOR'S NOTE

The journey through my mother's Holocaust experience has taken more than 80 years, a lifetime. The writing of this novel took two years. From my earliest childhood, my mother shared her stories with me. I was a truly inquisitive child who probed ever deeper into the world of darkness of my mother's teenage years between 1939-1945. Unable to comprehend how such horrors could have happened, I asked my mother time and again to tell me about her childhood, her family, and her life during the war.

My mother's story became seared in my own memory and those of my sister and brothers. Just as my mother could never forget, neither will I. Although reliving those years is still as painful as a new wound, I felt an urgency to share my mother's story. At the end of the war, my mother was one of the youngest survivors of the Holocaust. And with each passing year, the number of survivors dwindles.

The survivors carry the weight of what they lived through. They are witnesses to the worst genocide in our history, and eventually, they will pass on to the great beyond to join the souls of those who perished in the war. While Holocaust deniers spew forth their venom as they try to alter the historical record, the personal accounts from the flesh and blood survivors stand firm in the face of evil.

After the war, through the ensuing years, the fates of some of the people written about in this novel have been learned. I changed the names where necessary to protect their privacy, but the events have been unaltered and are as true now as the day they occurred.

Mrs. Felzenszwalbe, my mother's teacher in Radom, lived in a primarily Christian neighborhood. After the invasion of Germany and after the Jews had been resettled into the two ghettos, my mother ran into Mrs. Felzenszwalbe in a pharmacy on one of her illegal excursions out of the ghetto. There, for a few brief moments, they reunited and conversed. My mother learned that Mrs. Felzenszawalbe and her daughter had not been forced to move into the ghettos. A German officer had commandeered their home, and the two women were allowed to remain, cooking and cleaning for the officer. He must have known they were Jewish, but he chose to look the other way, pretending they were not. As far as is known, both mother and daughter survived the war.

Dina's maternal family in Brzeziny, except for her elderly blind grandfather, were all resettled in the Lodz ghetto and perished in Auschwitz. The Nazis declined to murder or resettle her fragile blind grandfather, a saintly old man who was revered by his Polish neighbors. Taking everyone else, they left him in the care of these same Polish neighbors, who pleaded for his welfare and purportedly cared for him until his death of natural causes sometime shortly after his family was taken to Auschwitz.

Dina's girlfriend, Lola Freidenreich, who escaped from A.V.L. with her brother Yaacov (Yannick), assumed a false identity as a Christian in Warsaw. She joined her sister, who had previously assumed a Christian alias. The sisters worked for a wealthy Polish family as live-in maids until one evening, Lola overheard her employers in a conversation. The mistress of the house suggested to her husband that she suspected the sisters of being Jews.

In fear that they would be denounced, the two sisters fled the home in the middle of the night. Their brother Yaacov worked as a construction laborer. The three siblings paid a Christian family to hide their mother and the husband of Lola's sister. They would visit them regularly in brief, happy moments. One day when Yaacov was visiting his mother, the SS surrounded the building and forced everyone out. All of the Polish residents, Lola's brother Yaacov, her mother, and brother-in-law were forced into the street where the Nazis (having probably been tipped off that Jews were hiding in the building) proceeded to execute everyone. Lola's brother Yaacov, her brother-in-law, and mother were all murdered on that day. The sisters, although devastated by their loss, continued to work in Warsaw as Christians until Warsaw's liberation by the Russians. After the war, the sisters emigrated to the United States. Lola married another survivor who had also lived as a Polish Christian during the war. They had one daughter and moved to California, where Lola made a good life for herself.

Hannah, Dina's young friend from Pionki, who disappeared in Auschwitz, survived the war and emigrated to the United States and lives on the East Coast.

Esterka Litwak, the beautiful Jewish girl who captivated *Unterscharfuhrer* Taube, survived the war and was liberated at Bergen-Belsen. I have searched the archives for information regarding the fate of *Unterscharfuhrer* Taube (commander at Hindenburg), but his fate is unknown. He was never captured or tried. However, this was not the case for *Hauptsturmfuhrer* Josef Kramer, commandant of Bergen-Belsen, who was tried and hanged on December 13, 1945.

Dina's dear girlfriend Lucia married her boyfriend Szymek and emigrated to the United States. They settled in Philadelphia and had two daughters. Dina and Lucia stayed in touch until Lucia's passing.

Dina's cousin, Nadja, who went to Sweden after the war, ended up emigrating to the United States, where she married another survivor named Morris, who was from Lodz. They had three children, Theodore, Larry, Sharon, and eight grandchildren. Dina and Nadja remained close until Nadja's death.

Dina's cousin Majer also emigrated to the United States, where he met and married Helen, who spent the war hidden as a Christian on a farm. Helen and Majer have two children, Abe and Mindy. Majer, who became known as Mike, passed a few years ago.

Dina, Majer, and Nadja were the only survivors of their immediate and extended families.

Hanezka Handelsman (Dina's roommate at Aglasterhausen) and Rakocz emigrated to Israel, where they married and had two daughters and a son.

Dina's boyfriend, Natek Korman, emigrated to Israel and participated in the birth of a nation. He married and had children. Dina visited Israel in 1981 with her daughter and son-in-law and enjoyed a wonderful and touching reunion with Natek.

After her arrival in New York, Dina was placed with a family in Philadelphia, where she attended Overbrook High School. She left Philadelphia for Los Angeles, where she found a relative, Pauline Solow. Pauline was the daughter of Dina's grandfather's brother, who had immigrated to the United States in the early twentieth century. Dina finished high school at Roosevelt High School in Los Angeles. Due to her financial circumstances, Dina entered the workforce after high school and was unable to attend college. Dina married Leo Balbien, a *kindertransport* survivor from Vienna, Austria. Leo spent the early part of the war at a trade school outside of London. When he turned eighteen, he followed his parents to the United States and enlisted in the US Army. He served in the Philippine Islands until the end of the war. Dina and Leo have four children, Tema, Joel, Joshua, and Sarah. They are also blessed with seven grandchildren. Dina lives in Southern California and is a devoted mother, grandmother, and great-grandmother. She is vibrant and healthy and often speaks at schools, temples, and organizations about her experiences during the Holocaust.

My mother told us everything about her childhood. Her stories have become my stories, too. As a child doing my homework in the kitchen, I would watch my mother at the stove. My mother was always in the kitchen cooking or baking something. Food has always been important to her, as it has been for other survivors. My mother adores cherries more than any other fruit, or any other food, for that matter, although no cherries in Southern California could ever stand up to the ones in her memory. The cherries in Fela's grandparents' orchard were the size of ping pong balls and the sweetest in the world.

Whenever I see a roadside stand with cherries, I find myself pulling to the side of the road, knowing my mother will beam her sunshine smile when I hand her the bag, and what could be better than my mother's smile.

BELLE AMI BOOK LIST

The Last Daughter
Based closely on the remarkable true story of Dina Frydman, one of the youngest survivors of the Holocaust, *The Last Daughter* will reaffirm your faith in the indomitability of the human spirit.

∼

OUT OF TIME THRILLER SERIES

The Girl Who Knew da Vinci
Book 1
Art historian Angela Renatus is haunted by dreams of a Leonardo da Vinci painting that—as far as the world knows—doesn't exist. When Angela is contacted by art detective Alex Caine, she's shocked he's searching for the same work of art. But someone else wants the lost masterpiece, someone who will stop at nothing to find it—even murder.

The Girl Who Loved Caravaggio
Book 2

Art historian Angela Renatus is different. She can see into the past—into the lives of the greatest artists of all time. Are her visions a gift or a curse? Angela and her fiancé, detective Alex Caine, search for a stolen Caravaggio painting, but the deeper they delve into the artist's tortured life, the more deadly the investigation becomes.

The Girl Who Adored Rembrandt
Book 3
In a psychic vision, art historian Angela Renatus witnesses the theft of a Rembrandt painting from the home of family friends. Working with the FBI, Angela and her detective fiancé Alex Caine investigate the theft. But nothing is ever what it seems as they trace the masterpiece to a deadly drug lord and a centuries-old Rembrandt family secret.

TIP OF THE SPEAR THRILLER SERIES

Escape
Book 1
Cyrus Hassani can kill a man fifty different ways barehanded. As a deep-cover Mossad agent in Iran, he walks a tightrope without a net. When Layla Wallace, a Jewish American grad student is kidnapped by Iranian forces, Cyrus blows his cover to rescue her. But facing deadly henchmen might be less dangerous than protecting a feisty redhead.

Vengeance
Book 2
Cyrus faces his worst fear when his wife Layla goes missing after the bombing of a restaurant in New York City. Although Layla is presumed dead, Cyrus doesn't believe it. He will find her and then he'll make the terrorists pay.

Ransom
Book 3

Cyrus is torn between protecting his family and heading up a mission to search for Aryeh Stern—a top agent with Mossad's Tip of the Spear elite team—who has gone missing in Beirut while on assignment with fellow agent, Zara Zayani.

Exposed
Book 4
When Jazmin Amin's family perishes in a London bombing, she turns to Mossad's Tip of the Spear agents for help. Cyrus and Layla—along with the rest of the team—track down crucial evidence behind the explosion, as fellow agents Zara and Mustafa embark on a daring rescue mission in Iran. Meanwhile, Aryeh is assigned to protect Jazmin—but can Jazmin trust her growing feelings for the notorious agent known as "The Lion" or is she risking more than her heart?

∿

THE BLUE COAT SAGA SERIES

A Time-travel romance set in the present day and in World War 2.
She has the power to save the future, but she must face the evil in the past.

In 1942 German-occupied Paris, nineteen-year-old Leah Manheim turns up the collar of her blue coat against a biting wind as she waits outside Saint-Ambroise Cathedral for English Marine Commando, Aidan McQueen. When she signed up with the resistance she knew all the risks. Luckily her friends smuggled her parents out of Paris and away from the looming danger of deportation. Leah must keep her wits about her, focus on her mission, and survive....

In present-day Brooklyn, librarian Rose Levi finds a tattered, old blue coat at the back of her late grandmother's closet. Keep? Donate? Throw away? A lifetime of memories to sort through, wrapped in faded tissue paper, sprinkled with dust. But it's the packet of Bubbie's letters tied up in a faded ribbon and tucked in a drawer that gives

Rose pause. Can she even believe the words? Rose must keep her wits about her and find the courage to accomplish the task her grandmother has given her….

The Rendezvous in Paris
Book 1

The Lost Legacy of Time
Book 2

The Secret Book of Names
Book 3

Boxed Set: The Blue Coat Saga (Books 1, 2, 3)

～

COMING in 2022

THE ONLY ONE SERIES (romantic suspense)

LOST IN TIME SERIES (time travel romantic suspense published by Dragonblade Publishing)

～

Sign up for Belle Ami's newsletter at belleamiauthor.com
Follow Belle Ami on BookBub

ABOUT THE AUTHOR

Belle Ami writes breathtaking international thrillers, compelling historical fiction, and riveting romantic suspense with a touch of sensual heat. A self-confessed news junkie, Belle loves to create cutting-edge stories, weaving world issues, espionage, fast-paced action, and of course, redemptive love. Belle's series and stand-alone novels include the following:

TIP OF THE SPEAR SERIES: A continuing, contemporary, international espionage, suspense-thriller series with romantic elements. TIP OF THE SPEAR includes the acclaimed *Escape*, *Vengeance*, *Ransom*, and *Exposed*.

OUT OF TIME SERIES: A continuing, time-travel, art-thriller series with romantic elements. OUT OF TIME includes the bestsellers *The Girl Who Knew da Vinci* and *The Girl Who Loved Caravaggio*, and the new release, *The Girl Who Adored Rembrandt*.

THE BLUE COAT SAGA: A three-part serial, time-travel, suspense thriller with romantic elements set in the present-day and in World War II. THE BLUE COAT SAGA includes *The Rendezvous in Paris*, *The Lost Legacy of Time*, and *The Secret Book of Names*.

The Last Daughter is a compelling and heart-wrenching World War II historical fiction novel. based on the remarkable life of Dina Frydman, one of the youngest survivors of the Holocaust. The story begins at the dawn of World War II and follows the Nazi invasion and occupation of Poland, focusing on the Nazi's six-year reign of terror on the Jews of Poland, and the horrors of the death camps at Bergen-Belsen and Auschwitz, where more than six-million Jews were slaughtered.

Belle is also writing a three-book, time-travel romance series for Dragonblade Publishing, one of the top-selling boutique historical romance publishers in North America. The first book in Belle's *LOST IN TIME* series will be out in May of 2022.

Belle is also the author of the romantic suspense series THE ONLY ONE, which includes *The One*, *The One & More*, and *One More Time is Not Enough*. This series will be revised and re-released in 2022.

Sign up for *The Belle Ami Journal* (Belle's newsletter) for updates on her upcoming books, sneak previews, contests, giveaways, and more.

A former Kathryn McBride scholar of Bryn Mawr College in Pennsylvania, Belle, is also thrilled to be a recipient of the RONE, RAVEN, Readers' Favorite Award, and the Book Excellence Award.

Belle's passions include hiking, boxing, skiing, cooking, travel, and of course, writing. She lives in Southern California with her husband Joe, her daughter Natasha, and her son Ben, along with a horse named Cindy Crawford, a senior-citizen Chihuahua named Giorgio Armani (who still has plenty of spark in his bark), a sassy-gal Chihuahua named Pebbles, and a loveable goofball pit bull rescue named Coco.

Belle loves to hear from readers. You can contact her directly: belle@belleamiauthor.com or connect with Belle on social media:
BookBub
Twitter: @BelleAmi5

Facebook
Instagram
Newsletter Signup

Made in the USA
Middletown, DE
17 March 2022

62828841R00196